Mrs. Ruth Ann Smith
November 18, 1952
(November selection)

RAMPOLE PLACE

RAMPOLE PLACE

BY
ISABELLA HOLT

THE BOBBS-MERRILL COMPANY, INC.

NEW YORK • INDIANAPOLIS • *Publishers*

RAMPOLE PLACE

Chapter *1*

AT SOME point between midnight and daybreak, in April of 1906, the telephone rang through the large spaces of Senator Rampole's house on the outskirts of Meridian—rang and went unanswered. It wakened young Victor in the children's wing and Augustus Henning in the servants' quarters, but neither of them took immediate action.

At this hour of the night the call would be from some drunken political underling, appealing to the Senator to get him out of a scrape with the police. When Horace Rampole was in residence he took care of these chores with sardonic good nature, accepting the fact that the Boys looked after him and he had to look after the Boys. But the drunk must be pretty far gone, or he would have remembered that the Senator was in Washington.

The bell brought Victor up, inch by inch, out of a blood-chilling dream of Indian fighting, so that it had an aura of alarm. As soon as he got his wits together, he burrowed back into his pillow. In his father's absence he took a junior responsibility for the affairs of the place, but on night telephone calls Augustus Henning outranked him. Augustus was the lifelong major-domo of the establishment, and he had a telephone extension on the wall directly outside his bedroom door.

But the bell went on drilling spasmodically into the silence, and Victor could not make his way back into the world of sleep.

He knew what was happening. Augustus was getting old and creaky. He and his wife, Jennie, were snug in their double bed, and the air was blowing nippy through the window. Augustus was letting the bell ring, in the hope that Mrs. Rampole would reach out and answer it from her pillow in the big front bedroom. Waking up was not the wrench to her that it was to Augustus. She had quicksilver in her; she was never entirely sleep-bound.

Ting-a-ling-a-ling, falsely sweet and insistent. Impatiently Victor set off in his bare feet on the long trip through the house to the sitting room downstairs.

He was in his balbriggan pajamas, and his strong black hair stood up in sprigs; but even so, he looked every inch a Rampole, and in Meridian a Rampole was a fine thing to look like. He was only fourteen, and his face was still unformed; but already he had the jutting family nose, the willful jaw, the ink-black eyebrows. If he kept on growing, he promised to be as big a man as his father. His eyes were not Rampole eyes, though—they had a dancing greenish-tawny glint that he took from his mother.

The house was spooky at this hour of the night. Victor made his way through the labyrinth of corridors, where the gas jets were turned down to mere beads of light. Down the great staircase and back through the cross corridor to the sitting room. By the time he arrived, the bell had rung itself into silence.

He spoke into the transmitter, but no one answered except Augustus. "Get along back to bed where you belong, Vic. If it rings again, I'll take care of it."

Augustus sounded edgy. He had been slack about answering the telephone, so now he was giving orders to Victor. Victor resolved to go back to bed when he chose and no sooner. There was something bold and ticklish about being at large in the house at such an unblessed hour.

Victor threaded the cluttered, cozy room to peer at the clock on the mantel. A quarter past four, a spooky time of night. A few embers were still winking on the hearth, and the game of checkers stood unfinished where he and Katie had left it when their mother sent them off to bed. It was still yesterday, and yet it was trying to be tomorrow.

He went over to the bay window and looked out toward the forest beyond the lawn. A pallor was coming into the sky, as if the ink of midnight were being diluted. The giant trees stirred and strained uneasily. It was an unchancy time of night, sure enough; and except that Augustus had ordered him back to bed, he would have been inclined to go.

All of downstairs was dead and empty. In Father's smoking room, next to the sitting room on the cross corridor, the roll-top desk was locked, and the pervading odor of cigars was musty. The portrait of Big Joe Rampole, Victor's grandfather, dominated the obscurity.

Victor prowled toward the front of the house, quaking pleasurably. The two parlors were like mausoleums, with the tall mirrors sending off an eerie gleam. Everything was ebony and spindled black lacquer, with tufted yellow satin sofas and a grand piano like a catafalque. Over the mantel hung the portrait of Father's first wife, a ghostly presence roped with ghostly pearls.

It was really creepy in the parlors. They were bracketed by a conservatory, where great ferns and rubber plants towered in grotesque silhouette; the wall fountain dripped a sluggish tattoo. Having exhausted the pleasures of disobedience, Victor had set his course toward his own bedroom when the telephone trilled again. He bounded to answer it.

But this time Augustus was ahead of him. He heard Augustus saying crustily, "Yes, this is Senator Rampole's house. Henning speaking."

Augustus had not gone back to his bed; he had stood in the drafty hall with his nightshirt flicking against his hairy old shanks. He had a foreboding that the call would be repeated, and he was disturbed—not so much because he had missed it the first time as because Mrs. Rampole had not answered it. That was not like her—it was unsettling. It might even mean that she had not come home safe from her meeting.

For that matter, it was out of character for her to go to a meeting at all, except when the Senator took her along to decorate a public platform with her prettiness. She was completely unpolitical and feminine.

The longer Augustus stood cogitating in the drafty corridor, the more uneasy he felt. He had been in charge of three generations of Rampoles, but Chloe was his pet and his darling. He had taken to her the moment she set foot inside the house, even before Horace married her. His feeling for the second Mrs. Rampole was deeper than any relationship of mistress and servant—more like the devotion of an uncouth old uncle for the flower of the tribe. The very girlishness that made him love her made him worry about her. He ought not to have gone to bed until he had let her back into the house and locked up after her.

The Senator was away so much that Chloe often went out without him in the evening—but never to meetings. She went down to her friends' houses on Adams Avenue, seven and eight miles nearer town. She went in the family car, with William to drive her, and she was always back by midnight. Augustus held that only a chauffeur was qualified to cope with a death-dealing engine like an automobile, and even a chauffeur had no defense against blowouts.

This evening's departure had been disturbingly different. She had taken a telephone call about eight-thirty, and twenty minutes later she was dressed and out of the house, in a flurry of pink motor veils. She hadn't even given Augustus time to open the front door for her; she had called over her shoulder, "Don't wait up for me, Gus. I'm going to a meeting, and I may be late."

And Augustus had been left with a confused impression that she had climbed in beside the driver of a flashy open roadster.

Only daredevils drove their own roadsters—only the young and intemperate. Week after week the papers carried reports of accidents on the highways. Someone—and Augustus wished he knew who it was—had arranged to exploit Mrs. Rampole's public position by carrying her off to a meeting in her husband's absence. She was no more use at a meeting than a kitten. Someone had taken advantage of her fathomless inexperience, her sweetness and good will.

He gave a sharp check to his forebodings. He mustn't be an old softy. The chances were a thousand to one that Chloe Rampole was sound asleep in her own bed, drugged by the sharpness of the April air. He started back to his own bed. . . .

The telephone rang again. "Yes, this is Senator Rampole's house," he said. "Henning speaking."

"We have a person-to-person call for Mrs. Horace Rampole. Can she come to the telephone?"

"Where you calling from?"

"This is the Doonville operator."

Doonville was fifty miles upstate. Augustus knew it only as the headquarters of the Nineteenth Congressional District. It had no possible connection with Chloe Rampole. His anxieties dissolved. "One second," he said, and pressed the buzzer that rang beside Mrs. Rampole's bed. The line hummed with a lonely wind-swept sound.

Chloe's extension did not answer. Victor's voice came in unexpectedly. "It's funny Mother doesn't answer, Gus. Shall I run upstairs and wake her? I'm down in the sitting room."

"Do that, Vic," Augustus said—curtly, because Victor had flouted his authority in the matter of staying up.

Victor ran up the stairs and rapped gently on his mother's door. Getting no response, he pushed it open and said, "Mother—telephone!" After a minute he struck a match and lighted the gas jet beside the door.

He was dumfounded—Mother was not in her bed.

The bed linen was uncreased, the lace-and-muslin nightgown laid out with the mules below it, just as Nora left them every evening. Across a chair lay the foulard dress Mother had been wearing when she kissed Victor good night; on the floor were the black silk stockings she had stripped off and the French-heeled slippers she had stepped out of. The bathroom door was open, and the bathroom empty.

For the first moment Victor was more surprised than frightened. Mother's absence was so queer that it could not be a fact. She couldn't have gone out, because when she did she always told him and Katie. They often sat in her room to watch her prettify. She was at her gayest when she was dressing for a party—the three of them sang rounds and went off into gales of laughter.

And yet the room looked as it did when she dressed in a hurry. Rice powder lay sprinkled on the dressing table. The drawer where she kept her bright-colored motor veils was half open.

4

A nasty premonition invaded him. He felt a churning in the pit of his stomach. He wished the telephone had never wakened him.

He picked up the telephone and spoke through to the back hall. "Mother's not here, Gus. Where in the world can she be?"

"Will you speak to anyone else?" the Meridian operator asked of Doonville.

A workaday voice answered, "Yes, put me on. Hello? This is Sergeant Littlejohn speaking, from police headquarters in Doonville. Who's talking?"

"Augustus Henning. I work here."

Augustus' terseness steadied Victor, even when the sergeant went on, "We've had a crash on the turnpike. Ottymobile hit a culvert and turned over. Both occupants killed."

"Well, that's too bad, Sergeant, but do you have to call the Senator at four in the morning? Can't you take care of your own drunks?"

The sergeant went on methodically. "I have a reason for calling. We've identified the man from papers in his wallet as Harold Ritter, of 817 South Boulevard, Meridian. Know anything about him?"

Victor had not known that a pain was tearing at him till it went away all at once. For three seconds he had had the idea that his mother, his lovely delightful mother, had been killed in an accident. But he was often called in to shake hands with the Boys in his father's smoking room, and he knew Mr. Ritter as one of the young hopefuls of the party organization. It was too bad Mr. Ritter had been killed, but he had no connection with Mother.

Augustus was saying just what Victor expected him to say. "Sure. Ritter is a party committeeman. That's quite a tragedy, Sergeant—young Ritter was coming up fast. Anything I can do at this end? The Senator's out of town."

The distant voice went on relentlessly. "It's about the lady I wanted to ask you. We haven't identified her—she had no papers on her. She was togged out in a pink dress, with one of them long dust coats over it, and her hat was tied on with a long pink veil."

Victor wanted to put down the receiver, but his hand held it frozen to his ear. He screwed his eyes tight shut, as if he could shut out the recollection of Mother's pink dress and motor veil. Plenty of women wore pink dresses. . . . The inexorable voice went on: "So long as Mrs. Rampole isn't at home, it's my duty to tell you that this woman's wedding ring is inscribed 'H.R. to C.C., June 12, 1891.' "

Augustus gasped audibly into the telephone. Victor went dizzy and stone-cold. You're crazy! his whole being was shouting to Sergeant Littlejohn—it's some other woman with the same initials. There's no way

5

it could be my mother. But the tentacles of evidence were getting him in their grip.

"Furthermore," the sergeant continued, "one of our patrolmen escorted Mrs. Rampole through town the time the Senator spoke at the Grange Hall, and he claims to identify her by her pretty chestnut hair. I hope to God he's wrong, Henning."

In his extremity Victor must have made some slight sound into the telephone. "Get off the line, Vic," Augustus ordered him gruffly.

Victor had no strength to hang up the receiver; it dangled in his hand, with cheeping sounds coming out of it. The force had seeped out of his knees, his elbows and his thumbs. The air smelled of nightmare. He was facing a horror. Only a superhuman effort could avert it; but he had no power to move hand or foot.

For fourteen enchanted years he had never faced a danger except of his own making, and his mother had been at hand to rescue him. The basis of his universe was being destroyed. He must shout into the telephone; he must silence these gibbering old men and exorcise the nightmare.

He managed to lift the receiver to his ear. Augustus was talking now. ". . . Well, you must bear with me, Sergeant. There wasn't a sweeter, cuter, fetchinger young lady in the whole United States, nor one that will be more missed. I'll have to call the Senator in Washington and relay his instructions to you. Likely he'll send up a man from Wentz's."

Wentz—that name settled it and left Victor without hope. Until he heard that name, he might have persuaded himself that his mother's death was a bad dream. But even a fourteen-year-old knew that Mr. Wentz handled all the best funerals in Meridian.

Sergeant Littlejohn hung up; Augustus hung up. Victor sat with the dead instrument in his hands. Somehow, somewhere, fifty miles away, his mother had been killed in Mr. Ritter's car. The fact was so improbable as to be monstrous, but Augustus accepted it as true.

He heard a series of clicks—Augustus was trying to signal the operator. Then Augustus spoke through to him. "You there, Vic? This is black news. Hang up, sonny, I want to reach Central."

"Central, Central! Aren't you doing anything to stop this crazy business? Mother can't be dead, Gus."

"You would listen in," Augustus said somberly, "So now you know. I feel as bad as you do, pretty near. I'm doing all that's left for me to do, so will you please get off the line?"

"Are you going to call F-father?"

"I want to get through to the Old Snorter first."

Victor was stupefied. "Aunt Louisa! What business is it of hers?"

6

"Plenty," Augustus said grimly. "Hang up and let me have the line."

"You ought to call Father the very first thing."

"Vic, this is going to be tough enough on your father, the best we can do. His sister is the one to break the news to him."

His aunt's intervention was more than Victor could endure. Aunt Louisa didn't really like Mother—she babied her and belittled her. He began stuttering incoherently into the telephone; his voice rose to a stringent squeak.

"Jennie," Augustus said over his shoulder, "go up and look after young Vic. He was on the line in his mother's room and he heard the whole thing. He's coming down with the shakes."

Victor hung up the receiver. Lights were springing up in the halls. From the servants' wing Nora let off a doglike howl that chilled his marrow.

He knew now that his mother was irrevocably dead. In a moment Jennie would take him in charge.

He made a tiptoe circuit of the room that still had Mother's life in it—her limp stockings on the carpet, her powder strewn across the dressing table. She might almost have been moving in the shadows behind him, just out of eyeshot—tossing her garments here and there, humming a little tune, smiling her tender half-smile.

Jennie stood in the doorway and said compassionately, "Come, laddie. Come down to the kitchen. There's fire in the back of the range, and I'll make you a nice cup of cocoa."

Her front hair was neatly parted, but the pigtail in the back was scuffed from sleeping. Her good, gaunt, capable frame was muffled in an immense dressing gown with white pearl buttons, and she was wearing a pair of her husband's shoes.

She put her arm around him, as she used to do when he was four and five years old. But he was too big—the gesture was physically awkward, and he couldn't cry as a little boy could. "Cocoa!" he said blastingly, drawing out of her embrace.

"This is your first trouble, Vic. Even if food don't change things, it puts the heart into you to bear them. Come along now."

After all, the kitchen was better. Victor let Jennie establish him in her own sacred rocking chair and tuck her afghan around his shaking knees. She shook down the stove, poured in coal which instantly began to snap and glow, set the cocoa to brewing and put on a pot of coffee.

The cocoa proved to be more of a solace than a humiliation; it muted the gnawing in his vitals.

A car swept into the driveway, and gravel spattered against the base-

7

ment windows beside him. "That'll be your auntie," said Jen. "You'll have to go up and speak to her."

"Not until I've talked to Gus," Victor said.

"He's been on the telephone," Jennie said. "He'll be down as soon as Mrs. Lassigne is through with him." But she obliged Victor by going to the dumb-waiter shaft, rattling the cord and shouting robustly, "Coffee, Gus."

"I don't understand what's going on. Why has Aunt Louisa got to come sticking her nose in?"

"This isn't anything you have to understand, Vic. It's just a misery, and you have to live through it. When anybody dies, there's a lot of machinery to set in motion. Gus will be down pretty soon."

It was a long time before Augustus came down, though. As Jennie moved about the kitchen she darted looks of concern in Victor's direction, searched for things to say, and gave up the attempt. A couple of tear-stained maids came down the basement stairs and asked what they could do.

"Not a thing in the world—not yet," Jennie told them. "Sit yourselves down with a good cup of coffee. You'll need your strength before the day's over." So they took their coffee off into their sitting room and mooed together like two mourning doves.

Victor sat with the empty cup on his knees—staring, staring.

If only Father had been at home—the overlord, the almighty presence—none of this would have happened. Father would have known better than to let Mother go skyrocketing off across country in the middle of the night in that unaccountable way. If he were at home even now, he would bring order back. In his absence Augustus and Aunt Louisa were squirreling away at their confounded arrangements, as if they were getting up a Fourth-of-July lawn party. Arrangements! Victor had a question to ask of Augustus, and it was more important than any arrangements.

In due course Augustus came clumping down the kitchen stairs and drank his coffee at the corner of the table. His mind was full of Mrs. Lassigne. "Trust her!" he grumbled admiringly, and he began to mimic her. " 'At a time like *this*, Augustus, I do think you might be *decently* dressed to answer the door.' "

Victor had expected never to laugh again—certainly not that night. But when he looked at Augustus, unshaved and unbrushed, with his nightshirt tucked into his trousers, a laugh forced itself out of him, and Jen added her curt country chuckle.

"She's the spit and image of Big Joe," Augustus went on. "There she sets, like General Grant in his tent, giving orders by telephone. She's

8

an old screech owl, but she's a jewel in time of trouble. Incidentally, Vic, she wants to talk to you."

"I don't want to talk to her."

"If you care anything about your mother, you've got to talk to her." And Augustus and Jennie looked at each other as if they understood something that was passing over Victor's head. The voice of maturity had spoken, and youth had to yield.

"All right—in a minute. But, Gus, Mother never told Katie or me that she was going up to Doonville tonight. She didn't say a word about it when she——" He stopped. He meant, When she kissed me good night.

"Ah, that was politics. The meeting was a deep dark secret. That was why she couldn't say anything about it."

"Politics! Mother didn't know a thing in the world about politics."

"Well, she got roped in on this. Her name carries weight. That's what the Snorter wants to explain to you. It was regular down-the-rat-hole stuff, but it's got to come out in the open now, and that's what your aunt's taken so long arranging. Let her tell you about it."

"I'll bet it was Aunt Louisa that roped her in." Aunt Louisa was a meddler, a finagler, a fixer from the word go.

"As a matter of fact, it was. Mrs. Lassigne was to have driven your mother up to the meeting in her own car, only Mr. Ollie got one of them precious stomach upsets of his and she had to turn the job over to young Ritter. Them Swedes upstate are on the rampage, and somebody had to sit on their heads."

"Then Aunt Louisa killed my mother."

Augustus said uneasily, "Don't let it rankle, Vic. She could have got killed driving to the grocery store."

"You don't even care about Mother being killed. All you think about is politics, politics!"

"My God! Do you think nobody cares but you? I'm doing what I have to do, Vic. Stop heckling me—go up and heckle your auntie. But first take my comb and give your hair a lick. You look like a fighting rooster."

While Victor was combing down his hair he felt like a fly wrestling against the flypaper. His instinct told him he was being diddled in connection with his mother's death.

He had sat too often on the pantry stool, while Augustus prevaricated into the telephone in the family interest, to be deceived. ". . . Tell him I took the earlier train, Gus—he needs a chance to cool off." . . . "Augusttus, please call Mrs. Grover and tell her I have a headache, so I can't

9

play bridge. Say I'm dreadfully sorry. . . ." Diddling was all right in its place—but not tonight, in the black shadow of tragedy.

Augustus read his doubts in his mirrored face. "You remember how it was, surely, Vic?" he urged. "Your mother packed you kids off early to bed, so she could dress and get going. It was all sub rosy—I didn't know myself till the Snorter told me just now. She used the telephone about eight-thirty, recollect? That was when young Ritter called to say he'd pick her up instead of Mrs. Lassigne."

Well, it all hung together. Mother had taken a call in the smoking room while he and Katie were setting up the checkerboard. He remembered something breathless and clinging in her good-night kiss. He remembered that when she left his room she went fairly flying down the hall.

The diddling originated with Aunt Louisa when she devised the lunatic plan of sending Mother to a political meeting. He would give Aunt Louisa a piece of his mind—— He set off up the stairs in high truculence and hatred.

The sitting room was not a show place, like the parlors and the conservatory. It had a box of candy standing open, and a litter of sheet music across the old upright piano. Mother had left the sewing machine and the dressmaker's dummy out. When she was a girl she had made her own clothes, and she still whipped up bright little frocks for Katie.

Now Aunt Louisa was using the room as staff headquarters. She was sitting at the desk when Victor came in, straight as a broom stick, between a telephone and a memorandum pad.

"My poor boy!" she intoned with splendid resonance. She had two voices—one practical, the other cultivated and organ-toned, and this was her second voice. "This is a dreadful catastrophe. Your poor father will be stricken to the heart."

Aunt Louisa didn't really mind Mother's being killed. She was enjoying herself, that's what she was doing—because she had a big funeral to manage. "You're a fine one to talk!" Victor burst out in a torment of bitterness.

Mrs. Lassigne was not one to tolerate insolence from the young. She reared, rather like a fighting swan, and then controlled herself.

"I make every allowance for your rudeness, my poor child. I must talk to you seriously. You and I, Victor, and all of us have a great responsibility to your father. He has lost two wives, two lovely young women. This must not be allowed to break him."

"How is Father? Is he all right?"

She hesitated before she answered, "He hasn't heard yet."

"You haven't told Father yet? Who do you think you are, taking everything on your own shoulders? Father had a right to be told before anybody."

Aunt Louisa was a Rampole, and no junior Rampole could roar her down. "I want to spare him as much as I can," she said steadily. "I want to be able to tell him everything is taken care of. I've sent Mr. Wentz up to Doonville, and I finally got through to Gentleman Dan——"

"Gentleman Dan! Do you have to drag even Dan Parmiter into this?"

"Dan is your father's right-hand man in political matters."

Victor's last restraint broke. "Politics, everlastingly politics! You sent Mother off to a meeting and got her killed, and *still* all you can think about is politics."

Mrs. Lassigne gave off an emanation of personal power that subdued Victor's clamor. "My boy, I must put it to you bluntly, and I hope you are mature enough to understand me. I am working to avoid a nasty scandal about your mother's death. You must know how badly it looks for a young married woman to be killed fifty miles from home, at four in the morning, in a car with a strange man. You must know what the *Sun-Record* will make of a story like that. That's why Augustus called me in."

She brought Victor up short. He felt small, cheap and childish. A coldness came into the pit of his stomach. He was sorry he had yelled at his aunt, and glad she had set promptly to work.

The *Sun-Record* was not allowed upstairs at Chestnut Point, but Augustus took it in the kitchen and Victor read it avidly. It was from the *Sun-Record* one learned about love nests, blackmailers, bigamists, miracle cures for unmentionable diseases, and the Katzenjammer Kids. It had a special animus against the established powers of the city, including the Rampole dynasty. Claggan, the editor, was a bogey to frighten little Rampoles with. Victor saw in an instant what the *Sun-Record* could make of his mother's death: HIGH JINKS IN HIGH PLACES.

Victor had been refusing to look squarely at his mother's death—not because he was too young to understand its implications, but because of the indecency of connecting Chloe Rampole with such nastiness. He knew too well what he would have thought if he read in the *Sun-Record* that some other woman in a pink frock had been killed on the Doonville turnpike.

"But . . . but she went to a meeting," he stammered. "All we have to do is tell them so."

"That's where the difficulty arises," his aunt said. "You must try to follow me." He did try, to the point of a physical ache in his head. "The facts are completely innocent, but secret, and I'm insisting that they must be brought out into the open. That's why I had to reach Dan Parmiter. You see, this little gathering of Arne Olsen's at Doonville was a conspiracy against Dan Parmiter and against orderly party government. You've heard about the Insurgents?"

Certainly Victor had heard about the Insurgents—wild-eyed partisans of Roosevelt, partisans of La Follette, anathema to the conservatives. He nodded.

"These misguided young men had made overtures to your father, hoping to enlist him in their revolt. Naturally they couldn't lead him astray. On the other hand, Dan Parmiter can be very rancorous with rebels, and Horace wanted to avoid a split in the party. If he had been at home, he would have attended the meeting and made the Insurgents see which side their bread was buttered on. Since he couldn't attend the meeting, he asked your mother and me to represent him, without letting Dan Parmiter know."

"*My father* sent Mother to that meeting?" The news knocked the last prop out from under Victor.

Father, at least, knew better than to send Mother to meetings. Father, Victor's last dependence, had wantonly used Mother as ammunition in a party uprising. If Father hadn't ordered her to Doonville, she would be asleep in her bed this minute. A core of dreadful anger against his father began to burn in him.

Aunt Louisa was still talking, but he was scarcely listening. "If I hadn't reached Dan at once, naturally he and Congressman Olsen would have given conflicting stories to the papers, since Dan hadn't been told about the meeting. The *Sun-Record* would have inferred that there was no meeting at all—that it was a story we Rampoles had cooked up to cover a scandal. Olsen and Parmiter have both been very fine about it, very loyal to your father. They've agreed to treat the meeting as an ordinary party conference."

"Well, Aunt Louisa, I guess you did the best you could." In her earth-bound way, she had. She had no scale on which to measure Mother's loveliness and Victor's loss. "Is it going to be all right about the *Sun-Record?*"

"I did what I could," Aunt Louisa said. She looked tired; her eyes, ordinarily handsome, were sunk in her head, with loose pouches under them. "I got Jim Claggan out of bed and gave him the same routine statement I gave the *Morning Telegram*. If he has any decency in him, he'll accept it. But I can't vouch for Jim Claggan's decency."

Victor still saw the night's events distorted and incredible. All that was clear was that his farther had sent his mother to her death. Father knew better—he knew that the Boys drank deep at their powwows; he knew that Mother was at a disadvantage with the Boys. She had been brought up on the scruples of Adams Avenue, she didn't drink at all. But she loved people, she loved parties. She was often in tearing spirits that could be mistaken for a blithe intoxication. The Boys probably sized her up as able to look out for herself—but Father knew she wasn't.

What did it matter now? For their own ignoble purposes Father and Aunt Louisa between them had squandered and destroyed Mother.

His misery forced itself upon his aunt. She said, in her grand-opera contralto, "I shall never, never forgive myself for not driving your mother in my own car this evening."

"I wish you had," he tried to say. He cleared his throat and repeated, "I wish you had."

"This is going to bear hard on your father. You must comfort him."

Victor said harshly, "If Father didn't want Mother killed, he needn't have sent her off to Doonville."

His aunt gave him a long scrutiny from her tired old eyes, and appeared to reject a number of comments. All she said in the end was "Victor, there are a great many things a young boy is not qualified to judge."

Victor was suddenly bored, empty and hopeless. He said, "Well, I might as well go up to bed."

Aunt Louisa hardly heard him. She was running down the list of her memoranda. "I believe everything is taken care of now," she said. "I can put in a call for Horace in Washington."

Chapter 2

KATIE wakened Victor in the morning by gently twitching the corner of his pillow. "What's going on, Vic? Doorbells, telephones, florists' trucks. Are we having a party I don't know about?"

Victor came bolt upright in bed, with a sense of doom upon him. There was nobody except himself to break the dreadful news to Katie. Did Katie even know what it meant to be killed? When they played cops-and-robbers it was etiquette for Victor to shout *bang* and for Katie to fall down dead; but the deadness ended with the game, and the corpse rose to its feet. How could he get it through to her that Mother was permanently dead?

He did not even consider ducking the assignment. He had always looked after Katie.

But this was going to be tough on Katie—poor little shrimp! Even tougher than it was on him. Katie wasn't really herself except in the shelter of Mother.

Victor was a boy; he got around more. Katie had a way with people that looked like arrogance, but it was really defensiveness.

Perhaps it was her looks. It was too bad she was a girl, because the Rampole looks, while they served well enough for a boy, didn't work out so well on an eleven-year-old girl. Her hair was straight and uncompromisingly black; her skin was like strong, smooth Manila paper fitted across her bones; and her nose took up the whole center of her face. When you knew Katie well you got awfully fond of her, but she was hard to know. She had a way of closing the shutters between herself and strangers; she spoke tartly, so that though you couldn't say she didn't have nice manners, they were forbidding; she wouldn't be got at. She wasn't going to give people a chance to snub her.

Consequently she never got any petting except from her mother, who was immune to Rampole noses. Nobody knew, except Mother and Victor, how Katie skylarked when she let her shutters down. Now Katie had lost her mainstay.

"It isn't a party, Katie. It's something terrible."

Katie fastened her owlish great eyes on him. Victor was always her commanding officer. Her eyes made things no easier.

"It's about Mother. Do you remember the time the two cars smashed together at the Doochee Bridge, and they had to carry the bodies away? Well, Mother was in an auto accident."

Katie said unbelievingly, "Mother wasn't even out in a car last night. She was with us right up to bedtime."

A strap tightened inside Victor. Her artless testimony confirmed his own sense of the queerness of last night. Mother needn't have gone out without telling her own children.

But what did it matter now? "Everybody knew she was going out, except us," he told her more roughly than he intended. "She went off to some sort of a meeting." He needn't go into the political involvements; they were confusing even to him, and they would be totally lost on Katie. "On the way back the car turned over." And he looked straight into her eyes, forcing upon her mind the words he couldn't pronounce— Mother was killed.

Her pupils dilated. She always played a game to the hilt, and now she was playing auto-accident. She was reaching the point——

"It was the worst you can possibly think of," he told her.

14

Katie didn't shriek, as he had feared she might. A long shudder traversed her body. Her hands locked together against her ribs.

"This is for keeps," Victor said. He was shy of touching her, but he had to break that locked state she was in. He pulled her down on the edge of the bed beside him and let her cry. He wished he could cry. The dryness of despair was worse than any torrent of tears.

But Katie still didn't really fathom what had happened to her. She was too young.

Nora brought up their breakfast to the playroom, because of the florists downstairs; and before they had finished, Granny Cummager made her appearance.

Granny was in black from head to foot, and the powder on her plump cheeks was grooved with tears. "My poor motherless lambs!" she mourned, and gathered the two of them to her large, soft bosom.

Katie stiffened, and put up her shutters. She loved only a few people, and Granny was not one of them.

Victor had loved Granny just enough to oblige his mother on Sundays. Mother had loved her with charming constancy. Every Tuesday, rain or shine, she had Gramp and Granny to dinner at Chestnut Point.

Victor had absorbed the basement view of his mother's parents. They were butts for Augustus and the maids, who begrudged them service. Augustus called Granny "the Puddin'."

In the first place, they weren't Old-Meridian. Thay had come to town when Mother was a tiny child, but nothing could alter the fact that they weren't born there.

Gramp had carried his head high in his younger days. He built up a flourishing chemical business in the growing city, which was a rival to Chicago, Detroit and Cleveland. Then, during Mother's girlhood, Gramp lost control of his business. A local syndicate took it over and pushed it to a success in which he had no part. He was left with nothing but his grievance. He clung to his membership in the Meridian Club and made a point of lunching there, but there were certain men whose hands he would never shake again. He told Victor about them on Tuesday evenings.

The Puddin' had kept a little money of her own, but the basement surmised that the Senator must help his father-in-law out, or how could he have hung onto his house on Adams Avenue? The basement discussed the shifts Granny was put to—doing her own housework and turning her old dresses.

The Cummagers, in short, were people to be tolerated and patronized at Chestnut Point—always on the stretch to maintain that they were as good as any Rampole.

To Augustus, and hence to Victor, they simply were not, because nobody was. Horace Rampole's mayoralty of Meridian, and now his senatorship, were mere newcome drops in the bucket of the family pre-eminence. When the Northwest Territory was opened up for settlement, the original Huck Rampole had arrived out of nowhere, striding the forest trails, and halting with prophetic instinct where the Doochee River flowed into the Cinnamon.

His son Luke brought the railroad in. Artemus, shortly before the Civil War, was a founder of banks and manufactures. It was he, who could barely write a grammatical letter, who endowed Meridian University in the backwoods.

Big Joe, the fourth in line, had seen the necessary connection between industry and politics. He had never run for office himself, but he was a kingmaker. It was he who held the state of Algonquin in the Republican column through the bad Democratic days of Grover Cleveland. He was a personal friend of Mark Hanna. He ran his son Horace for mayor, and later for senator.

In 1906 the family was perhaps not so outstanding as Augustus and Victor considered it. As the city ripened it developed a taste for subjects which the Rampoles left to their womenfolk—art, music and literature. Some elect persons considered the Rampole preoccupation with politics a comical defect in taste. But at least it was conceded that the Rampole blood had never run thin. While the descendants of the other early settlers rested back on their real estate, the Rampoles held their active primacy.

Meridian did not begrudge it to them. They had a fierce love for their community, and they did not sit on their money. They built up the university campus with a Memorial Chapel, a science laboratory and a stadium. The fountain in the center of the Riverfront Plaza had been erected by public subscription in payment of a debt of civic gratitude. Horace, carried on the tide of reform that came in with the new century, had been a better than average mayor. The old-timers who were familiar with Big Joe's methods acknowledged that the stream had risen higher than its source.

All this tribal lore was kneaded into Victor. So it was only for his mother's sake that he honored the Cummagers' absurd claims to equality with the Rampoles. This morning he did not slide out of his grandmother's pudding-soft embrace, although he wriggled.

But he liked Granny better than usual. He was glad to see her. Partly because, in an elderly way, she looked like Mother. Her hair was a dusty echo of Mother's chestnut crown, and she had the same cowlick over the temple. Her hazel eyes were Mother's. Her smile had the same quirk that gave Mother's smile its tender witchery.

And she was Mother's partisan, first, last and always. Her daughter was the loveliest daughter in the world, just as her husband was the most ill-used of men. Most people thought Chloe Cummager did a good day's business when she married Horace Rampole, but Granny hoped Horace appreciated his luck in persuading Chloe to marry him. So Victor let Granny clasp him to her bosom.

Granny had duties. It appeared that Victor must have a mourning arm band on his sleeve before anyone saw him, and that Katie's Sunday coat and her bright-colored dresses must be rushed out to the Sherwood Dyers. Till she had a proper black dress, Katie had better wear her white dress with a black hair ribbon. Granny stitched at the arm band as she talked.

"Who's going to see us?" Victor demanded fractiously. "We can cut down through the woods to the summerhouse and spend the day there."

Oh, no, that wouldn't do at all. Till their father got back from Washington, Victor and Katie represented the family. Dozens of people had left cards already. "Of course, I could receive them, except that I can't stay. My seamstress is coming in, and I must open my guest rooms. The Cummagers from Utica will be stopping with me for the funeral, and my sister Lucy from Minneapolis."

When they went downstairs both children must stay secluded in the sitting room. They could read their books, but they mustn't play checkers; and above all, Katie was not to play the piano. The ladies would think that heartless.

"What ladies?" Victor demanded. Granny explained that various family friends were keeping lists and dealing with callers.

Fortunately both the children were readers. They lived so far out of town that they had to be. Katie armed herself with the new copy of St. Nicholas, and Victor took along The Boys' King Arthur.

The ladies kept their voices low, as if they were in a sickroom. They poured their sympathy over Mrs. Cummager, and they had fulsome phrases on tap—dear Chloe, so lovely, so sweet, so wonderful. Their hearts were wrung for the poor dear Senator.

Katie's face came to quivering life. "I don't know how Father is going to get along without Mother," she said—she was a good little girl playing funeral now.

The ladies were properly touched. Mrs. Wyndham said, "You must be your father's little sunshine, Katie. You must take your mother's place. You're the lady of the house now."

17

This suggestion was so wide of the possibilities that it exasperated Victor, who was flayed and bleeding. Mrs. Wyndham might as well have advised Katie to take up a career on the flying trapeze. But it answered an emotional need in Katie. It engrossed her totally. After she and Victor went into the sitting room, her thoughts flickered across her face—she was casting herself as Father's little sunshine. She was filling Mother's place.

Victor couldn't endure being shut up in the sitting room. His mind was going round and round the treadmill of bitter memory. He must be on the move. For one thing, he wanted to get down to the kitchen and see what the *Sun-Record* had made of Mother's death. So when Granny set off for home he escorted her to the front door.

Several ladies joined the escort party, condoling with Granny's loss. When the front door closed they turned back in a cluster toward their headquarters in the back parlor.

Victor was headed for the basement stairs when he heard a sound that halted him. On any other day it would be the most normal sound in the world. Today it was the crackling twig that betrayed the enemy.

It was nothing but a short, light, natural laugh. In this house of mourning it signified that the ladies were laying aside their masks of sorrow. Victor needed to hear what those ladies had to say among themselves.

The parlors were admirably adapted for eavesdropping since both of them had archways opening into the conservatory. Victor went through the empty front parlor into the conservatory. He settled himself with his book in a Philippine chair with a back like the spread of a peacock's tail, out of eyeshot of the back parlor but well within earshot.

At first the ladies were too busy for gossip. They listed the wreaths and sprays that came in. They answered the telephone and recorded the calls. They conferred with Aunt Louisa, secluded in the smoking room with the ailing Uncle Ollie. Augustus screened the callers and ushered a select few into the back parlor.

Every time they rehearsed the accident, Victor came nearer to screaming like a steam whistle. They didn't really care. They were enjoying themselves. They were—what was the word?—they were ghouls.

". . . Yes, a calamity. Nobody was like Chloe. . . . The time of the funeral will be announced in the papers, when Mr. Wentz gets back from Doonville. . . . Yes, horrible. It was sweet of you to call."

It was almost lunchtime. The last visitor took her leave, with her words still hanging in the air, "What's so terrible is that it might have happened to any one of us."

Some lady was not able to resist adding, in her normal, frivolous voice,

"—Not unless we'd been out on the turnpike at four in the morning!"

Several little laughs were strangled, the tone of decorum broke. Victor began to seethe dangerously. But he had to listen.

Another woman said, in a captious voice, "I'm not a prude—I don't give a woman a bad name simply because she goes out in a car with a man. It's her secretiveness that's so hard to swallow."

"Who on earth was Harold Ritter—does anybody know? Where did she meet him?"

"He lived on South Boulevard, I understand," someone said damagingly.

"We mustn't leap to conclusions, you know," a falsely charitable voice put in. "It's quite possible this congressman did call a meeting upstate."

"The *Sun-Record* gave a pretty strong hint that there was no meeting. They called it an *alleged* political conference—don't you adore that? Imagine Chloe at an alleged political conference."

"Oh, the *Sun-Record,* my dear!"

"I'm not ashamed to read the *Sun-Record*. It prints what the *Telegram* keeps bottled up. They sent a correspondent racing out to this congressman's house, but nobody answered the doorbell. And not one soul in the neighborhood had noticed any cars outside the Olsen house yesterday evening."

"There's something so peculiar about this accident, so unsettling! It will be a dreadful shock to Horace Rampole. He'll hardly have the heart to marry a third time!"

Pain struck Victor, as if the woman had driven a red-hot spike into his brain. Somehow he found himself on his feet, facing the ladies from the conservatory arch.

"Yap-yap-yap, you bloodsucking old witches! You just love having my mother get killed. . . . There *was* a meeting!" he shrieked into their faces. "But don't ask anybody that really knows—don't ask Augustus, or Aunt Louisa, or Father! . . . Go on, read the *Sun-Record*, so you can have your fun slinging mud at Mother. . . ."

For another moment his own violence sustained him. Their faces were flaming—he had scorched them.

But his bones betrayed him—they began to tremble. Rather than let the ladies see him unmanned, he dashed furiously through the house and down the side-porch steps. He bounded across the lawn like a young stag, seeking the shelter of the forest.

He ran and leaped through the old timber, his lungs bursting, till he slowed to a stumbling walk. He let himself slump to the ground, between the roots of a great beech tree. He was not far from the summerhouse.

19

It didn't matter where he was, just so he was alone. He buried his face in his arms, drawing in the damp scent of leaf mold. Tears welled into his eyes, the first tears he had shed.

He cried for a long time, and wrestled against the strap that bound his heart so intolerably. The strap never gave an inch; he hurt nothing but himself. Everything was wrong, everything was wicked, except Mother; and Mother was dead.

He cried away every ounce of his strength, and lay quiet.

Chapter 3

THE path along the bluff to the summerhouse was beaten so soft that a footfall made no sound on the matted leaves. It was an old Indian trail to the ford of the Doochee; scalping parties had moved that way.

Victor heard a twig crack—someone was coming after him. He burrowed down into his arms. Nobody was going to drag him back to that venomous circle in the back parlor.

The footsteps passed him and paused at the summerhouse steps. Whoever the man was, he was not on Victor's trail. Victor braced himself on his elbow and reconnoitered.

He saw a man's back—a tall, fair head, a good gray overcoat. The man filled his pipe and settled himself for a smoke on the farther steps, looking down at the ford.

What could the man be up to? Did he belong on the place? He hadn't the look of an undertaker, nor exactly the look of a reporter.

Mother might be dead, and the ladies might be ghouls, but Victor had a duty to Chestnut Point. He got to his feet and sauntered along the edge of the bluff. When he got a look at the man's face he stopped and said with genuine surprise, "Why, is that you, Mr. Grover?"

Mother was awfully fond of Mr. Grover. She had grown up with him on Adams Avenue. Father pooh-poohed him, because he was a mugwump in politics. But people had respect for him, because one of his forebears had been the first Chief Justice of Algonquin. He had married a ridiculous, baby-talking out-of-town girl named Queenie, but Mother insisted on having the two of them to dinner for old times' sake. There was a Grover daughter at Miss Peebles' School, and she was asked to the birthday doings at Chestnut Point; but she was a quiet girl, in a grade between Victor's and Katie's, and neither of them knew her well.

"Well, Victor!" Mr. Grover said. "Want to sit down a minute?" Victor was self-conscious because of the tear tracks on his face, but Mr. Grover was not looking at them. He laid his hand on the sun-warmed steps, and Victor joined him.

Sitting quietly on the steps, looking down at the diamond dance of sunlight on the ford and on the glass-green pool beyond, catching the pungency of pipe smoke—this was the most comforting moment Victor had had since the telephone wakened him. The sun traversed the young green of the treetops, and the shadows shifted on the trail. The place was wilderness, just as the Indians had left it. Mother would be glad to know the hepaticas were out—— He jerked his mind away from that thought.

This was a happy place, all the same. Katie and Victor had built dams here when they were little. Mother had waded out to the big rock with her picnic basket; after lunch the children had washed the plates by plunging them arm-deep in the current.

"The Doochee Ford," Mr. Grover said at length, "has always reminded me of your mother."

A defensive shudder ran down Victor's spine. Let people be careful how they talked about his mother! Then everything told him that Mr. Grover was on Mother's side. "Me too," he said. "That was our picnic rock."

"That's not all I meant, although we used to picnic here when we were kids. I meant the river is like your mother. It's so fresh, and so various, and so different from other places.".

Victor understood now, and it was the sweetest, the most real thing anybody had said about Mother. It didn't call for an answer.

Mr. Grover went on, "Big Joe, your grandfather, let our class come out here for a picnic when we graduated from high school. Your father did the honors for old Joe that day, and that was where he first got his eye on your mother. A bonny thing she was in those days! I've known her longer than you have, remember. It's surprising how much I miss her."

"Yes, sir." And they shared an equable silence.

When Mr. Grover had relighted his pipe he said, "I was in love with her, you know. All through college. Then she married your father, right after your grandfather died."

Victor was liking Mr. Grover better and better; he didn't have to be on his guard against him. "It would have been funny if she'd married you," he said.

"She wouldn't have me. I never held it against her. She had more attention than any girl could handle. And I was too young—I had law school ahead of me. I got over it, and now I'm glad, because if I'd married Chloe, I couldn't have married Queenie."

Victor recalled an odd fact, much debated among Mother's intimates: Mr. Grover was blindly, besottedly devoted to the regrettable Queenie. That did seem a comedown, after being in love with Mother. However, the whole conception of grown-up, married people being in love was one that made Victor uneasy. Youngness was a part of love. Victor was in love, but wild horses would not have dragged the admission from him.

"You look awfully like her, you know," Mr Grover said next, comparing the river with Victor's face as if they were two photographs.

"I wish I did. Aunt Louisa says I'm all Rampole."

"Well, you're a Rampole, right enough. But, somehow, you have Doochee eyes. That's what I used to tell your mother—that she had Doochee eyes. She took it for a compliment, because she loved the river. . . . Well! I'd better be getting back to the house. I left Queenie to those buzzards in the parlor and sneaked out for a breath of fresh air."

"Buzzards!—that's the word. I'm not going back to the house till they clear out." And Victor added unwarily, "I was pretty fresh to them."

Mr. Grover was on his feet by this time, leaning against the rustic doorway. "Staying out in the woods won't bring your mother back to you, Victor." Then, with an amusement that ranged him on Victor's side: "What did you say to the buzzards?"

"They were gossiping," Victor said, flushing. The full weight of his misery came down on him again, after the respite.

Mr. Grover drew on his pipe, then said, as if he knew what he was talking about and wanted to share his knowledge with Victor, "People always gossip about delightful women. It's part of the price of being delightful. They started on Chloe before she was out of high school. They give Queenie a working-over, every so often. If you're lucky enough to love a delightful woman, Victor, you can afford to disregard the gossip about her."

It seemed easy enough to disregard it, out there in the sun-shafted forest. All the way up the trail Victor was taking Mr. Grover's advice to heart. Mr. Grover did know what he was talking about.

They came out of the forest and crossed the big lawn, past the old stables, the new garage, the greenhouse, the tennis court. The driveway was full of traffic. A car was nosing along, looking for a gap. The driver walked back toward the front portico ahead of Victor and Mr. Grover, trying to settle his silk hat on his large head.

Mr. Grover said dryly, "If he was going to borrow a hat at all, he should have borrowed a bigger one."

"He's a politician," Victor hazarded.

Before mounting the steps the politician polished his perspiring brow and gave the hat a despairing tug. He was a stalwart young hayseed— one of the Insurgents from upstate, most likely.

While Victor was lurking in the cross corridor, dodging the ladies, Augustus came through and announced to Aunt Louisa in the smoking room, "Mrs. Lassigne, Mr. Olsen has arrived from Doonville."

"Excellent," said Aunt Louisa, regally emerging. "I'll see him in the breakfast room, Augustus."

Congressman Olsen—the last man who had seen Mother before she was killed. And Aunt Louisa was seeing him in the breakfast room. The fetid smell of conspiracy came back to Victor. The breakfast room was where people went when they were determined to avoid eavesdroppers. It was a glass coop overlooking the east lawn, and the approach through the huge dining room provided no cover—no curtained recesses, no deep-backed chairs.

Aunt Louisa had talked to Mr. Olsen on the telephone the night before, and that ought to be enough. Meddle, meddle, meddle! She said she was protecting Mother's reputation, but if she didn't look out she would protect it so much that people would begin to think there was something wrong with it.

Victor could not hope to overhear the conference in the breakfast room, but there was no law against his watching it through the peephole in the pantry door.

Mr. Olsen was in view. His chair was too small for him, and he sat with his big palms pressed together between his knees. All that showed of Aunt Louisa was one long, autocratic hand, its forefinger tapping the tabletop as if she were hitting one typewriter key over and over. She was laying down the law to Mr. Olsen, and Mr. Olsen was nodding— Yes, ma'am, yes, ma'am—with a troubled, countrified look on his face.

The forefinger drew back, its work accomplished. Mr. Olsen held up one hand, palm forward, as if he were swearing allegiance to the flag.

Aunt Louisa came into view, steering Mr. Olsen with queenly condescension toward the entrance hall. He reclaimed his hat; the two of them shook hands, and Mr. Olsen set briskly off to execute his orders.

Aunt Louisa nearly trapped Victor by coming unexpectedly through the pantry door. The swinging door practically flattened him to the wall. Augustus was at the counter, refilling the sherry decanter.

"I knew we could count on Olsen," she said to Augustus in a voice of working partnership. "He understands that the papers mustn't be al-

23

lowed to make a mystery out of that meeting of his. He's going to persuade all those men to admit that they were at his house last night. Then
he'll drop in for dinner at the Belvedere Grill, where Jim Claggan always eats. Claggan will leap at the chance to get a statement out of
him—so there we are!" And she proceeded grandly toward the smoking
room.

Victor sauntered toward Augustus and helped himself to a piece of
cold cinnamon toast which had come out on a tray. Augustus gave him
a knife-edged glance, but said nothing.

"I never saw such a woman for getting her nose into things," Victor
said.

"You let your auntie alone," Augustus said, recorking the sherry bottle and setting it back in the liquor cupboard. "I told you she was a
jewel in time of trouble, and she is. It's a pity she wasn't born a man.
She's filled up her life with female flummery, but she's as sharp as a
razor and as quick as a rattlesnake."

Chapter 4

THE day wore on to suppertime. A crescendo was building up—the Senator was due in from Washington on the eight-o'clock
train. The whole of downstairs was astir with people who didn't want to
leave until they had said at least a word of sympathy to him.

Victor had been nerving himself for the difficult trip back from the
station. Mother had always taken him and Katie down to meet Father's
train. He blamed Father for sending Mother off to Doonville, and yet
in fairness he admitted that Father would not have had Mother killed
for the world. The mysterious meeting was a stupidity, not a wickedness. Victor had a flood of affection dammed up inside him, now that
his mother was gone, and he needed to release it upon his father. Once
he and Father met, the dam of bitterness would break.

Then it turned out that Aunt Louisa had pre-empted the job of meeting her dear bereaved brother. Trust her!—and yet it was a reprieve of a
sort. The meeting might pass off better at home.

The children had had supper in the playroom, away from the crowd.
Instead of eating her lamb chop Katie stared into space like an under-
sized Joan of Arc. "Do you know what, Victor?" she said. "I'm going to
practice every single day, so that I can play the piano to Father in the

evenings, the way Mother used to." Victor restrained himself from saying that five-finger exercises gave Father the fidgets, although this was a recognized fact.

Nora came into the room. "Your Sunday dress is back from the Sherwood Dyers. I can't think how they ever dyed it so quick. Shall I help you into it?"

Katie was eager to be costumed for her new role. A few minutes later she rushed half dressed into the corridor, shrieking that the Packard was coming up the drive. She hustled into her dress, and Nora gave her hair a lick and a promise.

"Do you know what we're like?" she said to Victor as they stood at the head of the stairs. "The Princes in the Tower. All in solemn black." And she descended as princelike as she could, with Victor ill at ease beside her, ringed by pitying eyes. Politicians lugubrious on the dining-room side, family friends crowding the parlor doorway for the spectacle.

Augustus opened the front door for Father and Aunt Louisa; William followed them in with a suitcase. The circle of watchers drew back, granting the Senator partial privacy for the meeting with his children.

Father's eyes were bloodshot, and his big face was dewlapped like a hound's. He looked almost dangerously right and left, and the watchers shrank farther back, as if in his distraction he might lash out. The Senator was taking this very hard—and a great many people were trying to read his face to see whether the *Sun-Record* version of the story had reached him.

Katie took three steps forward from the foot of the stairs. "Poor Father!" she said clearly and kindly. "We're here. You still have us."

The Senator's raging eyes came round and dwelt on his daughter in the ghastly silence.

Victor was suddenly aware of how shocking Katie looked. Nora hadn't Mother's hand with a brush and comb; Katie's hair was clumped into a mane, and the parting was askew. Nobody had ever seen her except in picture-book colors; now she was in black, and the dress had shrunk in the dyeing, so that she looked to be all joints, shins and shoulder blades. She looked like a young half-fledged crow.

"Good God!" was what Father said, devastatingly. And Victor knew he could never forgive his father.

It wasn't the profanity Victor minded. Victor himself had felt like swearing all day. Father had no idea he had spoken at all—because two minutes later, while ladies were coming forward to press his hand, he turned and said in a quite different tone, "And now, where are the children?"

25

But by that time it was too late. Katie had scorched upstairs, and for a long time no one could find her.

Yes, Victor was sorry for his father. But however badly Father felt, he had no right to flare out at Katie. Other people felt badly too. It was a dense, cruel, blundering thing to have done. It was a blindness to everyone's interests except his own, and it tied in with the fatal stupidity that had sent Mother to her death.

Everyone except the Senator joined in the hunt for Katie. William organized an outdoor searching crew among the men on the place.

Victor was afraid he knew where to look for Katie—afraid because it was the place where he least wanted to go. She would be in the Secret Cave.

The Secret Cave was the space under the valance of Mother's bed. In earlier days it had been Katie's privileged hideaway; but when Victor was wounded in a running fight with bandits she would take him in, and stanch the bleeding, and strengthen him with bits of graham cracker on a doll's plate. So that was where he went to look for her.

Mother's room was as orderly now as a hotel room. All the traces of living were gone. The dressing table was on parade, the cupboard drawers were closed, the chairs stood square to the walls. He forbade himself to look at anything.

He bent down and raised the dimity flounce. Two wild-animal eyes burned from the depths of the cave. He heard a sound of scrambling away from him.

As Katie's superior officer he had a long experience in handling her. He sat down cross-legged on the carpet. After a while he said, "I'm not doing anything much. I could read to you out of the *Five Little Peppers*."

After a pause for interior conflict Katie said in a detached voice, "Mother was in the middle of *Bob, Son of Battle*."

Victor had his own pause for conflict. He didn't think he could open the book where Mother had laid the bookmark only two days ago.

But he was ruggeder than Katie was, and what Father had just done to her might crack her to bits. He said, "Well, all right then," and to spare Katie the ignominy of creeping publicly out of her cave, he strolled back through the house to the playroom.

In a few minutes he heard her turning on her bath. Baths came just before reading.

He had five or ten minutes, so first he called off the search parties. Then he headed doggedly for the smoking room. For his own part, he never wanted to speak to Father again, but he must make Father do something kind for Katie.

He knocked on the smoking-room door, and then opened it.

He had never seen his father as he saw him now. He was sitting in front of the roll-top desk, with his head down on his forearms. The hand that showed was opening and clenching on the blotter, as Victor's did when the doctor put the seven stitches in his scalp. Every few seconds a spasm went through his back and shoulders.

Victor felt one moment of compassion. Then the strap tightened inside him. That's just fine, he thought—you specialize in busting people, and then being sorry when it's too late to do any good. Go on and agonize—you have it coming to you.

"Father——"

The Senator gave a twitch of his body, indicating that he was to be left alone.

Victor said firmly, "I have to speak to you, Father. Mother always used to kiss Katie good night. Somebody will have to attend to that."

The Senator reared his head. His face was shockingly lined, but his eyeballs were dry and his eyes were still dangerous. "Haven't you taken in that your mother has been killed? There are a lot of things we'll all have to get along without. Haven't you any consideration for me? I never kissed Katie good night in my life."

"You'll have to, just this once. Something awful will happen to Katie unless you show a little interest in her." Victor had never spoken up to his father before; the discipline of childhood was still strong upon him. He was on new ground, and he quaked; but his anger held him together.

He could hardly believe it—Father rose, and followed him upstairs.

Katie had got herself into bed, with *Bob, Son of Battle* lying open at Mother's bookmark. When her father came into the room her face froze and her pupils widened oddly.

She mustn't blow to bits, not tonight. To put out the fuse that was burning in her, Victor said, "Father came up to say good night to us."

Because he was Victor, she took her tone from him. He could fairly see the passing of a sponge across her memory of her father's swearing at her. "Why, hello, Father," she said with surprise and pleasure.

The Senator said, "I came up to—er—tell you you must be a brave little girl——"

"Are *you* going to read to us tonight?"

"Afraid not," he said in haste. "I'll just—er—kiss you good night."

Victor knew how silly his father felt, approaching his stubbled jowl to Katie's vellum cheek. Her wiry arms went up around his neck and clasped it.

Still, it was better than nothing. After he had gone, the Joan-of-Arc shine came back into her eyes. Propping her arms behind her head she

27

speculated, "I guess we are a comfort to Father, or he wouldn't have come up."

Victor ground his teeth, to keep from telling Katie it was he who had dragged Father upstairs. His whole effort would be wasted if he told her that.

More mumbo jumbo, more covering up. A taste of brass lay on his palate. It was more corroding than the taste of sorrow—it was the taste of all-enveloping falsity.

Chapter 5

Two days after the funeral Horace Rampole drove himself down to River Street for a word with Dan Parmiter. He had an apology to make and a question to ask, both of them ticklish and both necessary.

People eyed him as he tooled across town in his glittering automobile. He chose to show himself. He was not a broken man, not a deceived husband; his presence challenged those discreet innuendoes in the *Sun-Record*.

But his heart was heavy. This new trouble had him pinned beneath it. It was not only the loss of his wife—although Chloe had twined her way into the depths of his affections—it was the tarnish of her ambiguous death. He must stop brooding over it. He was a public man.

River Street antedated Adams Avenue, but its glory was far in the past. Dan lived in the old Justice Grover mansion, on a low bluff overlooking the river basin. But its white colonnade had been grimed to elephant-gray by the smoke from switch engines on the foreshore. The water front was a clutter of docks, warehouses, saloons and hock shops. Commerce had claimed River Street.

Dan's desk stood unoccupied inside a tall narrow window, on which was lettered:

D. S. PARMITER
Shipping Broker.

From these homely headquarters Dan exercized his power over the city. He could have bought and sold half the magnates in Meridian, but his manner of living served his legend, as Chestnut Point served the Rampoles.

Horace was a fine figure of a statesman as he went up the steps, swinging his motoring goggles by their strap. He had leathery forceful features and brown-coffee eyes beneath a crag of eyebrow; his strong-growing hair was just flaked with silver. He preferred not to remember how near he was to sixty.

In the back parlor he found a buxom, middle-aged woman, with her hair combed into a bun, stringing green beans.

"Why, Senator!" Mrs. Magruder kept her distance as Dan's housekeeper; she did not trade first names. She was separated from her husband, a patrolman, and more than professionally devoted to Dan; but she was too good a Catholic to divorce her husband and marry him. "Sure we feel terrible about your poor pretty wife."

"Thanks, Mrs. Magruder, I know you do. Dan around?"

"He's out snoozing in the hammock. He's not the man he was before he took that indigestion last summer."

Horace made his way down the back steps to the dooryard. Machine shops had encroached on the old garden ground, but the place had its amenity—a tangle of shrubs, a croquet set, a picnic table under a tree. Dan Parmiter lay in the hammock with a bandanna over his bald spot. Even in idleness he was trimly buttoned into his clothes. Neatness of mind and of person had given him his nickname of Gentleman Dan.

He darted across the lawn, his rosy little old face alight, his protruding affable gray eyes sending out beams of friendship. The two men had worked in partnership since they were boys. "Well, how are you bearing up, boy?"

"Fine." Dan's presence lightened Horace. Dan was an easy, useful little cuss. He claimed to have left school in the seventh grade, but life had sufficiently educated him.

Horace settled himself in a hickory rocker and lighted a cigar. He didn't know how to open up on Danny, and Danny seemed equally unwilling to grapple with him over the little conspiracy in Doonville.

For some time he parried idly while Dan scolded him about Theodore Roosevelt. The strain was familiar: Horace heard it in the Meridian Club and in the Senate rest rooms. At certain exasperated moments, when the Presidential hand had moved faster than the eye, he joined it himself. But sooner or later the regulars would have to recognize that Roosevelt was a magnificent President, in tune with the new century. The air felt fresher these days—it smelled of civic righteousness and high enterprise. Horace would never be a radical, but in middle life he had developed a niceness about keeping his feet out of the public trough. He had run for mayor on a reform ticket, and coerced Dan into helping him. He saw himself as a mediator between the mossbacks and the radicals in the party. And Dan was definitely among the mossbacks.

Dan grumbled along, working up a healthy pink in his cheeks. Trust busting . . . railroad rate regulation . . . what would be left of prosperity when Teddy got through with it? Even the Old Guard in the Senate had knuckled under. "You make me sick," he said. "He's bewitched the lot of you. Teddy yells, 'Come on, let's exterminate the big bad Interests,' and you all forget that the Interests are nothing but your own silly selves, and that you've made the country what it is. There was a time when a lot of little fellas would stay regular for nothing more than an annual railroad pass—and to get their pass they had to see me. What have you left me to trade with?"

"He has the weight of public opinion behind him——"

"Public opinion!—tell that to P. T. Barnum. The man's a megalomaniac. He's no better than a side-show barker—all in the interests of Theodore Roosevelt. He thinks he's bigger than the party that put him in office. You go on bootlicking Roosevelt, and you'll saddle us with him for a third term."

"He's not going to run again, Dan, he's said so. He's grooming Taft to succeed him."

"That I will believe when I see it," said Danny. Mrs. Magruder brought out two steins of beer. Danny dipped his blunt muzzle, wiped his upper lip and cast about for a more immediate topic. But he still evaded the sore point between himself and Horace. "You'll be glad to hear that we're squared away on the refunding of the Meridian Street Transit bonds. One little chore for you, and we're all set. And high time—the *Sun-Record* sent out a muckraker the other day to investigate us."

Horace said stiffly, "There's nothing about MST to investigate. We haven't passed a dividend in twenty-five years. We've all got rich trading in MST stock, and half the widows and orphans in Meridian are living off it."

Dan gave his friend a sidelong look of kindness. The MST had been one of Big Joe's creations, and Horace had a touchy loyalty to his rascally old father. Dan said delicately, "Five years in a row now, we've dipped into our sinking fund to pay dividends. It's getting kind of chronic."

"There must be bad management, then. In my father's day, the MST was a gold mine."

"We've got to open a new vein of gold. That's what I want to talk to you about. What we need is more passengers and more nickels."

On the face of it Dan's proposal had merit. The MST owned and operated the Rivergrove Amusement Park out at the end of the car line, and Rivergrove had been losing money. Dan was bringing in some new concessions to attract new patrons. "If we really promote Rivergrove, we can ring up a million new fares a season."

"With merry-go-rounds and salt-water taffy?" Horace scoffed.

"That's only part of it," Danny said. He sighed, plainly wishing that Horace would not press him. There were down-to-earth realities in life that Horace was squeamish about. But Horace kept an inquisitorial eye upon him, and he had to go on.

"When I said concessions—— Rivergrove is outside the city limits, Horry. I have the sheriff in my pocket. Well, we're letting in a high-class restaurant, with clubroom features, at a whacking big price, and it will attract the streetcar trade."

Horace turned mulberry-red with anger. "Gambling! When I was mayor I ran the gamblers out of town."

"And I helped you," said Danny coolly. "But where did those gamblers go, do you suppose? Not into monasteries. They moved out beyond the county line and set up in business for the automobile trade. And I say that's downright undemocratic. This is going to be strictly high-class—prettiest little casino you ever saw—the poor man's Monte Carlo."

"And liquor, I don't doubt. In a family resort?"

"Only to members," said Danny virtuously. "There's going to be a big demand for membership cards."

"Have you lost your wits entirely, Dan? The *Sun-Record* is just hankering for a good crusade against vice and crime generally, and particularly if they can tie it to our tail. Where is that going to leave us next November? We can't afford a stench like that."

Dan tossed his silver pocketknife and caught it—openly merry at Horace's artlessness. "Stench? Would I lay myself open to a stench? Likely you haven't heard there's a new owner bought into the *Sun-Record*. Only a minority interest, but he calls the tune, and he can be got at."

"So?" Horace said, frowning. Danny had scored on him. "I hadn't heard. I haven't lunched at the club, this trip."

"New fella in town. Fella named Anson Epps. He made a pot of money in the market, and bought out Burns & Halliday when it went bankrupt. You'll run across him. Smooth, slim, fine-looking fella with a nasty smile. Slick as paint."

"Democrat, I take it?"

"Five thousand to us, five thousand to the Democrats."

If there was one thing Horace distrusted, it was a man who hedged his bets against the Republican party. "And you're counting on a welcher like that to muzzle the *Sun-Record* for you? What is there in it for Epps? Is he in on the gambling racket?"

"Now, now! What he wants has no cash value at all, and you're the one to deliver it. He wants to get elected a member of the Meridian Club. I think his women folks are deviling him to put on style. You'd like him all right—he don't eat with his knife."

"It smells. It's blackmail." Dan had put Horace in a quandary. Horace had access to sacred ground that Dan never penetrated, and the Meridian Club was sacrosanct. Epps must be a shrewd, unscrupulous trader.

"I wouldn't ask you to do it if he was a bum," Danny urged. "Read the society columns—him and his wife get around everywhere. Half a dozen members would second him—he has his hooks into them."

Horace tugged at the end of his nose.

"Look," Dan said, "you're not so lily-white yourself. You lost your political virginity long ago. What's more important—one piddling little gambling joint, or the solvency of the MST? Give me two years—three years at the most—then you can gallop in on your white horse and clean up Rivergrove."

"I'll think it over" was all Horace would say. His hands were tied. He was a man ruled by loyalities; and the deepest of these, the sorest to the touch, was his loyalty to Big Joe, who had operated under the ethics of a grosser age.

Dan smiled wisely. Horace might wriggle, but he couldn't get off the hook. Dan had no desire to drive the barb in.

Horace plunged into the subject that had brought him to River Street. "Dan, I can't leave town without thanking you for being so decent about that Doonville business. You spiked the scandal, and I appreciate it—particularly as it was a mutiny against you. My father would have taken the back of a hairbrush to those young galoots upstate, and you had a right to."

Dan didn't like this subject any better than Horace did. He fiddled with his penknife. "A paddling isn't in order. That sister of yours, she forced all our hands. Chalk this up as a personal favor to you, Horace, in your time of trouble. . . . But that Louisa, she's a great little fixer! She takes after your dad."

"Too much of a fixer. Sometimes she covers more territory than she needs to." He waited for Dan to take him up.

But Dan was pursuing a fly that threatened his bald spot; his hand hovered for the kill. He obliged Horace to continue.

"Maybe she was justified in making bad blood between you and the

Boys upstate—but not between you and me, Dan, not after all these years."

Dan made a snatch, and closed his fist on his quarry. "Forget the whole damned thing, Horry. It's going to take a bigger girl than Louisa to make bad blood between us two."

"Get this, Dan. I might have met with those young Swedes and tried to straighten 'em out—but I'd have tipped you off, and reported back. The plain fact is, Dan, I—er—I was never asked up to Doonville. It was Louisa got wind of the meeting and decided to represent me—and then she couldn't go after all. The first I ever heard of it was when she met me at the train the other night—and that's what I wanted to get straight with you."

He counted on Dan to guffaw, slap his thigh and take Horace back into fellowship. But Danny withheld the guffaw. "Louisa is as smart as hell" was all he would say.

"Too damn smart. If she'd kept her long nose out, my wife wouldn't have been killed."

"Don't hold a grudge against Louisa. She used her best judgment—and she got results. Drop the whole business—it's served its purpose." His mildness was oppressive because it was uncharacteristic. Dan was an autocrat over his machine.

Horace got to his feet and said heavily, "Well, I must be moving." He still had not asked his question—it wasn't a question a man could ask. He took a turn across the grass and hefted one of the lopsided croquet balls in his paw. The question was destroying him, and he had to ask it. He took his stand in front of Danny's chair.

"Dan, did Louisa invent the whole story from beginning to end? Was there any meeting in Doonville? The *Sun-Record*——"

Dan sprang upright—terrier confronting mastiff. "Good Lord, Horry, this has knocked you cockeyed. There's a dozen witnesses to the meeting. You of all men ought to know better than to go by the *Sun-Record*."

A groan drove itself up from Horace's chest. "I haven't been sleeping, Dan. I get nightmares."

"Two double whiskies at bedtime," Dan said firmly. "That's my prescription, and I sleep like a baby. And the very minute it's decent, Horace, you ought to get married again."

"No! I've tried it twice now, and I'm licked. I'm not a woman's man."

"You have two youngsters to raise, Horry, and that's women's work."

"I'll raise 'em. No more wives for me. There aren't any more like Chloe."

"You'll see things clearer in a couple of months. I don't know how

I'd have made out without Mrs. Magruder. Get along back to Washington, and sink your teeth into something."

Chapter 6

THREE weeks after the Senator went back to Washington, Victor smashed a glass of jelly on the marble flooring of the front vestibule. He had to. If he hadn't done that, he would have done something worse.

The funeral had been bad enough, but the vacancy after it was intolerable. He was expected to go back to school as if nothing had happened, and to stay for athletics, and to go to dancing school on Friday evenings with a black band on his sleeve; and he could never get away from the eyes.

Eyes . . . eyes . . . spying at him and then glancing away . . . What does he think about Chloe's death? . . . Does he know more than he lets on? . . . Was there anything to that first story in the *Sun-Record?* . . . We must pretend we think everything was all right, we must act perfectly natural. . . .

Victor was equally determined to act perfectly natural. He thrust out his jaw and glared back at the eyes. His safest course was not to talk about Mother at all. Anything he said might be twisted into a doubt of her. But the repression was hard on his temper. He choked off impulses to be insolent to his teachers and to pick quarrels in the locker room; and it was only a matter of time before he smashed something.

He knew his father was being criticized for leaving two orphan children marooned, eight miles from anywhere, without providing for their well-being. That was all right—Victor gave people leave to criticize his father to their hearts' content; and he was dead against all the suggestions that were made.

For instance, Granny Cummager stood ready to move herself and her husband out to Chestnut Point and to take charge of her grandchildren. A fine state of affairs that would be!

When Aunt Louisa drove out to Chestnut Point she was outraged. The children had to be summoned from the basement to receive her, and they had cake frosting on their chins. What sort of a bringing-up would they get from Jennie and Augustus Henning? What they needed was a crack governess, to put spit and polish on them.

34

Neither of these threats troubled Victor much. He knew his father would stand firm against Granny Cummager; and as for dislodging the Hennings, that would be impossible. Even Grandmother Joe Rampole, a firmly ladylike woman, had had to put up with them. They were Old-Meridian. The tie between the Hennings and the Rampoles was hereditary.

But there was a more insidious threat. Everyone expected Horace Rampole to marry for a third time, and most of the unattached gentlewomen of Meridian put themselves in nomination. Victor, Katie, Jennie and Augustus stood shoulder to shoulder against these aspirants. They had no defense against the society women of Washington, but they held the trenches in Meridian.

All the warmth and ease the children had they drew from the kitchen. Jennie and Augustus missed Chloe Rampole and mourned her profoundly.

Jennie, knowing the proprieties of caste, tried to drive the children upstairs. . . . "Get along to your practicing, Katie—Miss Archibald will be here tomorrow. . . . Run outdoors and play now, the two of you, before it gets dark. . . ."

But she could no more get rid of them than she could have evicted a dog who was determined not to go. "In a minute," they'd say, and go on playing tittattoe on the margin of a newspaper. She hadn't the heart to be severe with them; the big rooms upstairs were as empty as tombs.

Augustus gossiped before them, freely and humorously, about the solicitous lady callers. "Miss Geneva Cutler called just now, to inquire for the dear little people. She fetched along a jar of currant jelly with a geranium leaf in it." And he deposited the jelly glass on the kitchen table, with a sly side look at his wife. "I'm to give it to the dear Senator the very night he gets home, with his dinner, to let him know"—here he fell into Miss Geneva's adenoidal tremolo—"that *somebody* is thinking about him."

"Currant jelly, for the cat's sake!" said Jennie, bristling at the slur on her professional competence. "That Geneva Cutler! It would be a sore trial to her to give up her nice room in a boardinghouse and take over as mistress here. But she's not one to shirk her duty."

Katie looked up from the game of boxes she and Victor were playing and asked despairingly, "Is there some rule that Father has to get married again?"

"No rule," said Gus, "just opportunities."

"I would despise a stepmother," Katie said. But she said it resignedly. She wasn't fighting the situation as Victor was; she was letting it flatten her. She was not angry at her father, as Victor was. She didn't know he had kissed her good night under compulsion. She didn't know he had sent Mother up to Doonville. She was sorry for him; she loved him. And Victor had scruples against enlightening her—if he did, he wouldn't leave her much of anything to love.

The longer Victor looked at the glass of jelly the more his fury mounted. There was an effrontery about it that brought the blood into his eyeballs.

Moving with deceptive quietness, he went over and took possession of it. Should he empty it into the sink? Should he drop it into the garbage pail? Should he feed it to the family of cats that infested the old stables? He was going to punish that glass of jelly somehow for presuming to usurp his mother's rights.

He took it upstairs with him. He could fairly see Miss Geneva Cutler delivering it in the vestibule. If he'd been there, he'd have booted her down the front steps. . . .

He opened the front door wide. He stepped back and calculated his hurling position. Then he wound up and let go with the jelly glass.

It crashed gloriously; the splinters flew, the jelly squirted in radiating globules. . . .

Then he stood trembling. What had he accomplished? He hadn't repelled the threat of a stepmother; he hadn't brought Mother back; he had not resolved the public doubt over the manner of her death. All he had done was make a gosh-awful mess in the front vestibule.

Augustus had heard the crash and had come upstairs to investigate. He laid a hand on Victor's shoulder.

"Don't let it get you down, Vic," he consoled him. "His Nibs won't ever marry a plain woman—he never has yet. Come back downstairs. Jen's just taking a batch of brownies out of the oven."

In the encompassing kindness of the kitchen Victor and Katie absorbed the lore of tribal greatness. Augustus was a bardic storyteller, and he spun his yarns with intention, these days, to take the children's minds off their troubles.

Jason Henning, first of his line in Meridian, had worked in the original trading post for Huck Rampole. But he hadn't the Rampole foresight in taking up land. His property developed into the city garbage dump, and he let his creditors foreclose on it. Artemus Rampole took care of the Hennings by setting them up as tenant farmers at Chestnut Point, long before the big house was built there, and there Augustus passed his boyhood.

When Augustus grew old enough he was brought down to Adams Avenue to work around the Rampole stables, so that he could attend the city high school. But he never finished his schooling. He got too much fun out of driving Big Joe Rampole's buggy and serving as equerry to young Horace.

"Your grandma never approved of me," he said. "She thought I put your pa up to mischief—and maybe I did. We knew this town backwards and forwards, from the billiard parlors down by the river to the ball teams on the sand lots. But I will say for myself that if I got Horry into scrapes, I always got him out of them. And Big Joe stood up for me. He didn't want his boy to turn out a mollycoddle—the day Horace was born, Big Joe marked him for a career in politics."

During Horace's college years Big Joe developed Chestnut Point. He needed an establishment of mark, where he could entertain traction magnates, university trustees, governors and Presidents. He built his famous smoking room off the side porch, so that the Boys could come and go without offending his lady wife. And he used Augustus, who knew the ground, as a deputy building superintendent. By the time Horace graduated from college, Augustus had made himself indispensable at Chestnut Point.

"Tell us how you got to be a butler," Katie would coax him. And Augustus was delighted to oblige.

It occurred during President Grant's historic visit to Chestnut Point. Mrs. Joseph had telegraphed to New York for a genuine, eighteen-carat English butler, straight from Cockalorum Castle. Augustus studied his style, and mimicked him for the benefit of the maids in the kitchen. "You should have seen me come sailing through the door with a tea tray," he said.

The day before the big doings Dwiggins began to crack. He tried to count out the silver for the banquet, and he couldn't count to forty-eight—Augustus had to keep tally for him. But he held himself together until the hired waiters rolled in. Mrs. Joseph had engaged colored boys from the old Belvedere House.

"They were crackerjacks, those boys—they could load plates all the way up their arm to the shoulders, and then set off running. But that wasn't the way things were done at Cockalorum Castle. 'Savages!' Dwiggin would groan out, and then he'd wring his hands and fortify himself with a nip out of a bottle.

"Well, there was an afternoon reception, with a marquee on the lawn, and then a banquet to follow. The reception was going full swing—the band was tootling like sixty—when in comes one of them colored boys at the gallop, grabs up a stack of plates that Dwiggins had set out ready for his banquet, and makes off with them. 'Come back, you scoundrel!'

shouts Dwiggins—and then if he didn't bust out crying! Boiled as an owl he was.

"So I poured the old goat a tumbler of neat whisky, and laid him away to cool, and took over myself. There was no time to get permission. I climbed into his tail coat and, come dinnertime, I marched those waiters at the double. It may have been more hash-house style than White House style, but I figured U. S. Grant wouldn't be the one to complain.

"Well, the banquet went off as smooth as butter. You should have seen the flabbergasted look in your grandma's eye when I announced dinner, instead of Dwiggins. But she dassn't say a word. So next day I says to Big Joe, 'That Dwiggins is all for show and none for blow. If I have to do his work, I might as well draw his pay.'

"And a year later I married me a green country girl out of the kitchen—and look what a picker I turned out to be! Jen can turn out a mousse or a galantine as good as any caterer. She's like me—she isn't suited with a job till she's done it up brown."

Augustus was trying to shake some life back into Katie. She laughed at his stories, but then she relapsed into a frightening passivity, a wantlessness. It was old Miss Archibald, her music teacher, who did the most for her.

Miss Archibald had studied the piano in Germany, and assimilated many of the characteristics of her music master—his low rich chuckle, his peppery expletives, his dithyrambic eloquence.

She could have exploited her richest pupil, but she was too scrupulous to say that Katie had more than a "nice little gift." Katie's five-finger exercises were ragged and her sonatinas were wooden. Miss Archibald's heart went out to the orphan waif. When Katie sat perched on the piano stool in the dark-looming front parlor she reminded Miss Archibald of a black exclamation point.

She knocked away at Schumann's "Happy Farmer." Bam-*bam*, (bip-bip), ban-*ban*, (bip-bip)——

"Make it dance, *Liebchen!* Make it sing."

"I'd feel silly."

"Music is a magician. It can break our hearts, and heal them. It can fill the empty cup of our lives."

Bam-*bam*, (bip-bip)——

"*Schätzchen*, you're so self-conscious. For our recital, in June, we must play some concerted music. I want you to be carried on a wind of harmony and rhythm."

"All right, Miss Archibald."

"Eight hands—you, and myself, and two other pupils. The Tchaikov-sky Serenade, I think. I will arrange it myself, and write out the parts."

"For mercy's sake, Miss Archibald, can you write music?"

"At our house we improvise constantly. I live with my widowed sister, you know. She plays the cello and violin. My nephew can play any instrument he picks up. Music is our language around the house."

"Why, how interesting, Miss Archibald!"

"But the rehearsing—— You have a car, and the other children haven't. ...ld you stop at my house after school?"

"I should imagine so, Miss Archibald."

When Katie went to Miss Archibald's house she was ill at ease. She knew Miss Archibald was poor, and as a Rampole she had been trained to be gracious to poor people. But this house wasn't pretentious and run-to-seed, like Granny's. Neither was it like the gardener's house at Chestnut Point. It stood in a row of little houses, and you could smell the soap factory pretty strong; and when you got inside the walls were thin, and Mrs. Godkin answered the door with a cooking spoon in her hand. But it wasn't exactly a poor-people's house. It had a beautiful big piano, an upright, and a cello standing in the corner.

"This is Bessie, and this is Lorna," Miss Archibald said. "And this is Katie Rampole."

"Where do you go to school, Katie?"

"I go to Miss Peebles'. Where do you go?"

"To Parmiter," said Lorna.

"Oh, yes," Katie cried with unnatural vivacity. She had never heard of the Parmiter School, but she knew old Mr. Parmiter, who showed her tricks with coins and pocket handkerchiefs. She knew now how gracious to be, and her self-consciousness abated.

They fell to work at their eight-hand arrangement. Miss Archibald sat at Katie's left. She was extraordinary. She seemed able to play all her own notes, while still having several hands left over—one to beat time, one to knock Katie's fingers off the wrong notes. "*One*-and-two-and," she counted; and by sheer will power she drove them together to the conclusion.

"It's awfully pretty," Katie said. When the other parts had come in around her, echoing and diverging, her cheeks had gone ruby-red with excitement.

"Repeat!" like a captain leading his troops into combat. "From the double bar."

Suddenly heavenly music rose to join them. It came down from upstairs. It was a flute, doubling the melody, following it in thirds, decking it with bird-song warblings, dying away. . . .

Katie was spellbound, ravished. She could hardly keep her fingers at work; yet if she faltered, she would break the trance of beauty. Her breathing was almost a sob as she pursued her piano part.

"What in the world was that?" Bessie cried when they had come victoriously through.

"That was only Roy, meddling in. My nephew."

"Oh, Miss Archibald, can't he play with us at the recital?"

"That would be most unethical. I can't claim him as a pupil."

William now rang the doorbell and reminded Katie that he had to pick Victor up and get home in time for supper.

Katie pleaded to go through the Serenade just once more. So they went through it, and Katie waited for the flute to enter. But the flute had lost interest. The dream was over. Katie put her music together.

While she was saying good-by Mrs. Godkin came in and said to her sister, "I'll have to give Roy his supper. He's rehearsing with the school orchestra tonight." And she began carrying in plates.

"I'll call him for you," Miss Archibald said. She struck two or three notes on the piano that said as plain as day, "Supper, Roy!"

And from upstairs the flute called back, "Half a jiffy!"

Bessie and Lorna were dawdling, to catch a glimpse of the mysterious flute player. Katie had no such impulse. He couldn't be anything except a person, and that would be a disenchantment. She took her leave.

Chapter 7

Two years after Chloe Cummager's death, the Senator came back from Washington for the Easter recess. He went straight from the train to his office, where his secretary had a dozen appointments laid out for him. He had committees to convene, speeches to make, enemies to confound and bartenders to get out of scrapes. The trustees of the university were in a pother, as usual. And Dan Parmiter was far from well.

Horace thought about his children only in passing. He had never got around to hiring a governess. He had a dynastic fondness, stronger naturally for the man-child than for the girl-child. But Victor was growing like a giraffe and going through a cranky adolescence. Such views as he had on public affairs he drew from the *Sun-Record*. He wanted to be let alone.

As for Katie, Horace left her to Louisa. Some day she would evolve into a charming young Rampole belle, and that would be time enough for Horace to begin being fond of her.

His own career was trundling along well enough. In the fall the party caucus would renominate him, and the voters would re-elect him. He would have to go through the motions of getting out the vote for Taft, on whom the mantle of Roosevelt had descended, but there would be no difficulty about that. Taft was a successor, a protégé—fat, honest, likable, intelligent, conciliatory. But the Roosevelt fireworks were over.

At midmorning Miss Wupper informed him, "Mrs. Lassigne is on the phone."

Being a gentleman, Horace never swore in front of Miss Wupper, except unconsciously. "You'd think she could give me half a day after I get off the train" was all he said.

"She's been trying to reach you all week."

"Good morning, Louisa my dear. What's wrong in your department?" It was a purely rhetorical question.

With her usual sonority Louisa informed him that she and Ollie were closing their house, storing their furniture, and moving to California for the balance of their lives.

He could not have been more horrified if the Riverfront Plaza had fallen into the Doochee. "You can't do that!" he cried. "Meridian will go to pieces without you."

"Then it will have to go to pieces. Ever since Ollie had his pneumonia last winter, Dr. Reed has insisted that I get him out of this climate."

"You'll die of boredom out there, Louisa, with nothing to do."

"Oh, we have plans. Ollie has always felt like a fish out of water, here in Meridian; he says we don't understand the meaning of leisure. We're going to build in Santa Barbara. And while I think of it, Horace, we'll need about a hundred thousand dollars. Will you attend to that?"

Horace was flummoxed by this irresponsibility in Louisa. He had as good a right to retire as she had; but his duty to his state, his nation and his party forbade him to dally with the notion.

"It's life-in-death," he protested. "You're in the flower of middle age——"

"I'm sixty-two."

He was reduced to a personal appeal. "I can handle Vic, I suppose, but how about Katie?"

Louisa said simply, "I've lost heart for that enterprise, Horace. I'm too old to bring up a young girl."

"Why, Louisa, you've done a magnificent job on Katie. What's wrong with the child?"

"I'll tell you what's wrong with both the children—they live too far out of town. They have no gang of friends such as we grew up with on Adams Avenue, Horace. They've never roller-skated on the sidewalk; they've never stopped for sodas at Toomey's after school. Now that you've bought that Ford runabout, Victor rampages all over town with no supervision. As for Katie, she has no friends. She spends her time at the piano—fiddling and daydreaming. It's abnormal."

"Well, what am I supposed to do about it? Don't go telling me to marry again. I loved Theresa, and she went and died on me. And then Chloe did the same thing. Now I don't love anybody, and a wife you don't love is the very devil—I've seen it too often."

Louisa said smoothly, "But you could, Horace, you could move back into this house of mine. It's a Rampole house——"

"Now, now!" said Horace, who had no intention of moving anywhere. "This is a tempest in a teapot, Louisa. When Katie blossoms out a little more, she'll make friends. She's only twelve."

"Thirteen," Louisa corrected him.

"And you know yourself, Louisa," voicing a truism, "that there's always a welcome in Meridian for a Rampole. Give me a few years more—just till she's married."

"Married!" Despair broke through the resonance of Louisa's voice. "Those children are a special breed of Rampole, Horace. They carry tomahawks. Sometimes I think they're throwbacks to that squaw."

This was a joke in poor taste.

Not, the Rampoles were scrupulous to explain, that they wouldn't have been proud to claim Indian blood if they were entitled to. But the squaw was a canard of the hard-slugging eighties, nothing more. A plausible canard, because the Rampoles were dark-skinned and large-beaked. But Big Joe had carried the libel through the courts and won damages of one dollar. Huck Rampole had no more recorded antecedents than the fallen leaves on the forest trails. There was no warrant for calling him a half-breed.

What really rubbed Horace the wrong way was not the squaw, but Louisa's criticism of his daughter. "I'll look Katie over," he vowed, "as soon as I get out to the house this evening."

"Don't look for her at home; she'll be at Little Bierbach's Spring Festival. You remember, Horace—the afternoon class graduates and joins the evening class where they dance with boys? Katie is asked to supper at the Grovers', and then she's to lead the grand march. I've had Madame Clarice make her a handsome frock. You'll get the bill."

"Well, what more do you want?" he challenged her.

"She is leading it," Louisa said significantly, "with young Tommy Epps."

"Epps! Little Bierbach must be letting down the bars."

"You needn't complain. Who proposed Anson Epps for the Meridian Club?"

"That was business," Horace said unhappily.

"One of these fine days, Tommy Epps or some other of that ilk is going to marry Katie for her money."

"Over my dead body!"

"Prevent it, then; I've warned you. But don't try to talk me out of moving to California, because my mind is made up."

All day, while appointments came and went, Horace was wiping the floor with an imaginary Louisa. She was dead wrong. By definition, his daughter was as fine a girl as ever lived.

In the middle of the evening he said good night to the Boys who were drinking and conferring in his office and set out for the dancing academy. A mile or two out Adams Avenue he turned on Walnut Street and parked highhandedly in front of the Bierbach Academy. He did so with seignorial innocence. Only a rookie patrolman had ever asked Senator Rampole to move on.

The door of the Academy stood open to the fresh spring evening; the lights touched the young leafage of the elms. Through the doors came the gay discord of fiddles tuning up. Horace tossed his cigar into the bushes before he made his entrance among the parents on the balcony.

Little Bierbach was so known, not on account of his size but because he was the son of the founder. The matrons of Adams Avenue had danced with him when they were in pigtails, at the old Masonic Hall on River Street, under Bierbach the First.

The parents—parents half a generation younger than Horace—were leaning out over the rail during a break in the dancing, exchanging signals of amity with their young. The women's statuesque shoulders were aureoled by the evening wraps they had thrown back.

"Why, if it isn't the Senator!" a general greeting arose.

Horace waved an imaginary cigar, while deciding where to take his seat. He transacted half his public business on the wing. Was there anyone—?

He knew them all by nickname, and their fathers and mothers before them. They were the pioneer blood of the town. But they made their civic contribution by subscribing to the symphony endowment, or presenting rare books to the library. The leadership had passed into tougher

43

and more realistic hands. No, there was nobody he needed to speak to.

Some he preferred not to speak to. In his public capacity Horace was brother to all mankind, but in private life he allowed himself the pleasures of Old-Meridian snobbery. Things had come to a pretty pass when the only vacant seats would throw him either with Queenie Grover or with Mrs. Anson Epps!

Mrs. Epps, indeed, was already brightly beckoning, with a hand that suggested too much sausage in a white kid casing. After Horace rammed her husband into the Meridian Club he had had the doubtful reward of dining at her house.

No one knew her Christian name. It was variously thought to be Pomona, Verona or Cremona, because her husband called her Onie, or Ducky. He was not notably faithful to her, but he dressed her to the nines. She formed herself on the model of Lillian Russell. Tonight she had on everything, including an aigrette. Her smile was unaffected and innocent.

He had no option except to sit beside Queenie Grover.

Queenie was at least entitled to be called a lady. She came from out of town, but she had been bridesmaiding for a cousin on Adams Avenue when Philip met and married her. Even in her girlhood, though, she earned the nickname of "Miss No-Brains."

For Chloe's sake—for the sake of not appearing jealous of Chloe's girlhood sweetheart—Horace had endured a good deal of the Grovers' company. He had taken Queenie in to dinner, and bent a courteous head to her baby talk.

The marriage was typical of some lack in Philip Grover that made him harmless and likable. He ought to have got somewhere in the world, instead of subsisting on a dwindling law practice and a shrinking heritage in real estate. He ought to have held the club tennis championship; but no matter how prettily he played, his opponent always took the set point. He ought to have carried Chloe Cummager off from under Horace's nose. His looks weren't a man's looks—he had the chiseled spareness of an ivory angel.

Horace presented an impenetrable shoulder to Mrs. Epps and said to Queenie, "It was nice of you to have my little girl to supper."

"I had Victor too," Queenie tinkled, smoothing the chiffon of her *décolletage*. Her early beauty was being overpowered by its own opulence. She had a voice like a small silver hand bell on a tea table. "There they go now!" She wigwagged girlishly toward the dance floor.

"Katie?" Horace asked sharply. He hadn't located Katie yet.

"No, Victor and Lissa. Oh, the rascal! He's pretending she's a horse, and driving her by her pigtails."

"The lout!" But Horace laughed all the same. Victor was so big, so spirited, so fine-looking; Melissa was so slim, straight and passive under the horseplay. She was more Philip's daughter than Queenie's, and Horace's heart warmed to her.

"Don't scold him about it," Queenie cooed. "Really, they're the best of friends."

Horace doubted that they were the best of friends. He credited his son with his own specialized taste in feminine beauty, and he responded to a velvet bloom, a sweet-toned laugh, a conquering air.

Just as Victor was making his Bierbach bow to Lissa a very different girl drifted past him, took his elbow and towed him away.

This girl was beautifully built, to a small scale. Her head had a saucy set to it. Her skirt was a whirl of flounces, her bodice was a scintillating corselet. She moved close and sinuous beside her captive.

Horace noted mentally that it was time he had a serious talk with Victor. He himself had met such girls in his youth. But he had not met them on the floor of the Bierbach Academy, and not when he was sixteen.

"Who's the girl that kidnaped Victor just now?" he asked Queenie.

"That girl! What the boys see in her—! It's Jodie Epps."

Epps again! Horace's very entrails revolted.

"I had to ask her to supper," Queenie went on, "because Tommy Epps is Katie's partner tonight, you know."

While Queenie babbled, Horace quartered the floor and searched it for his Katie. He located three or four black-haired girls, but he couldn't claim any of them.

Little Bierbach blew his whistle and announced one more two-step before the grand march.

Blue serge suits rose from gilt chairs, bowed, and set off in quest of their new partners. Three striplings contested Jodie's favors, and Victor was the winner. The orchestra struck up, and dancing couples took the floor.

Along the wall near the bandstand sat a row of young creatures, graduates from the afternoon class, with fixed smiles. One by one they were all picked off, except the farthest.

Horace's heart upheaved in his statesman's breast. There sat his Katie, the last of the wallflowers, casting no glances, expecting no rescue. She was fantastically decked out, in a dress Louisa might have worn the year she came out. Her hair had been crimped with an iron, but it had gone lank. Her Rampole nose stood large and firm, her collarbones pathetically young and bony.

Horace's pride took a tremendous blow. He would have liked to punch those young squirts who passed his daughter by. Katie sat out the dance in proud apathy, while her father spent five minutes in purgatory. He emerged a changed man.

He had been waiting till Victor turned tractable and Katie turned pretty, so that he could begin to love them. Victor was in the toils of a designing girl; and as for Katie, Louisa was right: Katie was a rejected girl.

And now he loved his two children as he had never loved any created beings. This love attacked him as the smallpox might attack a man after a lifelong immunity. He would make up to them for their mother's death, for the warping of their youth, for their isolation under the dictatorship of an aging aunt.

How he was to rescue them he didn't yet know. But he was a man of resource; his emotion would instruct his wits. "By God!" he said, mopping his forehead; it was a vow. He had told women he loved them, but now that parental love had hit him amidships, he knew he had lied.

The eternity of humiliation passed. Little Bierbach, antique and wizened but still sprightly, blew his whistle for silence.

"Now, as the climax to our fifty-second annual festival, I have the honor to present to you our queen, Miss Kate Rampole, and our king, Mr. Thomas Epps. Will their majesties please come forward to the rostrum for the coronation? After the ceremony you will all fall in line for the grand march."

A gust of anger shook Horace. Little Bierbach was in effect announcing, "Miss Rampole is your guarantee that you attend a select dancing academy."

There was some jiggery-pokery with cardboard crowns, a patter of kid gloves, a fanfare from the orchestra. During the coronation Victor and Jodie Epps danced absorbedly in a corner of the floor—a rudeness which Old Bierbach would never have countenanced.

The royal couple were escorted to the head of the line, and the others fell in behind them. Mr. Thomas Epps was a head shorter than his queen, and her hand fitted awkwardly through the crook of his elbow; but he looked uplifted. Katie might have been a wooden ceremonial image, decked out in satin and buckram for a *fiesta*.

The march began sedately enough with a circuit of the floor. Katie trudged along docile, bewildered and completely ridiculous.

But as Little Bierbach brought the column around for a second time, she glanced up at the balcony and caught sight of her father. She came touchingly to life. She flashed Horace a smile, and he glowed white-hot with love.

Then the little dancing master came into his own. Tripping backward in front of the advancing king and queen, he waved couples alternately right and left. He brought them toward the reviewing stand by fours, by eights and by sixteens. The orchestra picked up the tempo. The dancers advanced in a romping phalanx. If he had stood still, they would have trampled him; but he flitted backward on airy dancing pumps.

He sent them into an interwoven double circle, into pinwheels, into a serpentine. Then by consummate craftsmanship he resolved them back into a stately column of dark suits and bright dresses. The music steadied to a sonorous march, and the cortege withdrew in good order down the basement stairs to the supper room.

The fathers in the balcony picked up their wives' wraps and escorted them down to supper, which traditionally consisted of a chicken patty, a cup of cocoa, a pickle and a spun-sugar basket of ice cream.

Horace stayed alone on the balcony, gnawing an unlighted cigar. In his vitals burned the pain of love and pity.

What was going to happen to the children when he was gone? With the tragic prescience of his new love he saw them exploited as they had been exploited this evening. He saw Katie married for her money, he saw Victor entrapped by sirens in sequined frocks.

Distastefully he mulled over Louisa's suggestion that he should move back to Adams Avenue. Louisa had queened it there for thirty years. It stood on a full city block, and she had brought it up to date with a picture gallery and a music room.

But Adams Avenue these days was a runway for cars and trucks, with soot in the air and trash blowing along the curbs. He smelled migration in the air; he heard men talking about it at the club. Now that they had cars to drive, Adams Avenue constricted them. And this year there were almost a thousand cars registered in Meridian.

. . . Out to the country! Cars to drive——

Horace stopped short on the deserted balcony. He remembered suddenly the young whippersnapper whom Miss Wupper had eased out of his office just before lunch—a real-estate salesman.

A zealot, that lad! He had come armed with a plat of Chestnut Point, on which with bald impertinence he had penciled ten or a dozen building lots.

Horace had let the sales talk run in one ear and out the other, but his brain had recorded it in transit. Automobiles, noise, city dirt . . . the mass moved to the open spaces . . . "You have several hundred acres of land out there, rolling country, magnificent old forest, river on one side and creek on the other—sell like hot cakes. . . . Choice little development; Neighborhood Association; big iron gates leading in from Adams Avenue; green parkway down the center where your avenue runs now,

47

and an oval of access streets. Your own house would close the oval, and you'd still have a perfect wilderness of land running back to the Doochee Ford. Pretty sweet little proposition, don't you think, Senator?"

Horace had dismissed the intrusive young man with the geniality he reserved for cranks. "When I'm ready to subdivide my land, young fellow, I'll get in touch with you." Now he felt a sense of awe that Providence should have sent him this particular crank.

He walked his beat and pulled at his nose. If he were to sacrifice his privacy at all, he would do so on his own terms. This development was not to be sold by young men ringing random doorbells.

Horace knew a better way of going to work: a word here and a word there in the right quarter—a chance to get in on the ground floor of a Rampole venture . . .

To whom should he drop his word?

Why, to the very parents who were at this very moment eating chicken patties in the basement. The Dysarts, the Wyndhams, the Breens with their growing boys; the Whittys, the Suttons, the Bellamys; the Grovers.

He debated the Grovers. Queenie was a laughingstock, but everyone liked Philip. The Grovers had governors and justices in their pedigree. Grover was a good name.

Horace cast a vote in favor of the Grovers, stamped his gnawed cigar into the rubber matting and set off down the stairs to the supper room.

Chapter 8

ROENTGEN, the young man who had forced his way into the Senator's office, had struck a bonanza. What, except genius, could have suggested to him that the Rampoles would ever cut up their estate into building lots?

The firm of Roentgen & Cowles was well along with the drafting of a handsome prospectus when Horace knocked the props from under them by announcing that he had half the lots sold already. Roentgen & Cowles panted behind him, alternately praising God and cursing the Senator.

He moved powerfully with the city council in the matter of paving, lighting, sewers and water mains. He planned, he promoted, he expedited. He employed the cunning of an old elephant hunter; there was no limit to his capacity.

Indeed, he whipped the project into a runaway gallop that he had a hard time controlling. It could have been sold three times over—but not to the right people.

He reserved a veto on all contracts. The salesmen brought in signed agreements with binders paid down—and Horace vetoed. They brought him the best names on Adams Avenue—and still he vetoed.

"All right, Senator," Roentgen told him, "if you get us into these jams, you'll have to get us out of them. We want to stay in business even after Rampole Place is sold off."

There were jams aplenty. Louisa's cronies, in a body, wanted to pass their declining years in Rampole Place. They had ancestral claims on him, and no one questioned their social eligibility. When he resisted them, they talked spitefully about him.

He was sorry, but not to the point of weakening. And even these acute old ladies never smoked out his hidden motive. Rampole Place was self-explanatory. "Trust a Rampole for timing," people said. "Adams Avenue is getting intolerable. In another year all of us would have bought property somewhere else."

He ran into a snag with the budding Rampole Place Improvement Association. In this modern age even workmen were beginning to drive cars, and they took their families for Sunday outings. His new neighbors asked him to deed the central esplanade to the Association as a private park, so that they might put up gates and install a watchman against picnickers.

"I'm a public man," he told them evasively. "I can't go closing off public streets. We'll get the police to keep them from parking in the oval. Leave it to me."

"But it's your own land, Senator. And in years to come—" by which they meant, after you're dead and gone—"we ought to be protected. You know the *Sun-Record* is campaigning for a belt of outer parks."

"That's what makes the subject a hot potato right now."

It was a hotter potato than they knew. Horace had fully intended to turn the parkway over to the Association—till he began getting the title deeds in shape.

Chestnut Point had never passed out of Rampole hands. Huck's title went back to the early days before there was any settled county government. The survey took its bearings from oak trees which had long since fallen, and rivers which had cut new channels. The place had passed from Huck to Horace through a chain of family wills. There had never been a search of the title.

Now Horace's lawyer told him, "I've turned up a point of antiquarian interest. I'll bet you didn't know that originally there was a right of way that ran through your driveway to the Doochee Ford."

"No!" said Horace with interest. "I remember before we built the house the farmers' boys used to cut through there to go swimming, but the big stone gateposts scared them off. When was it vacated?"

"It must have been in October '72. When your father inherited from Artemus it showed as a dotted line on the plats. When you inherited from your father it was gone. But there's no record."

"We'll have to clear up that title."

"You can give them a clear title," O'Donnell said. "The easement covers nothing except your own entrance avenue. And I don't know how you'll clear that up at this late date. The reason I mentioned October '72 is that they had a little fire down at the County Building that year, and the records for October were destroyed. When we come to a gap in a title we lay it to the fire in the County Building—it's an established practice in Doochee County. If there ever was a right of way across your place, it's obsolete."

Horace didn't worry—not till he had consulted Dan Parmiter. Dan's chuckle disconcerted him. "Typical!" said Dan admiringly. "The old brigand. I never saw through that fire in the County Building till this minute. I knew Con Kelly had a hand in it, but—well, well, well! Some days I'm just plain homesick for old Joe."

Horace said hotly, "If you're laying it to my father, he had no call to burn records. He could have had the right of way vacated and the transaction properly recorded."

"You've built up a plaster image of your dad, with a halo on. There never was a day in Joe's life when he didn't have a fight on his hands, and they fought dirty in those days. If he'd petitioned to have the right of way closed off, Jake McGee the People's Friend would have run a line of charabancs straight through to the Doochee Ford. Anyway, Horace, your dad got his pleasure out of taking the short cuts to what he wanted. He liked to feel his strength."

"What's all this about Con Kelly? I don't remember any Con Kelly."

"Con Kelly? Oh, he fell off a railroad trestle fifteen years ago. Clever fella when he was sober, but he went on nine-day drunks. Con would do anything in the world for your dad. And I do know that at one time he worked for the Recorder of Deeds."

Horace left Dan Parmiter, with a nasty feeling in the pit of his stomach. He hoped this cock-and-bull story was nothing but one more example of Dan's mythmaking proclivities.

In any year except 1908 Horace could have petitioned the city council and set the record straight. No citizen would have felt deprived of any rights, since no living citizen had ever exercised them. The Rampoles had held the land, developed it and paid taxes on it for over a hundred years.

Now, however, the *Sun-Record* was beating the drum for outlying parks. Let it be known that Horace Rampole, the people's elected representative, was closing the people's access to a hidden beauty spot, and the dogs of journalism would be on his track.

The Improvement Association would simply have to leave the matter with Horace until the *Sun-Record* forgot about its Outer Park Belt.

Horace eyed his children's response to the new bustle on the place. Salesmen and their prospects went steeplechasing over the trenches and sewer crocks; surveyors squinted through their transits; steam shovels trundled into the oval.

Katie was delighted to stroll beside her father through the rising subdivision. But she was hardly an intelligent companion. She took no interest in power lines or sewer connections. "We used to walk down here with Mother to look at the new moon," she would say dreamily, while Horace was pacing off the foundations of a new house.

It was Victor's company Horace wanted. But Victor seemed to be looking for chances of putting him in the wrong. Had there been a period when Horace resented his own father? Not in boyhood, certainly. All through his youth Horace had found his father's smoking room a three-ring circus. Victor's sullenness bruised Horace and baffled him.

What ailed the boy? How could he resist climbing into excavations and driving steam shovels? And he was positively uncivil to the Adams Avenue families who drove out to inspect the progress of their building. Every Sunday after lunch he would get into the Ford and go roaring off into the unknown.

"You ought to hang around, son, and do the honors. The Bellamys are going to be neighbors of ours."

"I didn't ask them to move out here. I liked the place better when it was nothing but woods."

"We still have two hundred and fifty acres of woods."

"I suppose you ran short of money, or you wouldn't have cut up our place."

"I did not run short of money," Horace snapped. "I saw——" Then he stopped. If he let his children know that it was for their sakes he was sacrificing his splendid privacy, he would destroy the value of the sacrifice.

Katie outdid herself in obligingness to the visitors. She shook hands with whole roomfuls of guests; but certainly she had no social gift.

"Katie," he suggested, "why don't you take Delia Dysart down and show her where the Breens are putting in their tennis court?"

Katie said politely, "Delia, would you like to come with me?" and the two girls stalked together down the drive.

Nine minutes later they came stalking back, having executed their assignment, and sat themselves primly down in the circle of grownups. If Horace had not loved Katie so despairingly, he would have taken her out behind the pantry door and boxed her ears.

And what could a mature statesman do about a young girl's clothes? In her mother's day she had been elfish and brightly picturesque. But she had been smaller then. Now she was a gangling five-foot eight. Since Louisa had taken off for California, Granny Cummager had had the dressing of her, and Granny counteracted her plainness by getting her up like a French doll. For great occasions she put up Katie's straight black hair on curling kids. Between these curlicues Katie's bony face peered out like a young owl's; her legs grew longer and longer. If Horace ever married again, it would be to get rid of Granny Cummager.

Ground was broken, that first summer, for six out of the eight lots in Rampole Place. A fine little pocket it promised to be, each house standing on a couple of acres of lawn and woodland that sloped either west to the Doochee or east to Rampole Creek. They were handsomely designed for entertaining. The Whittys were pushing their construction, with a view to giving their oldest daughter a coming-out party on Thanksgiving Day. Horace's dream of a neighborhood was a reality.

Two lots stood vacant. The Grovers had bought Number Four, but Queenie and her architect were still elaborating their plans. Number Two, the one to the left of the entrance gates, was unsold.

Not for want of purchasers. "What can I tell them?" Roentgen demanded. "I can't say it's sold, because it isn't. What are you waiting for, Senator?"

"I won't be pushed, young fellow. Say I'm holding it for speculation. Say I'm saving it for one of my children to build on. Say anything you like, just so you remember who's boss around here."

"We've put ourselves to considerable promotion expense. We want to get our money out."

"My heart bleeds for you. I did your selling for you."

"We appreciate all that, Senator. But I'm warning you, you may lose your market. There's this Blossom Lawn development, selling like hot cakes. And Janeway Brothers are opening up a tract at Middleton, ten miles out in the hills. It's going to be a buyer's market by spring."

"I'll gamble on that," said Horace coolly.

"I can't see, for the life of me, why Anson Epps's money isn't good enough for you."

"Epps!"

Roentgen caught the flash in Horace's eye and misinterpreted it as cordiality.

"This client is working through a broker," he gossiped, "but I'm positive it's Epps. You'd be lucky to land him, Senator. You can ask Epps any price you like. They tell me he can write his check for a million dollars."

Horace forbore to say that he wasn't having Epps on any terms. "Epps won't be satisfied with two acres of land on a main highway," he parried. "I'm working for long-range stability out here, Roentgen, and inside of two years Epps would move out on us and sell to some greasy immigrant."

Roentgen shook his head. "Here's how I figure Anson Epps. He has a boy and a girl, see? He's no fool, he knows Adams Avenue is shot to hell. Another couple of years and it will be all rooming houses. You probably haven't noticed, but every family with young people is moving out of Adams Avenue. And the cream of them are right here in Rampole Place. Epps wants to be where the kids are."

"I dare say," said Horace dryly. "All the same, I'm holding onto the Number Two lot. Before snow flies, I'll turn you up a purchaser."

But he didn't. Blossom Lawn got off to a thriving start. At the last moment the Suttons decided not to move at all.

So Number Two sank to the status of a parking lot for workmen's cars. The workmen left milk bottles and old newspapers behind them, in spite of all that William and Augustus could do.

One fine Sunday afternoon in September, Horace was ambling down the esplanade, admiring the half-built houses.

A Ford car swooped in between the entrance pillars, pinwheeled across the curb and came to rest under the trees on Number Two. Out climbed a long-legged boy, then a girl provocatively dressed in red.

Trespassers! Spooners! Horace quickened his step.

"Hello, Father," said Victor, supporting the girl by the elbow while she picked her high-heeled way through the underbrush. His eyes gave back green-gold glints to the slanting sun. He was in his Sunday best, with a high starched collar; he was as likely-looking a young gallant as a girl could hope to ensnare.

"Father, I don't believe you've met Miss Jodie Epps."

Jodie said bewitchingly, "I'm just delighted to meet you, Senator. Mumsy and I are making Daddy buy us this lot, so I asked Victor to bring me out to look at it. This would be the front steps right about here, I should think."

Horace disapproved of her completely. But she did call up a response of gallantry in him, which prevented him from ordering her off the place.

He said warily, "I'd like nothing better than to sell to your father, but we've taken this lot off the market. I've—I've given an option on it."

The antagonism came into Victor's eyes. "To who, Father?" he inquired unbelievingly.

Horace disliked telling direct lies, particularly lies in which he would be caught. "Friend of your Aunt Louisa's," he invented uneasily. "I'm not at liberty to mention the name."

Jodie answered unperturbed. "Oh, well, you'll have to get rid of her. I told Daddy I'd run away from home if he wouldn't move to Rampole Place. You coax your father for me, Victy!"

Unnaturally brave with the eyes of the beloved upon him, Victor said to his father, "I told Mr. Epps this very afternoon not to take any excuses from you. I said you could always find some way of looking out for your friends." He was prompting Horace not to let him down.

"Isn't Victor wonderful?" Jodie caroled. "Daddy says Victor's quite a politician already. Daddy's crazy about Victor."

If Horace had yielded to his instincts, he would have given off a full-throated bellow of rage. But she was only a cat's-paw in her father's hands. Horace controlled himself. He said with dry asperity, "Victor, it happens that the Number Two lot is bespoken. You had no right to commit me. I seriously object to you young people putting in your oar in my business affairs, and if anything like this happens again, I shall have to suggest that you see less of each other."

Victor did not mask the black hostility of his eyes. But there was a limit to how far a parent could be pushed. "Vic," the Senator added, "you'd better run Jodie home now. Some of your friends are waiting for you, up at the tennis court."

He had dismissed Jodie in words of one syllable. Any other girl would have gone home crestfallen.

Jodie stood her ground. Her eye was bright and uncommunicative like a bird's. She cried girlishly, "Oh, goody, tennis! Let's play tennis, Vic—I don't have to be home for hours." And off they went, the two of them, in open defiance. Short of heaving Jodie bodily off the premises and provoking an open break with his son, Horace had no recourse.

But if Epps calculated that calf love was enough of a handle to swing the Senator by, he would learn how radically he erred. Horace positively looked forward to dealing with Epps's residential pretensions. He would make an opening before long.

Chapter 9

BEFORE he tackled Epps, it behooved Horace Rampole to be sure of his ground with regard to the poor man's Monte Carlo at Rivergrove. The whole expedient had been so distasteful to him that he had looked the other way.

Dan Parmiter gave him little comfort, however. "It's small potatoes," Dan said easily. "Just a couple of green tables up on the second floor, and a refined little bar over in the corner. One bit of noise, and their membership cards get lifted. If you went out to dinner at Giacomo's Restaurant, you'd never catch on. You might notice a good many customers going through a door beyond the coatroom, but if you asked the waiter what was going on, he'd tell you the manager was celebrating his birthday upstairs. It's as smooth a little operation as you'd ask for."

Smooth it might be, but it still left Horace in the position of having to placate Anson Epps and the *Sun-Record*. He had appeased him once by getting him into the Meridian Club, but the man was insatiable. Epps was asking a second payment for his silence. He must not be allowed in Rampole Place; but in turning down Epps's offer for the Number Two lot, Horace must put on a convincing show of goodheartedness. He sought Epps out at lunchtime at the club.

He drew up alongside the table where Epps was playing dominoes after lunch. After he had stood watching for a few minutes he said casually, "Too bad, Epps, you didn't come to me direct about that Number Two lot of ours. I wish I'd known, because by the time the offer reached me, I'd given an option to my cousin Corinne."

"Don't think any more about it," Anson said idly. He played a double five, and marked three X's on the score pad. "That never was a firm offer, it was more of a nibble. I'm just as glad to be out of that deal. I understand there's a slight cloud on the title."

Horace reddened dangerously. He tried to keep his voice level. "You understand wrong, then. It's as clean as a whistle. O'Donnell has passed on the title. That ought to be good enough for you."

And he stamped off to the library, where he climbed in behind the full spread of a New York newspaper to take counsel with himself.

Assuming the very worst—assuming that Epps had nosed out some old record relating to the extinguished right of way—the city had no claim that would stand up in court. Nevertheless, Epps, through the *Sun-Record,* could touch off quite a smudge pot in election year: SENATOR RAMPOLE DENIES PUBLIC ACCESS TO DOOCHEE FORD.

And the choice little community which Horace had been at such pains to transplant for his children's benefit would be blasted. The residents would feel, and justly, that the Senator had let them down. Looking over the hand he was called on to play, Horace found it weak in face cards.

The time hadn't come for throwing in his hand. Most likely, all Epps had to go on was a rumor from some disgruntled old county employee. The story was fantastic—that Big Joe Rampole plotted to set fire to public records! Dan Parmiter had spun that story out of his own woolly old wits, and it was high time he stopped blabbing.

All well and good—but did Epps know anything, or didn't he? The only way to find out was to ask him, and to ask him was as good as giving the game away.

The domino game broke up. Epps strolled into the library and began scanning magazines on the long table. "Why, Senator!" he exclaimed innocently. "I didn't see you at first. Hope I didn't break up your nap."

"I wasn't asleep."

"About that Number Two lot, Senator—" spinning a magazine and discarding it—"somebody gave me the wrong steer on that. Something about an old easement—but since you tell me I'm wrong, I wish I'd followed through on that nibble. My womenfolks don't give me a moment's peace."

Horace summoned up his sunniest candor. "You don't want to live there. As the thing is working out, it's a perfect bear garden of sandboxes and gocarts."

A hardness appeared in the muscle along Epps's smooth-shaven cheek. "You'll have to let me be the judge of where I choose to live. And if I don't press my own claims, nobody's going to press them for me. I learned that when I first moved into town."

"Don't get me wrong, Epps. I'm all in favor of new blood. There's nobody I'd rather sell to than you. Only—what have I got to sell you? Number Two is spoken for, and I can't back out on a promise to my own first cousin. My life wouldn't be worth living if I did."

"Well, it was my own fault for moving too slowly." Epps absorbed himself in an illustrated paper. While turning the pages he said negli-

56

gently, "If your cousin changes her plans, keep me in mind, will you? I might make you an offer."

"I'll bear it in mind."

"Don't bear it in mind too long," Anson said, unfurling an agreeable smile marred by wolf-tooth cuspids. "That young Roentgen of yours is deviling me to pick up a big tract of land up by the Cinnamon Gorge. And in that case, of course I wouldn't give a hoot whether the titles in Rampole Place were good or bad."

"They're as good as gold."

"They could be questioned," Epps said. "In fact, they've been questioned."

He turned in the archway for a last companionable word. "Seen anything of our friend Claggan since you got back? I hear he's gunning for you. I told him to cool off—I said you were a friend of mine." And with a wave of his hand he vanished.

Horace sat in contemplation for some time; and being a realist, he decided this hand was not worth playing out. Epps had set a price on his silence in the ticklish matter of the right of way. Rampole Place would have to assimilate one dubious neighbor.

He held his nose and swallowed the dose. He would have to sell to Anson Epps.

Chapter 10

THE Grover family was the last to move into Rampole Place, except of course for the Eppses, who were a year behind with their building. All winter the oval had been crowded with moving vans, cars and carriages. There was a bedlam of Christmas parties for the young. Horace viewed his handiwork like God on the seventh day, and saw that it was good.

Finally, during Lissa's spring vacation, the vans came to move the Grovers into their new house. It was fortunate that Lissa was available to help with the moving, because when Queenie worked too hard she got ill and had to take to her bed.

Into the new rooms, still smelling of plaster and wood shavings, came in procession the old furniture from Adams Avenue. The old clocks started ticking on the new mantels. Ella set the old tea kettle to boiling on the new stove, and by eleven in the morning Queenie was having a cup of tea on the old chaise longue in the new boudoir upstairs.

"Oh, thank you, Ella dear. This will make a new woman of me."

Ella replied gauntly, "Next time you want tea, will you send Lissa down after it? I have my hands full, unpacking all those barrels of china. I have no time nor strength for stair climbing."

Queenie directed a merry grimace at Ella's departing back. "Old crosspatch!" she murmured blithely. "Actually, she's perfectly devoted to us. . . . Aren't you excited, pet?"

"I'm terribly excited," Lissa answered obligingly. She was kneeling beside the chaise longue, stacking her mother's lingerie nightgowns inside a band of shirred pink elastic ribbon. She was deft with her hands, and in the midst of the clutter she was as straight and clean as a wax taper.

Queenie reached out her own beautiful hand and gave her daughter's nose an affectionate upward flip. "You little sobersides, you!"

Lissa was excited in her own way, but her excitement would be poured into her diary that night. For some reason beyond Lissa's control, the more her mother twittered the tighter she corked her own emotions.

"People will be running in and out of the house all day," Queenie said in a daydreaming voice Lissa found touching. All her life Queenie had been wanting a house where people ran in and out; but with the handicap of a quiet husband and a quiet daughter, her dream lay always just ahead of her. Lissa, who loved Queenie profoundly, hoped that Rampole Place would prove to be the end of the rainbow for her.

Queenie was suprisingly good at getting work out of other people. Today, from her chaise longue, fortified by successive cups of tea, she upraised her plaintive, tinkling voice: Would *somebody* please do something about the light bulbs? . . . Would *somebody* tack down the stair carpet, before Queenie went stark staring mad with the clatter?

The moving men laughed among themselves, but it was simpler to oblige her than to raise jurisdictional issues.

The vans rolled away, and the family was left in possession. Philip had been slogging all day—climbing ladders, hanging window shades, laying rugs and then shifting them under Queenie's orders. Now he passed the door of the boudoir, with two long mahogany boards under his arm. Lissa was sitting on the foot of the chaise longue, finishing some cold tea out of her mother's cup.

"Phil-ip——" Queenie had a birdlike way of breaking her husband's name into two chirps.

"I've just located the sideboards for Lissa's bed. They were stacked with the extra leaves of the dining table."

"Philip, darling——" It was an appeal. Queenie was exhausted. Her full throat and her flowery face were tilted back against the cushions. He laid down his load and went over to kiss her. She drew a quivering, childish breath and held his hand against her cheek.

"No wonder you're tired, sweet. You've done a superb job today."

"You ought to rest too, Philip. You're as gray as a ghost. Is anything stirring about dinner? We'll all feel better when we get some hot food inside us."

"I doubt it. Ella's been unpacking dishes, and scouring bathrooms, and Lord knows what all."

"But, darling, we can't live without food indefinitely."

Lissa piped up, "Ella is figuring on our eating some more of the cold ham we had for lunch."

Queenie made a visible effort at courage, but her lip quivered. "I'm sorry. I don't mean to be a nuisance. But I've worked so hard all day, and I have such a headache. I'll tell you what, Philip. Let's go out to dinner."

"Two considerations prevent," Philip said in his lawyerlike way. "First, I have to set up Lissa's bed——"

"Daddy, Ella made a very sensible suggestion. She said, why didn't I sleep on the library sofa tonight? Then we could all stop work."

"What a splendid idea!" cried Queenie, restored at once. "Such an old head my baby has on her shoulders." With a bird-wing sweep of her hands she gathered Lissa in and kissed her. "So now we can go out to dinner!"

"Except," Philip said, "that I haven't money enough left on me to pay for a meal. I've been shelling out all day, and I'm busted."

"Phil-ip! You're just like a small boy about money—you never plan ahead. But you're adorable, and I love you. So let's go down in the pantry and eat sandwiches, and laugh and have fun."

Philip and Lissa were glad to see her spirits rising. They counted on her for the gaiety they were born short of. Queenie had an inborn need to enjoy hurt feelings, to kiss and make up, to act out her moods. She surged, she sparkled, she billowed. She was tireless in pouring out her temperament on the two reserved creatures she had on her hands.

They went off to their new bathrooms to wash, and got silly and hilarious hunting for towels with their faces dripping wet. . . .

After their sandwiches the three of them, arm in arm, made a tour of their new domain.

Queenie was proudest of the living room, in which everything was new. Mr. Osmond O'Shea had brought the decorative gospel of Elsie De Wolfe to Meridian; so the living room was keyed to a chintz pattern of lilies, urns and pheasants. He had installed a kidney-shaped writing table with a quill pen standing in a dish of shot, and a bowl of cinnamon-scented potpourri. It was not a desk to write at, but it was undeniably modish.

Daddy's library was in the north wing. "Why, it isn't going to look half bad!" Queenie exclaimed as they halted on the threshold.

Philip and Lissa had no need to exchange a look. They were an inner circle of two, enclosed in the family circle of three. They didn't mean to shut Queenie out, but they had no control over their own geometry. While the rest of the house might be Queenie's, the library was theirs.

It would be days before the library was in shape. The floor was covered with crates of books. But its character was visible already.

"I wash my hands of your old library, Phil-ip," Queenie had said cheerfully when the room first appeared on the plans. "We have a living room and a reception room and a boudoir, and we don't need a library any more than a cat needs two tails. I'll put the old Grandfather Grover office furniture in there, where nobody will have to look at it."

Now Philip dropped luxuriously into one of the shabby Victorian black-leather armchairs, tufted with buttons. Queenie took possession of the sofa, and Lissa perched on a crate.

The empty oak bookshelves went from floor to ceiling and even across the tops of the windows. Grandfather Justice's enormous old desk stood in the bay window. The big Oriental rug was worn down to the warp, but the colors were pleasant.

"The old Justice looks quite at home, doesn't he?" Philip said. The old Justice was a fine portrait, but not keyed to the chintz in the living room, so Osmond had exiled him to the library mantelpiece. Philip put his hand inside his waistcoat in imitation of the portrait, and beetled his brow.

"Not good enough, Daddy," his daughter quipped. "Your collar ought to stick up out of your stock like points of toast around a casserole."

"Why don't we christen the new fireplace?" Queenie suggested. So Philip fetched some broken lumber from the packing cases and laid it across the andirons with the brass eagles on them. A rosy flicker suffused the room.

"I can hardly wait to begin asking people here," Queenie said. "That Lissa exasperates me so! She's as cool as a wet cake of soap."

Lissa sat looking into the fire, her long hands crisscrossed in her lap. Queenie was often candid about her daughter's shortcomings.

Lissa had no illusions about herself. She would never be popular—Queenie told her so, in the most affectionate way in the world. She had missed out on Queenie's looks, she was the image of her father—a Grover right down to the bone. "Fog-Eyes," Queenie called her, because her eyes were such a deep gray. She was sedate, she was old-ladyfied. She was her mother's adorable pet, of course, and even pretty in a way nobody would ever notice; but, frankly, Queenie couldn't conceive of a man ever kissing her.

It was only on her mother's account that Lissa regretted her own lack of bloom. Queenie would have so enjoyed a fetching, dimpled minx of a daughter! For her own part, Lissa knew that Daddy and Queenie loved her, and she had a wordless faith in the future. When she was born, some fairy godmother had torn a playing card in two and given her half of it to carry. Somewhere in the world was the knight, the prince, who was carrying the other half.

While Lissa was dreaming in the fireshine, a small cloud overspread the family felicity. It began to darken when Philip had an impulse to begin arranging his books. "Could you put your hand on my Lucretius, Lissa?" he asked her. "He's my talisman."

Lissa had packed most of the books. She went to the crate where she had put Lucretius.

"Your Lucretius, Phil-ip! Don't tell me you're going to sit up tonight reading Lucretius."

"I've never read him, and I never expect to. But he's the ancestor of my library. See here, on the flyleaf—'Phineas Grover, Harvard College, September 19, 1681.'"

"You call me extravagant, Philip," Queenie said, "but at least I don't build whole rooms for books I never intend to read. This room justifies my little extra cupboards."

"If you're talking about those sliding trays in your dressing room, don't feel guilty."

"When I said cupboards," Queenie said in a voice significantly small, "I had something else in mind. I had Osmond order one of those glass doors for my shower stall, like Lucy Breen's. It's much more practical than a draggly old curtain. And they'll have to tear out some of the tiling when they put it in, so I'm having them carry the tiling all the way to the ceiling. You've no idea how much better it's going to look."

"Darling, I wish you'd spoken to me first. We were 'way over our estimates, even without that." Lissa looked into the fire, uneasy and out of her depth. The dialogue was painfully familiar.

"Pooh!—estimates. Not a single house in Rampole Place stayed inside its estimates."

"But we," Philip said in his underemphasized voice, "we more or less agreed we had to stay inside them, if we were to build out here at all. And I've had rather a jolt about renting the house downtown. I was counting on a hundred a month, to carry the mortgage payments. But Adams Avenue is all to pot. Stew Whitty tells me he signed a lease at sixty-five for his house the other day, and damned glad to get it."

"Don't worry, sweet. Somebody will come along and give you a hundred a month. I'm dreadfully sorry. I didn't think you'd begrudge me a door to my shower."

"I don't begrudge you anything I can give you, dearest," he said gently. "I'm glad you're going to have your shower the way you want it."

Lissa exhaled a small sigh of relief. The cloud had blown over—a cloud she was too young to deal with.

No one could have been sweeter than Queenie about putting Lissa to bed on the leather sofa. She went all the way upstairs for the laciest of her chaise-longue pillows. "There!" She patted it. "That's for the best little daughter in the whole wide world. Sweet dreams, darling."

Lissa lay in a moony state between sleep and waking, her arms behind her head. The curtains were not hung yet, and the street light threw angular shadows on the empty bookshelves. Grandfather Justice brooded sardonically in the dimness. Part of Lissa was so tired that her whole being swung at its moorings.

The other part was not ready to fall asleep. She meant to turn on the light and write up her diary. During the moving it had traveled in the suitcase with her nightgown and her toothbrush.

Lissa was of the race of human beings for whom nothing exists until it has been put through the crucible of words. The move to a new community must be committed to paper this very night. A great door was swinging open; she was moving out of the narrow enchanted entry of childhood. By writing tonight, she must set up a bench mark against which she could check her explorations of the future.

She switched on the light and sat with the open ledger on her knees. But her material overpowered her. After she had sucked her pencil for a while, all she wrote down were a few memoranda:

Unpack books.

That was because Daddy was so tired already.

New grass watered.

Order doormats.

Those were things Queenie might forget unless she were reminded.

Kitchen table leg.

(Before Ella got really mad.)

Lissa put her pencil back in her mouth and devoted herself to the continuing problem of Ella.

It was all very well for Queenie to pride herself on Ella's lifelong devotion. Lissa viewed that devotion rather differently. It had lasted, indeed, since Lissa was a baby; but Lissa had to take the rasp of Ella's tongue as Queenie didn't.

Queenie had had a little trouble about moving Ella to Rampole Place. The new house there was large. Ella didn't see how she could keep up with the work singlehanded—her married daughter lived on the far side of town. . . .

In family conclave, Queenie had previously agreed to get along with one maid, at least until the mortgage was paid off. So she had had to persuade Ella to stay; but the persuasion had involved raising her from six dollars a week to eight dollars, a princely wage. Daddy hadn't been told yet about the raise.

"I'll break it to him when the bills begin to slacken off, Lissa," Queenie had said. "He'll come around to seeing it's an economy in the long run—infinitely cheaper than a second maid."

"I suppose we could get along without anybody for a while," Lissa had suggested—though without enthusiasm. Nobody except really poor people did their own housework.

"Darling, how grubby! Why, we'd be laughingstocks."

So there was really nothing Lissa could do about the family finances. She was too young. And, after all, the money never ran out. She could go to sleep. . . .

She drew a second underscore below *Kitchen table leg.* That was within her province. She started to close the diary.

No, there was another worry that perhaps was hers to tackle.

Popularness, she wrote. She meant Queenie's popularness.

Queenie wanted people running in and out of the house all day. She was certainly handicapped by that quietness of Daddy's and Lissa's.

Lissa had no hope that at this late date she and Daddy could suddenly begin being as jolly as grigs. Just as certain voices can sing only soprano and others only alto, the Grovers had to sing in their own register.

But there were a few things Queenie herself could do to be more popular, and possibly—just possibly—Lissa could drop her a hint. One of the disadvantages of being fifteen was that one began seeing one's parents through the eyes of outsiders.

Queenie didn't realize, for instance that other ladies drew her out and then made eyes at one another behind her back. For instance, one day while Mrs. Wyndham and Mrs. Dysart were paying a party call, and while Lissa was handing the cooky plate, they asked Queenie about the talented young architect she had discovered.

63

"I simply adore Osmond," Queenie said. "Those tragic forget-me-not eyes! He makes me want to mother him and cuddle him."

Now there was something funny enough in the picture of Mr. O'Shea sitting in Queenie's lap to warrant an outright laugh. What it did not warrant, but what it invited all the same, was a choking snicker that blew cooky crumbs all over the room. People weren't fair to that impulsive warmth of Queenie's.

Outsiders misinterpreted her. Outsiders had no way of knowing how perfectly the three Grovers complemented one another and how much love they had for one another at home.

Lissa drew a second line under *Popularness* and turned out the light.

Chapter 11

SUNDAY was Easter. Philip was finicking away at the arrangement of his books. Lissa was perched on the broad library window sill, watching the limousines load up for church.

Lissa would have liked to be going to church herself. But Sunday was Queenie's morning to sleep, and Daddy had a tennis match at eleven-thirty.

Lissa had the vague makings of a mystic in her. Her taste was for Gothic gloom, a rolling organ, candle flames symmetrically disposed. When occasionally her father took her to St. Stephen's they sat under the Grover window, in a pew marked with a Grover memorial tablet. But they hadn't gone regularly, even when they lived downtown, and now she didn't forsee that they would ever go.

No car came round to take the Rampole children to church. The Senator was a hereditary Methodist, but a lax one. Since their mother died, their grandmother took the children occasionally to St. Stephen's.

Pretty soon Lissa saw Victor Rampole come whistling along the oval. He had grown tremendously this winter—he was seventeen now. The sun struck high lights from the black casque of his hair. He walked with a prince's gait. He was the idol of the tenth-grade girls at Miss Peebles'. Yes, Rampole Place was going to be fun—Lissa felt a bright foreboding.

She did something she had never done before in her life. She was not a girl who made advances to boys, and this was not exactly an advance. But she did pick up a book at random, carry it out to the front steps and engross herself in it.

"Well, hello there," said Victor from the sidewalk. "All moved in, I see."

"Why, Victor!" To her great annoyance she blushed a burning red, but she hoped he was too far away to notice. "Isn't it nice out here in the sun?"

"Bully," said Victor, in imitation of Theodore Roosevelt. "Well, I'll see you one of these days." And he swung about, preparing to resume his stroll.

Then prudence smote him.

Victor had been trained from infancy to extend those small courtesies that make vassals hug their chains. His father had been at him all winter to be civil to his new neighbors.

Victor had shown himself contrary. He'd be darned if he'd drive little girls to dancing school. On this fine Easter morning, however, he was engaged in the long-range strategy of love. He had come down to inspect the progress of the Epps excavation on Number Two, so that he could report by telephone to Jodie and possibly make a date with her for that afternoon.

His father was as grumpy as the dickens about his taking Jodie out. It was the part of foresight to diffuse some harmless attentions among the neighboring girls.

"Look here!" he said, walking up the Grovers' front path. Lissa withdrew her eyes from her book. "You know, of course, about the cars that take us down to school. Tomorrow it's—let's see—it's the Breens in the morning and the Bellamys in the afternoon. You be at the gatepost at eight-twenty, and we'll squeeze you in. We sit on top of one another."

"Thanks just as much, but Daddy's going to drive me to school when he goes to the office."

"Well, heck! How are you going to get back?" It seemed a sad and sordid thing, to Victor, that Lissa Grover should have no car at her disposal.

"I can either wait at school till Daddy comes by for me, or I can take the interurban."

"The interurban!" Victor exclaimed with unconscious cruelty. Not even Jennie and Augustus rode the interurban—nobody but the lesser maids on their days off.

"It's not a bad trip. I get off at the Doochee Bridge, only a block from the gate to Rampole Place."

"It runs only once an hour!"

"That's all I ask it to do," Lissa said with her faint smile. It was her father's smile, and as such Victor was disposed to like it. It stirred submerged memories of a morning three years ago, when no one had given Victor any comfort until Mr. Grover did.

"But we have fun in the car," he urged. "We sing, and roughhouse, and whoop it up generally. And when anybody has any money, we all stop for a soda at Toomey's. Of course, if you mind getting squashed . . ."

Lissa's pearl-and-ivory face turned bright pink. "Oh, it's not that. It's——"

"It's what?" Why was she getting pink, as he'd never seen her pink before?

She lifted her chin in difficult pride. "I'd rather ride the interurban because I don't like to take lifts from people when I can't return them."

"Well, good for you," he said awkwardly. The Rampoles kept no balance sheet on benefits bestowed. "But you'll have to get used to Rampole Place. We all live miles from anywhere, so we give one another lifts. If you want to even things up, your father can run a carload of kids down to dancing school some night."

"Why, so he can!" said Lissa, brightening. She had wanted desperately to ride in the school limousine, to sing and stop for sodas.

Victor was entertained by the pinkness that kept reflooding Lissa's face. He was well aware of the princely impression he made on the tenth grade at Miss Peebles'. It was fun to watch her fighting that uncontrollable blush.

"Why don't you and I walk down the trail to the Doochee Ford?" he offered. "Now that you live here you ought to know your way."

"I'd—I'd love to," said Lissa, laying her book aside and blushing more furiously than ever. She was fifteen years old, but this was the first time she had ever gone anywhere with a boy.

"Phil-ip!" Queenie lilted over the banisters. "Philip! Look out the front window this very minute. You'll never believe it unless you see it. Our Lissa is walking up the oval with young Victor Rampole."

"Why, so she is," Philip replied with the moderation his wife found so trying. He went back up his book ladder. On his lips was a smile that drew its honey from the deeps of the past.

Victor and Lissa walked the length of the oval, up the Rampole drive and down a trail into the deep forest.

Lissa was so alive that her finger tips tingled. Perhaps this aliveness was what Queenie meant by excitement. It was something new to Lissa.

She was not so deluded to think that Victor was paying her a personal attention. He was being a good host on his own property, that was all. Jodie Epps was known to be Victor's girl. She told herself that what enlivened her was the opening of an entirely new book, gloriously colored, printed in a strange tongue, and titled "Rampole Place."

Two traits were ingrained in Lissa: reserve of bearing, and neat co-ordination of body. She stepped along with her usual economy of movement, while her interior being soared and circled.

She didn't want to talk. It was enough to smell leaf mold and young foliage, to quaff the torrent of bird song. The little creek on the right, brimming from the spring thaw, worried its banks with puppy fury. The Doochee River was still out of sight beyond a ridge of forest on the left; but the ridge narrowed, and at any moment the two streams might converge. The very topography of the trail built to a climax somewhere ahead.

Victor held an easy gait at her side. He had nothing of any consequence to say to her. He had his own interior tempest, which was not concerned with young Lissa Grover.

But you couldn't walk a girl all the way to the Doochee Ford without speaking. So after a while he said, "This is where we used to pick pussy willows. But they're gone now. The pussies have turned into leaves."

Lissa acknowledged the information by a harmless neutral sound.

After another hundred yards he stopped and scuffed away the dead leaves with his foot. "Here's what I was looking for—bloodroot. In another week the woods will be speckled white with it. And these narrow leaves with the gravy stains—they're dogtooth violet."

Lissa broke her trance of silence to say politely, "You know a lot about wild flowers."

"My mother was crazy about wild flowers. She walked Katie and me down this trail a million times. We used to go hunting for the first trillium——"

"M-hm," said Lissa absently.

She didn't notice how sharply he had cut himself off. He looked at her uneasily, to make sure she hadn't noticed. What had got into him?

In the three years since his mother died, he hadn't once brought her name into casual conversation. The strap around his vital organs still held tight. This was a pain he had to live with.

People were at him constantly to talk about his mother. Nobody had any business talking about his mother—no business being casual about her. No business keeping her wedding photograph on the piano, as Granny Cummager did—a travesty of her lost bright image.

Now he himself had launched a reference to his mother. It must be because Lissa had her father's smile. He thanked his stars she hadn't taken him up.

Lissa gave a sudden squeak of alarm, then relaxed. "Oh, he made it!"

"Who made what?"

"A squirrel, Victor. The crazy little thing took off from a branch and sailed right over to the next tree."

"They do it all the time. You don't know much about the woods, apparently."

"Not the woods. We go to the seashore every summer. Daddy and I take walks along the beach in the dark. The waves come creaming and creeping up around our feet. They never stop coming in, you know, even when nobody's there to watch them. They keep marching up to the shore, and tumbling on their noses, and trying again."

"M-hm," said Victor. This was an undemanding dialogue. Victor was glad, because it did not interrupt his reverie on the subject of Jodie Epps.

This reverie was a cavern thunderous with hidden waterfalls—dangerous going, endlessly enticing. A man could get lost in that cave; he could panic and lose his bearings. But he couldn't stay out of it.

Its nearest reaches, where the daylight still glimmered, had to do with dates. He had to think of places where he could take Jodie, and of ways and means.

Victor was not on an allowance; he had a drawing account with Augustus. But Augustus was a spiteful old codger. "Before I fork out any more money, I'll have to speak to your pa." And as for Father, Victor could butt till his skull ached, but he could not butt down his father's insane prejudice against Jodie Epps.

The darker intricacies of the cavern glittered with color and fantastic form. Lost and remote, the cataract thundered. The rock walls vibrated to its impact. Come life or death, Victor must explore that chasm.

But that lay far ahead. Around the next corner he might come upon an answer to the immediate question that devoured him: what would be the consequences if he took Jodie in his arms and kissed her?

There were times when he suspected he could have got away with it. The time she leaned so close and intoxicating over his shoulder to look at a magazine; the time he brought her home after the Cambridge School Senior Play, when her hands lay in his while he said good night. Waves of rainbow light had shimmered before his eyes. After all, fellows did give girls a good-night kiss.

But supposing a girl burst into tears, or slapped your face, or hooted with laughter, or yelled for her mother—where did that leave you? You took the risk of looking like a darn fool.

While Victor was getting up his courage, Jodie's mood had changed.

She batted the end of his nose with her finger. "'Night, silly," she said, and vanished on a ripple of amusement that left him raging.

"Victor!" Lissa cried suddenly. They had passed the summerhouse and had come out on the point that overhung the ford.

The Doochee came tumbling out of its glen and launched its mazy sun sparkles against the broad rocks. From the right, the creek slid into the glass-green pool below. On the surface of the pool, trails of foam moved in a slow spiral toward a dimpling core. Beyond the pool the augmented stream went its way down an arcade of forest.

Victor was delighted by the effect of the Doochee Ford on Lissa. It brought a transforming peach color into her face. He made her sit down in the sunshine on the bank, and told her old stories.

"This was the old trail to the trading post, where the Riverfront Plaza is now. The Indians used to lie in wait for the settlers, right at this ford where we're sitting. Once when I was a kid I found a tomahawk down under the bank."

But she was in a dream, she wasn't more than half listening. "Victor," she interrupted, "what are these clumps of little pale flowers all up and down the bank, with the velvety stems?"

"Hepaticas." That was enough: he had answered her question. But he heard himself add, "They were out three years ago, the day my mother died."

This time he took himself furiously in hand. He was enraged with this insidious pale-pink girl who wormed things out of him. It was time he broke away from the witchery of the ford, back to the house and the telephone, back to Jodie Epps. He was about to spring to his feet.

"Dear little plant," Lissa said under her breath to a furry, gray-stemmed rosette of hepatica beside her knee. She stretched out her hand and played with it, lost in her daydream. It was impossible to hold rancor against a young creature so detached.

And lovely in a way of her own. Not a temptress, a wood sprite. The sunlight turned her smooth hair to silver-gilt; it transfused the candor of her cheek and temple. Her downcast eyelids were curved like almonds. Jodie or no Jodie, Victor had an eye for beauty when he saw it.

He heard himself utter these incredible words: "Your father and I were down here that day. We sat and talked for quite a while."

"My father is a very comforting man," Lissa said, giving him her full attention. "I don't see how you lived through that day, Victor. Weren't you the one who got the message from the police?"

Now this girl had gone too far; she had shown her hand. That impassivity of hers was a blind. She had the art of slipping through his tightest defenses—a black art—sorcery.

"I suppose your father told you that," he said woundingly. "I suppose your father went straight home and told everybody he'd had a nice long talk with me."

Lissa's eyes came round to him—velvet-gray, soft and somber. "Why, no, he didn't, Victor—Ella did. If you knew Daddy at all well, you'd know he never, never betrays people's confidence."

"How did you know about those hepaticas, then?" For, somehow, the hepaticas were at the bottom of all this.

"Why, you told me yourself."

She was right: he had opened his mouth and told her all she knew about hepaticas. She made him feel like a fool, and nobody was allowed to do that to Victor Rampole.

I must get out of here! he told himself in panic. I must get away from Lissa Grover before she turns me completely inside out.

And meanwhile he heard himself say, bitingly, unbelievably, "I don't imagine you've ever kissed anybody, have you—any boy, I mean?"

As a *non sequitur* this was a masterpiece. Victor knew the cavern it had popped out of, but Lissa couldn't be expected to. However, he had asked the question, and he meant to see it through. He thrust out his chin and cocked his eyebrows.

For a number of seconds Lissa made no answer at all. Her eyes were on the bend where the river disappeared. She's getting ready to haul off and sock me, Victor thought. I have it coming.

That was one response which didn't occur to Lissa. She kept her head averted, and fondled the hepatica at her side. "No," she said finally, falling back on the simple truth. "Queenie says she can't conceive of any boy wanting to kiss me."

This answer cut the ground from under Victor and left him angrier than ever. "It's nothing to be so hoity-toity about," he said truculently. "Girls do get kissed, you know."

His brute unreasonableness brought a flush of true red into her cheeks. "You're the hoity-toity one, it seems to me," she said. "I simply don't know anything about it, so why should I pretend I do?"

Madness mounted in Victor. "It's high time you did, then, so you won't be so goldarn dumb!" He put both hands on her shoulders, turned her to face him, and planted a kiss on the defenseless pink velvet of her mouth.

The madness died as suddenly as it had risen. Her mouth was frighteningly soft. It was as soft as a flower bud. Except that a Rampole never turned and ran, Victor would have run from the scene of his own turpitude.

"You probably didn't like that very well," he said ineptly.

70

"I can't think why on earth you did it," Lissa said, moderate to the last. She hadn't screamed or scratched him; but those shadowy eyes of hers were searching him.

"It was a dirty trick, and I'm sorry. Probably the best thing to do is to forget that it ever happened."

He felt like a complete fool, and yet he felt assuaged. He had learned what he wanted to know, at Lissa's expense: he had learned that this kissing business was no insoluble problem after all.

"What's the good of having things happen at all, if you erase them as soon as they've happened?"

"This is one you'd better erase. I won't say anything about it. Well, I ought to be getting back to the house. I have a phone call to make." He got to his feet and gave her a hand up. He was ramping to get to Jodie.

Lissa stood for a moment, saying good-by to the Doochee Ford. Once she put her fingers up to her lips, as if to confirm that they were still part of her face.

"Well, anyway," she said as she turned to go, "thank you for bringing me down here. I never saw such a beautiful place. It's as beautiful as the ocean."

Chapter 12

During the summer of 1909 Senator Rampole began to feel repaid for the desecration of Chestnut Point. Victor was thrown constantly with the right sort of girls. Even Katie was beginning to have fun.

There were three levels of youth in Rampole Place. The seniors, who would be setting off for college in the fall, kept an Olympian distance. The tots moved under guard of nursemaids. The regnant gang was the one that bracketed Katie and Victor—a full dozen of boys and girls.

Augustus was vexed by the way the young fry swarmed down the trail to swim in the pool. "It's a blasted summer resort we're operating," he told his wife. He enlisted Victor's interest in blazing an alternate trail to the Swiming Rocks, along the Doochee bank. Then he hung signs at both ends of the old trail: "Keep Out—This Means You." The new residents laughed. Augustus was quite a character, they said.

Victor organized the Rampole Place Swimming Club, with himself as president, and set the members to work clearing the club trail—leveling, shoring up, rigging steps and guardrails. They built a fireplace on the big flat rock at the edge of the pool. As the summer heat came on, they were in and out of the water most of the day.

Katie was the youngest of the Gang—just barely eligible for membership because she had skipped a grade in school and landed level with Lissa Grover and Delia Dysart. Physically she towered like a moose among the girls, but emotionally she was still preadolescent.

Nonetheless she had a status in the group—and not entirely as a Rampole. She played a savage game of tennis, because she had had to return balls all her life to Victor. Even Lissa Grover, whose father coached her, couldn't beat Katie, although Lissa played a prettier game. Katie was in demand as a doubles partner. On the Swimming Rocks she was no Lorelei, but in a relay race she was as good as a boy.

During the evenings she effaced herself. Her only parlor accomplishment was playing sonatas, and she shrank from inflicting these on her friends.

One evening, however, Katie arrived ahead of a supper party at the Breens' and sat down idly at the piano. Ever since her rehearsals at Miss Archibald's she had tweedled in private.

Doc Breen came clumping downstairs, tying his necktie and roaring with more gusto than gift, "I've Been Working on the Railroad." Absently Katie struck chords to support him.

Her social fortune was made at that moment. The word spread that Katie Rampole could play by ear. Even Dorothea Whitty, who was a senior and a dashing executant, had to memorize her pieces. Be Katie never so shy, she was dragooned into playing while the others sang. She was considered a prodigy.

Political life was quiescent that summer. Taft had been inaugurated, and Theodore the Great had set off for Central Africa to shoot dik-diks and hartebeests.

Horace frankly missed the Roosevelt regime as a drunkard misses his dram. He missed the turbulence; he missed Roosevelt's spectacular achievements and his glorious willfulness, his maverick energy, his urchin's impatience and his pundit's erudition, his infallible instinct for government. If Horace hadn't had Rampole Place to occupy him, he would have gone slack.

One afternoon he came on a clump of youngsters surrounding the big piano in the front parlor. The Gang was roaring out a ragtime rhythm, and Katie was keeping up with them. Horace was struck by one of his large conceptions. He went to the smoking room and rang for Augustus.

"Gus, Katie has a birthday in September, just before school opens. She's going to be fifteen. It's time she had a party. You fix one up."

Augustus, in his own phrase, did not cotton to the idea. "What more of a party does she want than she's got this minute?" he grumbled.

"No, no, a regular party. Dancing. Orchestra. Supper on their laps, with waiters. Awning out in front. Doorman and carriage calls. The whole works, the way my wife used to do things."

"They'd tear the whole house to pieces. We'd have to do the floors over."

"When I tell you to get up a party I'm not looking for back talk, I'm looking for a party."

"Just as you say," said Augustus, cowed for once.

"And somehow," Horace pondered aloud, "I ought to get hold of a decent dress for her. There's something peculiar about her getup."

"If I was you, I'd ask Mrs. Bellamy. She dolls her girls up pretty good."

"You're right!" Horace exclaimed.

Katie had no words to deal with her rapture when her father, her glorious godlike father, told her she was to have a full-fledged birthday party. She rushed to her room, hugging her ecstasy.

She went over to her mirror to see whether she was any prettier. She had heard enough, first from Aunt Louisa and then from Granny, about what a hard child she was to dress, to have her own plainness stamped into her mind. But two different grownups that summer had been heard to say that her eyes were stunning. Perhaps she was reaching the point Aunt Louisa had talked about, when she would "come into her looks."

The mirror reassured her very little. She had, indeed, dark glowing eyes with eyebrows that would have looked well on a man. But she had no pink-and-whiteness, no dewiness. And smack in the middle of her face stood the unyielding Rampole nose. It was more nose than a girl had any use for.

She slipped down her chemise to inspect her shoulders. The Rampole women had a name for magnificent shoulders—Aunt Louisa said so, rearing swanlike as she spoke. There was nothing swanlike about Katie. Impatiently she pulled her shoulder straps back into place.

All the same she was having a party, an evening party, a dance. Like Mother's parties.

To remember Mother's parties Katie had to grope back through a limbo of empty years. Before Mother died there had been a stir, a sweetness in things; but Katie had been a little girl.

She poked through the attic clutter of her mind and raised a dust of myth. Being the sheriff and shooting Victor off an imaginary horse. Sucking a piece of maple sugar in bed in the dark. Being an angel in a Christmas play. Going to Ernest Thompson Seton's lecture on "Wild Animals I Have Known." Leading her goats Schwänli and Bärli up the Alp—no, no, that was a book, that was *Heidi*.

She sorted out her authentic memories of grown-up parties as seen from over the banisters.

At first nothing came back except herself and Victor in their pajamas, peeping down at the resplendent crowd. Hadn't the two of them scurried down the back stairs to the pantry for tidbits? Hadn't they hung out a third-story window, long after midnight, while the carriages were being called—and then pretended they were asleep when Mother came upstairs?

Now she remembered looking down from the landing into a square coop of potted palms, inside which fiddlers were sawing away like crabs, a harpist wafting notes from his open palms like chains of fairy soap bubbles. She remembered Augustus, next morning, pushing a broad broom through a romantic debris of torn dance cards and rose petals.

She remembered Mother waltzing in the empty hall. Mother like a young queen in pearls and lace and forget-me-not brocade, her cheek dimpling, her chestnut head tipped toward her partner's face. The two of them moved with absent grace, pivoting clockwise, counterclockwise, as if one mind controlled them. They took an endless time to get where they were going. When their pattern finally carried them through the archway it was as if a play had come to an end.

Mrs. Bellamy made quite a mystery about Katie's dress. She came over with a tapeline and sat visualizing with her eyes squinted. Then she nodded happily and told Katie to ask no questions. She would come over the afternoon of the party and dress her.

The mechanism of party-giving was oiled and tuned. Augustus ordered all manner of things, down to gold safety pins for the girls' dressing room. Granny Cummager sent out invitations to everyone from old Adams Avenue, even to college men. The scope of the party was tremendous.

Katie had one dreadful scare, when Augustus told her at breakfast that her father had set off on the midnight train for California. Mr. Ollie had up and died, Mrs. Lassigne was left alone in the world, and very likely the party would have to be called off.

But Augustus told her not to worry. The Senator's parting words had been "Tell Katie we'll give that party if it takes a leg."

It very nearly did take a leg. Horace had to persuade Louisa that the party was a children's party, that his children had lived too long already in the shadow of bereavement, and that times had changed.

He tried to persuade her to move back to Meridian where she belonged. She clung to the empty shrine of her married happiness, but she did consent to come east with him for a short visit.

Once she arrived, she could not restrain her managing gift. "I'm in deep mourning," she said—and this was an understatement. "I can't appear at the party. But I can sit out of the way, in the conservatory, and chat with my old friends." She revised the supper menu and invited several well-connected youngsters whom Granny had overlooked. And she engaged a trained-dog act for the intermission.

Mrs. Bellamy gave Katie orders to have her hair washed on the day of the party and to get herself into the new underclothes that had arrived from Whittaker's Department Store. She was setting the stage for a transformation scene of some sort. Katie had read magazine stories about plain girls who blossomed into beauties. Perhaps this was the day for a miracle.

The slip had real lace on it, and it hung to Katie's shins. The stockings were sheer black silk, such as grown-up ladies wore to parties. The dancing slippers had dear little French heels about an inch high. While she waited for Mrs. Bellamy, Katie minced before the mirror like a young egret. She practiced saying fashionably, "Won't you have another cup of sherbet, Mr.—Mr.—?" She had a vision of a college man bending over her, a cup of sherbet in his white-gloved hand.

Mrs. Bellamy came in, gay and mysterious, with a great box under her arm. "Sit down at the dressing table, child," she commanded. "Close your eyes, and don't open them until I give you leave, whatever I do."

Katie squinched up her eyes. She heard the unmistakable snip of scissors here and there around her head, and felt the lightness as flocks of hair fell to the carpet. She was thrillingly frightened. But she loyally kept her eyes closed, even when the scissors marched straight across her forehead.

Now Mrs. Bellamy was burnishing her hair as if she were a silver tea kettle. Scented mist from an atomizer enfolded her. Some sort of a fillet went round her head from crown to nape.

"Now you may look," Mrs. Bellamy said.

Well, it wasn't a complete miracle, but it was miracle enough for one day. The Rampole nose had not abdicated. Katie was not blond nor rosy. But the high forehead had retired behind a gleaming black bang, and below the bang the Rampole eyes came into their own. Her hair was as smooth as Black Beauty's coat, and it floated at shoulder level. And the headband was an intoxicating, ethereal azalea flame color. It framed her face like a locket.

Katie held her breath while Mrs. Bellamy lifted masses of tissue paper out of the dressmaker's box. The dress was flame-colored, like the fillet. Not a frill, not a scallop, not even a scrap of lace—a sheer, fine-pleated chiffon dress whose beauty was all in its palpitating tint and texture.

"Pretty?" Mrs. Bellamy asked happily while she adjusted the pleats that veiled Katie's leanness with a nymphlike flutter when she moved. "This is how your mother would have dressed you if she'd lived."

"Mrs. Bellamy, you perfect angel!"

"Run down now and show your father how nice you look." And she smiled after her, as Pygmalion smiled at the breathing Galatea.

The downstairs rooms were transformed with palms, festoons, bare floors and small gilt chairs. The party was as imminent as a sunrise—nothing could prevent it now.

Father rose to meet Katie in the smoking room, magnificent in his dress suit, with a gardenia in his button hole. "My little girl looks wonderful," he said, "almost like a big girl. I hope she's going to enjoy her party. I have a couple of things for you."

"Oh, nothing more, Father. I'm too happy already."

He turned back to his desk for a glossy white florist's box, and took out a nosegay of white rosebuds with a lace frill. He presented it with a bow, as if he were offering it to the President's wife in the White House. It was like a huge white snowflake against her dress.

Katie began to cry with happiness.

"Well then," he said jocularly, "perhaps I'd better not give you the other present I had for you."

"Father, don't tease me. It's just that I feel so wonderful."

He laughed, and picked up a battered leather jewel case with tiny brass hasps. "Your Aunt Louisa says you're old enough for this now. It's the necklace my grandfather gave my mother when she graduated from the seminary. Your own mother liked it, and wore it sometimes. I don't suppose you remember."

The minute Katie looked at the necklace on its crimson-velvet cushion she did remember. A sweetness flooded her, as if someone had brought lilies of the valley into the room. Sitting on Mother's floor, Victor and Katie . . . Watching Mother dress for a party . . . Trying to sing "Three Blind Mice" and dissolving into laughter. Mother had come back for a moment, waltzing in her fairy gown at the foot of the stairs; and now she came again, living and all at once, before she receded again into the world of dream. She withdrew smiling, with her fingers blowing a kiss in honor of Katie's party.

The necklace was a twisted rope of seed pearls, with a pearl medallion as delicate as a second, smaller snowflake. Her father fastened it around her neck.

For several minutes she couldn't stop crying. Her father comforted her against his massive shoulder. He was a wonderful, wonderful man.

By the time the party began to walk in, Katie was supersaturated. Joy was spilling over her brim and running to waste around her.

She stood beside her father and shook hands with a stream of guests, and thanked them for their birthday gifts, which she put unopened on the table beside her. Everyone said, "How grown-up you look, Katie! What a heavenly dress!"

Her dance card was scrabbled over with names. She danced in a blissful daze. The new slippers raised a blister on her heel, but pain had no hold on her this evening. She invited her escorts to have a cup of sherbet; she danced with boys so gloriously tall that her nose bumped their shirt fronts. She spoke politely, if vaguely, to Aunt Louisa's friends as they passed through to the conservatory.

Aunt Louisa was holding court there, in the peacock-tail chair. She talked loud and dogmatically about the good old days in Meridian; and boys who put their heads inside the conservatory ducked out in haste and went elsewhere.

Katie had clean forgotten about the trained-dog act, until she heard a fanfare and a roll of drums from the orchestra. This brave sound was punctuated by a series of yips.

Everyone surged around the dog trainer, who was setting out pedestals, hoops, rubber balls, clay pipes and comic hats at the foot of the stairs. Even Aunt Louisa's friends deserted her, and if she hadn't been in deep mourning she would have followed them. The dogs came barking out of their cages, and the specators formed a jam-packed semicircle.

Katie as a hostess let them crowd in front of her. She had enough to enjoy that evening without trained-dog acts. She was tired, and she wanted to slip her blistered heel out of her dancing pump. She wandered away through the deserted rooms into the back parlor, and sat leaning her head against the wall.

Horace was tired too. This was his moment for a high ball and a little chat with Louisa.

"Woof, woof, woof!" he mimicked spitefully, coming through from the front parlor into the conservatory, glass in hand. "I'm too old to watch dogs jump through hoops. What do you think of Katie's party, Louisa?" He let himself down into a chair.

"Very nice," she said temperately. "It was high time you had people to the house again. There's only one thing: How did those Epps youngsters get in?"

"They're building on our Number Two lot, you know."

"So I'd heard," Louisa said with pinched lips. "Mark my word, Horace, the Eppses will ruin the tone of Rampole Place."

To other critics Horace could dispense eyewash. Epps was coming up fast; he was a likable fellow. If Adams Avenue could put up with him, so could Rampole Place.

To Louisa he said candidly, "I don't like them any better than you do. But I have my reasons for keeping on the right side of Anson Epps."

"When your children marry Eppses don't say I didn't warn you."

"Pooh! Victor takes Jodie out, but he's only seventeen. When I was seventeen I was in love with a Polish girl who worked in a sausage-stuffing plant. And a mighty pretty girl she was too."

"Oh, Victor can take care of himself," she said. "It's Katie who worries me. The child is so—so defenseless. If Epps doesn't pick her off, some other climber will."

"I'm looking out for Katie," said Horace, bristling. "And if you'll pardon the remark, Louisa, I'm doing a whale of a lot better on her than you ever did."

"Except for this one point," Louisa conceded, "you've done wonders. Why, the child is almost popular tonight—I've been watching her. It was a stroke of genius, Horace, your moving a whole neighborhood into your dooryard."

"Now, now, don't go leaping to conclusions. I sold off the land as a matter of business."

"Tell that to the newspapers! You were under no compulsion to sell, and I know you didn't sell for your own pleasure. I see through you, and I give you credit. You and I know that Katie was as nearly impossible as a little girl could be. No looks, no charm, no femininity, nothing winning about her. I don't say she's winning even now, and no amount of dressing will make her pretty. But she isn't a wooden Indian any longer. If you can keep her out of the hands of the Eppses, some fine day she'll marry a presentable boy, from pure propinquity."

"You make me so damn mad! You never did appreciate Katie. She's maturing slowly, but she's on the way to being a delightful young woman."

"Don't try to pull the wool over my eyes about your fascinating daughter. Remember, we talked this all out before I moved to California. Katie was impossible. I say you've been an admirable father."

"Did you notice," he said, chuckling, "that Katie had her dance card filled before the music started?"

"That's the merit of giving a party. The boys are obliged to dance with their hostess."

Katie had been sitting in a gilt chair, with her slippers off and her head against the back-parlor wall. "Woof, woof, woof": she had heard every word of the conversation from the beginning. She had let the authoritative Rampole intonations drift in at one ear, while the yipping of dogs came in at the other.

By the time they launched on the sickening part of their discussion she couldn't rise and slip away, for fear of being seen through the archway. She must protect her father from knowing that after all his anxious care on her behalf she had overheard him. She worshiped him more than ever. Who except her father would have gone to such lengths to manufacture a social life for an impossible daughter?

But impossible she was—the point was conceded. She would never be one of the beautiful Rampole women; no amount of dressing would make her pretty. She was a blight, a misfit, a wooden Indian. Her father had moved eight families into new houses to supplement her shortcomings.

If she had been younger she would have rushed to sanctuary in the Secret Cave under her mother's bed. Being fifteen years old, she did nothing. She allowed the worms to burrow their way into her heart.

Woodenly she smiled, woodenly she danced out her program, woodenly she shook hands and said good night. Woodenly she thanked her father for giving her such a lovely time, and climbed the stairs to bed.

"What's gone wrong with the kid?" Horace asked, looking after her. "She must be tuckered out."

"She has a blister on her heel," said Victor, who was still in a condition of bounding energy after dancing most of the evening with Jodie.

"All she needs is a good night's sleep," said Louisa Lassigne.

Having gone to the trouble and expense of giving Katie a bang-up party, Horace was a little let down by her low spirits. But he reassembled his hope and patience, as a parent must.

Chapter 13

DURING the second winter in Rampole Place the school limousine lost favor with the mothers. Big boys held girls on their laps, and tickling and squealing took place. It was hardly decent.

So the neighborly solidarity of the first winter was whittled away. Families began getting their own children to school.

Victor commandeered the Ford, and drove a gang of big boys to the Cambridge School. When the Eppses moved into their new house he must be foot-loose, able to evict his male passengers and drive Jodie to Miss Peebles' every day.

Augustus was vexed at losing the use of the Ford. Since Victor had taken it over, the least Victor could do was drive Katie to school—so Augustus said.

Victor's darling dream was threatened, and he turned contrary as a mule. If he had a girl-child tagging at his heels, he would lose caste with the boys—Gus ought to understand that. What was to prevent William from driving Katie to school and back? He would put his right hand in the fire for Katie, but drive her to school he would not—and that was flat.

The balance was shifting in Victor's relations with Augustus. Victor was the son of the house and nearly a man grown. In the matter of getting Katie to school with Victor, Augustus was whipped. William would have to drive her. Augustus was very cross, but he had no authority over Victor.

Augustus was entitled to his grievance. He ran a large estate with a small, well-disciplined working force. William not only drove the limousine and ran the household errands, he provided thews and sinews for the heavy chores inside the house. But William had sweethearts in kitchens all up and down Adams Avenue. His school run took up most of the forenoon. Day after day he left Augustus shorthanded.

Augustus grumbled to his wife, "Why can't Katie stand turns with the other girls the way she did last year?"

"Most of the girls are older. They don't want a kid tagging along any more than Vic does. They want to talk secrets about their beaux. But Delia Dysart and Lissa Grover—they're in Katie's grade."

"Yah! Delia gets to ride to school in her big brother's car. You couldn't pry her loose. And you know as well as I do that Lissa Grover hitched rides all last winter."

Jennie dealt with this as with other problems by setting out a pot of coffee and a quarter of a cherry pie. She filled her own cup and sat across from her husband at the kitchen table.

"This is one thing I can't fix up for you, Gus. The mothers make these deals over the telephone. I can't call up Mrs. Wyndham and offer to trade rides—I'm only the help. I wish Katie's mama was here."

Relief came to Augustus from the last quarter where he would have looked for it—from Katie herself. "Gus—" hesitantly, for Katie had been on the fringe of these awkward discussions—"Lissa Grover was suggesting to me today that her father could drive us to school in the mornings, and maybe I could drive her home in the afternoons."

"It's an idea," Augustus said. "I didn't know Lissa Grover was such a pal of yours."

"We're the only two left over," Katie said with stoic realism.

"Well," said Augustus, "we'll try it out."

"Why don't it set well with you, Gus?" Jennie asked him when they were alone. "It's what you wanted. And Lissa will be a nice friend for poor Katie."

"That's the whole point—will she? But she's good enough to ride to school with, I guess."

Jennie countered with more spirit than usual, "Grover is one of the best names in the state of Algonquin. Some would put it **above** Rampole. And Lissa is a pretty-mannered girl enough."

"I'm not putting money on the good name of the Grovers from here in."

"Gus, are the boys still scandalizing about Mrs. Queenie?"

"Plenty," said Gus, supping his coffee. The boys his wife referred to were the housemen, chauffeurs and gardeners of the street. "Nights when her husband won't take her out she calls a taxi and sets off under her own steam. And there's always some dude fetches her home. Last Tuesday one of 'em took four minutes and forty seconds helping her get her key into the lock. Henderson clocked 'em."

Jennie made grieving sounds. "Poor silly soul! She don't mean a particle of harm."

"She owed a lot to our Chloe," Augustus said, slicing into his pie with his fork. "Now she's gone, Philip Grover's friends ask him and her to dinner once a year for old-times' sake, and the rest of the time they give 'em the go-by. So she traipses around with strangers and foreigners—not a one of them born in Meridian. It don't look good."

"Dear, dear! Philip Grover had the world at his feet when he was a young fellow."

"I'm not one mite sorry for Philip Grover. If Philip Grover wasn't a silly-Billy, he'd take away her shoes and make her set home nights and behave herself. I hate to think what I'd do to you, Jen, if you took to gallivantin' around in taxicabs."

"Well," said Jennie, draining her cup, "young Lissa takes after her father, and I stick to it that she won't do Katie any harm."

Lissa had not proposed driving Katie to school out of any sense of intimacy with her. For Lissa it was a desperate resource in a desperate situation.

Rampole Place was not that desired haven where people dropped in and out of the house all day. At least not Queenie's house. Sick at heart,

Lissa saw her mother sitting at the front window while her neighbors loaded into cars to go marketing together, lunching together, committeeing together. On gala evenings Rampole Place dined by fours and sixes, while Daddy and Queenie dined alone in their best clothes and drove off to the party.

No door was actually closed against Queenie. When Daddy played tennis she put on a flowered chiffon frock, a pair of high-heeled white kid slippers and her string of real pearls, and sat chatting on the side lines. A stranger watching her would not have known she was excluded. But she was never asked to join the Monday Bridge Club, which was the executive body of Rampole Place.

Lissa couldn't stop trying to decipher the neighbors' treatment of her mother. These old friends of Daddy's were the finest sort of people, even—in a way that humiliated her—her own sort of people. But she would not identify herself with a group that discriminated against Queenie. She was sick with bitterness. It would have cost the Monday Bridge Club so little to widen their charity and take Queenie in! And once they accepted her, her native sweetness would win them over. She was a flower that opened only to the sunlight.

For everybody's sake, Daddy had to make light of Queenie's hurt feelings. Perhaps he deceived even himself. That was a question Lissa could not ask.

At dinner: "What were you up to all day, Queenie?"

"I sat home the entire livelong day. The telephone never rang once, except the upholsterer."

"The crowd hasn't found its way here yet. We've barely got settled in the new house."

"We've lived here six months."

"Suppose I give the Colemans a ring and ask them over for some bridge this evening."

"Well, you can try. You know them better than I do."

While Philip was away from the table, Queenie's mood wavered. "I wish he'd ring off. They don't want to come here."

Philip reported back. "They're tied up with the Wyndhams tonight. But they want us to give them a ring the first of the week. Lissa, you remind me."

When Queenie was happy her voice had a pretty tinkling peal. When she was out of sorts it picked up a flawed overtone. Now her voice warned Lissa, and Lissa clenched her toes inside her shoes. "Did they mention any *specific* evening next week?"

"Well, that's pretty far ahead."

"I can guarantee they will be tied up Monday, Tuesday, Wednesday,

Thursday and Friday, right up to the next week end. They'll be frightfully sorry, and they'll make us promise to call them up week after next."

"Come now, Queenie dearest! I've known Pete Coleman since I was in first grade."

"Darling, you're so guileless! This isn't the first grade, it's Rampole Place."

"It's the same people."

Queenie poked at a teaspoon with her pretty forefinger. "Sometimes I think it's because we don't live up to their standards of style; we let them down. They all have regular staffs of servants."

"Queenie!" he protested, half laughing, half distressed.

"I wouldn't blame them. You saw how things went at dinner the other night. The dinner was stone-cold by the time Ella got it on the table. And when she cleared away she stacked the butter plates right on top of the dinner plates. I almost died of mortification."

Lissa said unhappily, "Ella's feet get to hurting her, so she has to save trips."

Philip said just as unhappily, "Well, when we have people to dinner why don't we get in a waiter from the club? I suppose that's a justifiable extravagance for us Rampole Place swells."

Queenie gave this proposal her attention, and then shook her head. "That isn't it, darling. It's more as if we were contagious, and everybody but ourselves could see the spots coming out on us. What *is* wrong with us?"

(No, Daddy, no! Lissa prayed to her father. Don't hunt for the answer to that question. We're better off without knowing.)

"Nothing's wrong with us, Queenie. We mustn't be touchy. When we lived in the city we were on the go all the time. We'll fall into our groove before long."

As the sun breaks over a flowering meadow, the brightness that Philip and Lissa loved came back into Queenie's face. "Oh, that reminds me!" Her voice chimed true again. "Maddy Thies wants us for dinner next Tuesday. She has some sort of a musician staying with her."

"Fine!" said Philip robustly. Then, after consulting his pocketbook, "Bother! That's the night of the Bar Association Committee."

"It won't kill you to skip one meeting."

"Not this one, honey. Grover and Westerling fought for the appointment to that committee. Sometimes they pass us over."

A danger signal showed itself on Queenie's infantile round brow. "You don't like Maddy Thies—you didn't know her in first grade. That's provincial of you, Philip. I happen to enjoy Maddy's parties very much."

Philip said in his deliberate way, "I find myself inadequate to Maddy Thies."

"Now what do you mean by that, Philip Grover? Explain yourself. Maddy is a fascinating, cosmopolitan woman. She's traveled everywhere and met everybody—even people with titles."

"I don't deny that," Philip said. He gave a small, naughty laugh and applied himself to his salad. "I'm the inadequate one."

"What do you mean—inadequate? You're as clever as any one of them."

"If you really want to know, she expects me to make love to her. She feels let down when I don't. She agrees with you that I'm provincial."

Queenie went off into a tinkling ecstasy of laughter. Philip joined her, and Lissa's toes came unclenched. The sweetness was back in the room.

"That, darling," she cried when she had subdued her mirth, "is the unbreakable alibi at last. I'll let you off Maddy's party—I'll go by myself. Maddy can always scare up an extra man."

That was all Queenie's night life amounted to—parties with Mrs. Thies's friends.

Unfortunately, though, Maddy's cavaliers stood out like sore thumbs in Rampole Place. They were too handsome, too alien. Even when they were nothing more formidable than advertising men they had the air of soldiers of fortune.

If Queenie could only have resisted chattering about them to the good matrons of the street! She was quite patronizing to the dear ladies of Rampole Place, who had no one but their own husbands to take them out.

Whenever Queenie took this conquering tone, Lissa clenched her toes in misery. She could see, from the smiles and side glances that went round, that the ladies were more amused than impressed. For her own peace of mind Lissa shirked going out with her mother in the grown-up world.

For a while she felt safe among the young. At that time she was still riding home from school with a crowd of girls. She made the morning trip with her father.

One morning, however, Daddy had to have breakfast with an out-of-town client at the club, so Lissa climbed into the school-going car. She was virtually unnoticed, and the girls took up their gossip where they had left it the morning before.

"One-fifteen last night," Vicky Bellamy reported. "A Stutz racing car this time."

Lissa turned frigid. She had heard the Stutz roar into the oval.

Sue Whitty jeered. "So you had your telescope to your eye at one in the morning?"

"They made so much noise they woke me up. They sat parked under the street light for ten solid minutes. Ask Mummy—she heard them. She mentioned it at breakfast, and Martha said, 'Yes'm, I heard 'em too!'"

Lissa felt sick and embarrassed. She made a small gentlewomanly sound to put them on warning of her presence.

There was a half second of panic silence, followed by an artificial change of subject.

Lissa positively could not ride home with those girls. She went to the school office and called her father, and asked him to pick her up in front of Toomey's Drugstore on his way home.

From three o'clock till five she walked the streets in the neighborhood of the school, huddling her coat about her ribs to keep from shivering. She was framing and reframing what she would say to Daddy. She must ask him to tell Queenie that she was being talked about in that horrid way.

It was only twelve minutes past five when his roadster slid up to the curb. His look was anxious and perceptive.

"This is an unexpected pleasure," he said as they drove off. "Did you get kept after school?" He was joking—Lissa was an "A" student and a teachers' pet.

"Yes, I got kept after school," she came back with wan facetiousness. She tried to go on, but her breathing was cut off by a balloon that kept inflating inside her. He waited, and she felt him waiting.

She stared at the kaleidoscope of colored signs that jeweled the raw twilight in the streets, and nerved herself to open the impossible subject. She couldn't be sure she wouldn't break out crying. At some point the fragile casket of family love might burst and spill its treasure.

"Anything go wrong today?" he asked sidelong.

Part of her craved to cast herself on Daddy's shoulder, to beg him to make everything safe again. The dominant part, the mature part, revolted against making Daddy the victim of her weakness. Nothing was really wrong, it just looked wrong to outsiders. Speaking would make everything worse for Daddy. Lissa was surely strong enough to carry her share of a load of trouble.

"Nothing particular," she answered him. The balloon inside her collapsed all in an instant, and the pressure eased. "I got sick of riding home with the Gang. They screech so, and they sit all over me."

He took it that she didn't want to be pressed. "I don't blame you," he said easily. "I'm a great one for going off by myself. I always feel better afterward."

But still Lissa couldn't bring herself to use the school limousine.

Nature dealt temporarily with Lissa's problem by making her throw up her breakfast, so that Queenie said she had better take a day in bed. By afternoon she had worked out a plan.

She slid into her clothes and walked up to Chestnut Point to make her proposal about sharing rides. Katie accepted it with hesitant pleasure. She knew she was a wooden Indian, and she was glad her family limousine had trading value.

Queenie was delighted to have her Lissa sharing rides with Katie Rampole. It was a tribute to the family status, and she often brought it into her conversation.

Katie and Lissa made out surprisingly well. Their insecurities were a mutual bulwark. They stopped at Toomey's for a soda on the way home, and spent the shank of the afternoon together—doing homework, playing checkers, eating apples and reading Philip's books.

Lissa liked several things about Katie. Naturally she enjoyed the unlimited layer cake and lemonade in the Rampole house. She liked Katie's tweedling on the piano, which was so much sweeter and more expressive than her conversation. When Katie forgot she was not alone, her fingers talked for her.

But Lissa particularly liked Katie's detachment. If a man called to take Queenie out tea dancing, Queenie could make a rustling perfumed transit down the stairs, she could call out a silvery good-by, and Katie would call back, "Good-by, Mrs. Grover," without so much as looking around. Obviously she forgot that sort of thing the minute it happened.

Late in the afternoon a carload of big boys was apt to invade the Rampole house. They thundered through to the pantry for provender, and then up to Victor's room. If Katie came along the corridor, a pointed silence fell. From day to day they brought in new dirty jokes, and they were wary of being overheard.

But they had graver business to transact—the negotiation of week-end dates. They conferred endlessly. "Well, if you want to take Dinah, I'll ask Franny." . . . "What'll you bet Tod Hampner has Franny signed up by this time?" . . . "Well, call her up, you big dumbbell, and find out."

For the young buckaroos of the Swimming Club were not giving any girl a chance to turn them down. What they needed was girls popular enough to do them credit, but not so popular as to be bespoken. They did their canvassing over the smoking-room telephone, with the door closed.

One winter afternoon, however, while Katie and Lissa were reading magazines in the sitting room, Victor came charging in. He closed the door behind him and dashed to the telephone on the desk. His urgency was such that he disregarded the two younger girls. He called Adams 4113 and asked for Miss Jodie Epps.

The boys in the next room had calls to make too. The instrument clicked as they signaled the operator.

"Here!" Victor handed the telephone to Katie. "Tell them you're making a call. I don't want them listening in on me."

Katie obediently spoke into the transmitter: "If you don't mind, I'm using the line."

"Thanks," said Victor, repossessing himself of the instrument. "I have to reach Jodie before anybody else does. Jedge Breen says that big baboon brother of his is trying to sign her up for Saturday night."

"You generally sign her up weeks ahead of time."

"Hello?" Victor barked into a blank telephone. Then he answered Katie: "I booked her up a week ago Sunday. But Doc Breen has a closed car and a tuxedo, and I don't like the sound of things. . . . When do you expect her home, Mrs. Epps? . . . Well, would you ask her to call Victor Rampole the very minute she gets home? It's as important as all get out, Mrs. Epps. Thanks very much, Mrs. Epps."

With a frantic gesture he swung out of the room.

Lissa asked in her collected, pretty little voice, "Is Victor in love with Jodie Epps?"

"Is water wet?" Katie replied sardonically.

"I don't understand about boys. I don't understand about boys at all."

"What's the point in trying? They're crazy." And Katie went back to her magazine. She was reading a richly heart-rending story about young love, but furtively, for fear that Lissa might think she had gone sappy.

"But boys—" Lissa persisted with an effort, her face flushing—"boys are what girls marry, Katie."

"I don't see why anybody bothers to get married," Katie said absently, and turned a page.

"Oh, I do. What would we do with ourselves when we finished school if we didn't get married?"

Katie's face clenched, and her wooden shutters came down. "I haven't the slightest idea. We'd save ourselves a lot of trouble, though."

Lissa's eyes were fastened on Katie in a fog-gray stare. Some need of enlightenment made her ask slowly, "Katie, did any boy ever just haul off and kiss you?"

The question was so extraordinary that Katie laid down her magazine. Lissa was entirely pink, and she was giving off flickers of feminity. Lissa, the safe friend, the friend with no nonsense about her, was getting spoony about boys. Desolation moved in on Katie. "If any boy tried it on me," she cried fiercely, "I'd sock him!"

"It was quite nice," Lissa said. "Nice, but confusing."

"Do you mean to tell me you go around kissing boys?"

"It never happened but that once, and it took me completely by surprise. That's what I don't understand. When these boys telephone to girls, are they expecting to kiss them?"

"Why are you asking me? Eavesdrop around the coatroom at school and maybe you'll find out."

"When this boy kissed me, I kept it to myself. I've never told anybody but you."

"Who was it?" Katie asked, rolling over on one hip to concentrate on Lissa's face.

"Oh, just somebody last spring. Nobody you'd ever guess. In a way it was quite wonderful."

"Are you in love with him?" Katie hardly believed this tall tale of Lissa's, but it had a dark fascination for her.

"Yes, I am."

"Well, you two have certainly kept it pretty dark."

"I didn't say he was in love with me. Only—why else should he have kissed me? I didn't do anything to bring it on. It came like a flash of lightning—and that was all there was to it. He hardly speaks to me now."

Katie felt a swooning anguish for the paradise that was denied her. She said gruffly, "Don't ask me to explain it—ask him."

"Oh, I'd die. I couldn't."

"Then for gracious sakes stop asking me!" Katie cried, beside herself. She was close to panic. Lissa, so cool and old-ladified—a boy had hauled off and kissed Lissa, like a flash of lightning, and it had been quite wonderful. No one in the whole world would ever kiss Katie Rampole except for her money.

To break off these unendurable confidences Katie went to the piano, set the metronome very fast, and practiced scales two-hands-together, up and down the keyboard, like a gale of wind through the trees.

But before long she was tearing chords apart under her hands. She was launching despondent minor phrases that arrived nowhere. She ended on a discord, and sat holding down the keys till the dissonance died away.

Chapter 14

As THE TIME drew nearer for the Epps family to move into Number Two Rampole Place—as the crates of imported furniture were unloaded, as the grenadier urns that flanked the entrance steps put forth shakos of salmon-pink geraniums—one topic took precedence at the Monday Bridge Club. When, and in what formation, were the ladies of Rampole Place to call on the Eppses?

Senator Rampole had put them in a tight spot, and it was hard to forgive him. They knew that as a politician the Senator had strange fish to fry, but they hadn't expected him to fry them in his own dooryard.

These pleasant matrons prided themselves on their good manners. The crudity of boycotting the Eppses entirely was beyond them. And quite frankly, they were dying to see the inside of the Epps palace.

But they did feel entitled to set bounds against intimacy. Jodie and Tommy couldn't be excluded from the Swimming Club—that would be brutal. Anson and Onie, however, must not be encouraged to troop in and out of their houses at odd hours, or to wander over to the Breens' tennis court as everybody did of a summer afternoon.

Churchgoing tailored suits, white gloves and calling cards, after a decent interval—that was the cue. One invitation a year, to the big catch-all parties a woman was obliged to give. Civility at arm's length.

All their forethought was wasted. One morning every family in Rampole Place received an invitation to the Eppses' housewarming.

As the postman trod his course around the oval, the telephone began ringing. "My dear, have you got yours yet?" . . . "I'm having it framed. I'm going to hang it over the mantelpiece." . . . "Where do people *buy* things like that?" . . . "It must be Onie's idea of style. Anson Epps has been around enough to know better."

On the face of the invitation, which was so large that it came in a special envelope, was a colored picture called "The Hanging of the Crane," full of Pilgrims and Puritans. Below this was a printed verse, beginning, "Well, Neighbor," and going on to something about the latchstring being out. Embodied in the verse were blanks for the day and hour of the housewarming—three o'clock until seven on Saturday. At the bottom was the handwritten word "Refreshments."

The neighborly intentions of the Monday Bridge Club curdled in its collective veins. Calling, in their own good time, was one thing; being shanghaied into calling was quite another.

One faction proposed that Rampole Place should stay away in a body. A training as deep as instinct rejected this solution. Active rudeness was degrading; it was lower-class. If you weren't nice about things, you often found a situation had got out of control; the baser passions took over.

"Furthermore," said Cassandra Bellamy, "it would look very odd if our children went and we didn't."

Screams rent the air. "Our children! . . . Why should our children go? . . . This is a grown-up party."

"Try and stop your children. Jodie has been asking them."

"How are you going to stop them," Cassandra asked, "without sounding too snobbish for words?"

Ethel Dysart said in her distinguished voice, "Why can't we simply be honest with our children? Why can't we say, 'The Eppses are ill-bred and undereducated and pushing. If you go, you'll put me under obligations to people I'd like to stay clear of.' Why can't we say that?"

"Because, ladies," Cassandra pointed out, "the good old days are gone when we asked Mamma's permission before we accepted an invitation. Speaking only for us Bellamys, I can't prevent my girls from going to the housewarming."

"And speaking as the mother of sons," Mrs. Wyndham contributed, "I find that once a boy has graduated from the Cambridge School, he wears no man's collar. He's a college man; he's a prefreshman, no less. We're having to handle Walt very differently this summer."

The playing cards lay neglected. Occasionally some woman riffled the pack with a lizard snap, but the club was in executive session.

All they could do was set a backfire. They arranged a vaudeville party for the evening of the housewarming. At least it set a terminus to the affair.

They further agreed that they and their husbands would put in an appearance at the Epps party for fifteen minutes, between five and five-thirty.

"Do I look all right?" Onie Epps asked her husband and daughter on Saturday afternoon, when she was dressed for the party.

"Turn around slowly," Anson said. He himself was looking trim and stylish in his new cutaway.

She turned with her usual docility. She was fatalistically conscious of her breadth of beam. The bugle and seed-pearl embroidery of her gown multiplied itself like a repeat of patterned wallpaper. But the saleslady had told her it was just the thing for an afternoon reception. She hoped, for Anson's sake and Jodie's, that she looked presentable.

Rampole Place was no dream of hers. She would have been perfectly contented to cook the family meals with her own hands; and Tommy would have helped her with the dishes. But Ance and Jodie were high-steppers, they were gallopers; and when they called on her for a sprint, she was willing to sprint till she ran out of wind.

"You look like a beautiful great peony," Anson said, kissing her. "You'll knock their eye out. You could double for Lillian Russell this minute."

"Ance!" she exclaimed, half embarrassed, half delighted.

How generous he was to keep on loving her—to overlook her corpulence, her too insistently brown coiffure, her synthetic peony bloom! How wrong Papa and Mama had been, back in Brainardsville, when they opposed her marrying him!

She moved away, smiling, for a last survey of the party arrangements. She might not know about architecture and interior decoration, but she did know housewifery. Her refreshments were to be of the choicest. The dimmest crannies of the house were clean enough to eat out of. She had taken a carpet beater to the antique chairs and tapestries. She had stood over her staff while they polished the marble and parquetry.

"Would you care to taste the punch, madam?" Ferrers offered.

He had received conflicting orders about the punch. Mrs. Epps, who had a complete set of village high principles, had given him a recipe based on fruit juice faintly tinged with claret. The master had told him to spike it with plenty of brandy when madam wasn't looking.

Onie sipped it dubiously. "You must have put in too much claret. I don't want the young people to get tipsy."

"I put in exactly the proportion the recipe called for, madam. Shall I dilute it with Apollinaris water?"

"Well, I don't know," she said uncertainly. "The ice will dilute it, I presume. I've used that recipe for years." And she cruised away like a galleon, to set some bric-a-brac mathematically straight.

Onie tacked about the drawing room on a light breeze of contentment. It was as good as a storybook, her life with Ance. It filled her with innocent wonder.

She could not account for Ance. His people, in Brainardsville, had been trash in comparison with her own substantial parents. His father had deserted Ance's mother, and his mother cooked for the commercial travelers at the Main Street Hotel. Anson had gone to work while he was in high school, clerking in stores, soliciting advertising for the Brainardsville *Courier*.

Onie had championed him in those days. She thought he deserved a lot of credit. But she was not emotionally interested in him. She was the belle of her class—a beauty, a stunner, a peach. Anson had no time for girls, no time for high jinks.

"The boy's too sharp," her father said. "He plays both ends against the middle. He's asked to use my name as a reference on his application for college, and that's all very well. But if I happened not to feel like giving him a good recommendation, I'd expect to find a damaging misprint in my next week's ad in the *Courier*."

"Papa, that's simply ridiculous."

"Well, it's no skin off my nose. Once Epps sets off for college, that's the last we'll see of him in Brainardsville."

Even Onie never dared probe into his experiences at college, which brought him back to Brainardsville in the middle of his sophomore year. Something had hurt him, but something had released him at the same time. College had nothing to offer him, he said—he wanted to go into business.

He had changed his type. He dressed, now, not only well but casually. He had picked up a new way of talking, easy and ironical. He couldn't have learned this nonchalance from the fraternity crowd, because he hadn't joined a fraternity.

He found time, now, for courting; and he made a dead set for Onie Shields. Onie fell helplessly in love, and one of the last objective thoughts she ever formulated about Anson was that he'd modeled himself on the boys who did get asked to join fraternities. Wasn't that a credit to his intelligence?

. . . So here she was, the duchess of a chateau on the outskirts of a great city. And to compound the marvel, her husband still loved her, unworthy though she was.

"Ferrers," she said, "you'd better set those American Beauties more to the front. They're from the directors of the First National Bank."

They had asked a good many people. When Ance suggested a housewarming she had assumed that he meant her to ask their new neighbors. Ance said that wasn't what he built his house for. He asked the whole membership of the Meridian Club and a lot of men he knew downtown, with their wives—and some of his gay friends.

Yes, Ance had gay friends. He often drove off in his car when Onie went to bed; he was a nighthawk. She couldn't keep up with his night life and she didn't want to. Even the women drank and told jokes that Onie thought were not nice.

But she'd married Ance with her eyes open. She'd never expected to put a race horse between the shafts of a milk wagon.

She brought her children up to know right from wrong. She kept a comfortable house and set a good table. And when Ance and Jodie called on her to soar, she obligingly flapped upward.

As five o'clock approached, cars were parked on Adams Avenue as far as the bridge. Telephones rang between the houses.

"We're starting now, Cassandra; we'll stop by for you." . . . "Don't, for heaven's sake, Lucy; the Whittys and the Wyndhams are going with us already. If we tramp in together, we'll look like a delegation at an alderman's funeral." . . . "Well then, we'll see you there. Look for us."

By fours and by sixes Rampole Place edged into the queue at the foot of the steps, in a tumbling surf of ostrich plumes and fur boas.

Cassandra Bellamy was the chartered original of the group. "You know," she now proclaimed, "this isn't a bit more ridiculous than the old Rampole parties at Chestnut Point."

"Ssh! Somebody will hear you."

A photographer who had been squatting on his heels let off a flash. A forward surge of the queue carried them into the vestibule.

They were now stacked perpendicularly in a mass of breathing and perspiring flesh, unable to move. This would have been a good time for the exercise of irony at the expense of the new house, but what was visible was in no way ridiculous. If crystal, bronze, brocade and tapestry were good—and no one questioned that they were good—the Eppses had an overpoweringly handsome house.

The receiving line moved like a drowsy anaconda toward the drawing room. Waiters were forcing a passage through the crowd, with trays of claret punch, lobster salad and hot tidbits; but courtesy required that the guests should shake hands before partaking.

The young fry of Rampole Place were all too visible, sliding like eels through gaps and flourishing cups of claret punch.

"Stewart! Go over and lay down the law to our Dinah. Tell her she's not to drink another drop of that stuff. It's outrageous, serving intoxicants to girls who aren't even out!"

"My dear, I can't budge hand or foot. The waiter tells me it's nothing but claret lemonade."

"It smells of brandy to me."

"All right then, you try to get through to her. I know when I'm licked."

After reflection Cassandra propounded, "Do you know, this is exactly the house Big Joe Rampole would have built if he'd been building today?"

"Cassie! That's not fair. The Rampoles built their house because they *were* prominent, not because they *wanted* to be prominent."

"Probably Anson Epps is prominent this very minute, only we don't know it."

"Not so loud, Cassie!"

They were almost to the head of the line now. Under her breath Dorothy Whitty hissed, "Do you see what I see?"

They certainly did. In the niche beyond the fireplace Queenie Grover was holding court on the window seat. She was looking as luscious as a full-blown pink water lily. Her laugh rippled, her voice gave off its silvery clink. She was surrounded by facetious, middle-aged men—men who exuded an air of quick-and-easy money.

The little delegation reached the head of the line. They found their white gloves sandwiched, successively, between Onie Epps's broad palms.

"Well, Mrs. Bellamy—Mr. Bellamy—it's downright sweet of you to drop in."

"We just want to—to welcome you to the neighborhood. Our children know your children."

"They're all here somewhere," Onie said, waving one hand while holding Cassandra tethered by the other. "I love seeing young people enjoy themselves, don't you? We're only young once, I always say. Well, be sure you get some refreshments before you go. And look around upstairs, anywhere you like. You must drop over some evening when things calm down."

"Well—er—we'll expect you to drop in on us. Your house is simply beautiful."

"Ance dear, this is Mr. and Mrs. Bellamy from up the street."

Anson's manner was within the limits of decorum, but he was upborne by something more potent than claret punch. His eye was bright, and his color was high. "Let's see, do you people know everybody? Queenie, my girl, stop flirting for a minute and see that the Bellamys find their way to the dining room."

"Oh, you!" Queenie replied skittishly. It was all too evident that she was, to put it delicately, a little squiffed.

One of Queenie's cavaliers pulled her down by the elbow, and she yeilded with a bubbling laugh. She was having an astonishingly good time. It took her back to her glamorous lost girlhood.

"Let's get out of here," Stewart Whitty said through his teeth. "I don't want to run into Philip Grover right now."

By a quarter past six the Monday Bridge Club with auxiliary husbands was holding a post-mortem on the Wyndhams' porch. The stentor voice of the carriage caller still rang through the glades.

They should never have gone to the housewarming. Far from setting up bounds against intimacy, they had weakly asked the Eppses to drop around some evening. And Queenie—Queenie revolted them.

"This must be the way she carries on when she goes to parties with those young men of hers.". . . "No wonder Philip stays away!"

By a quarter to seven they had worries closer to home.

It wasn't that their children didn't understand the plans for the evening. Each of the households was having a quick supper at six-thirty, and they had engaged several boxes for the vaudeville.

At ten minutes to seven none of the young people had reported in. "Do you think I should telephone the Epps house and ask to speak to Delia?" . . . "Give her a few more minutes. The housewarming closes officially at seven."

At a quarter past seven Dorothy Whitty did call her daughter Dorothea, who was the oldest girl involved. Dinner was on the table, she said; they'd be late to the vaudeville. . . .

Dorothea said vaguely that she would pass the word but that Mother needn't hold dinner for her, she was so full of lobster salad.

"You weren't invited to supper."

"Oh, yes, we were. Jodie asked all of us to hang around."

At twenty-five minutes to eight Stewart Whitty and Bert Bellamy were deputed to make a sortie and bring back their children. Their assignment was humiliating from a variety of angles, but they marched under orders.

Bert caught sight of one of his numerous daughters sitting on the grand staircase with several boys, eating Nesselrode pudding out of a paper case. "Perhaps," he said dryly, "it's slipped your mind that your parents are waiting to take you downtown to the theater. Mrs. Epps invited you from three o'clock till seven—not to spend the night."

The young people worked up expressions of surprise and regret that they should have overlooked the time. Jodie cut the ground from under them by appearing in the drawing-room archway. "Oh, Mr. Bellamy, Mr. Whitty—how horrible! I didn't realize there was another party to-night. Daddy asked the orchestra to stay on, and we were going to dance."

No one but an old bear could have ordered his children out of her house. She directed her eyelashes full upon them, and waited for them to surrender gracefully. Anson Epps came out from the dining room and took in the trying situation.

They wished now that they had invited Jodie to their vaudeville party.

Their children were gathering in a circle around Mr. Whitty and Mr. Bellamy, as solemn as owls, obviously wishing they didn't have to go to the tiresome old vaudeville.

"You come along with us, Jodie," Stewart said lamely. "We didn't know you were having dancing this evening, and we've taken five boxes at the Regent."

"I wish I had known," Jodie said, "and I wouldn't have let Daddy engage a whole orchestra to stay on." Her manner was still deferential, but she did not budge from her position. And clearly she had her father's backing. He kept his loafing posture, but his eyes burned a wicked green.

"Well, you kids will have to figure it out," Bert Bellamy said. "But I warn you that your mother and I are leaving for town in exactly fifteen minutes."

A good many motives operated in the silent choosing of sides that took place. Most of the girls were socially disciplined enough to start for home. Jedge Breen had been under parental discipline that week, and rather than bring down any fresh lightnings on his head, he said good night.

Jodie was left with an assortment of guests—three odd girls and a whole troop of boys. Delia Dysart decided that if her brothers were staying, she would stay too. Letty Coleman stayed. And Lissa Grover— who was a wet blanket at any party.

Lissa would have given a great deal to go home, but she couldn't; Ella had the evening off, the Grover house was locked and the key was in Daddy's pocket. Anson had swept the senior Grovers into the dining room for a bit of supper with himself and Onie.

Queenie was still skimming the stratosphere of joy. "It's such fun, having you next door!" she cried. "Phil-ip! Why don't we give a party as good as this one?"

"You made the party go, dearie," Onie Epps said, helping herself for the third time to lobster salad.

"Quite a little icebreaker, I'll say," Anson commented gallantly, raising his punch cup to Queenie. "She had the boys dizzy."

Lissa moped about the entrance hall, watching for the moment when Daddy and Queenie would be ready to take her home.

She couldn't bear to watch her mother playing up to Mr. Epps in a way that meant so little and looked so badly; so she drifted to the drawing-room door. Jodie was dancing the Boston with one of the Wyndhams, and Victor was glowering in a corner.

The Boston was not an easy dance—it took a knack. Jodie danced it

96

like a nymph in a glade. Delia and Letty did nothing but giggle, apologize, and bump their partners' knees.

Victor tried to cut in on Jodie, but she whirled into Doc Breen's arms. All she gave Victor was a taunting smile. Victor responded by kicking an ottoman.

Lissa loved Victor Rampole so much that she could gladly have choked Jodie Epps for trifling with him.

Jodie was the only girl worth dancing with. The other couples gave up and made for the punch table. Jodie took a startled look around the floor and went flying out to the dining room. "Daddy!" she said urgently. "The party is dying on my hands. They won't dance. They'll start going home any minute. Can't you do something?"

Anson met his daughter's eye. These two understood each other, more like brother and sister than father and daughter. "I'll tell you what—we'll go out to Rivergrove for the shank of the evening."

"Oh, Ance! Jodie's tuckered out," came Onie's motherly protest.

"If she is, it's the first time on record. Go ahead, Tootsie, round 'em up."

Jodie skimmed away on her glad errand.

"Ance," his wife said firmly, "I am not moving one step out of this house tonight. As soon as the silver is locked up I'm going to bed. My feet are killing me."

"I won't argue with you, sweetheart. But you—" turning to the Grovers—"you're game, aren't you?"

Speaking together, Philip said they couldn't think of it, and Queenie said it was the most adorable idea she'd ever heard.

Anson, still leaning back in his chair, looked from one to the other of them with a satanic twinkle in his eyes. "Now we'll find out which of the Grovers is boss," he dared them.

It ended, as so many of the Grovers' projects ended, in Philip's staying at home and Queenie's joining the party. "After all," she said with her tinkle-bell laugh, "they can't go without a chaperone."

"I suppose you'll be wanting to come, Lissa," Jodie said with no great warmth.

"I'd like to, thank you," Lissa said slowly. They didn't want her, and she didn't want to go. She wished Daddy were going. Since he wasn't, she would put the best face she could on things by trailing her mother.

Chapter 15

It was almost one in the morning when Queenie and Lissa let themselves in at their own front door. The arc light at the curb defined their shadows in a thin forbidding glare.

"S-sh! We mustn't wake Phil-ip. But did you ever have so much fun in your whole life?"

Like a small child, Lissa thought in her enervation and fatigue, who knows she has a spanking coming to her, so she sets herself to disarm her mentors with her prettiness! Only my mother is a small child of thirty-eight, and her innocence does not sit easy on her.

This barb of judgment came new and unwanted into Lissa's mind. It tangled with sixteen years of uncensorious love, and left her physically shaking.

Be fair, Lissa adjured herself. What's really running the red-hot knives through you isn't your mother—it's Jodie Epps. It's the spangled darkness at Rivergrove. It's being a bodiless ghost at a carnival. It's loving Victor Rampole while Jodie drags him captive.

Lissa set her foot on the stairs. Soon—tomorrow morning—she would have to speak her mind to Queenie. Tonight she felt too trampled and outdone.

"Dar-ling!" Queenie protested. "You're not going up yet! Let's have some milk to go to sleep on, and laugh about things. That's the way to get the good out of a party." She wandered back to the library and sank in creaming billows on the buttony old leather sofa.

Lissa went out to the pantry for two glasses of milk. Very well! If Queenie was asking for a bedtime review of the evening, she should have it. But there would be no between-us-girlishness about it.

And yet this isn't my job, it's Daddy's. I oughtn't to be put between the jaws of a wrench like this—loving Queenie so desperately and having to scold her, having to despise her. I'm nothing but her daughter. I'm entitled to keep her on a pedestal on the nursery mantelpiece.

Tears of self-pity came to Lissa's eyes, but she shook them away. She was not a child in a nursery. She was sixteen years old.

If Queenie wanted to be accepted in Rampole Place, it was not enough to be a good woman—in the sense in which Queenie was a thoroughly good woman; she must be a decorous woman. The price of acceptance had to be paid in the coin of discretion. And that was a price Queenie was unwilling to pay, when pleasure was in view.

Lissa came through the dark hall with her glasses of milk. Her hair hung fair and straight from her temples to her shoulders. She looked like an alabaster angel; she felt like a Kansas twister.

Queenie had kicked off her shoes. She was framing her arms into a ballerina arch about her head, and then letting them drift downward, delighting in their grace.

"Thanks, precious." Then, feeling her way toward an exoneration in her daughter's eyes, "Lissa, *did* my panties show when I slid down the Fun Tower? Anson is such a tease, you can't believe a word he says."

"Your panties didn't, but your garters did," Lissa replied concisely.

"Now, Old Goody Prim! It happens to everybody, it's part of going to an amusement park. In fact, darling, you acted too stuffy for words this evening. If you weren't going to enter into the spirit of things, you might better have stayed at home."

Lissa was thrown off balance by this counterattack. She said, "I never see any point in paying five cents to get banged around."

"I do wish you could let go and enjoy yourself the way I can. You miss so much." And for the thousandth time she said, "You're your father's daughter. I'm the changeling in this house."

"Queenie——" Lissa said. Her strength consolidated all at once. She would cut straight through to the facts, as they would be known the length of Rampole Place by morning. "It wasn't the Fun Tower I minded. It was your going gambling with Mr. Epps and taking most of the young people upstairs with you. I think you must all have gone crazy. You know how all the families are going to feel about it."

"Why, Melissa Pendleton Grover!"

Lissa gave her hair a discouraged sideward shake. Queenie did not tell lies, but she often sparred for time. She did it while Philip was furrowing his forehead over the monthly bills. But until tonight it had been a trait one overlooked, because it deceived nobody.

"The reason I know," Lissa said evenly, "is because the rest of you left me and Delia Dysart alone at that big restaurant table till closing time. The waiters kept asking if they could clear away. But we didn't know where else to go, so we asked them to let us keep on sitting. It was quite embarrassing, and Delia was very snappish about it."

"Precious, it wasn't so long as you think. It was a matter of minutes."

"Forty minutes."

"And what on earth makes you think we were gambling?"

"Well, there was a revolting big man at the next table to ours, and he boomed out that he was a stranger in town, and where could he get into a friendly game? So the waiter laughed and said, 'The boss throws a birthday party upstairs, five nights a week. You go through the door behind the coatroom and say Luigi sent you.'"

Queenie's eyes shifted, then came back, clear and sunny, to meet Lissa's. "Oh, that! It's a joke all over town. Osmond and I have been to Giacomo's birthday party several times. But as for calling it *gambling*—" she used mock-heroic mimicry—"I suppose you call it *gambling* when Philip and I lose fifty-five cents to the Colemans at bridge. This is a private club, Lissa, with membership cards. . . . What I do resent is your implying that Anson and I lured the young people up there. They found their way, one by one. Nobody need tell me they hadn't been there before."

"What you and your grown-up friends do is none of my business. What the boys do when they're out together is none of my business. But this is my business, whether I like it or not. You were in charge of the crowd."

"In charge! I was a guest. If anybody is to be held accountable, it's Anson Epps. He'll find out," bitterly, "what a square-toed, blue-nosed community he's moved into, but certainly it's no affair of mine. And in fact, unless somebody tattles, how are the families going to hear anything about it?"

"Delia Dysart is going to tell her mother all about it. She was just mad enough. She hates being left out of things."

"But she can't testify that there was any gambling, because you say yourself she never got upstairs."

"Queenie! After you and Mr. Epps had been gone from the table for a while, Art Wyndham looked very knowing and said he'd go find you. And then Walt went to find Arthur—till, one by one, everybody leaked away from the table except Delia and me. And when you did come downstairs the whole gang was whooping and laughing and showing rolls of money. The boys certainly behaved as if they'd been drinking."

"Well, so they had. Giacomo kept offering them drinks, and Anson and I had no way of stopping them. They thought they were regular young devils. We'd have come down long before we did, except that Doc Breen was winning and we couldn't get him away from the tables. Anson gave each of the boys five dollars for a little flutter, and we felt sure they'd lose it in the first five minutes and be ready to come home."

"How did you get up there in the first place? If you hadn't gone, nobody else would have thought of going."

"Well," Queenie said in a honeyed meditative croon, her voice chiming off key, "I suppose this will be built up into a great hullabaloo, but it was just one of those coincidences. I went out into the lobby, looking for the ladies' room, and along came Anson Epps talking to this Giacomo who runs the restaurant. And Giacomo said, in his cute little accent, 'Why don't you and your lady come up and blow out my birthday candles?' So Anson said, 'Next year, Jake,' and Giacomo said, 'Oh, Mrs. Grover has been my guest before this.' So Anson gave me that kind of twinkle out of the corner of his eye, and I saw he wanted to go up—so what could I do? He was my host, Lissa. I could hardly tell him he couldn't buy himself one drink." Queenie moved her pretty, silk-stockinged foot, appearing to congratulate herself on having such a creditable—and accurate—story to tell. "How the youngsters found their way up there, you'll have to ask them."

"Gambling," Lissa said inexorably, as Grandfather Justice might have spoken from his sepulcher. "Daddy was on some sort of a committee to stamp out gambling in Meridian. There was a tremendous fuss, and an election."

"Lissa, you little prig! You'll make people hate you."

"If Daddy had been along this evening, would he have liked it?"

Queenie gave an impatient laugh. "If Philip had been along, Giacomo would never have asked us upstairs."

"Then you shouldn't have gone."

Queenie drew a spectacularly patient breath. "Lissa, sweet, there's something I ought to say to you, now that you're growing up. You know what a lovely time the three of us have together—lovelier than anybody. You may think that's just the Grovers' good luck. Well, it's a lot more than that. I work at happiness. Sometimes when you think I haven't a care in the world, I'm making myself laugh and carry on—because somebody has to."

"We know that, Queenie. All the same——"

Queenie held up that lovely hand of hers for attention. "But Philip and I enjoy different things. This evening we both did as we chose—I went to Rivergrove and Philip read himself to sleep with a book."

Lissa sat forestalled. Queenie had flung her back into childhood, where grownups axiomatically know best.

"So if you're a wise little daughter, you won't stir your father up by telling him at second hand about that birthday party of Giacomo's. It sounds sort of degraded, when actually it was nothing but fun. I'll tell Philip when I get around to it."

She did not even wait for a pledge of silence from Lissa; she climbed to her feet, yawned, and stepped into her shoes for the trip upstairs.

Lissa walked out to the pantry with the empty milk glasses.

. . . I did not promise her. She takes for granted that I promised. But I cannot make a compact with her behind Daddy's back—not on this.

She won't see what she's done to herself in Rampole Place. Daddy's got to know; he's got to decide what to do next.

On Sunday morning Lissa got herself out of bed. She had a bone-deep fastidiousness in dress. She put on her fresh white linen dress, she brushed her hair as smooth as glass. But while she was primming her surface, her soul was still adrift in the howling waste where it had whirled all night. This was the day when she must speak to Daddy about Queenie.

In Rampole Place in 1910, families breakfasted in formation. Egg beaters were humming and finger bowls were clinking, in preparation for Sunday-morning breakfast.

At Number Four there were compromises with this ritual, because Ella worked singlehanded. Daddy got a good hot breakfast in the dining room, with oatmeal and sausages; Queenie rang for her tray some time before noon. Lissa, knowing how rushed Ella was and how her feet hurt, violated the rules of caste by taking her Sunday-morning bite at the corner of the kitchen table.

When Lissa came down the oatmeal was brewing in the double boiler and the granite coffeepot was set back on the stove, but the kitchen was empty. Ella's absence was a bad omen. Lissa knew it meant that storm warnings were being flown up and down Rampole Place.

Ella was fond of saying that she kept herself to herself, she didn't go gaggling up and down the street.

But Ella was human, and when the grapevine shrilled loudly enough she went a-gossiping with the rest.

Lissa served herself a bowl of oatmeal. The gluey pallor of the stuff persuaded her that she was not interested in breakfast. She took refuge in the library, and opened a big dusty book across her knees. Her hands lay narrow and parallel upon the pages.

She heard her father come down to the dining room. Her fingers pressed hard against the book. She granted herself a respite: she would let Daddy eat his breakfast first.

Pretty soon he strolled into the library and settled himself in the bay window with the Sunday paper. Presently he turned a flapping page and said casually, "You look like a virgin martyr in the arena," and ended on a question mark.

She couldn't open her mouth. Her eyes, gray and unfathomable, fixed themselves on her father's face.

"I'm sorry I ducked out of the Rivergrove expedition," he answered her eyes. "I might have been able to give you a hand."

"I wish you'd gone, Daddy."

He embarked on a formula of self-justification, leafing through the newspaper while he spoke. "You know—" (flap)—"when I do tag along on parties with Queenie I feel like a—" (flap) "—a scarecrow, an old hat on a broomstick. I—" (double flap)—"I used to trail her to Maddy Thies's. But it ended up with the rest of them sitting in a circle on the floor, dipping melted cheese out of a crock, and me—" (flap)—"sitting in a straight chair, with somebody bringing me a plate. You and I, Me-liss—" (discard of one section of the paper and taking up of another) —"we're rigged out of broomsticks. We might as well resign ourselves."

"Absolutely, Daddy, but you wouldn't have liked what went on at Rivergrove last night." . . . Ask me a straight question, Daddy. Help me out that far!

"Amusement parks," he continued, discarding the comic section of the paper, "are for puppies that enjoy squealing. But there's no great harm in them."

(You're dodging, Daddy, you're ducking. I excuse you, because I've done it myself for years. You think that's the way to hold onto being happy.)

"Daddy," she said distinctly, "last night Mr. Epps took most of the Gang to a professional gambling place, up over the restaurant. None of the families in Rampole Place are going to like it." (And they're going to lay the blame on Queenie, Daddy—that's what I'm trying to tell you.)

The quizzical modeling of his lips turned straight and stern under his neat mustache. He couldn't show distress about Queenie, but he could be angry at Anson Epps.

Every trace of the dilettante disappeared from his bearing. He was Philip Grover, attorney. He took Lissa through the evening's adventure as if he had her on the witness stand. Then he sat back and gnawed at his lip with his lower teeth.

Lissa, with her fingers interlaced on the big book, was inwardly asking his pardon. By her meddling she had cast him for a part he wasn't qualified to play—an aggressive part. He was miscast.

So was Queenie. Queenie was no Roman matron, but neither was she a convincing villainess. She was a full-blown flower, drenched in sweetness. She was herself—that was the best and the worst you could say about Queenie.

"You understand, Daddy, I'm not complaining on my own account," Lissa concluded with anxious accuracy. "Delia and I didn't go upstairs with the others. Probably Mr. Epps thought the rest of the crowd was old enough——"

"I can't understand Epps's motive. They've just moved into this neighborhood. He's no fool. And yet he thumbs his nose at all the decencies."

"Perhaps he was annoyed because the parents got up that theater party and left Jodie out."

"Lissa, I didn't raise any objection to his taking the party to Rivergrove. It's the gambling angle that's inexcusable."

"Probably where Mr. and Mrs. Epps come from they think gambling is all right."

Philip gave what amounted to a snarl. "Epps never sinned in ignorance in his whole slimy life. He's a corrupter of innocence. The whole Epps family will be boycotted, and they needn't blame anybody except Epps himself."

"Boycotted" was a sinister word. Lissa braced herself and said, "I don't care a particle what people do to the Eppses. All I hope is that they won't take this out on Queenie."

"They wouldn't be so unfair as all that. Epps took advantage of Queenie's good nature. If she were a tartar like Lucy Breen, she'd have spoken her mind. But thank the Lord, Queenie's no tartar." He was asking Lissa to reassure him.

Having braced up to the primary agony of speaking to Daddy, Lissa was not going to lull him with reassurances. She said, "What Letty and the boys are going to tell their families, to get themselves out of hot water, is that Queenie was having more fun than anybody. When they came downstairs again Queenie—well, if she'd been a schoolgirl, you'd have said she had the giggles. I'm not sure but what she won some money too."

"I'll have to move fast on this. By lunchtime every family in the street will have the story, with embellishments. We'll want to get together and take some kind of action against that gambling joint."

"I think the cat is out of the bag by this time," Lissa said miserably. "I came down at eight o'clock this morning and Ella was out gossiping."

"Then I'll go at once."

"Daddy . . . perhaps you'd better talk to Queenie first. I'm not sure she understands how spiteful people are going to be."

"She wouldn't, bless her heart."

"She seemed to think it was . . . priggish of me to raise objections. But I knew Delia Dysart would tell all she knew, and I thought you ought to know too."

"Quite correct. You and I were born on Adams Avenue, and one of the few advantages of being born on Adams Avenue is that we understand Adams Avenue. I'll have to make Queenie see that she's got herself out on a limb."

"Daddy . . ."

"Yes, Meliss?"

"It couldn't possibly be too late for Queenie to get herself back off her limb, could it?" That was the eye of the nightmare.

"Stuff and nonsense, Lissa, don't exaggerate," Philip said violently. "This isn't a major scandal—it's one of those summer whirlwinds that scatter the trash on the lawns and then blow away. Don't, I beseech you, go stalking around like the Muse of Tragedy—you could mess things up fearfully."

"Yes, Daddy," she said meekly. "I'd much rather you attended to it."

Chapter 16

ON SATURDAY NIGHT the young of Rampole Place counted on easing themselves inconspicuously into their beds. They faced a blaze of lights and a midnight conclave of elders. "What on earth have you been up to all this time? . . . I do believe you've been drinking!"

By a grievous oversight the young had neglected to get together on a story. Some of them came up with vague references to swings and roundabouts; one devised a falsehood about tire trouble on the way home; another ingeniously skirted the truth by saying they had sat around a restaurant table playing games till closing time.

They knew their parents would cross-check their stories in the morning. They foresaw a day of reckoning.

On Sunday morning a spontaneous clotting process set in through all the arteries of Rampole Place. The young foregathered at the Swimming Rocks, comparing notes and hunching their shoulders to the impending cloudburst.

The parents hived, immediately after breakfast, at the Breens' summerhouse. By common impulse none of them had so much as dressed for church; today their duty was to the tribe. Lucy Breen went so far as to break the Sabbath by fetching along her darning bag.

This was no pleasure party. As family after family contributed its fragment to the mosaic of inference, the picture took horrendous form.

Delia Dysart had not had much fun at Rivergrove. The long ignominious period when she and Lissa sat rejected at the restaurant table, sniffing high jinks in the offing, had dissolved Delia's loyalty to her generation. So she had given her mother an acid report on the events of the evening.

Bob Dysart, *père,* was not so downy a chick as not to have heard about the gambling rooms over the restaurant. The foremen at his plant held membership cards. He put two and two together. In sum, the ineffable Epps had taken the minors of Rampole Place to a low-grade professional gambling den.

Something had to be done.

The ladies first envisaged a massed frontal attack on Number Two Rampole Place, where they would give the Eppses to understand—well, what? They looked at one another.

"If they were normally decent people, they wouldn't need things spelled out for them."

"But they're not normally decent people—that's the whole point."

The ladies were always self-conscious about putting their code into words. They lived under the implicit tradition of Adams Avenue, under which certain freedoms might be exercised and certain transgressions forgiven, while others very similar lay outside the pale.

Cassandra Bellamy said with her well-known independence of judgment, "I don't believe Onie Epps means any harm. She just doesn't know anything. If we put ourselves out a little to make friends, I think we could steer Onie our way."

Someone said spitefully, "All right, Cassandra, you're so bighearted, you are hereby appointed best friend to Onie Epps, God help you!"

But unexpected support developed for her defense of Onie. "Onie didn't even go to Rivergrove." . . . "I'll warrant she spent the evening with her feet in a tub of Epsom salts." . . . "She can't handle that husband of hers." . . . "Or that daughter." . . . "Onie's a homebody, that's what Onie is, poor soul." There was something disarming about Onie.

"That's all very well," said Lucy Breen, driving her flickering needle across a gap in a sock, "but there's a question before the house."

The men made themselves heard above the clamor. "This is more than a personal matter. Rivergrove is supposed to be a decent family amusement park for the streetcar trade. It's run by the MST, and probably half of us own stock in the MST. If the gamblers are chiseling into Rivergrove, they ought to be run out."

"How long ago was it that Horace Rampole cleaned up the city?"

"All of ten years ago. First civic committee I ever served on."

"What a pity he's out of local politics!"

"Out of local politics! If Horace Rampole raised one finger . . ."

Lucy brought them back to the point. "You can't clean up Meridian between now and next week end, and in the meantime I want to make sure that my children go to bed sober. It's Rampole Place I want to clean up."

"There again it's up to the Senator. He brought the Eppses in here. It's for him to read the riot act to them."

"Speaking only for the Breens," Lucy said in a tone that even her dearest friends described as smug, "I am quite capable of reading the riot act to my own children." She snipped off her darning cotton with a precision that was a reproach to lesser parents.

"I wish you the best of luck," Dorothy Whitty said dryly. Through her daughters she had insight into the Breen boys which their mother lacked.

The men were conferring again—recalling the crusade of 1900. Rousing days. They had rung doorbells and got out the vote, and marched in a torchlight parade. It was a pity that the growing pressure of private business had deflected their activities. They were still all in favor of civic purity. But they were out of touch with the mechanisms.

"What's wrong with us—yelling for Horace Rampole to kiss the bump and make it well? The Senator works through Dan Parmiter. What's wrong with our going to Dan Parmiter?"

"Dan Parmiter operates on a strictly *quid-pro-quo* basis. I don't know Parmiter to say hello to."

"Philip Grover was our precinct captain, back in noughty-nought. He dealt with . . ."

A constraint laid hold of them. They were sick about poor old Philip. They had to leave Philip out of this. He was vulnerable through his wife.

Queenie was on the carpet now. The women took charge of her: "Queenie doesn't know black from white. Very likely she never noticed anything off color about the Rivergrove party."

"Didn't she, though! You notice she carefully maneuvered to leave Lissa and Delia on the side lines while she disported herself upstairs."

Betty Coleman, whose daughter Letty had not been so well protected as Lissa and Delia, said with concentrated fury, "Queenie Grover is never going to chaperone one of my daughters again."

"Till yesterday, I gave her the benefit of the doubt."

It was agreed that for poor old Philip's sake they had borne too long with Queenie Grover. Now her goose was cooked.

By lunchtime the program had taken shape.

First, as regarded the young people—even in the loose atmosphere of 1910, parents had certain defensive armament. Allowances could be stopped, cars could be impounded. The families issued a joint ukase: no more parties under Epps auspices.

"But who's to lay down the law to Victor Rampole? He runs wild in that Ford of his, and nobody calls time on him."

"That's one problem that really does belong to the Senator."

Next, within an hour after Horace Rampole got back to Meridian, the men of Rampole Place would wait on him in a body.

As for the Grovers, Lissa must not be penalized more than necessary, nor good old Philip. There must be no formal boycott. If Queenie chose to come up to the tennis courts, no one need feel bound to cut her dead. A cool "How are you, Queenie?" and very little more would keep the surface of life from eroding; and sooner or later even Queenie must take the hint.

As the fashionable young married set streamed prettily across the greensward toward its several Sunday dinners, someone alerted the rest: "There comes Philip now."

They took cover as gracefully as possible—all except the last three men, who were ashamed to scuttle away from him.

"No chance of a game right now, Philip," Cap Breen called to him. "Matter of fact, we never even got the net up."

Philip's walk was trigger-tense. "I'm not looking for a game. I wanted to talk to some of you fellows about the goings on last night at Rivergrove."

Breen, Whitty and Bellamy exchanged glances. "We've been meeting as a committee of the whole," Bellamy admitted. "I wish you'd dropped around earlier. Something has got to be done."

"Queenie didn't like it at all," Philip said. "But you know how Queenie is—no more fight to her than a blue-eyed rabbit. She says how *could* she take a stand when she was accepting the Eppses' hospitality? I told her—well, never mind all that. The point is, I'm not going to have my daughter dragged through the underworld at the age of sixteen."

"That makes it unanimous. And on the municipal level, we're going to put it up to Senator Rampole as soon as he gets home."

"That may be another month," Philip objected. "What are we waiting for? This Giacomo is small fry. We can get rid of him with a fly swatter."

"That was our first idea. But there's a technique to these things. We don't know the ropes. If we carried any weight with Dan Parmiter, we could put him to work on it. But, frankly, we don't."

"I carry some weight with Dan Parmiter," Philip said. He was a descendant of justices, governors and founding fathers generally. He had frittered away his birthright, but his forebears had been public men when Huck Rampole was a land-greedy gimcrack peddler. "I'd just as soon talk to him."

"You sleep on this, Philip," Cap Breen said uneasily. "We want just what you want, but we don't want to give the game away."

"I'll sleep on it." The fine-drawn muscles tensed at the corners of Philip's lips. "But not for any month."

"Do you want some of us to go with you?"

"I'll chance it singlehanded," Philip said. "After all, it's a routine matter of administration."

When he was out of range the three of them fell to speculating fiercely as to whether Queenie had been fool enough to babble at breakfast, or whether her husband had forced a confession out of her. His zeal embarrassed them. Their crusade, as he would learn all too soon, was partly directed against his wife Queenie.

Chapter 17

CHESTNUT POINT, lordly behind its porticoes, was the only house where the hornets were not buzzing.

Augustus heard what was afoot—certainly he heard; he had his sources. But he viewed the whole rumpus tolerantly. "I'll warrant them kids could tell their folks a couple things about night life in Meridian," he commented to Jennie.

And Katie was not involved in the howdy-do about Rivergrove. She hadn't even gone to the Epps housewarming. She had been practicing for her recital.

Holding the closing recital at Chestnut Point had been Miss Archibald's idea. She had put on her ancient jet-beaded hat and her mother's mink neck fur, and called on the Senator at his office.

"She's gone so far, Senator," Miss Archibald said, "that she has no incentive to go any farther. She plays well enough to satisfy her young friends when they want to sing. No one ever asks her to play serious music. I can't hold her to technical exercises—she monkeys instead of practicing."

"Well, you know, Miss Archibald—" he fingered his cigar—"even Katie's mother never had it in mind that the child should take up music—er—professionally."

"Naturally not. She's not qualified in the first place. And in the second place—" she smiled her ripe, dry maestro's smile—"she's too rich to make the necessary sacrifices for a career."

Horace recognized this candor with a smile of his own. "On the other hand, Miss Archibald, I'd feel badly if she stopped her lessons. Her music is a big part of her life. It gives her a—a standing in her little group."

Miss Archibald said punctiliously, "As I've reported to you before, Senator, Katie hasn't a great gift, but she has a genuine gift. I'm very fond of Katie. I've been sorry for her since her mother died—she's been cut off from normal girlhood. She's shy, she's *farouche*, she has no self-assurance. I believe her music represents her one chance of being something more than a rich man's daughter."

Horace drew on his cigar and contemplated this burly, formidable old woman. He recognized integrity when he saw it. He saw also that she shared his anxiety over Katie.

He drew her proposition out of her. "You've got hold of a fine idea there, Miss Archibald," he said heartily. "I'd like to have the recital at our house. Let's see now—we want this to go off with a bang."

"If you could send me a list of guests you'd like to include—Katie's friends . . ."

"I'll get Mrs. Herbert Bellamy to make you up a list. And I'll ask her to act as a hostess that afternoon. What's the date? June 30th, July 1st? I'll get home for it myself, if I can possibly make it. Excellent idea, Miss Archibald."

"Would you be offended, Senator, if I tried to get press coverage? Musically, I mean, of course, not socially. My pupils have professional ambitions, some of them, so I try to arrange that. I do have contacts with the newspapers."

His face broadened into a leathery grin. "You flatter me if you think I'm sensitive about getting my name in the papers. I'm in politics."

He escorted Miss Archibald all the way to the elevator—a sign that she was on his preferred list.

So Cassandra Bellamy set the recital in motion. She passed the word to the Monday Bridge Club that they were to turn out in force. She had the piano tuned; she ordered Katie a pretty dress. Unpretending women all over Meridian went out to buy new Merry Widow hats, and their husbands applied for an afternoon off from the office.

"I think," Miss Archibald said reflectively to Katie, "I can get you ready to play the Chopin Ballade."

"I'm not very sure of it, Miss Archibald."

"Because you haven't worked at it," her teacher said tartly. "I'm going to work you as you've never been worked in your lazy life, Katie Rampole. I'm going to put you last on the program."

"Oh, not last, Miss Archibald! Suppose I let you down?"

"If you let me down, I'll take a horsewhip to you. I'm risking more than you are, because I have a reputation to lose." She began writing an assignment in Katie's notebook. "Now this passage, bring it up to seventy-two this week, and next week to eighty. When you've got it letter-perfect at eighty we'll put the metronome behind us, and you're to play it every day for a month, as a master plays. I want you to make its beauty yours, so that you can pour it out to your audience."

No such demand had ever been made on Katie. Cold shivers of awe ran down her spine. Her hands crisped on the feeling of power.

At the end of her lesson, however, she came back to the question of the program. "At the very end—to cheer people up—do you know what would be nice? A concerted number, like what you used to write for us. Perhaps with—with your nephew playing a flute obbligato."

She made her teacher very angry. "My blessed young ignoramus, Roy Godkin is a professional musician. He's getting his diploma from the conservatory in Chicago. He's composed a string quartet that's being played on the university series. It would be suicide for him to appear at a pupils' recital!"

"I'm sorry, Miss Archibald, I had no idea. All I thought was how the audience would love it to go home on."

"You rich amateurs! You spoiled brats!"

"Miss Archibald, please excuse me."

"Roy and I will have a good laugh over this at supper tonight."

"Oh, he's not in Chicago?"

"He's been home for two weeks. He's playing in the dinner orchestra at the Belvedere Hotel this summer. *He* doesn't get his musical education handed to him on a platter."

This was Katie's first intimation that there might be an aristocracy with other quarterings than those recognized on Adams Avenue. She gathered that Miss Archibald was giving her one chance to play as well as if she had to play for her bread and butter.

So she didn't get to the Eppses' housewarming, and she didn't get to Rivergrove.

She took her solitary swim before breakfast every day, so that she could float undisturbed on her back in the pool and hear the Chopin Ballade orchestrated by the rush of the current. The rest of the day she spent at the piano.

On the day of the recital she gave no attention to the lining-up of the gilt chairs. Her father came in on the morning train from Washington, and she greeted him as abstractedly as if he had never been away.

Victor cut through her detachment at lunch by asking her unexpectedly, "Have you spoken to Lissa Grover about coming this afternoon?"

"Why should I?" Katie asked him blankly. "She wouldn't care about an old recital."

"The whole Gang is coming," Victor said with modest pride; he had given them their orders.

The prospect of playing before the Gang dynamited the dam of Katie's composure. She didn't much mind playing for grownups, but to play Chopin for the Gang would be putting on airs. From now on they would think they had to ask her to play her Piece. Her status was in jeopardy.

All the same, they were coming. In the kindness of his heart Victor had ordered them to come, and now nothing could stop them.

"If they're all coming, why did you ask me about Lissa particularly?"

Victor drew his broad, glossy brows into a knot. If Katie hadn't noticed the boycott, so much the better. It didn't bother him. He and Jodie still came and went as they chose, while the others lived in durance and went to bed at ten o'clock.

But Lissa Grover was another matter entirely. Lissa was caught in a boycott. And he wasn't going to have her penalized for a situation in which she was the white-feathered victim. Lissa was Katie's best and only real friend. Lissa kept Katie in countenance. Hence, Lissa had to be looked out for.

The Gang was taking out its frustrations on Lissa Grover and on Delia Dysart for tattling. Delia was of a fiber that could stand up to obloquy. She counterattacked. She had no apologies to make. And her thick-skinned aggressiveness was paying off. Delia was being taken back into fellowship.

What Lissa had done in reporting to her father was not tattling; it was the necessary consequence of being Queenie's daughter. If people cold-shouldered Lissa, she would never justify herself; she would square her chin, and walk her lonely way.

Victor knew all this about Lissa Grover because, unwarrantably for his own purposes, he had kissed her at the Doochee Ford. That kiss made him responsible for her.

"Well, you see," he answered Katie, "you're Lissa's best friend. And when you're snagged up in a recital she has nobody much to team up with. I thought she'd be more comfortable if you made a point of asking her."

"If they insist on coming, Lissa is certainly the one I want most."

"Call her up, then."

So Katie rang Lissa up. If Katie had not been so preoccupied, she would have wondered what made Lissa's regrets so stilted. Lissa had things to do with Daddy that afternoon. She was fearfully sorry. She wished Katie the best of luck. And she seemed anxious to get off the telephone.

It was time to dress for the recital. The performers and their mothers were already assembling in the sitting room, perking up hair ribbons and sniffing smelling salts. Miss Archibald, who was in a state of nerves, had sent word that she hoped Katie would be on hand to deal with the gentlemen of the press when they arrived, as she herself had a million other things to attend to.

Katie dragged herself upstairs with a most awful feeling in her vitals. Her luncheon didn't want to stay down. She had the gripes, she had the swoons. She fell across her bed and feebly rang for Nora.

"Nora," she said, "I am coming down with some fearful disease. I can't possibly get up. You'd better call the doctor, and let poor Miss Archibald know that I'm dropping out of the program."

"Sure, lovey, it's nothing but stage fright. I went through it the day of me confirmation. Like a busted clock I was. But the little girl next me, she gave me a quick kick in the shins. She bloodied me nice white stockings, but that's the last there was to me terrible disease. Stand up now and let me get you into your pretty new dress. The chairs are filling up downstairs. Everybody's asking for you, and Miss Archibald's in seven fits."

Nora got Katie into her clothes, and clumped her hair at the nape of her neck. "Ye look like a lady grown," she said encouragingly, as she gave her a smart shove between the shoulders to start her moving.

Mrs. Bellamy was welcoming the audience as it came in. The vogue of the cart-wheel hat, wider than the wearer's shoulders, made seating a problem. "There you are at last, Katie," she cried cheerfully. "Miss Archibald has been scouring the house for you." Then a shriek. "Darling, wait one second. Your petticoat shows!"

"I'll fix it," Katie promised, and at once forgot her promise. She went through the cross corridor to the emergency Artists' Room, where hysteria was in full swing. In Miss Archibald it took the form of a massive sarcasm.

"Well, Katie, how nice of you to condescend to appear! Of course, you're an amateur. You don't realize that punctuality is the courtesy of monarchs and of artists."

"I'm dreadfully sorry, Miss Archibald. Did you want me to talk to some reporters?"

"I particularly request you not to talk to any reporters. The audience has been seated for fifteen minutes, and the room is as hot as Tophet. Now that you're here, we can open our program."

The girls lined up in the corridor in order of height. All of them were dressed to the nines. Katie towered at the end of the queue.

The mothers created a confusion in their going. Their husbands were holding chairs for them, so they had to climb past legs, laps and Merry Widow hats. Miss Archibald, watching from the entrance, held her hand in air like a conductor waiting to give the down beat.

There was a second delay: Augustus was opening the front door for a pair of late-comers. Katie could see Mrs. Bellamy standing in the front-parlor entrance, scanning the room for places for Mrs. Grover and Mrs. Epps. She looked disturbed. She beckoned to William and had him carry in two of the heavy, high-backed hall chairs to a spot she pointed out.

"*Vorwärts!*" Miss Archibald exclaimed. She had regained mastery of herself during the pause. "Walk in quietly to the front row of chairs. Do not wave to your parents, and for the good God's sake, do not burst out crying when you step to the piano! Make a correct, gracious little bow."

Finally the line got under way. Facing the audience from the conservatory arch, behind the heel of the piano, sat Mrs. Grover and Mrs. Epps on their thrones, completely blocking the view of the spectators seated in the conservatory. They looked like two sea cows regnant, and they seemed to be attracting some indignation.

"Go ahead, Nellie," Miss Archibald prompted. Nellie, the smallest and hence the most fetching of the pupils, made a bow of sorts, played Schumann's "Happy Farmer" and retired to a fair modicum of applause.

The long windows on the portico were open, but no air penetrated; the room was stewing with heat. Women fanned themselves with their programs, and men with their straw hats.

Katie thought: this is the most ghastly ordeal I ever let myself in for. Nobody is listening to the music, and the music isn't worth listening to. I am elected the principal buffoon of this spectacle. I cap the climax, I finish the program. I know what I'll do. When my turn comes I will rise, I will make a correct gracious bow, I will play Schumann's "Happy Farmer" and walk out of the room—and not one soul will know the difference.

The recital was well along. Lorna, the girl who went to the Parmiter School, was in the middle of MacDowell's "To a Waterlily," with an impressive arm attack, when a crash of china from the dining room brought her to a standstill. She jumped out of her skin, lost her place and froze in position. "Go back to the beginning and start over," Miss Archibald coached her in a corrosive whisper.

When my turn comes, Katie amended, I will rise, make a correct gracious bow and walk out of the room without playing anything. It will be a kindness to all concerned.

I mustn't be ridiculous, she adjured herself. I mustn't let poor Miss Archibald down. I must stop being spiteful, I must think about what I'm going to play.

At this point she discovered that she had no faintest lingering recollection of Chopin's Ballade III, which she had been practicing eight hours a day. Miss Archibald had insisted that she play without notes, like a professional; so the blame lay on Miss Archibald's head. Katie found herself in the calm spot in the eye of the hurricane. She was not in the least disturbed; all hope was gone.

She looked dispassionately at Lorna's dress. She looked at Mrs. Epps and Mrs. Grover, with their white-gloved opulence of body. Her eye wandered out to the portico.

Two unlikely-looking men were leaning against a pillar. One had a pale, oblong face with large spectacles. The other was a beery old boy with his collar open. He might be a saloonkeeper, come to solicit a favor from the Senator. William ought to get these two loafers off the premises.

Katie was sitting next to Miss Archibald. She poked her teacher's large thigh, pointed inconspicuously and raised an interrogatory eyebrow.

Miss Archibald took her Svengali gaze from Lorna's fingers long enough for one envenomed hiss, "The press!"

The press! Katie didn't wonder at Miss Archibald's irascibility. The two papers had given the back of their hand to Miss Archibald and her recital.

Lorna finished, and Bessie went to the piano. Time was racing.

Suddenly Bessie reached the conclusion of Liszt's *Liebestraum,* and Katie's turn was upon her. The room was astir, conscious that Katie Rampole came next. At this moment Katie recalled that she had forgotten to adjust her drooping petticoat. Her members were locked. She couldn't even walk out of the room, because she couldn't move hand or foot.

Miss Archibald gave her a vicious prod, and she rose like a walking dead thing. A wave of applause greeted her. She clamped a meaningless skeleton grin on her jaw, and bent her head. Miss Archibald willed her into the pianist's chair.

She extended her long hands across the keys. She still had no information, direct or indirect, about the Ballade, except that it was in A-flat. Her fingers, which had a certain residue of aptitude in them, ran several arpeggios for her while her mind scrabbled for a clue.

But the arpeggios couldn't go on indefinitely, and no light broke. The only melody that came to her was Schumann's "Happy Farmer." Horror spread across her face. She was condemned to sit at that piano through all eternity, running off arpeggios till the audience broke into maniac laughter.

Through the open window came a light, liquid, infinitely melodious whistle. It was so fine-drawn that if any of the audience heard it through the arpeggios, they took it for a bird. It lined out the tilting, cloying, unmistakable opening phrase of the Ballade III.

With an inward hallelujah Katie brought her arpeggio to a conclusion, paused for an impressive moment and struck into the Ballade.

She had never played better. The notes lilted, they purled, they crashed masterfully under her hands. She closed to an honest smash of applause.

As she made her correct, gracious bows, two faces shone out at her from among the wildly pitpatting hands—Miss Archibald's, charcoal-red with triumph and emotion, and her father's, a harvest moon of glory.

She had a telescopic glimpse of a future. She was a concert artist. She bowed to cheering thousands who crowded down the aisles and refused to leave the hall till Miss Rampole had played one more encore.

Katie was holding court beside the piano. Hats converged from all sides, with ladies under them. The Gang trooped in, awed and inarticulate, but obviously not holding her triumph against her. Katie repeated dozens of times, "Thank you, I'm glad if you enjoyed it. You know my teacher, Miss Archibald? Thank you, I'm so glad . . ."

Fame was sweet but hampering. What Katie wanted most was to get out to the portico and thank that clairvoyant young man with the spectacles.

A voice cut through to her ear. It was Mrs. Breen's voice, with a rasp to it, and it came from under a hat as wide as a millstone. "Brazen, that's the only word for it!"

After one startled glance Katie concluded that the condemnation was directed at Mrs. Grover and Mrs. Epps, who were creating a traffic hazard in the conservatory arch. Numbers of the guests were trying to get past them and their chairs. But instead of saying straightforwardly, "Excuse me, may I get by?" they were squirming past them one by one, without speaking.

"Now, Lucy, we've got to be *nice* about things. They're headed this way. Let's duck out to the dining room."

Katie wondered idly what kind of a mare's nest the ladies of Rampole Place were stirring up now. "Hello, Mrs. Grover," she said brightly, "it was lovely of you to come. I hope Lissa changed her mind about being here."

"Lissa is enjoying a case of the gloomies," Queenie answered. "Now you're through with your recital, I hope you can coax her out of them. . . . Oh, Betty! Sorry I bumped you. Didn't Katie play beautifully?"

Mrs. Coleman didn't seem to hear Mrs. Grover's apology. "I have to catch somebody in the dining room," she proclaimed to whom it might concern, and scuttled out of range.

With marked vivacity and heightened color Queenie took Mrs. Epps's arm. "It's too hot for tea, Onie. Come down to our house and we'll make ourselves a long cold drink."

"Ance will be home by this time," Onie demurred.

"We'll telephone him to join us."

These middle-aged absurdities left no mark on Katie's mind. The crowd was thinning out now. She said, "Before we have our tea, Miss Archibald, could we say how-do-you-do to those critics from the papers?"

"I want no part of those music critics," Miss Archibald said sharply.

Katie had not been fifteen years a politician's daughter for nothing. "Why, Miss Archibald!" she cried. "Don't you want a good write-up?"

"I have no grievance against that poor old barfly from the *Sun-Record*. His paper sent him out, and it's not his fault that he's from the city-hall beat. But the other one . . ."

"He's from the *Morning Telegram*? He looks pretty young."

"The other one," Miss Archibald said with concentrated bitterness, "happens to be my own nephew."

"Your nephew! Not a critic at all?"

"A critic for one day. I did not deserve this treatment from the *Morning Telegram*."

"But you say yourself that your nephew is a thorough musician."

"He is the best musician in Meridian. But that does not alter the fact that he should have refused the assignment. Anything he writes will be taken for nepotism. I am thoroughly put out with Roy Godkin."

"All the same I'd like to meet him. He did something very kind."

"I was ashamed of you both. I'd rather you'd played without coaching, even if you broke down. The next time you play for an audience, you needn't think you'll have Roy Godkin on hand to whistle for you."

"All the same," Katie persisted, "I want to thank him."

"He's left. He goes on at the Belvedere at six o'clock."

"I wonder what he'll write."

"If he's honest," Miss Archibald said, suddenly discarding her bad temper, "he'll say that you played Chopin as well as a fifteen-year-old can play it. You did extremely well, Katie."

Chapter 18

THE Senator was going to have to take the train back to Washington the night after the recital. He had needed a restorative lungful of his native air. In Meridian a Rampole could still say, "Let there be light," and there was light.

Things were far otherwise in Washington; there seemed to be two wrong sides to every question. Under Taft the glittering Roosevelt bandwagon had deteriorated to the condition of a bumbling old omnibus, with the passengers calling the stops and complaining about the service.

Horace blamed the President, not for evil intentions—there wasn't a saving ounce of rascality in that cumbrous benevolent carcass—but for ineptitude.

Roosevelt had been a bull in a china shop, perhaps; but Taft was an ox, who could knock down as much bric-a-brac by turning around twice as Roosevelt could at full charge. He supported the losing side of every controversy. Ballinger, as Taft's Secretary of the Interior, had recently granted to private interests the development of some public lands in Alaska; Gifford Pinchot, the champion of conservation, had dashed into the fray giving the battle cry of God and Saint Theodore. Taft had supported his bureaucracy, and the facts were now obscured in the dust of partisan battle. The whole summer, with mid-term elections coming up in the fall, the headlines would be whooping it up for Pinchot versus Ballinger.

Horace felt, disturbingly, that he might have made the same mistakes Taft had made. Like Taft he was a regular, a party man, but with an itch for the millennium. He wasn't proud of his own committee work on the revision of the tariff. The western Progressives, and even the scoundrelly Democrats, could criticize it plausibly.

Oh, for the piping times of Theodore!—for the adulation of the mob!—for a whacking majority at the polls in November.

But the great Theodore had his own punctilio. Having set up a man of straw as his successor, he was giving portrayal of Cincinnatus returning to the plow. Roosevelt being the showman he was, this portrayal involved a semiregal transit among the crowned heads of Europe. But he was playing Cincinnatus all the same, and he would not open his mouth on public affairs.

The recital was a happy event for Horace. Katie's triumph at the piano honestly astonished him. He had thought of piano playing as something that a woman did prettily after dinner. Katie's playing converted music into a coin that Horace understood—the coin of prestige.

He promised himself a family evening with Vic and Katie.

Before dinner, though, he had a disquieting telephone call from Dan Parmiter.

"A deputation of your neighbors is headed your way," Dan said. "Be cagey till I get a chance to bring you up to date. They're fooling with dynamite."

"Dan, you old granny! If it's that easement, I can take care of it with one hand tied behind my back."

"Drop around in the morning, if you get a chance," Dan said with a wariness that told Horace he had company with him. "By that time I may have the picture filled in."

Horace gave two or three pulls to his nose, and then dismissed the riddle. Dan was losing his grip.

He was disappointed that Victor left the dinner table ahead of the finger bowls, saying he had a date. One more chance for breaking through to Victor had escaped him. Soon Vic's boyhood would be gone beyond recapture.

Horace asked himself whether the alienation was any fault of his. He knew he must have been heavy-handed with his two wives, since it must be more than coincidence that they had both eluded him by dying. He wasn't clever in the give-and-take of domestic life.

What more could he have done? He had made a real sacrifice for his children's sake, by slicing up his barony into a subdivision. He had made overtures to Vic, and Vic had consistently rejected them. Short of abandoning public life and turning himself into a nursery governess, what had Horace left undone?

He brought his brief case into the sitting room after dinner, but he was not disposed to buckle down to it. He wanted to talk and visit.

He looked over at Katie, who was sitting with her long legs hung over the arm of a chair, deep in blissful reverie.

"Where's Vic gone off to?" he asked as an opener.

With an effort Katie came up out of her daydream. She was spinning herself a yarn about going down to the Belvedere Hotel for dinner—about stepping over to the orchestra platform and saying to the young man with the oblong, spectacled face, "I'm Katie Rampole, and I want to thank you a million times for giving me that whistle through the window. You saved my life."

Like any daydream, this one had to overleap the probabilities. No young girl from Rampole Place ever dined at a hotel. But Katie gave herself license to dine at the Belvedere.

The daydream was going great guns. The young man, violin in hand, was just saying, in a respectful but intense voice, "Miss Rampole, your Chopin stirred me to the depths. You couldn't—" he was getting up his courage, because after all she was Katie Rampole and he was nothing but an orchestra player—"we couldn't have lunch together one of these days? We have so much to say to each other." Their eyes met. . . . This was how things advanced in magazine stories.

Now Father was asking her where Victor had gone.

"He's probably out with Jodie," she said absently.

"Doesn't he take notice of any of the nice girls around here?"

"He thinks Jodie is the nicest. They're always paired off."

"Does everybody around here take Jodie Epps at her face value?"

Katie laced her fingers behind her head. She was more tolerant of young love than she had been. "The Gang knows Jodie is Vic's girl. Aside from that, she'd stop belonging to the Gang—she's not especially popular. But she's perfectly nice."

"Katie, why does Vic duck out on me the way he does? Here I'm at home for just one evening. . ."

While she was searching for a consolatory reply Augustus came to the doorway.

"Some men from down the street are here looking for you, Senator. I put 'em in the smoking room."

"So soon?" said Horace, laying aside his papers. They must be really roused about something.

Four—five—six, he counted mentally as he greeted them. Every last householder in Rampole Place except Epps and Grover.

They even had a spokesman—Bill Coleman. Horace still thought of these middle-aged citizens as boys. They had never played the part of men in the city. They had factories, yes, and family businesses; but they cut no ice.

Horace planted his guests in comfortable deep seats, but he himself took the swivel chair in front of his desk and swung it around toward the circle. In conference, he rode this chair as a general rides a charger, whirling with terrifying speed from one flank to the other.

The smoking room was like a theater so ripe in tradition that it could afford some aging in its material fabric. The leather chairs were deep and durable, in spite of a lacing of surface crackles. The big Oriental rug was still a better rug than anybody could buy now. On a marble-topped table in the bay window stood a terra-cotta Rogers group of two old boys playing checkers, a relic of the first Adams Avenue house. A bronze bust of Abraham Lincoln in a toga sat on top of the clock; and above the mantel Big Joe's portrait presided over the scene, his ham hand thrust statesmanlike into the bosom of his Prince Albert.

Horace sat foursquare and granite firm, and gave Bill Coleman an opening.

"I'm doing the talking, Senator, because this hits me hardest. My daughter Letty was in it, up to the neck."

Isn't there anything, Horace asked himself sardonically, isn't there one single thing these men can handle for themselves? I'm to make their children behave—that's what we've come to now.

But as Coleman spun his sorry tale, he grew hot within. His mind raced far ahead of the story; it drew inferences that inflamed him further.

Not that he feared the young of Rampole Place would be ruined for life by laying a few chips on a roulette table. If at their age they had that much innocence to lose, he thought poorly of their enterprise.

What made his blood boil was the name, constantly recurring, of Anson Epps. Whenever their paths crossed, his mistrust deepened.

The delegation didn't dig into the question that engaged Horace—of why Epps was so breezy about violating the canons of Rampole Place on the very day when he made his bid for social acceptance. They accounted for him as a self-made man, a rounder, who didn't know any better.

Horace knew Epps as a man of deep calculation. It came to him in a blood-red flash that if Epps paraded his underworld connections, it was because he was not afraid to. It was a defiance—a defiance to the ruling caste of Meridian.

This was a long leap of inference, sparked by personal hatred, and Horace knew better than to pass it on to the ingenuous delegation which sat before him. He had no evidence that Epps's ties with the underworld were anything more than casual. Horace must keep his personal vendetta with Epps separated from what was, after all, a routine problem of political administration—the cleaning out of one gambling joint. If he and Dan Parmiter couldn't handle that, they were not worth their salt.

What was the warning Dan had given him over the telephone—that the delegation was playing with dynamite—that Horace was to move cautiously?

"Do I understand," he asked, "that you've taken some steps already?"

"We haven't, sir—Philip Grover has. Naturally he's red-hot to get the Rivergrove Casino cleaned up. We're sorry for old Philip, but we—well, we rather felt he might embarrass our committee. On account of Queenie. He's working independently of us."

"Did Philip get anywhere with Dan?" Horace asked dryly.

"Dan told him to wait till you got back."

"Philip doesn't carry much weight, in Parmiter's terms."

Stewart Whitty was of the old Meridian blood. He said stiffly, "Philip carries considerable weight of ancestry."

"Ancestors don't get out the vote, my boy."

It was a bald verdict of incompetence, which the committee was at liberty to extend to itself. The Senator had pity on them. "Gentlemen," he said magisterially, "I'm glad you came to me about this Rivergrove incident. There's an effrontery about it that's disturbing. It's a reversion to the bad old days we worked so hard to put behind us."

"That's it exactly, sir."

"You're thinking in terms of crusades and mayoralty elections. That won't be necessary. The machinery we set up ten years ago is still functioning. We may not even need to raid the casino. All this Giacomo needs is a hint that Rivergrove is not healthy for him."

His trained dogs, so eager, so blameless, climbed down from their perches with evident relief. The Senator had taken charge. Horace rang, and Augustus circulated the second-best whisky.

Horace escorted the delegation genially to the front door and then stood alone on the portico. In his fatigue he tended to feel the tentacles of evil groping toward him through the darkness. Meridian was no improvement on Washington. This was a luckless year.

He fought against his mood. He had no one to blame except himself for letting Anson Epps make use of him as a wedge into the Meridian Club, into Rampole Place. If Horace had stood his ground against the first intrusion, his son would not now be in pawn to the enemy.

He lectured himself: even assuming—which was unproved—that Anson Epps was a merchant of corruption, on what grounds could Horace stand superior to him? Plenty of pitch had stuck to Big Joe's fingers. In spite of Horace's own reforming trend, the Rampole money stank of pitch.

But we weren't bloodsuckers, Horace thought fiercely. Father took a lot out of Meridian, but he poured a lot back into it. He increased the blood flow of the community. It will be a long time before Anson Epps has a fountain erected in his honor on the river front.

Two ambiguous deities reigned over the smoking-room mantel, and Horace paid homage to both. Abraham Lincoln and Big Joe Rampole. The tension between these two images was the tension that ruled Horace's maturity.

His job for tomorrow was to clean up the Rivergrove Casino. His long-term job was to neutralize Anson Epps.

To combat his sense of futility he did setting-up exercises before he got into bed. They re-established him in his own eyes. Any man who could touch his toes a hundred times was a man for malefactors to beware of.

By Sunday morning Horace was ashamed of his overnight panic. Out of excessive, anxious love for his son he had created a bogey to frighten himself with, and named it Anson Epps. Epps, by daylight, was nothing more than a smart operator on the make, with a taste for night life. Meridian had digested, or ejected, a thousand of him.

Dan wasn't downstairs when Horace walked into the house; he wasn't in the garden. Mrs. Magruder was not darning or shelling peas in the back parlor, and the parlor was dusty.

Then he heard sounds from overhead, suggestive of an old gentleman in a temper. Bureau drawers were being yanked out and slammed back. The whole house resounded with a foghorn bray: "A-meeeel-ia!"

Amelia! What under the canopy had happened to Mrs. Magruder? "Stop bellowing," Horace said from the foot of the stairs, "and come on down."

"Oh, it's you," said Dan ungraciously, popping his head out of the bedroom door. "If you want to see me you'll have to come on up. That leprous misbegotten hag hasn't left me a shirt or a sock fit to go out in."

"I never knew you to go into a tantrum," Horace said, mounting the stairs to Dan's room.

The huge bed, the bureau and the wardrobe had shallow overhanging cornices, so tormented with carving that they looked like the low curly foreheads of three rams. The fastidious Danny was standing in his underdrawers, one foot bare and the other clad in a sock with a big hole in the toe. The unmade bed was littered with garments that Dan had cast aside. "Button off," he said bitterly. "Cuffs frayed. . . . Three buttons off. . . . Rip in the shoulder. . . . Hole in the toe. . . . Hole in the heel. . . . A-meeel-ia! She wouldn't miss Mass for the world, the slut, not if I had to walk down River Street in my bare feet!"

"Where's Mrs. Magruder?"

"Mrs. Magruder has gone to Ireland." Dan was enjoying the mystification on Horace's face; his bad temper began to evaporate.

"For keeps? After all these years?"

"God, I hope not!" Dan began putting on the sock with the smallest hole and the shirt with the most buttons. "Mrs. Magruder's old mother was dying and asking for her. So I shipped her off, and she got in this critter to look after me. . . . There! My vest will cover the gap. . . . You know, Horry, I never realized what I owed to Mrs. Magruder .She's been living in mortal sin all these years, for my convenience, and if she'd died, she'd have gone straight to hell. But never a peep out of her, till it all came out when she was crying about her mother."

In their long years together, Dan had never said as much about Mrs. Magruder; but under Amelia's ministrations he missed his good companion too sorely to keep silence. Horace took permission to discuss her openly. "Then you have broken up?"

"Not a bit of it. She's a fine woman, Horace. She means all the world to me. I wish we'd had children."

"But if she's making her peace with God, where does that leave you? Are you taking vows of celibacy?"

Dan gave a shy and very human smile. "I wouldn't say this to anybody but you, Horace, but time passes and health goes. I'm not much of a man any more. She and I could sleep side by side in that bed as innocent as two lambs in a bassinet." He shook himself down inside his well-tailored coat, buttoned his vest and strung his watch chain across his paunch. "Now, sir, I'm ready to talk business."

They proceeded companionably down the stairs, and made their way to the kitchen.

"Bitter as lye by now, I'll warrant," Dan said, shaking the coffeepot that was set back on the range. "But you'll take a cup with me? Fine lumpy oatmeal—brick-bat biscuits—slice of ham like the sole of my shoe." Tripping birdlike between stove and icebox, he assembled his morning meal and led the way into the garden.

"Now then, Horry," he said, leaning back after his first swig of coffee, "I see you've got your crusading suit on. My advice to you is to hang it back in the closet."

"How did the story reach you? It's stirred up a furor in Rampole Place."

"Oh, one of those Rollo boys of yours—his folks used to live in this house. His lady wife got led astray by the villainous Epps, he tells me. That's what's at the bottom of his outburst of civic zeal."

"You and I can't disclaim responsibility for a gambling joint on MST property. I'm sorry we ever let it in there. It makes me out a fool, or a knave, or a hypocrite."

"One of which you were," Dan said with some asperity. "You gave me a free hand with the casino concession, and it was you that made the pay-off. We had our reasons, and we got results. The MST is back on its pins. And if anybody is a fool, a knave or a hypocrite, it's not me."

"All's well and good, Dan, but I particularly said it must be a temporary arrangement. Now three years later we find it running wide-open, catering to juveniles. It must be operating under protection."

"You catch on quick. Bright as a button, you are."

"Big protection. Top protection." Horace didn't like to say it, but he had to. "You know the political value of clean hands as well as I do, Dan Parmiter. In the long run, they pay off better than kickbacks do."

He had nettled the little boss. "It's years since I took a dirty dollar from anybody. And this pained surprise of yours, Horace—if you don't mind my saying so, it smells of fish."

Horace dismounted willy-nilly from his high horse and asked practically, "Well, if this Giacomo hasn't got to you, who has he got to? Who's backing him?"

"That's what I wish I knew," Dan said, letting his coffee cool. "It's just one more straw in the wind. There's goings on in this town I don't like. That's why I told you it was dynamite for society reformers to meddle with. I had some of the Boys in here last night when you telephoned, checking up on campaign contributions, and they're having trouble getting the money in."

"Money's always hard to get in."

"This is no ordinary sales resistance, Horace. I got a report from Mike Dolek. Perhaps you remember him—saloonkeeper down in the Twelfth Ward—regular as they come. Mike pretty near had tears in his eyes when he cut his subscription in half. He claims he's being bled to death keeping on the right side of the police. Says they had him up in court a month ago—for some little two-for-a-penny violation, mind you."

"Did he come to you about it?"

"He came, and I passed the word to go easy on him. But there's a kink in the line somewhere. The judge gave him a tough time. He had to get his own lawyer, a lawyer that was recommended to him, and it cost him plenty to get squared."

Horace's big mouth puckered with distaste. It was an old and sordid story, and one he had outgrown. But he couldn't walk away from it. It would be a fine thing if an organization could keep its hand completely clean, but a machine could purify itself out of existence. To get out the vote and control the patronage, it had to work with the human material at hand. It had to be freehanded with influence, with bail with coal orders and saloon licenses. It had to look after its own.

The give-and-take of disciplines and rewards was in Dan Parmiter's province. And Dan wasn't much of a man any more—he'd said so himself. Horace must climb down off his statesman's pedestal and take a hand in the local chores.

"Who have you got down in the Twelfth Ward now? Who's the fellow to give Giacomo his walking papers?"

"By rights it's McQueen, the police captain at the South End Station."

"If you won't speak to him, I will."

Dan gave the Senator a leery look. "McQueen is ducking me," he admitted. "Three times I've called him in, and three times he's had the fishiest kind of a previous engagement. I'd like to have seen him pull that stuff on Big Joe—he'd have been out on the sidewalk on the seat of his breeches! So I got myself out to a bean feast at Twelfth Ward headquarters, and I sounded him out on the gambling situation in the South End. He said, (a) what did I mean, gambling?—and (b) when he does try to clean up his district all he does is make himself unpopular. The citizens want to gamble, he says, and they're down on the blue laws."

"Why, Dan, that's the story the police captains were giving us fifteen years ago, before the big house cleaning. Have we got it all to do over again? Have things got out of hand?"

Dan had pushed back his chair from his untouched meal. He gave a small belch, surprising in a gentlemanly little man like him. "Maybe it hadn't struck you, Horry," he said with a sort of compunction, "that the two of us are getting no younger. One of these days we'll have to step down."

"And let the town run wide-open?"

"We're not so lily-white ourselves, Horace. You've heard the old saying, 'If you can't fight 'em, join 'em'?"

"Join whom, for God's sake?"

"It ain't city-wide. My troubles are all down in the South End. The City Hall is solid, so far as I know. All I had in mind was, we might absorb 'em."

"Speak for yourself, Dan. This is one fight I won't back away from."

"Don't forget the *Sun-Record*. Our side don't smell entirely of lily of the valley, remember. Can you afford to bring Claggan down on you?"

"I've done it before, and I've lived through it. Why, Dan, this is a natural. The *Morning Telegram* would come in, and the churches, and the Voters' League. Remember our old team? Jim Jacques——"

"We made Jim Jacques a name in the district attorney's office, and he's built him a private law practice on the strength of it. He's through sticking his neck out."

"Well, Cahill then. Cahill stood up like a bull pup to those plug-uglies in the Thirteenth Ward."

"Cahill's worked up to Deputy Superintendent, and he's bought him a house that he never paid for out of a policeman's salary."

"Streck—he was a hound-dog on the trail of a story . . ."

Danny grew more acid as Horace called the roll of the ex-combatants. "You can't pick last year's apples this fall, Horry. Where have you been? The *Sun-Record* took Streck over when the *Evening Courier* folded.

If you want a crusade, you'll have to recruit a brand-new lot of crusaders."

Horace resisted Dan's defeatism. "Well, you and I haven't sold out yet."

"I tell you fair and square, Horace, I won't lift a finger to Giacomo till after election. And if you have the good of the organization at heart, you won't either. It's too risky."

"Who has you over a barrel, Dan? If you can't take 'em on, I can."

"Can you?" Dan asked, eying him. "Can you afford to get the *Sun-Record* on your tail? It's you I'm thinking of, more than me."

"What can the *Sun-Record* do to me?"

"I got it pretty straight," Dan said, taking out his silver pocketknife and tossing it, "that you were on shaky ground in the matter of the Outer Park Belt. Somebody's caught on to that old right of way across your place."

"How does that come into a cleanup of the South End?"

"Epps owns the paper now, you know. Now that your neighbors have set out to discipline him, he's likely to make a personal feud out of this Rivergrove business."

"Epps!" Horace said with concentrated venom. "Is that where the trail leads?" The bogey loomed again, showing its fangs in a vulpine long-toothed smile.

"Now, now! You're warped on the subject of Epps. Epps is a businessman, and the only thing you have against him is that he's working his way to the top and crowding you. But you start closing up the joint at Rivergrove, and Epps is bound to show you you can't do that to him—and he'll do it through his paper."

"I'll chance that. Hang it, Danny, Epps doesn't want Rampole Place turned into a public runway any more than I do. He lives there. That ties his hands."

"Nobody's rolled out the red carpet for him. He can sell out any day he likes, to anybody he chooses, and move outside the city. He'll figure you have more to loose than he has."

"When was he giving you all this tripe?"

"Other day in the County Building. He don't come right out with it, you realize—he hints around. Cross your heart, Horry, has he got anything on you about that old right of way—or was he bluffing?"

Some organ inside of Horace turned a sickening flip-flop, like a cold hot-water bottle. But he asserted stoutly, "He was bluffing, Dan Parmiter, and you bit. McConnell says I could fight it through the courts and win hands down."

"Yes, and let the *Sun-Record* crucify you and all your ancestors, just before election. I'd hate to see what Streck would make of that story about the title. He could twist it into fishhooks."

Horace said in despair, "You've gone yellow, Dan. You've sat in your hammock and let a gang of boodlers get too big for you to handle. I don't ask you to stand up and fight. Give me names, give me facts, and I'll take over."

"Get out and do some of your own legwork!" Danny snapped. "I'm six years older than you are, and my insides have gone back on me. I'm too old to sit around at Polish weddings and Irish field days, and drink in bars with the boys. Milk, that's my tipple now—ever hear of the stuff? There is a ring, that's as much as I can tell you, and the South End is the place to begin looking."

"Thanks a thousand times. So I'm to go down to the South End and then ask some passer-by to direct me to the man they pay protection to?"

Dan said with well-founded scorn, "You great big reformer, you—coming to me with pad and pencil for the names of the rascals you want to throw out! You're puffed up with glory like a bullfrog, Horry, but there's nothing inside you but wind." He stopped, appalled, and reviewed the bad names they had been slinging back and forth. He said in a contrite voice, "Horry, let's stop yammering at each other like two old loonies on the porch of the County Home. We've had our fun, that's the long and the short of it."

"I am six years younger than you," Horace said, rising, "and this is one fight I'm going to take on. As soon as Congress adjourns, I'll roll up my sleeves and wade in."

"That's a spunky lad!" Dan said—but whether sincerely or ironically it was hard to tell.

Chapter 19

THIS summer Jodie Epps filled the entire foreground of Victor's world. He had been proconsul of Chestnut Point for so long that he automatically took notice of the Rivergrove rumpus. But it had no importance. Even his own graduation from the Cambridge School and his promotion to the status of a subfreshman at Meridian University had no particular meaning for him.

He took a cavalier view of the rumpus; it would blow itself out. He could have told Mr. Epps and Mrs. Grover, on that momentous Saturday evening, that they were making trouble for themselves. Victor and his gang had explored worse dives than the Rivergrove Casino—not in viciousness, but out of curiosity; but they had covered their tracks. Mr. Epps and Mrs. Grover were old enough to know better, and he had no sympathy to waste on them.

The rumpus worked to his personal advantage, because the other boys were subject to a disciplinary curfew and he had Jodie more to himself. She couldn't resist playing him off against other boys; she enjoyed making him jealous. At Rivergrove she had driven wanton spikes through his heart.

During these blissful weeks of the curfew he had a monopoly of her. A girl, naturally, liked to be taken out and to have money spent on her; so he took her to the zoo; he took her out on the grubby old excursion boat that waddled up and down the Cinnamon River; he took her to Toomey's for sodas. He liked best their idle afternoons on the Swimming Rocks—endlessly fencing with her, endlessly probing her guard, with the constant delicious terror that her rapier might pink him and draw blood.

Sometimes, for one honeyed moment, he caught her in a mood to be kissed. But even this rapture raised a question—whether she allowed other boys the same privilege. Her kisses didn't commit her. You could no more pin Jodie down than you could pin down a hummingbird. She darted away at an angle, with aerial equilibrium, in a quiver of rainbow brilliance.

One event that penetrated his narcosis was Katie's recital. Deep in Victor, below the drag of the emotional tides, lay the granite of Rampole loyalty to Rampole; and he gloried in Katie's triumph.

He had another feudal loyalty—to Lissa Grover. She was the only victim he felt sorry for. He took on the job of bringing that kid back out of the wasteland. He got the girls back into the routine of their tennis; he coached them. One day Augustus sent him down to old Mrs. Cummager's with a crate of garden raspberries; so he took Katie and Lissa along and treated them to a soda on the way back. Their reverence for him poulticed the bruises Jodie inflicted on him.

Not that they were little girls any longer. It wasn't only that their figures were developing—they were becoming unpredictable.

Lissa, for instance, had toes to be trod on; one condescending note from Victor and she was off like a bird. She had to be getting home, she'd say—she and Queenie had shopping to do. Love me, love my Queenie—that was her ultimatum.

Katie was a prey to April moods. She laughed when no laugh was called for, then cut herself short as if she had betrayed herself by laughing. Her daydream was often impenetrable, and she looked through Lissa and Victor with visionary eyes.

One morning, after tennis, he and Katie were lying in the shade at the edge of the courts. She nibbled at a sprig of sorrel and eyed him portentously.

He deflected his mind from Jodie and gave her an opening—she had something on her mind.

Katie blinked, and dived off the high board. "I have a very childish craving," she said apologetically. "I'd like to see Trovo the Great Magician at the Lyceum this week."

"That's perfectly simple. You buy a ticket, and you go in and sit down."

"But who could I go with? The Gang must have done something bad—they're not being allowed to use their families' cars. I can't just have William drive me down—I'd feel silly."

Katie wanted more than a trip to the theater; she wanted a treat. She was entitled to it. Victor rapidly considered asking Jodie to go with him and taking Katie along. But that was not Jodie's notion of a date.

Victor had a long-standing date with Jodie for Saturday. After one pang, he dedicated the previous evening to Katie. "I could take you on Friday," he offered. "And so long as we're going, let's make a party of it. Let's take Lissa along. She never gets around anywhere."

It was a handsome offer, but it intensified Katie's subsurface twitters. "I'd adore it," she said provisionally. "But that's not all, Victor. I'd like . . ."

"Come on, out with it. I won't bite you."

"I'd like to have dinner downtown first. I'd pay for it myself," she assured him hastily.

"You needn't pay anything. I'll sign a check at the Meridian Club, and it will go on Father's bill."

"Oh, but I've been there!" she almost wailed. "And it's no more exciting than eating at Granny Cummager's. I wanted to go somewhere *gay!*"

"Well, as I live and breathe!" Victor exclaimed. He had imagination himself, but he had never vaulted so high as to consider taking Jodie to a public restaurant. Young girls didn't dine in restaurants.

Of course, in social terms, a boy could take his sister out to dinner as often as he liked—only he never liked. It was a crazy thing to do, when they had a good hot dinner cooked for them at home.

He looked at Katie with new respect for her originality. "What is your idea of something gay?" he inquired with real interest.

"Some place with an orchestra," she brought out with a monstrous air of deviousness. "Like the New Willard in Washington."

"The nearest we come in Meridian to the New Willard is the good old Belvedere, and that's not very near."

"Well, if we can't do any better," she conceded in a world-weary tone that did not deceive her brother, "let's make the best of it and go to the Belvedere."

So that was what she wanted! Very likely one of the housemaids had told her the Belvedere was an "illegant" place.

Well, he'd promised to take her, and take her he would. It wouldn't kill him.

He never did find out what she had expected out of this great experience. Somewhat sheepishly he escorted his two young charges into the hotel dining room and sat between them during the shabby wonders of the performance at the Lyceum.

Katie was wearing the dress Mrs. Bellamy had ordered her for the recital. She ate scarcely anything, and she let Victor and Lissa talk across her.

At one point, between courses, she did say, "You know, Miss Archibald's nephew plays the violin in that orchestra."

"Which is he?" Victor asked, turning in his chair.

"I've never met him," Katie said. "I imagine he's the young-looking one, with spectacles. I think Miss Archibald would like it if I went over and spoke to him. He came all the way out to the recital and she wanted me to meet him, but I never got a chance."

"Well, go ahead," Victor said unconcernedly. That was the Rampole coming out in Katie. Like royalty, the Rampoles knew how to gratify unimportant people with small attentions.

He hardly watched while she threaded her way among the tables. The musicians were idling and turning over their music.

The young man with the spectacles stepped to the edge of the dais, carrying bow and fiddle in his left hand, and exchanged a few civil phrases with Katie. They ended by shaking hands. He took her condescension in his stride; and when the other players twitted him afterward, he took that in his stride too, without smirking. A businesslike fellow with his living to earn—nothing Bohemian or dangerous about him. Victor didn't give him two thoughts. Katie had nothing to report about him.

But when they came home she thanked her brother extravagantly for a divine evening. Lissa thanked him too.

Chapter 20

HAVING given Katie the big treat she asked for, Victor had a free field for Saturday. He was taking Jodie on a picnic to the Cinnamon Gorge.

His mother had taken him and Katie there when they were little. In those days it was an all-day adventure in a horse and buggy. He had been there several times since, in cars, but he had always remembered it as he saw it first—impossibly romantic. He and Mother and Katie had made believe that the castellated rocks were brigand strongholds, and that they were in great danger. Victor had stood guard with an improvised gun over his shoulder while the women ate.

In taking Jodie to the gorge, Victor was taking advantage of Mrs. Epps's ignorance of social niceties. For some reason shopgirls and servant maids could go sweethearting where they chose, but a girl in society was subject to chaperonage.

These standards were breached from year to year as the automobile enlarged the social radius. But a mother who knew her world would never have let Jodie junket about in Victor's car as Mrs. Epps did. Mrs. Epps's indulgence suited Victor to a *T*. And Jodie was in good hands when she was with him. He wouldn't hurt a hair of her head.

After luncheon he got Jennie to put up the picnic equipment for him. He looked in the almanac to find when the moon rose. It was a full midsummer day, yeasty with sunlight, and the evening would be deliciously mild.

She came skimming down the steps to meet him, fluctuant as a bird in flight. How pretty, how pretty she looked! She was wearing her long white linen duster, and the white chiffon scarf around her hat described a triangle that ended in a big loose bow under the chin. In this geometric frame her face was like a valentine come to life.

He helped her into the car, and off they spun.

But something was amiss between them. Every subject he opened was the wrong subject. He drove, and called on his stores of patience. The gorge would work its alchemy on her.

The Cinnamon Gorge belonged to somebody, as was evidenced by a weathered No-Trespassing sign at the gap in the fence. But trespassers were no great problem, because the gorge was so hard to reach. The road was unimproved, miles and miles of it, with ruts and mud wallows. To drive a car that would take you to the gorge was a sort of caste mark in Meridian, and only the gentry knew the place at all.

When you left the road, you followed a wagon track through several superannuated gates; and when the ground rose broken and forbidding along the ridge, you parked your car and took to your legs, carrying your picnic basket over the outcrop of rock.

Finally Victor and Jodie stood at the rim of the gorge.

It would not have impressed a visiting Alpinist; it was a small-scale Midwestern spectacle. But the rusty castles still flanked the river, and the stream still plunged in discontinuous cataracts over a series of dropping ledges. The trees were giants, rich with sap. The rocks were ferny. All in all, it was the best gorge Meridian had to offer.

Jodie was impressed. While the fire was burning down to the steak-broiling phase, they clambered together to the bottom of the glen and sat on a deep divan of moss within the drift of the spray, listening to the undecipherable chords and harmonies of the thundering water. They held hands while the sunset inscribed the zenith with fiery flakes of cloud.

But there was nothing total about her compliance. All through supper a suspense built up insupportably between the two of them.

"Now," she proposed briskly when supper was over, "let's pack up and start for home."

"If you want to go home, you can start walking. I came to see the gorge by moonlight, and I'm not leaving till I've seen it. Come and sit down like a good girl." And he patted the ground beside him. He had pulled a blanket over his shoulders like a cope. Sooner or later he meant Jodie to share that mantle.

She dropped to the ground and sat facing him, straight as a Burmese idol above her crisscrossed legs. "It is a privilege," she said with high sarcasm, "to be allowed to beguile Your Highness' leisure."

"Jodie, for the love of Pete, what's got into you? What have I done now?"

"You are completely self-centered. I have no feelings, of course, so it's perfectly all right."

"I can't imagine what you're talking about."

"I've been a fool. I've put myself completely in your hands. Now you have me where you want me, and the very first chance you get, you drop me."

"Drop you! Is this what you call dropping you?" Bitterly he indicated the scenic effect of which they were the center. "I've been living all week for this picnic."

"I cried all of yesterday evening," she said, her voice shaking, "Till long after you brought Lissa Grover home from dinner and the theater. Lissa Grover, of all people! It's as much as to say that any girl in the world is good enough to take out, just so long as it isn't Jodie Epps. Bewitching, *irresistible* Lissa Grover."

He gave his full shout of laughter. He couldn't help himself. "So that's how far out of the way you have to go to pick a fight."

"I don't say you're in love with her—that would be physically impossible unless you were blind and deaf. All I say is, you used her to show me where I get off."

"You're as crazy as a bug, Jodie. That was Katie's party, from start to finish. She never has any dates, and she never gets to go anywhere, so I let her write her own ticket. I could have told her it was a hopeless sort of a party, and it was."

"And Katie asked you to take Lissa along, I suppose?"

Victor was not above telling a lie, but he couldn't lie to Jodie. He must stand foursquare with her. "Not exactly. Lissa is Katie's best friend, and we both look after her. She's having a wretched time right now."

"Since Rivergrove, you mean?"

The girl was beginning to see reason. "That's right," he agreed. "Her mother, and all."

She rounded on him like a young leopardess. "There! That's the point. Your heart bleeds for Lissa Grover because she's Old-Meridian. Your precious friends in Rampole Place are treating my family a lot worse than they're treating the Grover family. You'd think we were a load of garbage that got dumped on the Number Two lot. They walk around us in a wide circle, holding their noses. Day after day Mumsy has tea and sandwiches laid out for party callers, and nobody darkens our door. After simply glutting themselves with lobster salad at our housewarming!"

"Well, it was that gambling business that put everybody's back up."

"Daddy had a perfect right to take Mrs. Grover up to a club that he belongs to. The rest of us tagged along after him, as you know perfectly well, and Daddy would rather die than be a spoilsport. Rampole Place is one great gluey gob of spoilsports. I can tell you one thing—Daddy is furious. For three cents he'd sell his house to some old banana man and move back to Adams Avenue."

It was a direct prick to his heart. "Golly, you can't let him do that!"

Her answer came slow and broodingly. "I'm not a bit sure I want to live there. I'm an article on approval. If you don't keep me, nobody else in Rampole Place has any use for me."

A blast of exultation detonated in Victor. Jodie's guard had finally broken down. This was a naked appeal for reassurance.

He had no eloquence ready. His arms, his kisses would have to speak for the upsurge of his heart. "There's no problem, then," he said. "If you can't depend on me, you can't depend on the moon coming up at eight-twenty-two." And he moved closer to her.

But Jodie still sat upright as a candle in a socket. Her tension had not reached the point of release. Even in the summer darkness he felt the veto of her eyes.

"People think——" She stopped, and began again. "Even before River-grove, people kept me at arm's length. They think I've set my cap for you."

"Rats! I've been in love with you ever since dancing school."

"Then that's not the reason you're so highhanded with me?"

"Highhanded!" he exploded. "You're a fine one to talk. You've played cat-and-mouse with me. You've treated me like the very devil, and you've enjoyed it. Highhanded!"

Jodie disposed of his complaint negligently. "Silly, that's the way a girl has to play it. . . . Then you never did think—?"

"It never once entered my head. I'm no catch, Lord knows, for a girl like you."

"It's true all the same. But not because you're Victor Rampole and live at Chestnut Point. I wouldn't care if you were a—a newsboy and peddled papers for a living. Grandness doesn't mean anything to me, Vic. It's you yourself. You have a—a terrific effect on me. I could tell you the very necktie you had on the evening Little Bierbach introduced us. The only reason I dragged my family out to Rampole Place—and I did—was to be near you."

Glory flooded over Victor. This was more than anything he had hoped from his picnic, this complete surrender. His arms went toward her in longing.

Her palm still held him back. "Let me finish. Lately I've been scared, Vic. I feel in my bones that Rampole Place is going to come between us."

"Just let them try, that's all!"

She said plangently, "If you don't love me, Vic, way down deep, don't pretend you do. I dragged my family into Rampole Place, and I can drag them out again. To make me stay there and fight a losing fight for you—that would be cruel. I couldn't live through it."

"Nobody even tries to come between us, Jodie darling. They all know you're my girl."

She gave a long sigh and took his kiss on her flowering lips. But her lack of response told him that he had let her down.

He knew what more she wanted—not in his mind, but in his blood and bones. Jodie was farther along the road to womanhood than he was to manhood. She was ripe for a proposal, an engagement.

He loved Jodie with all fervency—and he expected to love her while he drew breath—but with a boy's love. His undefined hope was to skylark with Jodie, forever young, through the blue brightness of eternity.

He would like to oblige her, but the words wouldn't come. Deep below thought, deep below passion, Victor's center stood firm for the male prerogative of taking the initiative at his own time.

The only course left to him was to temporize. "You work on your family," he urged her miserably. "Make them sit tight till this rumpus blows over."

"Well, I'll do my best," she promised, just as unhappily. "Daddy gets boiling mad when people are mean to Mumsy and me. She didn't have a thing to do with the rumpus—everybody knows that. If they'd treat her civilly, Daddy would cool off."

It was Victor's turn to sigh. For Jodie's sake he would have walked on red-hot coals, but he knew no way of making the neighbors take Mrs. Epps to their bosom. "People in Rampole Place are slow starters, that's all," he offered his awkward consolation. "They don't begin liking you till they're used to you."

"Not even then, in some cases," she said caustically. "But in the case of the Grovers, who can blame them? Mrs. Queenie is sucking up to Mumsy, now she has nobody else to go round with, and Mumsy doesn't see through her." It was as if she put out her hand and gave him a small intentional jab with a needle. She couldn't take issue with the real injury he had done her by not asking her to marry him, so she made the Grovers a pretext for drawing one drop of blood. He had taken Lissa to dinner and the theater, and she didn't intend him to forget it.

But he had a stand to make too against her premature claims. And the Grovers were as good a pretext as any. "Mr. Grover and Lissa are nice people," he said argumentatively. "And as for Queenie, she has no brains, but there's no harm in her."

"How can you say that? She acts up. With half the men in town. And don't you tell me she doesn't, because I hear her coming home, all girlish and giggling, at two in the morning."

Victor was famished with unfilled ecstasy; he was caught in a rip tide of passion and resistance to passion. His own answer stunned him like the discharge of lightning from a loaded cloud. "Don't *you* gang up with the buzzards!" was what he said ferociously.

"Why, Victor Rampole, what have I done, for gracious sake?" She popped upright out of his arm, as if he had released a spring in her.

"Women are bitches about other women," he ground out between his teeth.

She was too affronted to speak. She sat straight and separate, and he made no effort to recapture her. "One of these days," he threshed along, "they'll gang up on *you* and pick your eyes out, and then you'll know what I'm talking about."

"So Mrs. Queenie Grover is your ideal of womanhood," she blasted him.

He shook his head to drive out the bewilderment. Those Stutzes in the oval were a midnight abomination. Why had he been so prompt in her defense? "I don't know a thing about her private life," he amended his position. "All I say is, it's not your business and not mine."

"So you call me a bitch for repeating what everybody says about her? Daddy hears it downtown, Mumsy hears it at lunch parties. I hear it from the girls at school."

"Any girl I love has got to cut out the smutty talk about other women."

"Any man I love," she replied with spirit, "has got to let me say what I choose, without calling me dirty names." Then she went on balefully, "I guess the Rampoles have their own standards about this sort of thing—so I've always heard, but I never believed it till now." She waited for him to ask her what she was talking about, but he didn't dare ask. A horror of blackness was closing down on him, and all he could do was wait it out. Breathing furiously, she went on, "Let me tell you one thing, Victor Rampole. After we're married——"

She launched the new word between them, the forbidden word. It drove a delicious barb into his vitals, but he fought against the blade.

He took her up viciously. "Oh, so I'm marrying you, is that it? Thanks for telling me."

It was a whiplash question. It brought Jodie to her feet. "I wouldn't marry you," she cried, "if I were an old maid and worked in a pickle factory. Not after this evening."

And she was off up the side of the gorge—skimming, stumbling, righting herself, till she reached the car. "Take me home this very minute," she gasped when he overtook her. "I'd walk if I could. But don't you dare speak one word to me on the way home."

For the first few miles of the return trip from paradise Victor kept commanding the bad dream to vanish. How, on the very evening when Jodie had admitted she loved him, had they blundered into a quarrel about the Grovers—about the Grovers, of all inconsequential people!

But she met all his overtures by shivering, and huddling against the farther door of the car.

"I don't wonder I frightened you," he said, abasing himself. "I frightened myself. I went loco all of a sudden."

She strained her face farther away from him. All he could see was the back of her hat in its swathing of diaphanous white.

He left her on her own front steps, and she slammed the house door in his face.

Chapter 21

Until the day of Katie's recital, there had been a good chance that the Rivergrove rumpus would blow over and that Queenie would be taken back into comity. The boycott had been a thing that couldn't be pinned down—it slid through one's fingers. It was simply that people always happened to be looking the other way when Queenie tried to wave at them.

Lissa had felt sick when she heard Queenie making arrangements to take Onie Epps to the recital. It was no crime, certainly, to show courtesy to a newcomer, but in Rampole Place it was bound to be considered an insolence—a planned insolence. Whereas, actually, Queenie was incapable of anything resembling a campaign. Her mind didn't work that way.

While Queenie was telephoning to Mrs. Epps on the morning of the recital, Lissa had followed her father into the study. "Daddy," she said urgently, "this isn't a good idea of Queenie's."

"I agree with you, my dear. But she says she's called everybody else in the street and they've all made other plans. She's got to have somebody to keep her in countenance." This was as near as the two of them came to admitting that anything was wrong.

"Couldn't you—oh, I don't know—couldn't you take the three of us on a picnic or something this afternoon?"

"That would be knuckling under. Katie's recital is quite an occasion in our little frog pond. Queenie wants to go."

"Well, I can't bring myself to go."

"Don't then," Philip said in the Grover tradition of *laissez faire*.

For one rebellious moment Lissa wished Daddy were a man who averted troubles by action. He saw the torment in her face.

"Honey," he said gently, "you can prevent a bird from flying. But what alternative have you to offer him?"

Lissa gave her father one of her long gray-velvet looks. She was applying his analogy to himself. Daddy had no alternative to being himself. To expect him to turn into a family autocrat was futile. She loved him, she yearned over him; so she would shoulder as much of his burden as she could.

. . . But not to the point of going to that recital. Lissa had her limits too.

When Queenie and Onie came back from the recital Queenie was merry to the point of hysteria. She caroled a greeting to Mr. Epps across the lawn and persuaded him over for a drink. Mr. Epps put on almost a parody of domestic behavior, with only a quirk of the eyelid to betray his satirical amusement.

That evening Lissa dreaded the letdown, when Queenie should stop putting up a front.

But Queenie laid an astonishing and touching discipline on herself. She sat brooding all evening over a game of solitaire. Her face was suffused with heavy pinkness; but she didn't shed a single tear or demand a single reassurance. She was showing courage after her fashion.

Her husband and daughter appointed themselves her bodyguard. Every evening Philip came home primed with proposals: why not run down to Adams Avenue and pay a call on Old Aunt Caroline? . . . How about asking the young Treadways out for a game of bridge? . . . Oughtn't they to have Herman and Maddy to dinner before Maddy sailed for Europe?

Lissa took the daytime shift. There was one indulgence she could not deny herself—her morning tennis with Katie and Victor. But she did not go near the Swimming Rocks, she did not play ping-pong at the Wyndhams'. She stuck to her mother like a shadow.

"Queenie, would you teach me to play bridge—just the two of us, till I learn my way around?"

"Why, darling, what fun! I didn't know you cared for cards."

That killed ever so many afternoons.

"Queenie, oughtn't we to look over my summer dresses before we start for the Endicott Inn, and take them to Mrs. Somerville to be let down?"

This was an inspiration. It led to several fittings, and a trip downtown for dress shields and seam binding. So one more day was checked off.

And of course there was still Maddy Thies's crowd. Queenie was their pet, Queenie was the china shepherdess of their salon. Now that the weather was hot, they made the Grover porch their rendezvous. Ice tinkled, masculine laughter rang the length of Rampole Place.

Lissa had a divided mind about Maddy's crowd. She was thankful Queenie had companionship. On the other hand, the companions came in Stutzes; and even at five in the afternoon the Stutzes had the look of night birds. And though the topic might be Monet's paintings or Midwestern Philistinism, at a distance it had a saturnalian sound.

Lissa planted herself obdurately on the porch while the young men paid their devoirs.

It was awkward, this duennaship. Queenie seemed embarrassed, not at being chaperoned, but at having a daughter so obviously unpopular. "Why don't you run down for a swim, darling?" . . . "Why don't you call Katie Rampole and ask her to come over? You're getting to be a regular little bookworm."

Lissa provided herself with properties for her self-appointed vigil. If Queenie didn't mind, she had a lot of book reports to write during the summer, and this was the coolest place she could find.

She kept a notebook open on the arm of the chair, and a volume of Meredith or Hardy on her lap. She sat as composed as a Tanagra figurine over her book, her eyelids veiling her troubled eyes.

One of Maddy's young men was an interior decorator who had studied in Europe. "You know, Queenie," he said, as if Lissa were inanimate and deaf, "that daughter of yours is the most beautiful work of God in all Meridian. She's like the Sleeping Beauty. I'd like to be around the day she comes to life."

"It's simply darling of you to say so," Queenie answered. She herself had no illusions about her daughter's beauty.

Lissa was not always reading when she appeared to be. Sometimes half an hour went by before she turned a page. She might not have been able to last out the humiliating vigil she had laid upon herself, except that she had a great resource—she had Victor Rampole to think about.

She did not contest his love for Jodie Epps. Even that miracle evening at the Belvedere Hotel was nothing she could take to herself personally. She had no standing with Victor except as Katie's friend.

But that evening existed, and Jodie had no claim on it. It was food and fire to Lissa. If she chose to spin fancies of beautiful things he had said to her, that was nobody's business but her own.

She had one other memory even more precious to her—and yet it was nothing. Katie had seen all there was to see, and had paid no attention.

Victor had been standing beside the court, watching the two girls rally. "Hit through!" he coached them, impatient with their pitpat game. "Follow through. Put some steam behind your stroke."

Finally he stepped out on Lissa's side of the court and came up behind her. He took her left upper arm in his left hand and put his sinewy paw over hers on the handle of the racket, so that they were coupled together like two railroad cars. Then he drew back her right arm with his own, and sent the racket through with piston force, their two linked bodies rotating with one impetus.

"There! See what I mean about follow-through?" he asked. The next minute he had walked off in the direction of the Swimming Rocks.

Lissa couldn't answer him to save her life. The vigor he had transmitted to her left her dazed. She went to sleep recalling it in every fiber of her young body, she woke up hungry to experience it again. While she appeared to be reading George Meredith on the porch, she was reliving that glorious impact.

She took up her pencil and pretended to make a note on her reading. She wrote *Victor Rampole*. Beneath that she wrote *Melissa Pendleton Grover*. She began canceling out the letters to see whether he loved her. In a fury of embarrassment at her own childishness she rubbed out the two names with her eraser. And to make sure they couldn't be deciphered she wrote over the erasure *Sir Willoughby Patterne—selfish and egotistical*.

One afternoon toward the end of July, Mr. O'Shea drove Mrs. Thies out to the house to say good-by. Mrs. Thies was leaving on the morning train for Europe. On the whole, Lissa was sorry Mrs. Thies was going. She did provide a framework of movement for poor Queenie.

Even if Queenie had had the initiative to keep Maddy's circle in being, she would have been hopelessly handicapped—by lack of money for easy hospitality, by Ella's sore feet, and by that woodenness in her husband and daughter which put a damper on any Bohemian party. Lissa recognized these limiting factors.

Well, the vacuum had a limit in time. On the first of every August, like migrant birds, the Grover family set off by hereditary impulse for the Endicott Inn on the Maine coast. Philip and Lissa might get Queenie to the Endicott Inn one jump ahead of emotional collapse. And by fall the boycott might have passed into limbo.

It was the hottest day of the summer. The whole heartland of America lay prostrate under the onslaught of the sun.

Osmond O'Shea had brought along the apparatus for an old project of his—a pastel portrait of Queenie. "I see you as a Renoir," he was accustomed to say, narrowing his eyelids, "half goddess and half nectarine."

He propped his drawing board against a chair and set to work in his shirt sleeves. He scrubbed his drawing with his handkerchief, and then his perspiring brow, till his face was streaked with colored chalk dust—though it still maintained its air of damaged and harmless handsomeness.

Maddy took her ease in the chaise longue. She was a compact, engaging, European little woman with blond bangs. When she smiled, her cheeks bunched up beneath her merry black eyes. She was openly wearing rouge and lipstick, she was smoking one cigarette after another, and—though it was hard to believe—she appeared to have celebrated the heat wave by leaving her corsets at home. In an Adams Avenue woman these would have been three marks of depravity, but in a foreigner one had to suspend judgment.

Lissa did not think that Osmond's drawing was very good. He was rendering Queenie like an architectural façade, accurate and dead.

Life was the palpitant essence of Queenie's beauty, and she was all life this afternoon. She was deliciously given over to the heat; her round forehead and her upper lip were frosted with a minute bloom of perspiration. Her dress disposed itself in cumulus billows. She was a pink water lily, full open to the afternoon.

Having something to watch was distracting Lissa from her reading. Osmond was planning to run over to Paris in September, and he and Maddy were hoping to connect with each other. "Oh, how I envy you both!" Queenie cried.

"I wish you were coming wizz me, Queenie," Maddy said. She had a pungent little buzz in her speech, not quite amounting to mispronunciation. "It doesn't cost me a penny more zan you spend at zat old Endicott Inn of yours. I visit my friends. Herman saves money by sending me abroad every summer."

"Why don't you take her up, Queenie?" Osmond asked, picking through the box of pastels. "How long is it since you've been over?"

"Don't torture me," cried Queenie on an airy note. "I have never been abroad."

"Never been abroad!" Osmond echoed her incredulously. He laid down his pastels and scanned her deprivation out of his caverned forget-me-not eyes. "But what can be wrong with that husband of yours?"

Queenie leaped to Philip's defense. "Oh, Philip has great plans for taking Lissa and me—perhaps the summer after she graduates from Miss Peebles'."

"But why wait?"

"Money, Ozzie darling, money! You're going to Europe on our money. We've had to take out an odious old mortgage. It's as bad as a tapeworm."

"But Maddy assures you it doesn't cost any more——"

"Now, Ozzie!" Queenie said with charming spirit. "I simply won't go without Philip and Lissa. And furthermore, I don't want to go at all if we have to carry our own sandwiches. Shall I tell you my ideal of Europe?" She broke her pose, her face naïvely lighted. "It's Paris—Paris—Paris. It's dining at smart restaurants and having diplomats twirl their mustaches at me. It's wearing a ravishing frock to the races, and having photographers snap me as I sweep by under my parasol. It's——"

"Don't let it go too long," he warned her darkly. "It's less fun going to the races in a wheel chair."

"Oh, don't!" There was nothing airy or affected about her cry of pain. Her eyes took on a haunted horror. "That's what keeps breathing down my neck. A few days go by, and a few more days, till all of a sudden your hair's gray and life is over before it's ever begun." And she shivered.

"Yet knowing all that," Osmond said venomously, "you still commit slow suicide at the Endicott Inn, summer after summer."

Lissa had stopped any pretense of reading. It had never occurred to her that the Endicott Inn was not the paradise to Queenie that it was to Philip and herself. Perhaps it was not even the resource they needed for the present crisis.

As for the family trip to Europe, Lissa suspected that was a mirage. The money pressure on the household never relaxed. The mortgage was an anaconda, strangling the three of them.

Without premeditation Lissa spoke up. "Queenie, why don't you go over with Mrs. Thies? That wouldn't prevent your going with us later."

"Why, dar-ling! Are you—" her voice was unsteady—"are you trying to get rid of me?"

"Nonsense," Osmond cut in. "Don't set up as a martyr. Herman Thies survives Maddy's absence very nicely, and he's all the fonder of her when she gets back."

"I guess you don't understand our family very well," Queenie said, rejecting the analogy with the Thieses. "We're as close as *that*." She clasped her fingers tight together.

"Somebody ought to put it up to Philip," Osmond said. "For ten cents I'd speak to him myself. He may seem obtuse, but I've always felt he was fundamentally fond of you."

"I am going first to Wiesbaden." Maddy dangled the enchanting prospect. "I am staying at my aunt's villa. I promise she would be delighted to take you in."

Queenie was tempted. Her glance traveled from face to face.

Lissa resented Osmond's tone. "Don't bother speaking to Daddy, Mr.

O'Shea," she said. "I'll speak to him myself, if Queenie decides she wants me to."

"Don't everybody push me!" Queenie cried in protest. "I'm frightened, somehow. I think Philip and I need each other more than most people do."

Maddy rose, and shook herself down inside her uncorseted dress. "Well, sink it over, my pet. Only you must sink fast, because ze boat sails on Sursday. You can come into my cabin—zere will be no trouble about zat. . . . Come, Ozzie, drive me home. You are not getting anywhere wizz your vork. I have a million sings to do. *Auf Wiedersehen,* darling. I hope your Phee-leep lets you come wizz me."

After they were gone, Queenie sat poking absently at the mint that was drowning in melted ice in the bottom of her glass. Lissa was frightened by her own intrusion into adult affairs.

"There's Philip driving in!" Queenie exclaimed.

"Shall I say anything—?"

"Just tell him what Maddy suggested. But don't give him the impression I want to go, because I'm in a complete fog."

Lissa would have given her soul to get out of this pickle. But Queenie followed her as far as the living room and lingered there, to overhear what Philip would say. Lissa had no choice: she must let Daddy know what trouble she had launched.

Philip came through the side entry, drawing in grateful breaths of the coolness of his own house. "Now for a deep chair and a tall drink!" he said. "It was hotter than Tophet downtown."

"Daddy . . ." Lissa began. And she told him what was afoot.

She felt the triple filaments that connected the little group—filaments spun out of love and desperation. No one could say what they were all thinking: "This is an escape for Queenie."

"Let's go out on the porch," Philip said. "You're throwing this at me pretty fast." He sank down into his particular chair and pressed his fingers against his eyeballs for a moment.

"Queenie, if your heart's set on it, I'll find some way of sending you. Lissa and I will be like lost souls without you, but I dare say we'll make out. Tell me, do you want to go?"

Queenie dredged up a question from the depths. "Do you want me to go, Philip?"

"Answer yes or no?" He sent her a bittersweet smile. "Let's put it that I can endure to have you go, and you're entitled to go. However, there's a new factor to be considered. You might as well know about a piece of bad luck that hit me today.

"Not bad luck," he corrected himself. "A deserved calamity." He seemed to have difficulty in proceeding. "You know Jock Richards. He's my biggest and most litigious client. Jock and I inherited each other from our two fathers. Well, today Jock dropped around at the office, and he hemmed and hawed and paid me all manner of compliments on what a hell of a good lawyer I was. But he has a ticklish case coming up in court, and he's putting it in the hands of Swayne & Leatherby. He says right now he needs a lawyer with more ginger to him. And the worst of it is, he's right."

Queenie was instantly the consoling goddess. She bent over him and took his face between her beautiful hands. "I never had any use for Jock Richards," she said warmly. "You can just go out and get some other clients. And when Jock begs you to take him back you can say you're too busy."

Philip took possession of one of her wrists and turned her hand before his eyes like a *bibelot*. His smile was mockingly tender. "That will make Jock Richards feel very badly indeed," he said. "But until I put salt on the tails of those clients, I shall be two or three thousand a year out of pocket."

"Daddy!" Lissa breathed dolorously.

"It's only temporary," Queenie insisted in her capacity as family optimist. "You can sell off some of your grandfather's real estate to tide you over."

"The market's very dead for residence property in the old part of town. I have half a dozen properties standing vacant. I've borrowed pretty heavily at the banks to keep up taxes, and they aren't anxious to lend me any more."

Queenie perched on the arm of Philip's chair and stared into vacancy. "I don't understand," she said. "We economize and economize, and yet we never get any good out of our economies. Other people go to Europe; other people keep two cars and four servants. What's wrong with us? When you and I got married, Philip, the Grover family had as much money as anybody."

Philip gave his rueful smile. "You married the wrong man. It breaks my heart to keep you short, Queenie, but the fact is, I'm not a good provider."

She laid her cheek against his hair and emitted loyal, reassuring murmurs. But after a while she sat up straight and said in a voice like the sound given off by a cracked china plate, "Then the trip to Europe is out of the question."

"No, dearest. I said if you wanted to go——"

"But you made it perfectly clear you had no money."

"Queenie——"

"We won't discuss it any more." And Queenie's whole attitude of affront proclaimed that now that the glory of renunciation was taken out of her hands, she wanted very much to go to Europe.

She made a regal exit. Philip and Lissa heard her moving slowly up the stairs and closing the door of her room.

In the happy days before Rivergrove an outburst of temperament like this had been an April shower, soon over. Now they had run out of happy options. What confronted them was a matter of pure endurance of the unendurable. Queenie had no leeway left for blue moods and rainbow recoveries.

Philip and Lissa avoided each other's eyes. But they could not close their ears to the piteous sounds that reached them. Queenie was crying like a forsaken child.

Lissa said miserably, "I could bite my tongue out for suggesting that she should go abroad."

"It was a pretty good idea, on the face of it. . . . I'm going upstairs."

"Can you do anything for her?"

"I may be worthless in most ways," Philip said with unexpected spirit, "but I understand my own wife."

And apparently he did. It took a long time, but the crying stopped. An hour later the two of them came downstairs bathed and freshly dressed. Philip had had the inspiration of asking Queenie to go dancing with him at the open-air Magyar Pavilion on the river, where they had danced when they were engaged. And she was leaving for Europe the next day.

Chapter 22

"WELL, GUS?" the Senator said, late in an August afternoon. He was just back from a statesman's junket, and an hour earlier he had rung for Augustus. Augustus had come fortified with his account books. In the Senator's absence he had a large executive freedom on the place, and he rendered a periodical accounting.

Once the agenda were cleared, Horace asked Augustus to join him in a drink; and behind closed doors they took their ease like the lifelong cronies they were.

Augustus made himself comfortable in an armchair and prepared to bring the Senator up to date on the neighborhood. "Street's pretty well closed down, I notice," Horace said, tilting back in his swivel chair. "Has everybody cleared out?"

Augustus gave evidence of husbanding some prime tidbits of news. "Not everybody. A few of the men are baching it till they can get away."

"Epps out of town?"

"No, but his womenfolks are. Overnight, you might say, they picked up and skedaddled for the mountains. Her Royal Highness Miss Jodie cracked the whip, so I hear."

A glow spread through Horace's vitals. "I expected Jodie would be making hay this summer, while everybody was away."

"Oh, but her and Victor are on the outs." This was one of Augustus' hoarded nuggets, and he took real pleasure in displaying it.

"You don't tell me! Well, calf love is like the measles—one day they're sick enough to die, and the next day they're out roller-skating."

"Vic's taking it pretty hard. He's in the devil of a temper most of the time."

"He'll outgrow it," Horace said. If he had ever been ravaged by adolescent love, he had forgotten it. In his colthood he had pranced and whinnied like the rest; but if tears had been shed, they had not been shed by Horace. His children had a Cummager admixture—an inwardness of sentiment, which revealed itself like the flicker of heat lightning. But with or without tremors, a boy outgrew his calf love.

"Then the children have nobody to keep them company?" he asked.

"Sure they have. They're just like Siamese twins with young Melissa Grover. And there's a goings on for you!" This was Augustus' second nugget. He gave it a shine on his cuff.

"Aren't the Grovers away in Maine?"

"Not this year. They were all set to leave, and Ella Hedges was going off for her month's vacation as usual. Then—bam!—Mrs. Queenie's off to Europe in a cloud of dust, and her husband and daughter cancel their reservations and decide to stay home for the summer. This is the last straw for Ella Hedges, I can tell you that much."

"Queenie Grover couldn't get as far as Cleveland by herself."

"Nor she didn't go off by herself. She trailed along with that Thies woman she's so thick with. They're going to visit in a castle on the Rhine, Ella tells me."

"Thies," Horace said damningly. Herman Thies had had the bad taste to come to town without introductions and to make his money without asking favors of the ruling clique. "This will settle Queenie's hash, I'm afraid."

"Her hash is pretty well settled already. Nobody so much as passes the time of day with her, since the rumpus at Rivergrove. She'd reached the point of laying down on her bed and squalling like a baby. You could hear her all up and down the street."

Horace tut-tutted. "She ought to have ridden it out. By September they'd have forgotten what they were mad about. They'll never forgive her for careering around Europe with the Thies woman. Philip ought to have kept her tied up behind the house this summer."

"Philip Grover is too goddamned easygoing. He ought to take a strap to her."

"Does the daughter take after her mother?"

"She's all Grover."

"Good stock," said Horace, "good stock." In fancy he welcomed a Grover daughter-in-law into the family.

Augustus read his face. "Mind you," he qualified, "Vic's not sweet on her. It's more like he was training a puppy. She's sweet on him, if you like—it sticks out all over her."

"We're running ahead of ourselves. Vic has to finish college and get a start in business before he can take on a wife." This was Adams Avenue gospel. Only loafers and no-goods set up as gentlemen of leisure. That had been the trouble with Ollie Lassigne. "Well, I'll look the kids over at dinner."

The colloquy was over. Augustus rose, and picked up his tray.

At first Victor hardly took his breach with Jodie seriously. They had quarreled, yes. He was willing to go any length to make peace, short of asking Jodie to marry him. How gladly he would throw Queenie Grover to the wolves—if that was the price required of him!

But as for marrying Jodie, why in the world should Jodie want to get married—Jodie, who had her whole bright youth to squander first? So far as he could see, she was not in the grip of physical desire as he was. Her caresses had to be coaxed out of her.

Most men did marry—but not at seventeen and eighteen. Marriage was a treadmill for the superannuated. Its pleasures began, and ended, in bed. Married men worked in offices to support their wives. After dinner they watered the lawn; at ten-thirty they walked the dog and turned out the lights. To Victor, all this was a waste of life's possibilities.

But he might have to propose to the girl to get back on speaking terms with her. She wouldn't come to the telephone. When he appeared at the Swimming Rocks she pointedly picked up her bath towel and withdrew. She made eyes at his best friends.

To Victor, Rampole Place in July was the enchanted castle one explores on tiptoe—the fire burning on the hearth, the cat dozing on the window sill, and the beloved inaccessible.

148

Then in August the street emptied. The blinds came down, the dust covers were spread. Surely now, when she had no one else to flirt with, Jodie would sue for peace.

He kept out of Lissa Grover's way. Jodie's jealousy was irrational, but it had to be reckoned with. Avoiding Lissa was not easy; she and Katie were inseparable. They read, they pressed flowers, they got Jennie to teach them to make cookies.

Katie had a new talking machine. Hour after hour she played operatic records. The huge splendor of Caruso's voice flooded the house: *"Ridi, pagliaccio . . ."* That record was a knife straight through Victor. From the opening phrase, *"Vesti la giubba,"* his tension mounted with the singer's agony up to the last measures where the heart actually, almost physically broke.

Victor made weary work of filling his time. He worked with the crew of men who were cleaning up the woods. With rare piety he drove Katie down to see their Grandmother Cummager. He played only in men's doubles on the tennis courts. Faithful unto death—that was Victor's motto.

Jodie had not taken the veil, by any means. She enticed brash youths with roadsters, from the wrong side of town, to swim at the sacred rocks. When she ran into Victor she looked straight through him and out the other side.

From day to day he expected her to come down off her high horse—until the day she left town. And that leaving was not Lissa's fault, but she was certainly the occasion of it.

One day Victor was on his way home from the city—his car was just rolling up the ramp of the Doochee Bridge. The bridge crossed a pocket of marsh and bottomland cluttered with tin cans, but also rich in waterside flowers. He caught sight of Katie and Lissa scrambling up the bank, their arms laden with loosestrife. In a brotherly way he stopped to give them a lift home. He was not more than a few hundred yards from the entrance to Rampole Place. By evil hap, during this short transit an outgoing car swept past him; and in that car was Jodie. Her eye was the eye of Medusa, which freezes the heart to stone.

He tried to reach her with explanations. He told the whole story to Mrs. Epps and asked her to intercede with Jodie. Mrs. Epps chuckled and said to leave Jodie to her.

Mrs. Epps miscalculated her powers. That evening an expressman called at Number Two and took a pile of trunks to the station. Overnight the Epps ladies followed their baggage.

Victor had come to the end of his scruples. He would be doggoned if he would waste any more time living up to Jodie's demands. If there had been any real girls to take out, he would have taken them. Since there were none, he devoted his empty days to Katie and Lissa.

Despair gentled him in more ways than one. Not only did he swim and play tennis with the girls, he was reduced to taking an interest in his father. He talked politics at the dinner table. The great man was disproportionately flattered. He let himself hope that Victor had lived through his cranky spell.

Horace was working at his trade these days—making his rounds, dropping in at saloons, pool halls and athletic meets in the disaffected area, and pumping his henchmen for information.

He had left them to their own devices too long. They had gone soft. They carried snapshots of their grandchildren, and babbled about the chicken farms they were buying against their retirement.

Twenty years ago there had been constant pressure from young fellows eager to make their way to the top—tough lads with drive to them. Now the young blood had been drawn off into national politics, Progressive and even Democratic. The Republican stalwarts were nothing but a lot of aging wheel horses. He kept his eye peeled for likely new recruits. He had them up to his office or his smoking room; he gave them lifts in his eye-compelling great car. He asked their advice without letting them know what game he was stalking.

For this work he had one disadvantage: his face was known all over town. He couldn't drop into a bar with a convincing air of casualness.

In this predicament he happened to take Victor to a baseball game. There was a saloon across from the ball park where the politicos foregathered; and after the game he and Victor dropped in for a glass of beer. Victor proved to be an ideal screen for his operations.

"Well, Terry!" the senator would cry with a mighty handclasp. "Want you to meet this boy of mine. . . . Vic, this is a man you want to remember. Your grandfather broke him in and put him on the auditor's pay roll, and he's gone straight up the ladder. . . . Will you ever forget that old fellow with the glass eye, Terry?" And off they would go into reminiscence.

And before they parted, the Senator would have found some favor to do for Terry, from getting his aunt into the County Home to recommending his grandson for a scholarship at the university. In return, Terry would be giving away information without realizing he was being pumped.

Victor was driven to conclude that his father was an astonishingly able man. He enjoyed watching him work.

Regularly once a month every young girl in Rampole Place took a day in bed. The girls made farfetched excuses for defaulting their tennis matches, and the boys accepted the excuses with embarrassment, since the whole subject was unholy, titillating and faintly nasty.

Even Katie, who was as strong as a young elk, was subject to this taboo. Jennie would have been doing less than her duty if she had let Katie up out of bed. So, one morning well along in August, Victor proceeded alone to the tennis court to tell Lissa that Katie was under the weather and wouldn't be out for her usual morning game.

Lissa blushed, and headed meekly for home.

"We might as well play a set," said Victor, who was at a loose end. "I'll spot you thirty."

"I couldn't take thirty," said Lissa, bridling. She never wanted to accept odds in her favor.

"Fifteen then—but I'll lick the hide off you."

"Well, we'll try a set at fifteen."

So they played at fifteen. Victor began with chivalrous easy serves. She returned them with wicked neatness. Fabulous to relate, Lissa won the first game.

When he came to serve again the games were one-all. He had smashed his returns, but in her flitting, underemphasized way she had arrived in time to keep them in play, and she had run the score to deuce.

"You're darned good," Victor said. "You play better when Katie's not around. From now on, there are no holds barred." And he set himself to trounce her properly.

Lissa moved well behind the back line. Victor writhed powerfully and launched a thunderbolt of a serve; it seared the court.

"Outside," Lissa said regretfully. It had been out a mile.

His second serve was tempered. . . . "Let!" came Lissa's polite, deprecatory little voice.

The third serve was a marvel of conservatism. Lissa returned it, long and level, to the pestiferous corner where Victor wasn't. The game balanced at deuce, vantage, deuce; but Lissa won it. The games were one-two.

She did not win the match. Victor called on God, and took three games in a row. But the set was no notable triumph.

"You go on playing like that," Victor said handsomely as the two of them dropped down on the shady grass to gather breath, "and you can enter the Ladies' City Tournament next summer."

"I'm not a tournament player."

"Tennis means a lot to you, though."

"It means a lot to Daddy. He wants me to get good enough to be a doubles partner for him."

Victor was at the stage of maturity where new perceptions go off inside the skull like Roman candles. He read the Grover situation. For Lissa and her father, life was narrowing down. Excellence in tennis—so small an excellence in the Rampole scale of values—was still open to them.

This all seemed sad to Victor. He hoped Lissa would play an outstanding game of tennis.

"That's a wretched racket of yours," he said, picking up the offending object and twanging it.

"It's an old one of Daddy's. He's been meaning to restring it for me."

"It's past restringing. I have a spare racket in better shape than this."

"Daddy's been frightfully busy," she made excuse.

"That's why you didn't go down to Maine, I suppose," he said tentatively.

"That was one reason." She fell silent, and he waited. The pressure of Lissa's need to confide in him was almost palpable in the air between them.

"Staying at home was really my idea," she finally admitted, sending a dark-gray glance that brushed his face and then skimmed away. "When Queenie left, Daddy and I were headed for the Endicott Inn as usual. We'll tell her when she gets home." Then, suddenly contrite, she added, "I'd rather you didn't pass that on."

"I won't. But what was the idea?"

Lissa clasped her hands about her knees and gazed into a vista of forest. "Well, you see, Queenie had this chance to go to Europe with Mrs. Thies, and she's never been, and she doesn't like Maine as much as Daddy and I do, so we both urged her to go while we went to the seashore. But Daddy has been having trouble about money ever since we built our house. So the evening after Queenie left, it came over me that we'd just moved out into the country, and why need we go away at all? So we're staying at home."

"We never go away. Granny Cummager used to have a cottage in northern Michigan, and my mother used to take us up there when we were kids."

This memory, so distant, so overlaid, slipped out without any conflict. It seemed natural to remember the crescent of beach, the tin sand bucket and the small striped bathing suit—to remember his mother wading out with him into waist-high water, supporting him under his ribs and scooting him playfully through the lake. "Swim, Victor, swim like mad!" she'd cried, with a bubble of laughter in her voice. "You're almost there!" That was a pretty time to remember.

Lissa was easy too; she was assuaged by talking. "Everything has gone so wrong since we moved out here, Daddy and I would like to make things up to Queenie. You have no idea how sweet she is, and how defenseless. Nobody knows except Daddy and me."

One subject Victor could not discuss with Lissa was her abominable mother. He stirred, and suggested, "Come on up to the house. I want to see if I can locate that old racket of mine."

He led the way to his own room. He wouldn't have brought Jodie up there; but Lissa was only Lissa, and Katie was in bed next door—to satisfy Mrs. Grundy, in case Mrs. Grundy cared.

But Lissa was self-conscious about following him. She turned off into Katie's room and perched on the end of the bed, describing with innocent vanity how she had carried the set to 6-4 against Victor. He rummaged in his closet and came up with the racket clamped into its frame. "Come here, Lissa!" he shouted impatiently. He wasn't going to stand for any prunes-and-prisms about staying out of his room.

But she had been right and he had been wrong. Neither of them could shake off their troubling sense that she was a feminine presence in a masculine sanctum.

She stood poised like an oread for flight. Her eyes took in glimpses of the forbidden place.

A framed photograph of Jodie stood on the chest of drawers. Two neckties dangled disparagingly across the face of it. One brilliant, long-lashed eye gazed out between the neckties.

"Here, try this racket," he said, trying to sound easy. "I want to see if the grip is too big for your hand."

She gave the racket a provisional swing. "I can tell better on the court," she said. "I ought to be running along now. It infuriates Ella when I keep lunch waiting."

"It's nowhere near lunchtime. Wait one second—there's something I want to show you, if I can put my hand on it."

He went scavenging through the lower drawer of his desk, turning out a boy's treasury of rubbish on the carpet. "Yes, here it is."

At the instant he handed her the photograph, he called himself eight kinds of a fool. Why did he have to go and drag out his mother's picture, which had lain face downward for years under pairs of pliers, boxes of marbles and the group photograph of the tenth-grade football squad? The old creepy feeling came over him, that Lissa was a witch who had the power of sucking his heart's secrets out of him.

But the picture was between her long slim hands by this time, and he couldn't get it back without a commotion. She was looking from the photograph to Victor without knowing what to say.

It was a bride, with a tiny waist and a bustled white-satin skirt. Her gloved hands were clasped on a round nosegay of white roses and maidenhair. Under a diadem of orange blossom her eyes smiled out, and Lissa saw that they were Victor's eyes. But she was only a photograph, faded to mustard-brown. She looked infinitely old-fashioned.

"Is it—is it Mrs. Cummager?" Lissa ventured.

"It's my mother," he said harshly. . . . Stupid girl! . . . "She was more alive than that."

"Of course," Lissa said, so absently that he stared at her. Her eyes were velvet-dark and unfathomable, focused on nothing. A transparent color was coming and going in her face.

He recalled, shamefacedly, how pink she had turned that Easter morning when she bewitched him into talking about his mother and the hepaticas. Could she possibly suspect him of luring her up to kiss her again?

That was one memory Victor had been obliged to close the door on. He had taken advantage of Lissa's inexperience. It had been a low-down trick, and only a cur would try to repeat it. Could he tell her that?

Obviously not. He was in a swivet to reclaim his picture and get Lissa out of his room.

"Victor," Lissa said out of her brown study, "when your mother drove around in cars in the middle of the night—did people use to talk about her and turn up their noses at her?"

In asking this extraordinary question he saw that she was drawing comfort from an analogy between his old trouble and her own. Everything about her was pliant and trusting.

Victor had been wrong—abominably wrong—in suspecting her of angling after a cheap kiss. Asking that question was the highest compliment she could have paid him. Perhaps he had the disturbing power over her that she had over him—of sucking out secrets.

Something came to him from the black forgotten day of his mother's death. "Look, Lissa. The day my mother died, your father said the only good thing to me that anybody said. He said, 'People always gossip about a delightful woman. Don't pay any attention—just go on loving her.'"

"Daddy said that?" she cried under her breath. The brightness in her face was sweet to watch. Her voice was a dreaming silvery music.

Victor nodded. "He told me that while he was in college, before either of them married, he was in love with my mother."

They stared at each other. A miracle of coincidence had flowered between them, rooted in past and present. Their eyes mirrored it back and forth.

"I'm so thankful you told me that," Lissa said. "Thank you for showing me your mother's picture. She was darling, wasn't she?"

As he put the picture away he felt that he was a fine fellow. At no expense to himself he had performed a healing work upon young Lissa Grover.

Chapter 23

It was some time before Senator Rampole made any progress in identifying the trespassing element in Meridian. A number of men in his own organization had been tampered with. But to whom—to what—were they transferring their allegiance? The threat was faceless, and yet it was real. There was a slippage of power in the city government.

He kept hoping that the trail would lead to Anson Epps. But that hope sprang from personal bias, and he must not let it cloud his clearheadedness. He indulged himself by making inquiries about Epps, but they were a private side line.

He chatted with bankers and men at the club, and with Titus Cream at the Chamber of Commerce. He learned that no one individual could count the pies Anson had his finger in. Taken separately, they were not oversized pies. Epps owned a plumbing-supply plant. He had offices and a showroom in the Cinnamon Block, where he jobbed half a dozen lines of builders' equipment; but he had no monopoly in this field. He had bought into the *Sun-Record* and later absorbed it, and into several other unrelated businesses. He was a promoter and a middleman for anything that turned up. He had made money for his friends and trouble for his enemies. The characteristic oddity of all his connections was that the men who worked with him hesitated to admit their tie. The solid citizens of Meridian, to a man, let it be known that he was some other fellow's best friend, not theirs. So much for Epps.

On the political question, Horace picked up a valuable clue from His Honor the Mayor.

When he moved up to the Senate he had handed on the mayoralty to one Peter Wellworth. Pete cut a fine figure at banquets, and he was the idol of the school children, because he had donated an elephant to the zoo. For the rest, he was a well-diciplined nonenity who never made a decision without consulting Dan Parmiter. The Parmiter machine had won his elections for him as a matter of routine.

Now Pete made an appointment at Horace's office; and, behind a carefully closed door, he divulged his worries about the fall election. Gregg, the Democratic candidate, was making a disturbingly good campaign.

"You nervous Nelly, you!" Horace jeered good-naturedly. "What was your plurality last time? Something like eighty thousand?"

"That can melt away fast. I'm sorry we let Greeg run off with the issue of the Outer Park Belt—that's a natural."

If Pete would sit tight for a while, Horace would present him with a rousing issue—"Boot the Boodlers Out!" But the time hadn't come for disclosing that slogan. "Run on your record—Ten Years of Clean Government. We'll whip up something spectacular for the State Fair this October. Scale model of Meridian the City Beautiful, little flags and arrows pointing to the improvements during your administration. Beautiful girl on a float—crown her—kiss her—get your name in the papers—and leave it to Danny to get out the vote."

Wellworth's handsome face puckered with distress. "I wish I was sure of that. Dan's losing his grip, Senator."

Horace countered sharply, "Dan's got more grip in one finger than you or I have in two fists." He didn't like this sort of talk about old Dan. "Incidentally, Pete, is the Police Department solid?"

"There! That's what I mean." Pete leaped at the chance to unburden himself. "Time after time I make suggestions about personnel, or I drop a hint to go easy—and nothing goes through. They always give me an alibi, but there was a time when I didn't have to swallow alibis. I admit the *Sun-Record* is chasing the department right off its legs. You probably read how they got two patrolmen demoted this year for drunkenness—off duty, mind you. Damned unreasonable. But the *Sun-Record* raised a stink and got the boys demoted. So now the force feels we let 'em down. The spirit's not good, down at headquarters. The Chief don't seem to be able to deal with it."

Horace said bitterly, "I'd like to demote Jim Claggan! Who's he to break a cop for drinking?"

"That reminds me, Senator. If I want the Anti-Saloon League endorsement, I've got to come out for a bone-dry Meridian. How am I going to deal with that?"

Horace was familiar with this new genie which had come out of its bottle to confuse practical politicians. Congress was full of men who owed their election to the Anti-Saloon League. State after state was going dry. Horace had no sympathy with the Prohibition movement, but he took off his hat to its generalship. The Drys cut across party lines and elected their candidates. Their endorsement swung the churchgoing vote.

"My position on that has been consistent for years," he said. "I'm for a regulated liquor traffic. I'm for keeping the brewers and distillers in line. But I'm not for closing the corner saloon. I for one don't know how you can run a political organization on soda pop and soft-drink parlors. . . . Nor does Gregg. The Democrats can't come out for prohibition—not and keep a straight face."

"Gregg would perjure himself to hell for twenty votes," Wellworth said with partisan spite. "And as for enforcement, he'd let the blind pigs run wide-open. The whole thing gives me the shakes."

"Let me tell you something, Pete," Horace said masterfully. "Dan Parmiter and I are working up a red-hot issue for you. You keep joining lodges and kissing babies—you're doing fine. Just leave it in my hands for a while, will you? We've never let you down yet."

The mayor said he knew that.

"I'm wondering, Pete, if we'd strengthen ourselves by a shake-up in the South End Police Station."

"Things don't suit me down in that end of town," Pete admitted. "But I got a warning to keep my nose out of there."

"A warning! From whom, pray? Not from Parmiter."

"No. It came straight down from Parlor B."

"Parlor B!" Horace reacted fast enough to infuse his voice with scorn instead of amazement. A twig had crackled; the prey was approaching the blind where Horace had crouched so long. "Since when do you take your orders from Parlor B?"

"I don't take my orders from Parlor B!" Wellworth retorted in outrage. "But I have to live on my salary, Senator. You know how it is."

"I've a good mind to march straight down to Parlor B and let 'em know who's boss."

"I wouldn't do that, Senator. They'd make a monkey of you."

"The thing is, I've never been there. Could you take me?"

"Not for a farm," Wellworth said with unaffected horror.

"Well, how do I get past the door?"

"I don't eat there," Wellworth said with some stiffness. "But I understand there's no password, no doorman, no nothing. You just walk in the entrance at lunchtime, and up the stairs, and down the second-floor hall to the back. But I urge you not to go. What would you accomplish?"

"Well, maybe I'll take your advice," said Horace as he showed the mayor out of the office with every evidence of esteem.

He had never had any intention of invading Parlor B; he had been

157

fishing to find out where it was. It was in a club, a hotel, a bar—some place where men ate at noon. The field was limited. Horace had dined or speechified in all the places of public resort.

Parlor B—it wasn't at the Belvedere House. Parlor B must be in one of the older hotels or minor clubs.

This was not an inquiry he could delegate. He would look like a fool, sending out an underling to locate Parlor B for him.

He telephoned the Wayne Hotel, the McKinley House and the Deutschesverein, in each case inquiring about a room for a luncheon meeting. They were all delighted to serve him. He said he would let them know if he found he needed the room. None of them had offered him Parlor A, Parlor B or Parlor anything; they used a different nomenclature.

He stood in his office window, pulling at the tip of his nose and looking down into the warren of the financial district. Twenty stories below him, in exaggerated perspective, squatted the old Thomason mansion, caught among the banks and office buildings, and unrecognizable behind a plate-glass front. When he was a boy he had picked up his pretty cousin Corinne there time after time and escorted her to dancing school. The house was a restaurant now, much frequented by men who did not belong to clubs. Schmolck's Hofbrau—it served an excellent dollar lunch, and good draught beer. Lunch clubs met there. . . .

He invited Victor to join him for lunch the next day at Schmolck's Hofbrau. He did not mean to go up to Parlor B; he meant to see who did go up.

He arrived, intentionally, fifteen minutes ahead of Victor, to spy out the enemy country and dispose his forces. Eitel, the headwaiter, had once been the steward of the Meridian Club, and he did the honors for Senator Rampole.

Horace refused the secluded corner that Eitel offered him in the main restaurant. "I want to keep my eye on the door," he said. "My son is meeting me here for lunch, and he might miss me. I'll wait in the bar."

The big dining room made out of the Thomasons' old front and back parlors was to the right of the entrance. It still had two mantels of carved walnut and dark-veined marble. The tables were laid with heavy damask and silver. An odor of rich cookery pervaded the establishment. A dollar was a high price for a lunch, but the Hofbrau gave value for the money.

The bar, to the left of the entrance, had been Uncle Ben Thomason's study. A semiprivacy was provided by a swinging half-door of slats. A fabulous free lunch was laid out at the end of the bar, and on the inner wall, where no woman's eye could be offended by it, hung a painting of a succulent nude model lying on one hip and feeding strawberries to a kitten. It was a bar in the best tradition.

Horace, suppressing his hunter's excitement, leaned one elbow on the corner of the bar, so that he might watch the parade of heads that passed the swinging door.

He dismissed those prospects who halted in the lobby, conferred with Eitel, checked their hats and turned into the main dining room. What he watched was the heads that moved straight across his line of vision to the foot of the stairway.

A large proportion of these he screened out—nobodies, who roused no associations in his encyclopedic memory. He inferred that there must be a salesmen's luncheon upstairs, in some other room.

Three or four faces he did identify, without surprise. They were already represented by pins in his mental campaign map. A ward leader, a prosperous contractor, a police-court magistrate whom the machine recognized as a liability. The whiff of the Beast came strong to his nostrils, but the Beast had not come into view.

He realized that he was attracting notice. Two of Danny's henchmen were drinking together and eying him uncomfortably.

He turned on his geniality and greeted them by name. "Waiting for my boy to have lunch with me," he explained his presence. "The young scamp is late."

Fortunately at this moment Victor corroborated him by making his appearance. Horace hallooed him into the bar and introduced him. "I thought it was time he knew what German cooking can be like. . . . Best dark beer in town, son—better try one."

His father's eye instructed Victor that he had better want a beer. "Bring some of that good-looking cheese and pumpernickel over to the corner table," Horace said, "and we'll get a head start on our meal."

Sitting like a watchful spider in his corner, he guardedly let Victor know that he was watching the stairs. Victor lounged in his chair, made conversation, and watched too.

"Almost nobody goes up," he objected.

Almost nobody did go up. The salesmen had assembled at twelve o'clock, and the traffic had thinned.

Indicating a customer at the bar, Victor asked idly, "Isn't that your pal Terry Somebody, who wanted to get his mother into the County Infirmary?"

It was indeed. He had foregathered with Horace's two other acquaintances, and the three of them appeared discomfited by Horace's presence.

One by one they detached themselves, and straggled with exaggerated aimlessness through a door marked "Gents" at the rear of the room. They did not come back, even after an appropriate interval.

Horace uttered a large blasphemy. "How many of 'em have gone right past me and up the back stairs, while I had my eye glued to the front stairs? I've let 'em slip through my fingers, great ninny that I am. We'll have to sit them out and watch them come down."

He spoke to the bartender and asked if his luncheon could be served in the bar. For the Senator—strictly for the Senator—yes, that could be arranged. Damask and silver were laid at the corner table, and the two Rampoles gave their attention to Schmolck's excellent dollar lunch. They spun it out for an hour and a half, and their buttons were bursting by the time they had dealt with the strudel. But still nobody came down either stairs except negligibles.

"I have given my all for clean government," Victor announced at length. "Don't ask me to put one more spoonful of anything in my mouth, or I'll blow up in your face."

"Another cup of coffee?" his father besought him. "Waiter, some more coffee."

"I'll bet you they duck out through the alley," Victor said gloomily.

The Senator was considering this possibility when his luck changed. The washroom door opened, and Anson Epps put his head into the bar. This was better than Horace could have hoped; it linked his private vendetta with his public one.

The bartender greeted Epps with "The usual, sir?"

"Not today, Steve, I can't wait. Look here, Steve, if an old party with a mustache comes in asking for me, tell him he's too late—I've gone. I'll be upstairs, but don't tell him that."

He caught sight of Horace and Victor. His greeting was fairly scintillant with affability. "Well, Senator! A little off your beat, aren't you?" and he came to the table with a gladsome step. Victor rose awkwardly to his feet, overwhelmed with memories of his lost Jodie.

"I eat here every so often," Horace answered coolly. "I've been introducing Vic to the delights of hasenpfeffer."

Swinging toward Victor, Anson said benignly, "We miss your cheery face around the house." The olive glint of his eye was ambiguous; it gave no indication of how much he knew about the great rift between Victor and Jodie.

"Have you—have you had any word from Jodie, sir?" Victor stammered.

"Plenty," Anson said with cryptic cheerfulness. "She's leading her poor mother a dance, I can tell you. Last time Onie wrote, she had just prevented Jodie from eloping with the tennis professional at the hotel."

He nodded, and made his leisurely way back through the door of the Gents' Room.

Horace saw that Victor had taken a dagger between the ribs. He himself was rapt in calculation, relating all his piecemeal detective work to a pattern centering around Epps.

"Let's get out on the Esplanade and stretch our legs," he said abruptly. The ambush at the water hole was over. "Waiter, the check."

Victor's suffering was so intolerable that in self-protection he tried to take an intelligent interest in his father's long and apparently successful stalk. "I don't get it, Father. What does it all add up to? You were on the trail of something big. Then along came nobody but Mr. Epps."

"Nobody but Mr. Epps!" Horace halted, his hands in his trouser pockets, his head tipped forward, his darkling eyes fastened on Victor's face as if he were gauging a risk. "Vic, what's your estimate of Anson Epps? Is he a man you're drawn to?"

Victor was genuinely engaged and taken out of himself by the turn of the conversation; but he had difficulty in answering his father. What did he think of Mr. Epps? First and always, that he was Jodie's father. He could not see Mr. Epps except through a fire-tinged blur of Jodie, Jodie, Jodie. . . .

"Why, I don't know," be blundered among his impressions. "He's always seemed awfully pleasant around home. He and Jodie make you laugh when they're together—they roughhouse like puppies. He pretends to spank her, and that sort of thing. But there's no hard feeling— they laugh right in the middle of the spanking. She always gets her own way in the long run."

Horace did not consider his question answered; he waited.

"That Rivergrove rumpus," Victor continued, trying to oblige, "well, he was a sap to think he could carry it off. I sometimes think he doesn't quite know his way around."

The slight softening of his father's mouth was a sign that he was on the right track now. He persevered. "And I hear he's quite a rounder when he gets out on the town. Not the best husband in the world," Victor said delicately. "How does he strike *you?*"

"If I tell you, I don't want it to get back to Epps through that daughter of his."

"Small danger!" said Victor, the blood congesting his face. "Jodie has no use for me. You heard just now that she's carrying on with some shrimp of a tennis teacher."

"Have you any use for her?" Horace asked searchingly.

"I love her like hell. But if she went on her knees to me, I wouldn't take her out again." The loathsome image of the tennis teacher scorched into his soul.

Horace took a turn along the pavement, and then sat down on a bench facing the river to light his cigar. The familiar scene stirred him as it always did; it was a palimpsest of past and present, with the names of his forebears inscribed and superscribed.

The warehouses across the river danced in a checkerboard shimmer of reflected light; a trolley car lumbered through a hazy receding perspective of workmen's houses toward the bland hills of the horizon. A couple of sand barges were whistling for the Cinnamon Bridge. Behind the Plaza, Meridian's several twenty-story skyscrapers were laying fingers of afternoon shadow across the open area. The city was in a mid-August trance of quiet, and the clop of a horse's hoofs was startling.

"Anson Epps," Horace said, weighing every word, "is Mr. Brains for the boodlers' gang." And over the match he was applying to the tip of his cigar he watched his son's reaction.

"You're crazy," Victor said. "Why, Mr. Epps belongs to the Meridian Club. He lives in Rampole Place just like anybody. He'd—why, he'd pass practically anywhere. That's prejudice, Father. It isn't his fault he wasn't brought up on Adams Avenue."

Having gone so far, Horace must go farther and convince his son.

"You say he belongs to the club, and he lives on our land. Well—his methods in arriving at both those goals are what put me wise to him in the first place. Unscrupulous, underhanded methods," said Horace, not choosing to particularize. "He's as slick as a whistle, he's pretty nearly unbeatable. I've had my suspicions of him for a long time. Seeing him in Schmolck's today put the clincher on it. Parlor B, on the second floor of the Hofbrau, is his headquarters. That's where the orders go out from, and it's Epps that gives the orders."

"How do you know?"

"You can take my word for it. Giacomo's, to take a minor instance that you know about—Giacomo's is in his pocket, and he's protecting it. The police don't dare touch it."

Victor had read the muckraking magazines, he knew about the unholy alliance of underworld and government. But Mr. Epps simply did not fit his conception of a vice lord. Mr. Epps was Jodie's father, and wore very good suits.

Horace read the disbelief in Victor's face, and went on. "Oh, he'll never lay himself open to prosecution. If an officer is bribed, it will never be Epps's money that's found in his pocket. He'll never go bail for a gunman, but he'll find bail for him. He'll never hold title to a bawdy-house. It's subtler than that. Mind you, I know how Epps works, because he's worked on me. It's the application of pressure where it hurts the worst. It's making the fortunes of men who play along with Epps, and wrecking men that stand up to him."

"And I suppose Mr. Epps has confided in you?"

"Your ancestors, Vic—they pretty near created Meridian out of dust. I gave six of the toughest years of my life to getting it shipshape. I'm not going to see my work pulled down around my ears. The Epps gang is in the first phase of gaining power. It isn't too late to chase them out, and if it's the last job I tackle, I'll tackle that one."

"Well, more power to you," Victor said vaguely. He was all in favor of Meridian, but he couldn't afford to be dragged into this particular feud. Somewhere, some time, Jodie would come back to his arms—it was kismet; and when that time came, he did not want to play Montague to the Eppses' Capulets.

"Father," he said seriously, "haven't you gone off the handle for once? Aren't you building quite a card castle out of the simple fact that you saw Mr. Epps come out of a washroom? I know there's mischief on the loose, but I can't accept a man like Mr. Epps as a rascal."

"Well, son," said Horace, "wait and see." He had moved too fast in trying to alienate Victor from the Epps influence. He had very nearly uprooted the shallow growth of confidence between himself and Victor.

No matter. He felt sure that the facts, as they developed, would bear him out; and Victor would be convinced.

Chapter 24

ELLA HEDGES had plenty to engage her mind during August while she went about her housework at Number Four Rampole Place. Her dentures did not fit, and she had a habit or working them into place with her jaw; so when she went on all fours with pail and scrubbing brush she suggested a bony ruminant cow.

She had a grievance to mull over. With all this switching of summer plans, she had been done out of her vacation. When Mrs. Q got back from skylarking around Europe, Ella would let her hear about that.

Actually, if Mr. Philip had told her to clear out for August, she would have felt deprived. With no breakfast trays and teapots to carry up at odd hours, with no lingerie nightgowns to do up and organdy dresses to press, with no company dinners to cook and no telephone calls to write down, she got through her work in jig time. She gave Mr. Philip and Lissa of her best in the matter of dinners; and Mrs. Q would be pretty surprised if she could see how stylishly Ella served at table when she wasn't being pushed.

Her allegiance was to the Grover blood. She had worked as a young woman for Old Miz Grover on Adams Avenue, when the Grovers held their heads higher than anybody. To oblige her old mistress she had moved over to Mr. Philip's helter-skelter menage. The care and pampering of Mr. Philip and Lissa were a charge that Old Miz Grover had left with her.

Ella was sorry the Grover money was running out, because she didn't know where they would turn for more when it was gone; Mr. Philip was no money-maker. She felt condescension and pity for the Grovers, because she banked money every week. But there was something high-toned about being too good to earn a living.

Anyway, it was Mrs. Q's fault. Mrs. Q was like a sponge for soaking up money and having nothing to show for it. Mrs. Q was nothing but an interloper. Ella would have given her her walking papers long ago if she'd been Mr. Philip. A wife had no claim to board and keep when she fell down on her job like Mrs. Q did. " 'I'm going to raise your wages, Ella *dear,*' " Ella quoted nastily into her scrub bucket, and gave her rag a flap.

Ella often speculated on whether Mr. Philip could be as fond of his wife as he made out. Seemingly he was. "He's just like a baby," she said—working alone all day, she talked to herself a good deal—"hanging on for dear life to a dirty old stuffed flannel dog that he's used to cuddling."

But Old Miz Grover would have gone into conniption fits to see the carryings-on this past winter. Men underfoot everywhere you looked!

It tickled Ella pink to watch the change that came over the real Grovers when they got shut of Mrs. Q. They were forever talking about how they missed Queenie, and asking if a letter had come. But they were more themselves, like. They made jokes 'way over Ella's head, out of books. They didn't have to be forever playing up to Mrs. Q's baby talk.

Ella wasn't going to spoil Lissa with compliments, but she doted on the child.

When Ella cleaned the silver there was one little cream pitcher that she made a pet of. It had come down from one of the great-grandmothers. It wasn't more than five inches high, and it wasn't fancy. But it was so satiny, its lip and its handle sat so prettily, that Ella nicknamed it

Melissa. "You, Melissa! stand still now and let me wash under your chin. . . ."

All Lissa had ever lacked was spryness. And this summer she was sprier than spry.

You couldn't fool Ella—she knew that Lissa was sweet on Victor Rampole. He wasn't courting her, but he was going around with her—and Jodie Epps had better look out or she'd get left. Jodie was a flashy beauty—one of those that ripens too young and rots too young, thought Ella, who took comfort in the transcience of beauty. Miss Jodie better land him quick, thought Ella, or he'll get off the hook.

She gave her bucket a hitch, and inundated a new crescent of the floor with her circling brush. The match between Lissa and Victor Rampole was one that Old Miz Grover would have approved. A Rampole wasn't so good as a Grover—the Rampoles had an ordinary streak; they came by it honestly, from old Huck the half-breed peddler. But a Rampole was about as good as you could get these days; and to folks who didn't know the ins and outs of Meridian as Ella did, Victor was a match for any girl in town.

Philip Grover held his breath, watching the miracle of his daughter's flowering. Somehow he hadn't been prepared for Lissa's growing up and falling in love. He had always found her exquisite, but he had never thought she was everybody's dish. For years Queenie had harped ruefully on Lissa's lack of girlish spirits.

This summer her voice chimed, her feet skimmed the ground. She was a cream-white daffodil poised to take the wind of spring.

What a mercy, Philip thought, that this preoccupation of love had come to take her mind off her mother! It was right for a young girl to detach herself from the absorbing center of her family's life.

Philip took love seriously. He knew Lissa would take it seriously when her turn came.

He doubted that this was the deep love of Lissa's life. He did not even hope it.

This was dawn love. Victor would be to Lissa what Chloe Cummager had been to Philip—the initiation, the ordeal that qualifies. Losing Victor would be a minor death to Lissa—Philip remembered. But he didn't ask that his darling child should be spared the initiation.

If Queenie had been a better correspondent, he would not have been so bereft this summer. Queenie communicated on picture post cards crammed with superlatives. Ella was wrong in thinking he enjoyed his wife's absence. The long habit of sweetness had built itself into his senses and his spirit. He would not have thanked Ella for comparing

Queenie to a stuffed flannel dog, but she was right about the emotional tie. Queenie might not be everybody's treasure, but she was the treasure for him.

In his lonely bed he solaced himself with memories of their meeting. Love at first sight.

He had been an usher at Harry Stokes's wedding, and Queenie was the bride's cousin, the out-of-town bridesmaid. The girls were dressed in baby-blue taffeta and bowknots, with a rainfall of ostrich plumes across their hats. He stood opposite her in the semicircle around the altar, and stared till he brought her eyes to his. Throughout the ceremony they never broke that tranced interchange of eyes, and as the minister intoned the noble vows, Philip took them in his heart. To love and to cherish, till death us do part.

When she pulled off her white glove to take a nibble of bride's cake, the disclosure of her beautiful hand was like the loosening of the maiden zone. She was all beauty that day. Her complexion had a breath-taking luminosity. Her waist was supple and tiny beneath the feminine opulence of her corsage. Silver coquetry of voice, lucence of eye, touching ingenuousness of brow and lip . . . he brought her image back before him in the darkness.

She loved him as he loved her, that was the miracle. He married her under no illusion that she was clever. He wanted her just as she stood. He asked for the responsibility of loving and cherishing her, and praised God that she committed herself to his care.

No, Philip had no bone to pick with destiny, not even when Queenie involved herself in trouble. The only person he reproached was himself. After assuming those vows, he had given her a shabby sort of care.

He had kept her in genteel poverty—Queenie, who had had magnates at her feet. He was overcivilized, he was the last of an old breed. He had never been a money-maker; he had kept her on short commons. This empty August was a penance, and he must mend his ways.

He should have gone with her to Rivergrove. There was no such thing as changing Queenie; it was he who must change. He had never tried, except halfheartedly—he had played scarecrow in the cornfield.

Then, he must buckle down to earning a living for his family. He had inherited a first-rate practice, and he had let two thirds of it drift away from him. During this penitential month he must recover some of his lost ground.

He must prepare in another way for Queenie's return: he must break the boycott. If he bestirred himself, by the time his friends got back from their summer cottages he would be at the head of a bustling little reform movement that would overshadow Queenie's visit to the Rivergrove Casino. The name of Grover would stand for assiduity in the public interest.

This was a job he really worked at.

He began by talking to the lawyers he met in his daily round. The lawyers were slow to ignite. They were busy men. This was somebody else's crusade, not theirs. They would go so far as to make a small subscription, but as for serving on a committee—they couldn't think of it, old man.

By following likely and unlikely leads he ran down an odd assortment of sympathizers. A clergyman with a civic conscience; two social workers and a YMCA secretary; the lady president of a temperance society; a professor of sociology from the university and a couple of his graduate students. His real find was young Treadway in his own office. Theodore Roosevelt had inoculated Treadway with the itch for public service. And Treadway brought in several young lawyers of his own school of thought.

These volunteers were a bobtailed assortment to march against the walls of Jericho, but they generated the common spark that turns an organization into an organism. Working under no precedents, they set out adventurously to make their own survey and assemble their own evidence. They prowled by night through dens of depravity from which they came back with wide-eyed reports on the wickedness of Meridian after dark. Because they were nameless people they moved more easily than Horace Rampole could; and in a few weeks they had collected a surprising mass of unco-ordinated data.

Philip would have preferred to approach the Senator when the job was farther along. But after Labor Day his neighbors would come trooping back to town, and Queenie was due to land early in September. He set his heart on having a committee in being, which he could ask the good burghers of Rampole Place to join.

On a Saturday afternoon he put his memoranda in his pocket and strolled up the street to Chestnut Point.

Augustus directed him into the woods. The Senator was out inspecting the labors of the cutting crew in the forest.

Philip surprised Horace out of costume for once. The Senator had two categories of clothing—the richly tailored habiliments of a public man, and a secondary class aimed at the upstate voters. He bought these from a mail-order catalogue, with the express intention that they should not fit too well; they represented a farmer's blue-serge conception of Sunday best. He never abandoned the distinctive black felt hat which was his trade mark—it was, so to speak, a part of his head.

Today he was patrolling his domain in his electioneering clothes; and as the day was hot, he had hung his stiff collar and his necktie on a tree.

His personal majesty overrode the handicap of his costume. "Nice to see you, Philip," he said. "What's the word from your wandering wife?"

Philip exchanged civilities, and then launched into his story.

"It's heartening," the Senator said when it came his turn to speak, "to come across the self-correcting tendency of the community. It makes me believe in my fellow Americans."

This was a fine encomium, but it fell short of practicality.

"We're amateurs, sir. What we're hoping is that some of the professionals will take us over. Now for instance—where's the best point of attack? I'm a lawyer, so my instinct would be to go after Judge Rodebaugh. Would Rodebaugh be a profitable target?"

"That depends," Horace said guardedly. He was not sure yet how far he wanted to commit himself. Philip had made an astonishingly good start, but Horace had seen good starts peter out. What he wanted was to nurse the reformers along till after the fall elections. "It depends on whether Rodebaugh is one rotten apple in a barrel."

"Your opinion on that ought to be better than mine, Senator."

After all, Philip Grover was an intelligent man, and a man with a personal incentive. "I don't mind telling you in confidence," Horace decided to say, "that you and I are working on parallel lines. Rodebaugh's a weakling. I'm after the higher-ups. You follow your leads and I'll follow mine, but look behind the little men for the hand that pulls the strings. Later, we'll pool our data and get down to work."

"I'm coming around to the opinion," Philip said, "that the Drys have the right of it. So long as there's a profit to be made out of human vices you can't expect the purveyors to be too scrupulous."

Horace lighted a fresh cigar, and said quizzically, "Philip, you're one of those lucky or unlucky fellows that are put together without vices. If liquor selling were illegal, it would be no great hardship to you to go on the wagon. Well, it would to me, and it would to nine men out of ten. Look what's happened in the dry states—the rich get their liquor through the mails, and the poor go to blind tigers. I don't even call drinking a vice, unless it's immoderate. I don't say gambling is inherently vicious. To be perfectly honest with you, prostitution—well, you're never going to legislate it out of existence. I'm a realist, my boy. I confine my ambition to keeping human nature within bounds."

"Well, Senator, we both want to get rid of the rotten apples. Won't you head up the committee and lay out a campaign for us? Nobody knows more about cleaning up the town than you do."

"Not so fast," said Horace, tapping his cigar to release the shapely ash. "Last time I had an advantage I've lost now. My father was no reformer, God knows, but his machine was as tight as a drum, and in his old age he turned it over to me to play with."

"You still have a machine, unless the newspapers have grossly deceived me."

"Um, yes," Horace said noncommittally.

"Can't we set up a target and begin firing at it?"

Horace sat drumming on the knee of his blue-serge trousers. This greenhorn enthusiast was rushing him. "You and I will have to divide our energies for the time being. We're running some Progressives for Congress that will have to be broken to harness, or we won't have any organization nationally *or* locally."

"How do you break them to harness?" Philip asked with casual amusement.

"Through the purse strings," Horace answered simply. "Even getting elected dogcatcher costs money—and I don't mean dirty money either. That, Philip, in case you didn't know it, is politics, and that's job enough for me this fall."

"Well, then," said Philip, rising from his log and dusting off the ants, "you can't give us any active help."

His bluntness disturbed the Senator. "I didn't say that. I said, Give me time. If you've noticed, all the real work gets done between elections, and 1911 will be an off year. That's when we'll go after the boodlers. I can give you some tips right now that I have no time to follow up. Got a piece of paper on you?"

Philip handed him an old envelope and a pencil. Horace drew a line down the middle of it. He had come to a resolution to trust Philip Grover.

"On the left here, I'm jotting down names of men who might work with you. You're not to say I suggested them—a suggestion from me is an order, and if they disregard the order, they're rebels. And if the word got around that I'm in on this, it might spill the beans entirely."

He erased and rewrote till he had a list that satisfied him.

"On the right," he continued, "I'm giving you a few names that will bear investigating—the fellows that have stopped coming when I whistle. Some of them may get a clean bill of health. You screen them out."

"Yes, sir," said Philip, breathing fast. His fingers itched to get hold of that list.

Horace sat beating a tattoo on the envelope, weighing risks. He was putting himself in the hands of ignoramuses. But his deepest feelings were engaged.

"I have one more tip for you. I shan't even write it down, because it *must not* fall into the wrong hands. You understand, Philip, when you set up in opposition to the underworld it isn't like a tennis match, where you win or lose, and jump the net, and shake hands. Reformers run the risk of getting tarred with scandal and driven out of town."

"We realize that, sir," said Philip, who had not quite realized that. He had in fact thought of this crusade of his as an undertaking in which a good try was what counted. For half a second, till his courage rose to the Senator's challenge, he would have been thankful to be out of the whole thing. "Yes, sir," he confirmed himself, after a pause. "We do realize that." He felt he had taken an oath on his sword.

"I think I've located the headquarters of the new gang. They eat lunch in Parlor B, over Schmolck's Hofbrau. Some of them do, at any rate, and the question is who goes there and who doesn't. They don't like to be seen—they go through the men's washroom off the bar, and up the back stairs. There may be an alley entrance as well. I can't be caught crouching behind a garbage can, and I haven't taken anyone into my confidence till this minute. There's an assignment for some young chap on your committee. . . . Cops and robbers, eh?"

"Parlor B!" Philip exclaimed. "Why, with my own ears I heard that shyster Lippold say to Rodebaugh in the corridor, 'See you in Parlor B about one o'clock.'"

Horace and Philip exchanged a look of delight. Their findings were beginning to dovetail. Philip was on fire to call a meeting of his committee. He put the envelope away with precaution and reverence.

"One last tip," Horace said. "And I wouldn't want this to reach even your committee. When Anson Epps isn't eating lunch at the club, you're likely to find him eating in Parlor B."

Philip's response was all Horace could have wished. Philip had his own grounds for hating Anson Epps.

"Well, there's your long-range target," Horace said. "You can see now why we can't begin taking pot shots at the little fellows. This isn't a skirmish, it's a campaign."

Chapter 25

Two Queenies were sitting inside one skin in the green-plush Pullman section as the train clacketed across the Algonquin countryside.

The exterior Queenie could not help being gratified by the astounded backward looks she drew from commercial travelers on their way to the diner. It wasn't often they had a look at cosmopolitan beauty, fresh from the modistes and couturiers of Paris.

She was wearing a black tailleur, coquettish in its severity; a hand-made blouse that was a miracle of needlework; shoes with long, pointed toes; and her peach-basket hat—so new, so arresting in contrast to the outmoded cart wheel. She had learned tricks of make-up too subtle to be detected. She wafted perfume on the air. Her white suède gloves were still folded in tissue paper on the seat beside her; she would put them on at the last minute. She had ordered a dozen pairs.

Lissa and Philip must be waiting on the station platform by now. At the thought of meeting them she gave a spontaneous smile of delight.

The interior Queenie was an orphan child, on her way back to the orphanage after a dazzling party with a birthday cake and toy balloons. A child who had perhaps been naughty in going to the party at all, and a very little bit naughty while she was there, but who would know for the rest of her life that happiness existed.

"Clackety-home-again, clackety-home-again," the wheels reiterated idiotically, on purpose to taunt her. The landscape was veiled in autumnal wood smoke. Fields rough with stubble or raw from the plowshare undulated tediously to the horizon. The telegraph poles pivoted past the windows with hypnotizing regularity. Villages whirled by, with the train gates down and farm wagons waiting at the crossings.

It was not an arresting countryside. It depended on a wooded ridge, a willowy creek bottom, a gravel cut in a hillside, for all the drama it had to offer. Nothing ivy-grown, nothing crumbling under the weight of centuries . . . Queenie closed her eyes. How many times had she made this westward trip? Dozens and dozens of times. It had lost all power over her imagination.

The porter brushed her off and carried her suitcases with their foreign labels to the vestibule. "Land sakes," he said as he accepted her quarter, "I 'most forgot your flowers."

"Don't bother," Queenie said—but so faintly that he did not hear her. In a moment he had set the florist's box on the seat beside her.

Her violets—she closed her eyes again. Strictly speaking, she would do better to abandon them on the train—they would be hard to explain. On the other hand, she had been splendidly loyal to Philip; she had rushed away from New York for the very purpose of not seeing Rudy again. And she was immensely sorry for Rudy. . . .

She opened the box, and the violet fragrance mounted to her nostrils. The unsigned card was still in its envelope. "Forgive us our trespasses," it read. The very phrasing, rightly understood, was testimony to Queenie's womanly goodness.

The problem of Rudy had not arisen till she was homeward bound. All summer, among the continental men whom Maddy presented to her, she had kept her head. She had fended them off with just the right blend of sophistication and regret. Her technique had come to her out of some pre-existence when she had curtsied in royal courts, and broken hearts on battlements beneath the moon.

Poor Rudy, on the boat coming back, was another matter.

Maddy had taken a dislike to him from the moment he made their acquaintance at a ship's concert. "He is a bad one," Maddy had said. "More zan likely he is a cardsharper or an international jewel thief. Keep a sharp eye on your pearls, pet."

That was dense and spiteful of Maddy. Queenie knew all about Rudy. She should, after his hour-long outpourings in the deserted writing room or on the boat deck. He was destroying himself with drink and self-pity, but he was no criminal. Maddy would have been surprised to learn that Queenie was persuading Rudy to go back to his wife.

Rudy was half Polish and half American. His mother had died of the transplantation to America; his father had put Rudy into the wholesale grain business, when all he wanted was to play the piano. Rudy had married, and made his wife so unhappy that she had become a morphine addict. Rudy's father had lost patience with him and told him to clear out.

He had roamed Europe for two years, always intending to buckle down to his music, always dogged by a fatality that blocked his intention. He told Queenie in his extravagant way, "We carry our sentence of damnation stamped behind our eyeballs."

Whatever Maddy thought, Rudy did not even try to make love to Queenie during their long disappearances. She would not have gone with him a second time if he had. Queenie had a definite code. She would dangle any man on the edge of a kiss, but at the last spilt second she would dodge and say something startlingly noble that stopped him in his tracks. It was a little game at which Queenie was a past mistress, and if she had ever lost a round, she would have renounced the game.

On the last night of the voyage Rudy had taken her up to the boat deck. There, in the very midst of one of his long lamentations, he suddenly enfolded her in a frightening embrace. He kissed her mouth and her shoulders while she struggled with him in horror. Finally she fought free. "Shame on you!" she gasped. "It isn't even as if you had the excuse of being in love with me."

His only answer, with his hag-ridden eyes burning through the darkness between them, was "There's a great deal about love that you don't understand, Queenie. Sooner or later you'll have to learn."

She didn't sleep that night. She was unbearably roused. She felt scorched by her own shame—she had been desecrated; and yet those famished kisses were nothing a woman could wipe out of her memory. They raised the issue of whether Queenie did know all there was to know about love. Philip had never kissed her so disturbingly.

She and Maddy had meant to spend one night at the Plaza on their way home. Rudy knew this. She dared not be there to receive him if he called. This must stop. She was not a woman of iron. She could not answer for herself if Rudy got out of hand again.

In a rush and scramble she got herself aboard the night train for Meridian. She told Maddy she would not wait another day to see Philip and Lissa.

The porter brought her Rudy's violets after the train was under way. "Forgive us our trespasses"—that told the whole story. It was a tribute from a lost soul to a bright spirit beyond his reach.

One thing Queenie was sure of: none of those dowdy prudes in Rampole Place had ever had such a temptation to resist. She had come through it well. She would remember the experience for the rest of her life.

"Passengers for Meridian, out this way!" She laid down the violets, and stood up.

Then, across the river, she caught sight of the spindly scaffoldings of Rivergrove, the Ferris wheel, the giant swings, the roller coaster, the casino spick-and-span under its striped awnings. Rivergrove brought an acrid taste into her mouth. In a spirit of defiance she looked at herself in the strip of mirror between the windows, while she pinned Rudy's violets at her waist.

She came slowly down the platform, her head a little bent. Except for Philip and Lissa she would have been thankful never to set foot in Meridian again. In Meridian she was despised for the very qualities that made her welcome in a wider world.

The passers-by were still paying her the tribute of a stare. A woman of extreme beauty and elegance, lost in reverie, with violets at her belt. She was not Anna Karenina, but she was a strayed denizen of Anna's world.

In another moment she was folded in the tepid sweetness of a husbandly embrace.

She knew how glad they were to see her. She knew Philip would give her a real kissing when they were alone. All the same, her welcome was somewhat of a letdown. She might as well have been Lucy Breen getting back from her summer cottage on the lake.

"I'll bring the car around to the main entrance," Philip said.

"Mind you don't lose us in the crowd," she said archly, knowing she was nothing that could be overlooked in any crowd.

Surely Philip might have made some gallant reply. Instead he said, "Don't worry. I'd have to be blind before I could lose track of *that hat*." And he laughed.

Philip considered her hat funny.

She made excuses for him. It was only because his eye was not trained to Parisian chic. But the last remaining carbonation went out of her cup of pleasure. She lost the vision of herself as Anna Karenina. The Meridian terminal was not the Nevsky Prospekt, and Philip's roadster was not a troika. Philip enforced his own view upon her: she was a middle-aged wife got up like a side-show freak. She was back at home now, sure enough.

She took up her cross. While they drove through the wholesale district, across the Plaza with its fringe of skyscrapers, and out the deathly familiarity of Adams Avenue, she rattled back gay answers to the family questions.

She would have been flustered by a question about her violets, but she was provoked by the absence of such a question. Philip and Lissa disregarded the violets, which they appeared to consider a part of the routine of foreign travel, like labels on one's luggage.

All Europe underwent a deflation at their hands. They tried to be interested; but she had no words for conveying the savor of Europe to the untraveled. Better not to talk about it.

"Tell me about the inn!" she cried. "How many sailing races did you win, Phil-ip? You don't look so tanned as usual. Who did old Mr. Quisenberry find to dance with in my absence?"

Philip and Lissa exchanged a look of delighted conspiracy. Their turn had come now; they were waiting to talk about the dear old Endicott Inn.

"Search me," Philip said with elaborate nonchalance. "We didn't go east at all. We passed an agreeable August under our own vine and fig tree."

"What do you mean? Don't tease me."

"Melissa pointed out that we had a summer resort at our own doorstep. We had a fine time, didn't we, Meliss? If we'd had you with us, we'd have been perfectly happy."

Queenie sat confounded. The car was embarked now on the endless stretch of second-rate shops that ran to the Doochee Bridge. Queenie looked at them with loathing.

Her silence was so strained that Philip and Lissa took their turn at being deflated.

Queenie said finally, "I suppose you did it to save money." She let all her distaste for penny pinching show in her voice.

"It did save money," Philip said cheerfully. "Without pain."

"Why didn't you put up a billboard on the front lawn?" Queenie asked bitterly. " 'If You See Me Without Shoes, It Is Because My Wife Is Gadding Around Europe At My Expense.' . . . A nice situation you've put me in, Philip! The spoiled, extravagant wife, the downtrodden husband. You've given Rampole Place one more rope to hang me by."

All at once, now it was too late, Philip saw that that was exactly what the neighbors would say.

"It has been perfectly lovely at home," Lissa put in. "Ella took beautiful care of us."

"Ella! You didn't give Ella any vacation?"

"Well, she didn't raise any objection."

"But you know, Philip—you know as well as I do—that the only way I've kept Ella all these years is by giving her a month's vacation in the summer."

"She'll have to take her vacation later," Philip said with his nearest approach to sulkiness. He was bewildered, he was ashamed, by this squabbling that had broken out the very minute Queenie got back to town. After all, he had given up his vacation on her account. If he had saved money, it was so that he need not stint Queenie. The committee to which he had given so much energy was for Queenie's benefit. She was misusing his best gifts and putting him in the wrong.

"Let's not talk about it," Queenie said, while Philip was saying, "I may have been stupid, but my intentions were good."

"Here we are," Queenie cried. "How pretty the house looks! . . . How are you, Ella dear? I hear you've been taking wonderful care of the family while I was away. I've brought you a little present from Paris."

Philip carried in the bags. There was unwrapping of gifts, display of bargains in gloves and French lingerie. They made merry together around the lunch table.

But when Philip had gone to the office, Queenie found herself alarmingly tired. It was not physical fatigue; it was the fatigue of facing the empty future.

Through the windows she followed the sociable stir of Rampole Place, from which she was excluded. Betty Coleman and Dorothy Whitty set out in a car with their golf clubs. Lucy Breen and Ethel Wyndham strolled side by side up the Dysarts' front walk with their workbags.

None of these women would be dropping in to exclaim over her lingerie and sniff her French perfumes. In Rampole Place there was not one soul who wished her well. Her uphill destiny was to keep on creating an impression of membership in the human race.

She could escape into a nap. She could lie down for an hour and drift off to sleep over an analysis of Rudy's character and intentions. She could cuddle down in her pink flannel bathrobe against the coldheartedness of Rampole Place and let time pass over her head.

She went to the dressing-room closet where her bathrobe hung.

Chapter 26

IF IT HADN'T been the bathrobe it would have been something else. So Queenie thought, during the years when she looked back. Some inconsequential thing sets off the eruption of the volcano, and one loses one's power of choice. In this case it was the bathrobe.

She never got to the point of putting it on. While it still hung limp on its hanger, her eye fastened on the front breadth.

Down the front ran a cottony web of moth tracks and a peppering of visible holes.

Every housewife in Meridian waged unremitting war against moths, with a good half of the victories going to the enemy. She and Ella had not been recreant; they had done all that two women with whisk brooms could do, and no single woolen object had been admitted into the new house without a clean bill of health.

"Ella!" she shrieked, at a pitch that brought Ella hotfoot from the kitchen. "Ella! The moths have got into my closet!"

"Good grief!" said Ella in her dry-gravel voice. "The way you yelled I thought the house was afire." She munched her lips together. "It should have been hung away in the cedar closet when you took it off." But this, she made plain, was no responsibility of hers.

"Well, why didn't you put it away then?" Queenie demanded, half frantic. "You've just made work for yourself, because now every one of my woolen dresses will have to be brushed and aired, and all Mr. Philip's winter suits."

Ella fired right back, in that insolent way of hers, "The woolens were all put away, excepting this bathrobe. You wore it till the very day you left. You were wearing it that time you had the big crying spell. You stuck it back in your own cupboard, I suppose. If you wanted me to take care of it, why didn't you say so?"

Her manner was beyond endurance. Queenie had made concessions, she had overlooked, she had appeased, to keep Ella from leaving. She had had about enough of Ella.

Nevertheless, Ella did the work of three women. So Queenie placated her. "I hadn't time to think of everything. I left for Europe on twenty-four hours' notice."

"And when had I any time to think of things? 'Ella dear, pack us up for the Endicott Inn.' . . . Sneakers, bathing suits, smelly old oil-skins. . . . 'Ella dear, tear the trunks apart and pack me up for Europe. Press all my folderols and wash out my white gloves.' . . . 'Ella, we've changed our minds, we're staying home for the summer.' . . . And on top of that—" the note of hysteria came into Ella's voice—"I worked like a horse, right through the heat of the summer, when I'd been counting on a month's vacation."

"I know, Ella. Mr. Philip and Lissa upset everything this summer. I don't know what possessed them."

"They stayed home—" Ella gestured toward the fripperies strewn across the bed—"so's they could save money for you to sling around." Total dislike for Queenie glared through Ella's glasses. A notice to quit was framing itself on her lips.

Not even Philip could expect Queenie to put up with this treatment. She opened her mouth to give Ella a week's notice.

Ella got her word in first. "I've been waiting for you to get home, Miz Grover, to ask you to look for somebody else. I have money saved, and my daughter's been at me to take life easier. You've never been satisfied with me. You can hunt up somebody to suit your swell ideas."

The words had been spoken before—in fact, they had been spoken once a year. But always under forms of civility. This time Ella had gone too far.

"Perhaps that will be just as well, Ella. I thought you were happy in your work—I thought you liked us. If you don't, you might as well look for another place."

"I'll stay out my week," Ella said.

"I'd rather you went right now," Queenie said glacially.

Ella went out, and closed the door behind her.

Queenie stood in the middle of her bedroom floor, her hands clasped in front of her. If the weight of one feather were laid on her, she would fly to pieces.

A few months ago she would have flung herself face down on the bed and cried till Philip came home from the office; then the skies would have cleared, Ella would have withdrawn her notice, the picnic of life would have got back into its stride.

But in going to Europe, Queenie had passed through a door that had swung shut behind her. She had shut herself away from warmth and protection. Everything was different, everything was threatening. She couldn't afford the self-indulgence of a good cry. She would be risking too much.

For one thing, she would be risking her beauty, which was all she had. When she cried she looked bloated and debauched, she looked every day of forty years old. Formerly, before she passed through that door, she had counted on Philip's fathomless devotion to overlook her collapses. Nothing had happened to his devotion—surely nothing had happened to it. But this morning he had laughed at her hat and belittled her trip to Europe; and during the summer he had put her in a false position with her neighbors.

She had always had the power to change her mood—it was her form of courage.

I must get right out of this house, she thought. I might go down to Aunt Caroline's and take her her present.

But Aunt Caroline was a morose old lady. One didn't go to see Aunt Caroline in any expectation of being cheered up.

Who else was there? In all Meridian, who was there that loved Queenie as she deserved to be loved?

She went over to the bay window and stood playing with the tassel of the shade. Rampole Place lay dead under the afternoon sun; there was no help in Rampole Place.

A town car turned into the oval and discharged Onie Epps at her own doorstep.

Onie must have been to the beauty parlor; her head was as firmly ornate as a Grinling Gibbons wood carving. Her chauffeur, laden with dress boxes, followed her up the steps. Onie dawdled. She nipped off dead geraniums from the urns. Onie had time on her hands.

"Well, why not?" Queenie said aloud.

She climbed back into her Paris clothes, wrestling with the crocheted loops and buttons down the back of her blouse. She brought back her prettiness by recourse to her little pots and bottles. She did a first-rate job on herself. She rather hoped some of her ill-disposed neighbors would observe her transit down her own front walk.

She found Onie in the High-Renaissance sun parlor drinking hot chocolate with whipped cream.

The call was a satisfactory one. Queenie's black mood blew away on the wind of chitchat. Onie showed the most generous admiration for Queenie's new costume, and wanted to hear every word about Europe.

After Queenie had talked herself out on that theme, she opened the subjects most on her mind: "What do you do about moths, Onie?" and "How do you go about getting a satisfactory maid, Onie?"

Onie couldn't be expected to solve either of these age-old riddles, but she had wrestled with them both. Lowering her voice, she told Queenie exactly how mad she was at that Withers of hers, who considered himself too good to turn the ice-cream freezer.

Queenie was on her third cup of hot chocolate when Anson Epps got home from the office. He could be heard in the front hall asking questions of Withers.

"Goodness, it's dinnertime. I must fly."

"It isn't but five o'clock," Onie contradicted her hospitably. "Ance! come out to the sun parlor and say hello. Here's somebody you like, just back from Europe."

"Who's that, ducky?" he inquired from the archway. His eye lighted on Queenie, and his eyebrows paid tribute to her. He, at any rate, did not think her peach-basket hat was funny.

"Well, if it isn't our Queenie!" He came forward to take both her hands. His eyes gave an ice-green flicker.

Queenie had not lived thirty-eight years in a man's world—she had not fended off the amorous males of Europe—without being able to pick up a signal. She had no idea she had received and filed a communication, but she began to feel very much at ease. Anson's eye had said to her, "You and I have things to talk over, Queenie. But not now. Hold everything till later. Watch me be a family man."

Even before he released her hands he was talking across her to Onie. Almost as if she weren't in the room. It was an odd conversation.

"Where's that young hellion gone off to? Withers doesn't know."

The young hellion—that couldn't be Tommy. Tommy took after his mother in never making headlines, good or bad. The young hellion was Jodie.

"She's out with Victor Rampole. She hadn't been home twenty minutes before he was lallygagging on the doorstep." Jodie had stayed east after her mother came home, to pay a visit; she was just off the train that morning.

Queenie listened with an eagerness she tried to mask. She had learned at luncheon something the Eppses did not seem to know—that her Lissa was giving Jodie Epps a run for her money. She caught a supercilious little smile on her lips, and hastily removed it.

"Made up her mind yet?" he asked his wife. "I don't know how much longer they'll hold a place for her."

"Now relax, Ance. We can't settle anything before evening. And I warn you, Anson Epps, if you put one single ounce of pressure on Jodie, either for or against, I'll walk right out of this house for keeps." She spoke with uncommon spirit.

"Yes, ma'am," he answered with a mocking docility.

"You are a thousand times smarter than I am, Anson," she persisted, "but if there's one thing I do understand, it's sweethearting. If Papa and Mama had taken any notice of our spats when we were courting, I'd have been so mortified I'd have jumped right off the town bridge."

Queenie sat trying to put two and two together. They couldn't be expecting Victor Rampole to *marry* Jodie between now and dinnertime. What on earth were they talking about? All Queenie could say was, they were counting their chickens before they were hatched.

"They're having it out," Onie continued, "about that tennis teacher. Victor was bellowing. I could hear him all the way upstairs."

"Excellent!" said Anson, jingling the coins in his trousers pocket.

"Excellent?—it's perfectly horrible! It was all smoke and no fire, but it's the kind of a story you don't like to have get around. I can't imagine how it got to his ears."

"I told him myself. On purpose."

"Anson, you are outrageous. I don't know what to do about you."

"I thought I'd slip an extra ace into her pocket."

"Sometimes I wonder why I ever married you," she said helplessly.

He chucked her blithely under the chin. "You would marry me," he twitted her, Darby to Joan. "I never was any different, even when I was in high school. I guess you're stuck with me. . . . But here we are, neglecting our guest. This is all Greek to you, I suppose, Queenie? You'll have to excuse us. It's a question of sending Jodie away to boarding school."

"For pity's sake!"

"I'm glad you came over. You are the only member of your family that I have any use for. I'm a little put out with your husband."

"Why, Ance! . . . Don't pay any attention to him, Queenie."

Queenie popped out without thinking, "I'm a little put out with him myself. What has he done to you?"

"He's got himself a committee to clear up the bad smell you and I left behind us at Rivergrove." His eyes drove little probes into her.

Queenie barely listened. She was feeling what Peter felt when the cock crowed thrice; she had betrayed her master. "I'm a little put out with him myself"—trifling words, spoken lightly by trifling wives. All her pain came back upon her. What had gone wrong? What had happened to their deep security?

"Oh, committees," she said impatiently. "I don't know one committee from another."

She must get home to Philip. She must shore up the ominous breach between them. She rose, and drew on her white gloves.

"I'll walk you home across the lawn," Anson offered.

"What's all this about your being annoyed at your husband, Queenie?" he asked her as soon as they were outside the house. He had come away with her on purpose to ask her.

"That was a ridiculous thing for me to say. Philip never hurt me in his whole life—not intentionally."

" 'Each man kills the thing he loves,' " Anson quoted negligently, for her to pick up or not as she chose.

Her eyes darkened in a woeful stare. "Don't even say things like that!" she cried. "All Philip did was . . ." But she could hardly tell Anson Epps the series of troubles Philip had launched by staying home from the seashore.

They were picking their way through Onie's new-planted border of red salvias toward a convenient gap in Onie's new-planted hedge. Anson was holding a branch out of the way of Queenie's Paris hat. He stopped, branch in hand, to look down at her. "You must be very fond of your husband," he said. "Nothing else would have held you in Rampole Place. When you went off this summer I made a bet with myself that you'd gone for keeps."

"Anson Epps, don't you dare to say such a thing!" Great forces churned Queenie round and over: her desperate love for Philip; her rancor against Rampole Place; her shame that this stranger should allude to the boycott. "I belong right here. I belong with Philip."

"That's what I said," Anson answered her without taking cognizance of her distress. "I said you must love your husband a great deal. And he wouldn't hurt you for the world—not intentionally. All he's done is starve you to death. Because it's obvious—" his faint smile appeared— "that you don't belong here any more than I do. Now don't get up on your high horse—that's a compliment. I consider Rampole Place completely smug and limited and self-righteous. I've taken it on, and naturally I've got to lick it. But you—why should you wear your heart out trying to stand up to a little clique of has-beens?"

"Because this is where Philip and Lissa live."

"You're a darling! I take off my hat to you. But give me leave to be just a little sad about you. I've known women like you, Queenie, and

I've seen how they bloomed when they got transplanted into the right soil. Why, even at Rivergrove you were a different being. You were gay, you were irresistible. You were yourself."

Through the turbulence of her feelings Queenie could not help warming to appreciation like this. She had had little enough of it.

"Europe was the same way," she admitted. The mention of Europe brought little bells into her voice.

"You don't need to tell me. You must have driven the men wild."

"It was quite fun," she said, dimpling. In her memory, as in reduplicating mirrors, a long perspective of men receded into infinity, men who had found her irresistible.

"You tell Philip Grover, from me, that he's a lucky devil," Anson said.

Queenie turned her head to follow Anson's eye, and saw that Philip was home. He was coming along the driveway from the garage; he was looking straight ahead of him, and the muscles of his jaw were working.

How tiresome! The malign destiny that ruled this day had decreed that Philip should find her in a situation open to misinterpretation. She must begin by justifying herself, when all she wanted was to hurl herself into his arms.

Anson held open the gap in the bushes for her and turned back toward his own house. "Philip!" she cried, hurrying toward him in her pointed French shoes and her peach-basket hat. Her face was bright with tenderest love.

Chapter 27

PHILIP was offish, no doubt about that. He gave her a constricted smile. They went in together through the side entrance.

He went into the coatroom to wash up, and she preceded him into the library. What fun it would be—what a refreshment—to make a good rousing scene and then flush away the bitterness in a cascade of happy tears on his shoulder!

But that door had closed behind her. She must be self-controlled.

"Darling," she said, the moment he came into the room, "I've been waiting all day to tell you how much I appreciated your staying at home this summer. It would have been a wonderful idea—" then she remembered about Ella, and she could not resist adding, "if only it hadn't gone wrong."

That sounded ungracious. Before he could accept it as an apology she would have to tell him about Ella, about the moths—yes, about poor Rudy and the violets and "Forgive us our trespasses." Not about what Anson had said in the shrubbery—that was inadmissible, even to Queenie herself.

"Before we go into that," he said, "there's another point I'd like to clear up with you." He picked up the paper knife from the desk and walked about the room.

She knew that manner of his. It came of his being a lawyer. He was measuring out words before he delivered them, like an apothecary measuring out drugs. "Will you please," he said, "keep Anson Epps off my property?"

"Why, Phil-ip!" She sat looking at him blankly. Could he possibly have heard those impertinences of Anson's? If he had, he must know that she had taken a very proper wifely tone. But it might have been even more loyal of her to cut Anson short before he said quite so much.

He couldn't have overheard. The tableau itself was enough to account for his crossness—the arch of shrubbery, and the long grave colloquy.

"Philip, there's no reason for you to be annoyed with Anson. I ran over to see Onie and tell her about my trip. Anson walked me home. We were only discussing——" She checked herself. "I was telling him how happy I was to be back at home with you and Lissa."

Her own ear told her that the flaw, the dissonance had come into her voice. She was not cut out for a prevaricator.

"I have never protested against your standing around in the shrubbery," Philip said. "I'm telling you that on account of a . . . business situation which I'm not at liberty to go into, Anson Epps is one man you must not be seen with. If you are, my good faith will be called into question."

"Now, darling, that's prejudice. You mustn't be Adams-Avenue. The Eppses treat me kindly and pleasantly, which is more than anybody else does. Do you want me to sit alone at home till I go stark staring mad? I'm—I'm frightened, Philip."

A real, living look flashed back into his face. "I know, darling. I wouldn't ask you to stay in solitary confinement indefinitely. But I do wish you could have had patience for a few days. All the time you've been gone, I've been working to break down the—the fence that's been built up around you. I've taken a public position against that discreditable affair at Rivergrove, and in doing that I've had to align myself against Epps."

"Oho! Your committee."

"How did you hear about my committee?" he asked, sharp and startled.

"Why, Anson was complaining about it."

The current of sympathy broke between them. Philip stopped thinking about Queenie at all, he was so agitated about his committee. "There must have been a leak," he said. "There was supposed to be the most absolute secrecy."

"I don't see what good all this committeeing is going to do me."

"You were the victim of an attack on the decencies——"

"Darling! A little fun at an amusement park—and it gets to be an attack on the decencies. You sound as if Anson Epps were getting up a monstrous great conspiracy."

"I didn't mean to sound that way," he cut her off, suddenly taciturn. "I should simply have asked you to keep clear of the Eppses. It never occurred to me that on your very first day at home you'd dress up like a plush horse and go calling on Onie Epps."

"The very first day at home!" she repeated. "It happens to have been one of the most ghastly days of my whole life. I had to go somewhere."

"What all went wrong?" he asked—too unconcerned, too husbandly. The dam of her afflictions broke. She poured out the sequence of calamity, beginning with the moths in the bathrobe and ending with Ella's giving notice.

"But she gives notice every few months, dear."

"This time," Queenie said in a shaking voice, "I'm not even trying to keep her. I've lost heart for coaxing her. I don't want her anywhere around me. She hates me, Philip."

"Well, I wish I'd given her her vacation," he said ruefully. "We'll have to get somebody else."

"All right. You go out and find an iron woman who will run twenty-four hours a day on a quart of kerosene. I can't."

"We'll find somebody," he soothed her with masculine obtuseness.

She leaned her head against the black-leather chair, and her tears began to stream down. "We won't, we won't," she kept repeating.

"And why not?"

"I've lost heart, I tell you. I'm tired of holding this household together. I'm tired of Meridian. Nothing holds me here except you—and even you aren't the same as you were. It's been ghastly, coming back."

"I was afraid of this," he said. "I've had nightmares about this. I haven't much to offer you."

She couldn't contradict him wholeheartedly. The best she could do was to say, "What you do give me is p-perfectly wonderful. Oh, if we all three of us go away together, we could be so happy! We're buried alive. We're missing all the experiences that make life worth living."

The muscles around his mouth grew taut and bleak, so that he did not look like the Philip she loved. She had violated his fundamental loyalty to Adams-Avenue.

"It would hardly be practical," he said in that infuriatingly repressed way of his, "for the three of us to spend our lives making the grand tour of Europe."

"Don't twist what I say!" she cried. "Did I mention Europe? I'm talking about the spark of life. Change. Stimulation. Getting out of our rut."

He took two complete turns up and down the room, fiddling with his paper knife, measuring out his words. "I realize, Queenie, that you're dependent on having men make love to you. Now, now—" he held up his hand to silence her furious protest—"I didn't say you made love to them. But I thought you got your dosage at Maddy Thies's."

She was on her feet, blazing with anger. "If you knew—if you knew!— what I've gone through keeping men from making love to me. Because our love was so sacred. I've told them that, time after time, and I believed it. And this is the thanks I get! This cynicism. These insults. I don't seem to know you, Philip. You're not the man I thought I was married to."

"I'm the same man I always was," he said with a twist of the lips that was meant for a smile. "The man who's loved you from the minute he saw you. But there seems to be a limit to the amount of pain I can take without showing it. I've given you what I had to give, Queenie, but you make it plain that it hasn't been what you wanted."

Anson Epps's words came back into her mind: "All he's done is starve you to death." She said, "If I had even a kitten that I loved, I'd see that it got something to eat."

She was hurting him dreadfully. His color had gone gray, and he seemed to be physically flinching.

A sense of power, utterly new, swept over Queenie. For the first time she had the ascendancy over Philip. His godlike self-control was breaking. She longed almost irresistibly to throw herself into his arms and make peace.

But not on his terms. That would be to throw away the battle at the point of a breath-taking victory.

"All we'd have to do," she said, "would be to move away from Meridian and turn over a new leaf. We could move to New York. You'd love it, once you got out of your rut."

"You ask me to live in New York?" he asked slowly, as if she had uttered an obscenity.

On this day of doom she had twice spoken words that could never be unsaid. She had told Ella to look for another place. She had asked Philip to move to New York.

"Moving me to New York," he said, "would be like trying to transplant a tree in a crack in the pavement. I'll meet you halfway, Queenie, or three quarters of the way, but I can't go the whole way. I wouldn't be much good to you in New York. I'd be the same old scarecrow I am in Meridian."

She crumpled down in the corner of the sofa, staring at the pattern of the rug. She had made her effort, she had failed. The effort was a folly never to be retrieved. Bound hand and foot by love, she was a captive in the enemy's country. Meridian till the end of time; Rampole Place and its slights; a procession of inferior maids through her house, with moths in the carpets and cobwebs in the corners; endless niggling over money; self-conscious stiffness with Maddy's young men—and Anson Epps grimacing at her through the hedge, Anson Epps who understood her too well.

She fought back her tears. If she once abandoned herself to crying, there was no reason why she should ever stop.

"Queenie," Philip said, pausing in his endless prowl through the room, "who gave you those violets you were wearing this morning?"

Her head came up sharply in a kind of terror. "Why, nobody particular," she stammered. "A man from the boat. What made you bring that up?"

"You're under some new influence. I can't get through to you."

"I haven't noticed you trying to get through to me. It's you who's changed, Philip. While I was away you decided I was an expense to you and a disgrace to you. You even got up committees about me."

He did not reply. "Didn't you?" she demanded.

"Have you fallen in love with some other man?"

"That is unforgivable. I rushed home from New York a day ahead of time, on purpose to avoid him."

"Thank you for that. But you kept his violets."

A blush engulfed Queenie's whole body. The violets were sitting at this moment in a specially choice crystal goblet on her dressing table.

"Philip, you're twisting a trifle into a horrible accusation."

All he did was stand and watch that fathomless recurring blush of hers. "Let me tell you about it," she said desperately, and she stumbled through the story of Rudy on the boat. It came out jumbled and unconvincing. "I *didn't* lead him on," she cried. "I can see it sounds as if I did—but you ask Maddy Thies."

"No, Queenie," he said, tired and gentle. "It sounds as if you were being a good girl. But even that man—that spineless outcast—gave you something I can't give you."

He laid down his paper knife at last. He walked over to the window and stood looking out across the lawn, his hands resting on the window frame.

"What it comes down to," he said, "is that you don't belong here, and I don't belong anywhere else. I love you too much, Queenie, to want to be your jailer."

"Philip, I'd die without you."

"No," he said reflectively. "No, you wouldn't die. You'd miss some things about me, but you'd make a new life for yourself, and I have no right to hold you back."

"Philip, have you gone mad? What's going on in your mind?"

"What you've said, Queenie. All that's in my mind is what you've put into it."

"Are you suggesting that we—that we b-break up?"

"I'm suggesting that you leave Meridian for a few months. Go to New York, go back to Europe. Get this out of your system. Perhaps you'll find you never want to come back. It will have to be your decision."

If he had come to her, if he had touched her, she would have melted into a storm of tears; she would have groveled at his feet. She would have met him on his terms.

"I'll send you half of all the income that comes in," he went on. "You'll have to make it do."

"Oh, money!" she cried scorchingly. She could not make herself go to this stranger.

After two minutes of pregnant silence Philip turned and walked out of the room.

Chapter 28

IT WAS THE middle of the morning, but Victor was still sleeping like the dead. Katie simply had to ask his advice, so she went into his room and gently twitched at his pillow.

Victor came back to consciousness with the agony of a man resuscitated after drowning. Jodie Epps had been back in town for twenty-four hours, and this sleep of his was a respite between one bout of rack and thumbscrew and the next.

Ever since he heard from Anson Epps about Jodie's tennis instructor he had been preparing the grilling he was going to give her.

But as for giving him any satisfaction! She was as hard to land a blow on as a mosquito.

Why, yes, she'd seen a lot of Cliff. She began being nice to him because people treated him as if he were one of the lower animals.

What was all this about an elopement? Victor demanded.

Jodie went off into spirals of airy laughter. "We thought the old biddies on the veranda needed stirring up" was all she would say.

"Did you let him think you were serious?"

"I'm never serious."

"You were serious enough, out at the Cinnamon Gorge."

But Jodie seemed to have forgotten all about the Cinnamon Gorge. "Did you let him kiss you?"

There was an interplay of naughty dimples across Jodie's cheeks.

He threatened her, he thundered at her. He tried to force a confession out of her, or else a firm protestation of innocence.

"Wow-wow-wow-wow," Jodie gave him back, with an irreverent imitation of his scowl.

He warned her that unless she was honest with him, he was through with her for good and all.

"I didn't realize I was responsible to you for my actions," she said.

"That may be. All the same, you'll have a pretty thin time this winter if you don't have me at your beck and call."

"Oh, this winter!" She was blithe as a breeze.

And yet all the time he was pretty certain that she was in love with him. She kept the ball in play, hour after hour. When, periodically, he set himself to leave her, she launched her voice after him like a messenger bird, "Don't run out on me, Victor. Don't be horrid."

"You should have thought twice before you started deviling that unfortunate tennis pro."

"Victor, it was you that brought this whole subject up. I wasn't planning to say a word about it."

He answered this sophistry with an animal growl through his teeth.

"You'd been perfectly vile to me, Victor. You'd called me a b-bitch."

"I never did."

"I heard you with my own ears. What else did you think I was so mad about?"

"Jodie, did you let that man kiss you?"

"Daddy feels very strongly that I ought to get to know lots of men before I settle down," she replied demurely.

"So his ever-obedient daughter goes out and spoons with the tennis teacher."

"I don't have to take your bullying, Victor. Daddy has thought up a very nice plan for me this winter. The worse you act, the nicer it sounds. I have till this evening to decide, and what I decide depends entirely on how you treat me today."

"What is this wonderful plan?" He did not believe a word she said.

"You'll find out soon enough."

. . . Round and round and round. The fight raged from the sun parlor to the Swimming Rocks, and after luncheon it resumed in the cathedral vistas of the Doochee Trail.

Once, infuriatingly, she surprised him by a moth kiss on the end of the nose. "You're so cute when you're mad!" she said caressingly.

But in another second she was off and away; and five minutes later they were at it again, hammer and tongs.

Victor could not remember eating either lunch or dinner. He put himself to bed on half a pie he found in the pantry, but it was Dead Sea fruit.

When Katie wakened him at midmorning his first glance was toward the chest of drawers. If he had known Katie was coming into his room he would not have indulged himself—as he had done—by turning Jodie's framed photograph face downward and weighting it with a pair of tennis shoes. This war between himself and Jodie was strictly private.

"I'm terrible sorry to wake you up, Vic," Katie apologized, "but something is dreadfully wrong over at the Grover house."

All he could call to mind about the Grovers was that they were one of the families who lived down the street. He nuzzled down into his pillow and grasped at oblivion.

"Well, all right," Katie said. But she still stood looking at him. "You're the only person Lissa really talks to."

He couldn't get back to sleep while Katie stood there with those great eyes fastened on him. "There's always hell to pay at the Grover house when Queenie's at home," he said. "What's up this time?"

"Everything seemed fine yesterday afternoon, and Lissa was so happy about her mother being back. We made a date for early tennis this morning. Well, Lissa didn't show up, so I walked down to her house. It was positively creepy down there. The front hall was full of suitcases with things spilling out. The dining room was all higgledy-piggledy— just some dirty coffee cups on the corner of the table, and an empty milk bottle. . . . And the most peculiar sounds coming down from the front bedroom! A low, steady, talking noise—that was Mr. Grover, and moaning sounds, like when a dog gets run over—that was Mrs. Grover."

"That Queenie is a trouble breeder," Victor said darkly. "Where was Lissa all this while?"

"You know that pergola down at the edge of their woods? Well, Lissa was standing there just like Mrs. Noah out of the ark, with her hands straight at her sides, as stiff as that!" Katie rapped the bedpost.

"You mean she'd had an attack or something?" Victor asked with real anxiety.

"Oh, no, no. 'I shan't be able to play this morning,' she told me. I saw that my being there made her tighten up worse than ever, so I came away. When Lissa's in trouble she doesn't want anbody to talk to her about it—except you."

"Well, I'm sorry about Lissa, but I have troubles enough of my own." He knew why Katie had come to him. She wanted him to make a few magical passes over Lissa and unfreeze her. He had the power.

But it was dynamite. Any time he gave to Lissa would be charged against him in Jodie's books.

Furthermore, the kid was in love with him, and he didn't give a whoop about her. Unfreezing her would be a doubtful kindness.

"Look, Katie," he demurred. "What Lissa needs is a good sweat on the tennis court, and I can't play this morning—I'm busy. Drag her out, run her off her legs. By afternoon the skies will clear, and Queenie will be all tinkle bells."

"You couldn't just telephone her—not saying I'd told you anything— and give her a little pep talk about her game?"

"No, I couldn't," Victor said baldly. "I have enough on my mind, and I can't go into that."

The second day's fighting between Victor and Jodie had to be postponed till after lunch. Mrs. Epps met Victor kindly, but she refused to wake Jodie. The child had prowled the house all night like a panther, she said, and now she'd dropped off to sleep.

"Mrs. Epps, what's all this about Jodie's mysterious plans for the winter?"

"Well, I don't know what to say. Of course I'd rather have her at home, but it sounds like a pleasant enough school. The girls don't study any too hard, and they come and go around New York almost as if they were living with their own families. Her father feels she ought to have some advantages."

He stared at Mrs. Epps, his eyes glassy with horror. A school—a school in New York?

There was no point in lambasting poor Mrs. Epps. Victor thanked her and took himself off.

This was the key to Jodie's independent air. She had a bona fide alternative to life in Rampole Place.

He walked slowly back up the oval, kicking the fallen leaves ahead of him. Instead of going home to lunch he tramped off down the Doochee Trail.

He had no argument to put forward against this precious plan. The undoubted fact that he would bleed to death at the deep heart's core if she went away was unlikely to sway anyone except himself. Rampole Place had been unkind to Jodie, and it would be even unkinder this winter.

He saw now why Jodie had given him one last chance to be nice—and the inference swept him suddenly up into high heaven. She loved him. She must love him. She had said her decision depended on him. She loved him enough to stay at home and endure ostracism, if she could count on him.

But why, then, had she been so secretive about her plans? Why had she given him only a blindfold choice?

Well, he had glimmerings about that. Glorious glimmerings they were. If she truly loved him—and only if she truly loved him—she would be too proud to club him into docility. She had blindfolded him to leave him free.

The question decided itself. He could not let Jodie go. But what would be her price for staying at home?

If he gave her leave to kiss all the tennis teachers she liked, would that hold her? The words might gag him, but he could try to get them out.

No, they would not be enough. Deep in his bones Victor knew Jodie's price: it was matrimony, and nothing less. Girls had a mania for getting married.

. . . And fair enough, after all. Marriage was the only career open to them. This bore hard on men, who had a lot of bachelor in them. On the other hand, the ivy paid the ultimate compliment to the oak by twining round it.

While he walked the quiet reaches of the Doochee Trail, Victor fought his way out of the chrysalis of boyhood. He could see clear now. To make her his at all, he must make her his for life.

He began to foresee the unimagined pleasures of being responsible for Jodie, of taming the tameless fire in her, of building an enclosure around himself and her.

So viewed, even watering a lawn took on significance. He balked at the prospect of pushing a baby carriage—but that was far over the horizon.

Indeed it was. It was a man's business to support his wife. And while it was barely conceivable that Horace Rampole might subsidize a suitable marriage at a suitable age, the hypothesis that he might subsidize Victor's marriage to Anson Epps's daughter was not worth wasting time on.

True, Victor had a little money of his own now. Last March, on his eighteenth birthday, Mr. O'Donnell had called him down to the office and explained to him that under his mother's will he was now to receive five thousand dollars with accrued interest. She had had, it appeared, fifty thousand dollars from her husband as a wedding present, and quite properly she had left most of it to her father and mother.

This vision of dazzling wealth had proved to be a mirage. Mr. O'Donnell was acting on the Senator's instructions; and the Senator, who was his guardian until he came of age, had told Mr. O'Donnell to reinvest the entire amount in six-per-cent bonds. All Victor carried away in his pocket was an odd $28.23. Every March and every September the lawyer undertook to send Victor a check for a hundred and fifty dollars.

Promptly on the first of September the first check had arrived. But Victor knew a man couldn't support a wife on three hundred dollars a year. It might be enough for an engagement ring. Another Meridian axiom was that you could not get engaged to a girl without a ring to bind the bargain.

Having taken a survey of his situation, Victor swung on his heel and set off for Jodie's house.

He had hoped to get her down to the Doochee Ford for the sacred moment. He and she, however, were at cross-purposes—she naturally picking up their fight where they had dropped it the night before. To cut her short, Victor tumbled out his proposal, hind side to, before they had crossed the Breens' driveway.

At once the stormy waves grew still, the sun shone out in splendor. Her eyes probed his, in incredulity and dawning joy.

"You're sure, Vic?"

"Plumb certain sure, Jodie."

"That's all I need to know," she said; and he saw the heavy weight of anger slip from her shoulders.

Her sweetness overwhelmed him. No firecrackers and shooting stars—she seemed to be walking softly for fear she should wake herself up. She slipped her hand into his, and they set off by a common impulse for the deep forest.

At first it seemed as if a hundred afternoons would not be enough for all their love-making and all their talking.

"You do see why I had to behave so horribly, don't you, Vic?"

"I most certainly do. All the same, the next time you play anybody off against me, I will black both your eyes."

"Well, I should hope so."

"We'll have to be engaged forever and a day. If I hump myself, I can probably get through college in three years, but that's the best I can hope for before I go to work."

"That's not so terribly, terribly long," she said.

"I'm going downtown tomorrow to buy you a ring." And he told her about his windfall of a hundred and fifty dollars.

She was so silent that he offered her a penny for her thoughts.

"It's sort of a peculiar situation," she said. "Of course any ring you buy me will be heavenly, Victor—only an engagement ring is something you wear all the rest of your life. And don't you think it would look sort of squinchy for Mrs. Victor Rampole to go around flashing an itty-bitty chip of a diamond?"

Victor saw her point. Aunt Louisa's rings were a magnificent load on her old knuckles. Mother's ring had been a coruscation. Possibly a hundred and fifty dollars wouldn't buy a really Rampole ring. Jodie must know.

"I should more or less think," she went on hesitantly, "that in a family like yours there would be family diamonds."

"Father must have some put away, but I wouldn't have the cheek to ask him for them." (And don't urge me to. Father is a little biased against you.)

"Victor, you'll get another hundred and fifty dollars next March, and so on? I'd really rather let that money pile up, till you get me a ring that's visible to the naked eye."

"But then we wouldn't be engaged till God knows when!"

"Silly!" she said tenderly. "It isn't the ring that makes the engagement, it's the promise. Only don't let's tell anybody, because I certainly would feel like thirty cents if I didn't have a ring to show them."

They hadn't spent their beatific afternoon yet. Jodie leaned back against his shoulder, infinitely at peace.

"There's one other thing I want to clear up," Victor said. "I'd have brought it up long before this, except for that confounded tennis pro. You remember that fight we had at the Cinnamon Gorge? Well, you were right about Queenie Grover and I was wrong. I don't know what got into me."

"I'm glad you've come back to your senses," she said without stirring from her nest. How pale this controversy seemed, in the great blaze of love!

"There's only one thing," she went on. "You're inconsistent, Vic. If that's the way you feel about Queenie Grover, I should think for my sake you could have found someone to spend your entire time with this summer besides Lissa Grover."

"Who says I did?"

"Don't be ridiculous. Anybody in the street could have told me. Actually, it was Netta, our upstairs maid. I hadn't been home twenty minutes before she took pains to let me know, while she was unpacking me."

Victor felt sheepish, and covered his embarrassment by a touch of yesterday's bluster. "You're a fine one to talk—you and your Clifford What's-his-name!"

"That's entirely different." And he could feel the tightening of her muscles against his side.

"It certainly is different." His crispness echoed hers. "Lissa Grover is a decent kid in a peck of trouble. This Clifford of yours is a matinee-idol type with an eye for a rich girl."

How familiar it all was, and how hideous—the withdrawal from his shoulder, the upright poise above the crisscrossed legs, the spiny darts of her eyes! "Jodie!" he tried to call her back to Elysium.

"You're putty in their hands!" she exclaimed, low and bitterly.

"In whose hands, for goodness gracious sake? In Lissa Grover's hands? Where's your sense of humor, darling? She and Katie are both sisters of mine."

"Fiddledeedee! Lissa Grover is nobody's kid sister. She's sixteen years old, just a year younger than I am, and don't you think she hasn't got her eye on the main chance! Daddy says her mother thinks she has you hooked—he says it was written all over her face yesterday. Lissa has simply got to marry, and marry well, before the whole Grover family blows up in one big scandalous mess."

Victor had the effrontery to reach out and take Jodie's head between his hands and to shake it gently. "There's something loose inside here," he said. He tried to sound humorous, but she really was a little touched on this one subject. "How often do I have to tell you——"

"Don't bother to tell me you're not in love with her. I'm not an utter idiot, and I know better than that. But I *would* be an idiot if I didn't know that Lissa is after you. Why else did she stay home from the seashore this summer? Why does she butter up to Katie the way she does? Why does she make such a point of playing tennis morning, noon and night?"

Victor struggled with the bombardment of questions, but she rode him

194

down. "At the very least, you put me in the position of looking like a fool. Suppose we're secretly engaged and Lissa is still hot on your trail. Everybody in Rampole Place will be betting on which of us is going to land you, and they'll trip me every chance they get. Lissa belongs. Jodie's an outsider."

The more he loved Jodie, the more essential it was to knock this pernicious spitefulness out of her. "You remind me of a cute little ant," he said, "trying to drag a great big dead beetle across the sidewalk. It won't drag, Jodie—give it up. Lissa Grover would rather die than chase any boy. She's so ladylike that she leans over backward."

"And I am not ladylike. I throw myself at your head. Is that it?"

"Now, Jodie! I've chased you ever since our dancing-school days, and you've been damned hard to catch. Can't you leave poor Lissa Grover alone?"

"No, I can't, and I'll tell you why. Because she's insidious. She's deep. She puts on that prunes-and-prisms act—but don't forget she's Queenie Grover's daughter, and Queenie is a man-eater. Lissa has her father's cold, secretive brains and her mother's hunting instinct. Her father's on the verge of bankruptcy——"

Something deep in Victor put the snarl into his voice. "How far are you going to chase this wild goose? Can't you even leave poor Philip Grover out of it?"

"I'm only telling you what Daddy says. He says Mr. Grover had a terrible time raising the money to ship Queenie to Europe. He tried to put a second mortgage on his house, and he got turned down."

Jodie was going to have to learn the uncharted boundaries of the permissible. "What this all boils down to," he interrupted her brusquely, "is that you want me to promise never to speak to Lissa Grover again. It wouldn't be any hardship to me. But I definitely will not send a nice kid to Coventry simply because you're jealous of her."

She stood up in one resilient movement, vibrating like a bowstring. He was terrified. His little lesson had gone wrong.

"There! that's exactly it. Lissa Grover is a beautiful soul. She must be sheltered from every wind that blows. Jodie Epps is common clay, she can take punishment. I think," Jodie said slowly, "Daddy is right about my getting out of here. I think I will go away to school this winter."

He had forgotten that she held an ace and that he had no trump for it. Fool that he was! He couldn't stand up to her. He could not live without her.

"Have it your own way," he said sullenly. "I won't promise to cut Lissa on the street, but I'll—well, let's say I'll treat her exactly the way

I treat Delia Dysart." That put it in a nutshell. Delia was a minor, junior, unpopular, negligible member of the Gang. It was his highest offer.

The flash of triumph in her face set off one last spark of defiance in him. If he had to yield, at least he could yield gracelessly. "Understand," he told her, "the only reason I go as far as that is because you're completely unreasonable."

"Idiot!" With one of her hummingbird dartings she went deep into his arms. "I'm completely unreasonable because I'm completely in love with you."

Glory rolled back over Victor. Owning a woman wasn't easy; it was like owning a thoroughbred horse. In the early stages the horse might unseat the rider, but in the long run it would take the bit, because the man was the superior being.

Chapter 29

VICTOR left Jodie at her house and walked back up the oval in the persimmon-red afterglow. Wood smoke hung in the air. The beatitude of the evening encompassed him.

Meanwhile, however, he was late for dinner, and he was ravening like one of the great carnivores. He couldn't remember when he had eaten a square meal. He would go down into the kitchen and coax as many as four helpings of everything out of Jennie.

He turned up the side-porch steps, heading for the cross corridor.

While his feet were clicking across the porch a voice punctured his reverie. "Victor—please?"

He turned and stood stock-still, appalled. Lissa Grover was sitting impassive, dim white against a dim-white pillar.

"I've got to go in to dinner," he muttered uneasily, and started to pass her.

"Could I speak to you just a minute? I wouldn't bother you, only something terrible is happening."

The next instant was a complete arrest in time. Victor had never, till this moment, faced a choice between two alternatives, one just as wrong as the other.

His ethical code was a conglomerate. From his mother he had picked up an inclination to kindness, particularly where Katie was involved.

From his father a sense of responsibility for his vassals. From Augustus a dry disdain for toadies and cowards. From books a hodgepodge of idolatries—for King Arthur, for Robin Hood, for the debonair sultan Haroun-al-Raschid. From Theodore Roosevelt an enthusiasm for all that was manly, boisterous and generally splendid.

Occasionally he did something he knew was bad: he lied, he eavesdropped, he brutalized some boy he disliked. He chalked up a moderate score of guilt on these counts; but by and large he considered himself a decent sort of a boy.

There were a very few incidents in his life that his code made no provision for—his kissing Lissa at the Doochee Ford, his flying out at Jodie in insensate rage at the Cinnamon Gorge. He had to deal with these episodes by putting them out of his mind.

But what was he to do now? Neither King Arthur, Robin Hood, nor Theodore Roosevelt would have broken his solemn promise to Jodie Epps; still less would they have thrown out Lissa when she came asking for help.

He had promised to treat Lissa as he treated Delia Dysart. But Lissa was not Delia. Only an extremity would have forced Lissa to lie in wait for him—it must have nearly killed her.

His decision was not heroic. If Jodie had been watching him, he would have walked away from Lissa and her troubles—because Jodie came first. But Jodie was safe at her own dinner table, and there was a good gambling chance that he could talk to Lissa without getting caught.

"Katie told me there were ructions down at your house," he said. "What's going on?"

"You couldn't walk up to the tennis court, could you?" she suggested. "It's something nobody ought to hear."

The tennis court was a better place for a secret conference than the side-porch steps. There was one particular bench that was not overlooked from any part of the grounds. Fortunately Lissa was no more anxious to be seen than he was. No one saw them as they cut across to the court.

"Everything has gone to pieces in our family," Lissa said, "and it is all my fault."

"Your father and mother, I suppose?"

She nodded. "They're making the most outrageous plans for Queenie to spend the winter in New York—just as casually as you might go into the city for the day, depending on the weather."

Victor was being properly paid for breaking his promise to Jodie. He thought Queenie's family was well rid of her, but that was not a consolation he could offer to Lissa.

"I'm as sorry as all get out, Lissa," he said. "But is there much of anything I can do about it?"

"There must be something," she cried, clasping her temples painfully with her hands. "It's like in fairy stories when the old witch comes along and turns people into frogs. It's as lunatic as that. And I am the old witch. But I didn't know, I didn't know——"

"Lissa, don't you take the blame for it! Grownups do things that simply don't make sense."

"In the fairy tales the good fairy waves her wand and turns the frogs back into people. I want to make things un-happen."

"Things don't un-happen, except in fairy stories."

"That's what I'm afraid of," she whispered. "Queenie's had the blues before and come out of them, but this time Daddy's stopped helping her."

"Perhaps Mr. Grover is giving her a chance to find out how unhappy she'll be if she goes away."

"I—I'm not sure he wants her to come back. Queenie says dreadful things, you know, when she's upset, but then they melt right out of her. They sink down into Daddy and stay there. He looks as if he'd been gouged with ice picks."

"What can you do except let her go? Even if she stayed, that wouldn't bring the old times back."

"They're going to be wretched without each other."

"Could—could your mother possibly have fallen in love with somebody else this summer?"

"But, Victor! Daddy and Queenie are *married*."

"Yes," he agreed glumly. In Rampole Place in 1910, marriage was bedrock. It was only in the newspapers that one read about people who got divorces and married again. "What sort of advice are you expecting me to give you?"

"I need a wand to wave. I was the bad fairy that turned them into frogs. Queenie's trip to Europe was my idea. Staying home from the Endicott Inn was my idea—and that's what makes Queenie the maddest, because she says people will criticize her for it. I wish I'd cut my tongue out first."

"You meant well. If suggestions as sensible as that went wrong, the wrongness was there already."

"But it might not have come out where Daddy and Queenie and I had to recognize it," she cried poignantly.

Victor understood that cry. It threw him back to the night when his mother was killed. His memories of that night writhed underground like fighting snakes, and he winced back from the horror. Somehow, even after allotting all due blame to the Senator and to Aunt Louisa, the sequence of fact did not quite add up to the tragic consequence. Chloe's death had been a case of trouble coming out where Victor had not been able to avert his eyes from it. Something had been wrong when Mother set off for Doonville. . . .

That channel of thought was forbidden. He forced his attention back to Lissa's problem.

But what could Lissa do? She was only the daughter of her house.

He tried to say that to Lissa. He told her she could not go through life carrying a pair of grownups on her shoulders. But he was not comforting her.

She said, "But how am I going to live through it? It's like being hung up by the thumbs for the rest of my life." And she began to cry.

Lissa's crying was not like Jodie's, which was a natural spillway for the overflow of temperament. It threatened the whole framework of her nature. It isolated her at an arctic pole. If it was the last thing Victor ever did, he must bring her back from her polar icecap.

He laid his hand on her forearm. She skittered away from his touch, but he maintained the light, steady pressure. "In the first place, the chances are a million to one your mother won't go when it comes to the point. But even if she does go, Lissa, you aren't hung up by the thumbs for life. I didn't like my mother's being killed, but I couldn't undo it. What I found out—and what you'll find out—is that your own life gets so interesting that it rescues you."

She was listening. She was holding back her noiseless rending sobs to listen.

"For instance," he drove ahead doggedly, "one of these days you'll fall in love, and then you'll find out how little the grownups matter. You're more than a third wheel on somebody else's tricycle."

Well, he'd said it. He was half glad and half sorry. A moment ago her arm had been as inert as the hood of a car with the engine turned off. Now the engine was running.

"Oh, I know what you mean, Victor! I—I—— That was why I had to talk to you and nobody else."

Great Scott! In another minute the kid would be telling him she loved him. "I won't be around when that happens," he said hurriedly. "But when I come down the line to shake hands at your wedding, I'll say, 'See, what did I tell you back in 1910?' "

"It won't be quite like that," Lissa said—and he would have sworn it was a different girl talking. She even laughed a little.

"Well, I've got to be going, Liss," he said, rising from the bench. "I haven't had my dinner, and I have a date this evening."

"Thank you ever so much, Victor. You're probably right—Queenie will change her mind ten minutes before traintime and stay at home."

"Find somebody else to talk to, Lissa," he besought her. "I'm the wrong age. Talk to your father, for goodness sake. Talk to Katie—talk to Ella."

"I don't need to talk to anybody but you," she said serenely. "You straighten me out the way nobody else does."

"You can't count on talking to me!" he exclaimed in a frenzy of avoidance. "It's all wrong. There are . . . reasons."

"Reasons?"

He couldn't tell her he and Jodie were engaged, because that was the sacred secret of his life. He couldn't possibly tell her he had promised to treat her as if she were Delia Dysart—that would be too offensive.

"I don't even want to talk to you. I couldn't look your father or your mother in the eye if they found out I'd been discussing them behind their backs."

"Well, they'll never find out from me." She had her composure back. She rose, and drifted away into the engulfing twilight toward the forest.

When he got down to the kitchen it was twenty minutes past seven, and he had contracted to pick Jodie up at half past. "Could I grab a bite of something, Jen?" he beguiled the good old lady who was rocking beside the stove while the underlings washed up.

"You're making a lot of trouble for Augustus these days," she complained. "Meal after meal he keeps a plate warm for you, and then you don't eat it. Then in the middle of the night you eat up all my pies."

"Come off it, Jen! I'm hollow right down to the knees. I could eat a kangaroo."

"Well, I've just put a duck in the icebox, but I wanted it for lunch."

"Fine!" He vanished into the kitchen pantry.

"There's a bowl of applesauce, and some peas," she called after him.

He came back laden to the kitchen table. By good luck he had discovered, to top off his meal, a wedge of peach shortcake quilted with whipped cream.

"Oh, well," Jennie grumbled, hoisting herself out of her chair, "I might as well make you some fresh coffee."

Victor ate as fast as he could, but a duck is nothing that can be gulped down; it requires surgical intervention. He could have eaten two ducks. He scraped the bowl of applesauce, and polished off the peas. The shortcake was too good to wolf down. He pursued the last fragments, and then supped the ambrosial juices.

"Thanks from the heart," he said, going over to the sink to wash his hands. "I've got to scoot. I'm late."

"She'll wait," Jennie said dryly. "Your coffee will be ready in half a minute."

The aroma from the steaming spout was irresistible. Victor waited for his coffee. Naturally he couldn't drink it at boiling temperature, so he lost another two or three minutes.

"It's ten minutes to eight," Jodie said when he picked her up. "Whatever kept you so long?" She was not cross—merely wifely.

"My dinner. I hadn't eaten a square meal since you got back to town. I certainly did enjoy my dinner. Did you break it to your father that you had changed your mind about going away to school?"

"M-hm," she purred as happily as a kitten.

"How did he take it?"

"Laughed, and jingled his money. He didn't seem much surprised. . . . Victor?"

"Yes, honeybunch?"

"What all did you eat for dinner that took you so long?"

It was a fair question, since she had taken on a responsibility for feeding him. But he wished he didn't have to equivocate about the passage of time. "Well, I finished up the scrag end of a duck that I found in the icebox——"

"In the icebox! But what did you eat at the dinner table?"

"Well, the other part of the duck. And peas," he added, searching his vacant memory. He saw now what a tight spot he was in. "And—applesauce. Oh, how do I know what I ate? I wasn't thinking about my food, I was just stoking it in. I tell you you had me starved."

"Was it the company at your house that slowed you down?"

"Company?" he asked blankly. Then he remembered that two strange cars had been standing in front of the portico. Yes, of course there was company. "I'm riding a pink cloud, I tell you. I don't notice things." He caught the menace of her tightened mouth and saw what a hash he was making of his explanations.

"I'll own up," he said. "I didn't eat with the family. I—I just roamed around after I left you, and ended up on that bench beside the tennis court. I don't know where the time went. When I came to, dinner was over. If you want to check my story, try kissing me—there's duck on my breath."

She was deep in thought; Victor grew more and more uneasy. His first story hadn't rung true—had the revision given satisfaction?

She said, "I'd promised myself to trust you, now that we're engaged. But you'll have to excuse me for cross-questioning you this once."

"Fire away," he said with a sinking heart. He hated lying to Jodie, and he lied badly.

"Victor, after dinner I wanted to be all alone to think about you, so I went out on the front steps and watched the moon coming up over the trees."

"Just like me at the tennis court."

"I sat there a long time, glorying about everything. Then, about five minutes before you picked me up, Lissa Grover came spooking along the oval from the—the direction of your driveway, Victor, and turned in at her own house."

"Well?" He brought out the word easily, but he was charged with rancor against Lissa Grover, who had a faculty for ruining his life.

"That's what I say, Victor: Well?"

"Probably she was taking a walk," he suggested with what conviction he could.

"It was a queer time and place to take a walk."

"Well, the Grovers are eccentric. If you think I was helping her take her walk, ask Jen—she'll tell you I'd been in her kitchen for twenty minutes, eating her out of house and home."

"Victor, answer me carefully, because a lot depends on it. Did you talk to Lissa after I left you?"

"I passed the time of day with her. I never promised you I wouldn't."

"Was she with you at the tennis court when you lost all track of time?"

"Gosh, Jodie, I couldn't help it if she came up on purpose to talk to me. She had no way of knowing I was through with her."

Jodie's self-control was more frightening than any amount of smoke and lava. "And you told me she never chased you. You said she positively leaned over backward to avoid you. What have I got to depend on when you lie to me like this?"

"I begged her to talk to anybody else except me. I told her I had reasons for not wanting to get mixed up in her affairs."

"But she did manage to talk to you."

"She's never come after me before. She was in such a state of nerves that she scared me."

"That's a standard opening," Jodie said ironically.

He raged in the toils. "You've got it all wrong. It was nothing personal."

"Am I to understand that she was in a state of nerves about her *algebra?*"

"Heck, Jodie, it was something confidential, or I'd tell you. About her family."

"Well, that clears everything up splendidly. It shows me just where I stand—second in line to Miss Melissa Pendleton Grover. To keep me quiet, you make me a solemn promise to have nothing to do with her. But obviously when Lissa comes creepy-crawling after you, you can't be expected to keep a promise like that. Naturally you have to kiss the bump and make it well—and trust to luck that good old Jodie won't catch you."

"Jodie! If I could tell you what the trouble was, you'd admit that it was real trouble."

"I'm waiting," said Jodie, cold as Medusa.

"Well, then—" flinging Lissa to the sharks—"Queenie is going off to live in New York, and poor Lissa manages to blame herself, because *she* sent Queenie off to Europe and *she* kept her father home from the seashore." He paused, hopefully. Surely, by betraying Lissa's confidence, he had bought forgiveness for himself.

"I'm still waiting."

"What for? That's the whole story."

"I'm merely waiting to hear how you consoled your poor sensitive little friend Lissa. Did you tell her it wasn't her fault, and she must look on the bright side, and tomorrow would be another day?"

"Well, more or less. Anybody would have."

"Did you offer her your manly shoulder to weep on?"

"I did not."

"Did you dry her tears?"

"Well, she calmed down before I left. Damn it, Jodie, you're a stony-hearted girl."

"How did you stop her crying? Did you hold her hand in a brotherly way and tell her she could count on you?"

"I told her explicitly that she could not count on me. I told her I was bad for her."

"That remark," Jodie said venomously, "will bear close analysis."

"Well, Jodie, it's no secret that the kid has a sort of crush on me. I was trying to foist her off on somebody else—anybody else."

"But you didn't tell her that you and I were engaged?"

"Why, no. We agreed——"

"If you're so good at breaking confidences, that was one confidence I'd have excused you for breaking. If you'd really wanted to shake her off, you'd have told her. It flatters you to have her dying with hopeless love."

"If you'll give me leave, I'll telephone her tomorrow and tell her. It would be a load off my chest."

"Don't bother. Don't cause her needless pain. Don't, for the world, tell her anything that isn't true." She drew a deep breath. "You and I are not engaged any longer."

He gave a great animal cry of agony.

"Will you take me home now, please? I want to catch Daddy before he wires the school that I'm not coming."

They quarreled till two in the morning. He pleaded, he abased himself. He cried.

Jodie cried more than he did, but her tears did not soften her heart.

"We love each other, Jodie."

"Unfortunately, I love you. When you say you love me, all you mean is that you want me to kiss *you* and not the tennis teacher. You reserve the privilege of cheating on me, and lying to me, and keeping Lissa Grover dangling. . . ."

Round and round and round, love whetting itself on the grindstone of hatred. It was like living through a hurricane; when one thought the storm must have reached its peak, a more terrible blast struck.

"What could I do that would satisfy you, Jodie?" Whatever price she set, he would have to pay it.

"Oh, I don't know," she cried in anguish. "A Rampole isn't like anybody else. A Rampole promise doesn't mean anything. There's nothing to tie to."

"Could we leave my family out of this?" he asked her harshly.

"We could, except that you're just like your family. The money your family slings around so magnificently is dirty money that Big Joe stole and salted away."

He would have enjoyed strangling her, but he heaved Big Joe to the sharks behind Lissa Grover. "How did my grandfather get into this? He died before I was born."

"Your father didn't die before you were born, and he's worse than Old Joe, because he's sanctimonious. He bleats about civic purity, and all the while he's feathering his own nest. Daddy says so."

"Your father says that about my father? That's rich, that's really rich." In his indignation, Victor's tongue ran away with him. "Why, your father is so crooked that there's a committee collecting evidence this very minute to run him out of town."

"Is . . . that . . . so!" Her weighted pauses gave Victor time to realize the enormity he had perpetrated. What he had betrayed to Jodie would go straight to Anson Epps. The situation was past salvaging.

"Jodie," he labored desperately, "let's skip our ancestors. This is between you and me. It's our whole lives."

"That's it exactly." Jodie was as distracted as he was himself. "If you cheat on me the very day you get engaged, what will you be like after we're married? If I didn't love you, I could put up with your double crossing for the sake of being Mrs. Victor Rampole. It's because I do love you that I can't marry you."

"Your father has been filling you up with lies."

"That's typical. You can call my father names, but I'm not to call your father names."

"Mr. Epps judges everybody by himself. It's perfectly well known that he keeps a blonde in an apartment on South Boulevard—and what's more, it's a different blonde every few months."

"Who told you that?" she demanded in a tingling voice.

"I'm sorry I said that, but you had it coming to you."

"Who told you that?" she repeated.

"Augustus Henning."

Jodie absorbed the thrust in seething silence. He was ashamed of himself for the crude accusation, but perhaps it would be the basis for a truce.

He had underestimated Jodie's catamount spirit. "So sweet of you to bring that up," she purred. "So different from your mother and Harold Ritter. At least Daddy hasn't *killed* any of his blondes."

His hands trembled with the restraint he put upon them to keep from taking her by the throat.

She shrank away from him, but she was not surrendering. Her words pelted around his head like a clatter of hailstones. "No, that's what I mustn't mention, not to a Rampole. When any low creature dares to whisper that Chloe Rampole got killed in her lover's car, it's like Peeping Tom and Lady Godiva. If he had any proper feelings he'd look the other way. The Rampoles gang up to keep it out of the papers. They frame up a cock-and-bull story about a political meeting that never happened, and get their political henchmen to perjure themselves. Everybody sends the most expensive flowers to the funeral——"

"Jodie, are you insane? Haven't I told you——"

"I've heard your version," she said wearily. "It happens I've also heard the facts. You may remember that Daddy owns the *Sun-Record,* and it was he who told Mr. Claggan to kill the story. In those days, when he first moved to Meridian, he was willing to live and let live. Later he discovered that it was a case of dog eat dog."

She had driven Victor to a point where even strangling her would have been no satisfaction to him. He was stunned into silence. He never wanted to see Jodie Epps again. He wasn't sure he wanted to go on living in the vile world.

"You are an unholy liar," he said as he deposited her at her own front door. "You'll probably find scope for your talents in New York."

Chapter 30

WHEN Lissa came down from the tennis court she took every precaution not to involve herself with her family. Daddy was reading in the library; Queenie's door was closed. Lissa flitted upstairs without turning on the lights. Tomorrow, and tomorrow, and tomorrow, she would give herself to her parents' problems. Tonight she needed to be alone with her new climate of hope. She not only closed her door, she locked it.

She did like her room. Mr. O'Shea had conceived it in nunlike paneled white; Queenie had enlivened it with festoons of flowered organdy, and some day she meant to furnish it in cane and white enamel. Meanwhile Lissa had fallen heir to some severe old mahogany pieces and an old blue-and-crimson Oriental rug. Lissa enjoyed the resulting hodgepodge—it was her sanctuary.

She waited for several minutes, to make sure no parent came rapping at her door. What she was about to do was so ridiculous that she positively could not be caught at it. It was the sort of thing girls did in her class at school. It was a nightly ritual.

Very gently, without making a sound, she swung the secretary a few inches out from its corner. She took a small pair of candlesticks from her dressing table and lighted the candles. Then she inserted herself through the gap behind the secretary into the triangular niche and set the burning candles symmetrically on the floor.

There was a black cloth stretched across the back of the bookshelves. It had been there since her grandmother's day. Granny had installed it to cover a split in the back panel.

Lissa took out the thumbtacks that held this cloth in place. Under the cloth she had arranged a sort of altarpiece, tacked to the wooden panel.

In the center was a snapshot of Victor Rampole at the Swimming Rocks. He was leaning back on one elbow, facing into the sun like an eagle, his head thrown back in a godlike laugh. Katie Rampole had taken the picture, and Lissa had stolen it from Katie's room. She had never stolen anything else; but this theft was in a category beyond good and evil.

Other objects were tacked to the panel. There was a picture of a hepatica plant, cut out of a wild-flower manual. There was a picture post card of the residence of Senator Horace Rampole. There was a clipping about a May Festival at the Bierbach Academy. There was the stub of a ticket to the Lyceum Theater. There was a soiled bit of adhesive tape, with which Victor had taped a blister on Lissa's tennis hand.

In the second most sacred position was a tiny fleck of brown leather, glued to a card. This was a frayed bit off the grip of the racket with which Victor had taught Lissa to follow through on her stroke. His hand had touched it.

Lissa had cast off her self-consciousness by this time. She took her place between the candles, knelt down, clasped her hands and gave herself to recollection. When her devotional mood had ripened she began reciting, in a low, level voice, several of the *Sonnets from the Portuguese*. She had a head full of poetry, and Mrs. Browning was her favorite poet.

> "Unlike are we, unlike, O princely Heart!
> Unlike our uses and our destinies. . . .
> What hast *thou* to do
> With looking from the lattice-lights at me? . . .
> The chrism is on thine head,—on mine, the dew,—
> And Death must dig the level where these agree.

> "How do I love thee? Let me count the ways.
> I love thee to the depth and breadth and height
> My soul can reach. . . .
> I love thee with the breath,
> Smiles, tears, of all my life!—and, if God choose,
> I shall but love thee better after death."

When a sufficient time had passed she rose from her knees and touched the photograph of Victor with a kiss, butterfly-delicate. Then she tacked down the cloth, blew out the candles and pushed the secretary back across its corner.

Now for her diary.

She was so neat by nature that it had been hard for her to create an artificial confusion in which her diary could lose itself. But the diarizing addiction had grown on her. To let any human being look into it would be the equivalent of finding herself naked in a public street.

Neither Daddy nor Queenie would read anything they knew was confidential; but in Lissa's early days she had been childishly proud of her neat line-a-day entries, and the volume had been in the public domain. She had often left it about the house, and they had often looked into it. Now that the ledger was crammed with exaltations and miseries, even to ask her parents to leave it alone would amount to giving herself away.

So in the drawer of an old sewing table Lissa had created an artificial clutter like that in the drawer where Victor kept his mother's photograph. Undarned stockings, old tennis balls, a broken bracelet, tubes of sunburn remedy, colored pencils, a packet of compositions from school. As a clutter it was a work of high inventiveness. The ledger fitted precisely into the bottom of the drawer, under the shelf paper.

She reread her entry of the previous night. How hysterical it sounded, now that Victor had given her back her peace! She had despaired too soon.

Her pen winged its way across the page, line after line, with pauses for review. She began by making a verbatim record of every word she and Victor had exchanged. Then she passed to her commentary.

What it amounts to is that Queenie won't go away after all, if Daddy and I can distract her attention from the idea. I might get him to ask Cousin Frank Kennedy and Cousin Rosa over from Cleveland for a visit. That would mean parties. People would be obliged to be civil to the Kennedys, because they are related to everybody.

Ella would come back if Daddy asked her to. If she won't, I can speak to the Dysarts' Cassie. She has about a thousand relatives at her beck and call. This house is getting into such a mess that I don't blame Queenie for wanting to move out of it.

What this REALLY amounts to is that there is plenty of action for me to take, instead of wailing and gnashing my teeth. I am not a little girl any more. Somebody has got to break this stupid deadlock, and it looks as if it had better be me.

I didn't tell V. how wrong he was about coming to my wedding. I shall never marry anybody. I would rather have Victor's hand on my arm for one minute—even if he is in love with J.E.—than be married to the most prominent man in the world.

Dear Victor dear Victor thank you dear Victor. . . .

School opened the following day at Miss Peebles'. Lissa calculated, correctly, that if she didn't mention the fact, neither her father nor her mother would remember the date. She called Katie Rampole and told her she could not drive her down that morning.

"I'll bring you your assignments," Katie said. She added, on a discursive note, "Nobody seems to be starting to school on time. This is the morning for Victor to register at the university, but when I banged on his door and reminded him he growled at me like an enraged bear. He and Jodie must have had a frightful row last night."

Lissa's heart leaped wickedly at the news, but she built no deluding hopes on it. They were forever having frightful rows, but they always made up. There was an Olympian magnificence to their quarrels; they darkened the whole sky around them. If that was the essence of being in love, Lissa was disqualified in advance.

She turned to her own affairs as she had planned them overnight. She talked to her father over his breakfast and caught him in a compunctious mood. He not only accepted her proposal for inviting the Kennedys over from Cleveland, he went to the telephone and put in a long-distance call. And while the Kennedys didn't agree to come at once, they took a favorable view of coming over to spend Thanksgiving. That would do well enough; it would give Queenie something to anticipate.

Exalted by her first success, Lissa pressed on. She couldn't reach Ella by telephone; so she walked up the street and conferred with the Dysarts' Cassie. Cassie undertook to send in one of her nieces by the day, till Mrs. Grover should have suited herself with a resident maid.

Cassie put Lissa through a grilling. Why had Ella left so suddenly? . . . On account of her health; she gave Queenie notice before Queenie started for Europe. . . . Was anything wrong with Mrs. Grover? She seemed to be keeping her bedroom shades down all the time. . . . No, no; Queenie wasn't ill, she was tired after her long journey; but she'd had a lovely time, and brought back the most beautiful presents.

It was plain that malicious eyes were focused on Number Four Rampole Place. But they couldn't be sure there was anything amiss, they could merely suspect. If Lissa could only succeed in holding her mother at home for a few weeks, the suspicion would blow over and no one would have a story to tell against Queenie.

With her triumphs in her pocket, Lissa went back to set up her mother's breakfast tray. The coffee was tolerable by amateur standards, although it had a good many grounds in it.

She carried the tray to Queenie's bedside and sat on the foot of the bed while Queenie ate.

Queenie looked dreadful. Her face was puffed from crying and her color was blotched. But she was compunctious too. The flowers on the tray brought tears of tenderness to her eyes. "You're such a sweetheart," she said, "and I've been so awful to you."

Timing her advance, gauging the tonic influence of the coffee, Lissa doled out her glad tidings. Adeline, Cassie's niece, was coming tomorrow morning to help out. Wasn't that a stroke of luck?

"Angel! It's a miracle. How did you work it?" Queenie began to unfold, like a primrose after long drought.

"And what do you think? Daddy happened to be talking to the Kennedys on the telephone, and they want to come over from Cleveland for Thanksgiving."

Queenie arrested her coffee cup in midair. Would she be in Meridian for Thanksgiving herself? She set down her cup and stared out the window. Lissa followed her thoughts across her face. . . . Parties for the Kennedys. The irrefutable claims of the Kennedys on their lifelong friends in Meridian. . . . Lissa didn't often pray, but she prayed while she watched her mother's ingenuous face. . . . Philip must have invited the Kennedys because he wants me to stay here. He's trying to be nice.

"Why, how lovely!" Queenie said at last. By those three words she renounced her trip to New York; the whole project withdrew into the nebulous realm of the might-have-been, the never-had-been. It had never been announced; nobody knew about it; it didn't exist.

"Do you know what we ought to do this morning, Queenie?" Lissa pressed her advantage. "We ought to unpack you. Your new dresses will be a mass of wrinkles."

Queenie had refused to be unpacked till she was committed to Meridian. Now she and Lissa emptied the trunks. She even hummed as she worked. "I'd forgotten how convenient my dressing room is," she said. "There's nothing in Europe to compare with it."

Late in the afternoon Lissa and Queenie were putting the screened porch in order. All day Lissa had kept up a flow of suggestions for little jobs that had to be done, and Queenie had followed her lead. As it was a fine Indian-summer day, they were preparing to serve a cold supper on the porch. Lissa wanted Daddy to admire her day's achievements; and Queenie felt reconciliation in the wind.

Lissa was dusting the rattan furniture and Queenie was arranging a big jar of autumn foliage when they saw Anson Epps run his car into his driveway. He came out of his garage and stood with his hands in his trousers pockets, inspecting the rear of his own house with a proprietor's complacence.

Then his eye swiveled around toward the Grover porch. He was too far off for his expression to be visible, but his figure came out of its easy slouch. After an instant he swung purposefully across his side lawn and made for the gap in the hedge.

"What does *he* want?" Lissa murmured resentfully. The word Epps spelled trouble in her vocabulary. Queenie was in precarious balance, and a breath could overset her.

"Why, he's just dropping in to say hello." Queenie knew she looked pretty in her housewifely ruffled apron, among the great branches of colored foliage. She ran her side combs through the ash-brown crinkles of her pompadour and moored them in place.

By the time Anson reached the porch steps he had recaptured his lounging gait, but Lissa still felt purpose in him.

"You'll have to overlook the mess," Queenie greeted him. "Lissa and I are getting straightened up after the summer."

"You astound me," Mr. Epps said easily. His eyes were sending darts of greenness one way and another, like a mirror turned in the hand. "I understood you were off to New York for the winter. As a matter of fact, I didn't think it was a bad idea. But, of course, it's even pleasanter to have you next door to us."

Queenie stood transfixed. The frond of scarlet maple in her hand began to quiver. She laid it down, and steadied herself against the table top.

Lissa read the turmoil in her mother's mind by the turmoil in her own. How could Anson Epps have heard, except through Philip? Could Philip have violated his own character so far?

Queenie's face flew distress signals. She was saying to herself: People know. They know Philip is through with me—he's told them. If I stay at home, they'll think it's because I haven't nerve enough to clear out. Even if the Kennedys come over, the visit will be a fiasco. People will fill them full of tales about me.

And Lissa, with such small knowledge as she had of the world, could not help agreeing with Queenie.

Anson continued. "I stopped in to ask a favor of you. I was going to ask you to be good to Jodie this winter in New York. You've probably heard that we've shipped her off to a finishing school—she left this morning. She thinks it's going to be all beer and skittles, but I prophesy she'll be homesick. I thought if you had an apartment in New York, you could have her to lunch or something. In fact, I'd gone so far as to hope you'd give the two of us lunch when I go down to see her."

Devil! Lissa thought fiercely. It was the first time she had ever hated anyone. Mr. Epps was tempting Queenie with a vision of the life of a great city—men dropping in, theaters, smart little lunch parties, shopping expeditions and fittings. Queenie had always adored the pleasures of New York.

Queenie's face was ghastly between the blotches of red, but she clung with a drowning grasp to her nonchalance. "The plan may still go through. I've asked Philip to get me a reservation for tomorrow night, just in case."

The question was no longer open; it was closed. Anson Epps had closed it, and he had closed it intentionally.

"Excuse me, Mr. Epps." Lissa's voice was not nonchalant, but she clamped it steady above the earthquake that was rocking her. "Can you remember who told you about this plan of Queenie's? We haven't discussed it with anyone." If it was Daddy, Queenie had a right to leave him.

"Why, certainly. Jodie told me. She picked it up somewhere." It was a question he was delighted to be asked, a question he had provoked. He gave his answer straight into her staring face, as if he were asking her what she proposed to do about *that*.

Mr. Epps took his departure leisurely across the lawn. Queenie held herself rigid until he was out of sight; then she struck out at her tall vase of foliage with a sidelong sweep of the arm. The jar toppled and crashed, with an outpour of water and scattered branches. She was shaking from head to foot. "That settles it," she said.

"Queenie! It wasn't Daddy that told him. It was——" How could Lissa force out her shameful confession? It was Jodie, who heard it from Victor, who heard it from Lissa herself. The treachery was Victor's, but the blame led back to Lissa.

"I don't care who told him," Queenie wrenched out through the chattering of her teeth. "I'm being mocked at, up and down Rampole Place. They all know Philip has asked me to leave him, and they're all glad—don't try to tell me they're not. How can you expect me to stay here and face them?"

"They don't all know—nobody except the Eppses and Victor—and I told Victor." There, she had driven herself to full confession.

"They will know," Queenie said blackly. "Even you can't keep it to yourself—that's Adams Avenue for you! Don't talk to me any more, Lissa—I'm going upstairs."

A point comes when one has no strength left for pulling the other victims aboard the raft—a point of individual survival.

Philip's car was turning into the driveway. He and Queenie would have to settle their account on their own terms. Lissa flew up to her own room, driven on a shrieking wind of betrayal.

She locked her door. She pulled the big secretary roughly out into the room. She ripped away the black cloth that covered her shrine. Her breath came dry and choking while she tore with her nails at her altarpiece. She shredded the snapshot of Victor into small bits and flushed the whole debris down the toilet.

After some uncounted length of time she got out her diary. She knew what she wanted to write. Mrs. Browning had spoken for her.

> I tell you, hopeless grief is passionless; . . .
> Most like a monumental statue set
> In everlasting watch and moveless woe
> Till itself crumble to the dust beneath.
> Touch it; the marble eyelids are not wet:
> If it could weep, it could arise and go.

She was clamped into a mold, with concrete being poured around her. She felt the heavy creep of it. When it reached her heart she would stop feeling. It would close over her head and solidify around her meaningless wooden smile.

The fleck of leather from the tennis racket had escaped her fury; it lay on the floor under the secretary. She held the card in her fingers, despising herself but unable to throw it away.

After a while she detached it from its card and dropped it into her clutter drawer. It was unidentifiable. Some day a housemaid's cloth would dispose of it with the rest of the dust.

But she chose to retain this minute tangible reminder that in her youth she had been mawkishly in love with a boy named Victor Rampole.

Chapter 31

GROWING pains—for sixteen years Katie Rampole had had no trouble with growing pains. Growing came all too easy to her. Her mirror told her she was not in the line of the Rampole beauties. She was built like a big thoroughbred colt, and her mane was as black as a colt's.

She rejected any pretensions to feminine grace; she carried her chin high and clipped her words short. She might be impossible, but at least she would not lay herself open to ridicule.

Suddenly, this winter, she developed growing pains of the heart. They were as real as Jennie's rheumatism. She wished she could move back into her private world of fantasy, where there were no consequences. She had been a princess, a captive, a bandit, a shipwrecked mariner, a hunted stag; she had loaded the settlers' muskets while the scalping party howled outside. She had progressed to being the world's greatest concert pianist, with the students dragging her carriage through the streets; she had been an international hostess, doing the honors for Ignace Paderewski. She had been, in a thousand aspects, the Immortal Beloved. There had been no price to pay for this whirligig of experience. She had enjoyed it behind a rampart of living people whom she trusted.

Since her mother's death she had known exactly who mattered to her. On the topmost plane, her father and her brother. Recently Lissa Grover had been promoted to this level. Below these, a very few others: Jennie and Augustus; Miss Archibald; Mrs. Bellamy, who was so untiringly sweet about buying her clothes. All others were silhouettes in a mist, menacing because even when their overtures seemed kind, one had to assume they were insincere.

Just once she had stretched out her hand through the curtain of dream—the evening when she coaxed Victor to take her downtown to dinner. She had met Roy Godkin as she planned, but on a note of prose. No deathless words had passed between them. She retired him into the middle distance of her reveries.

Now her three flesh-and-blood beloveds were in trouble, and it behooved her to help them. She wished she were not so stupid in human relations.

Aside from the concern about Victor that overhung the whole house, she knew her father was worried about the fall elections. This was a chronic worry at Chestnut Point, but for some reason this year was more critical.

Once or twice a week, old Mr. Parmiter came out to dinner. He and Father brought files of papers to the table, and fretted over the reports from the precincts. The betting was on the Democrats, five to four.

Katie was expected to be fond of Mr. Parmiter. She could not like him very well. He blarneyed her as if she were still a ten-year-old; and when he put a fatherly arm around her waist he was half a head too short, and his breath had a sickly taint. But she made an effort to like him, on Father's account; and she listened at the dinner table.

Until ten days before election, their fretting had a routine, tolerable quality. They had to keep the upstate Progressives in some semblance of party regularity; they had to make pledges to the Anti-Saloon League which they would have to wriggle out of later.

Then one afternoon Mr. Parmiter came out and closeted himself with the Senator in the smoking room, and it was evident that the sky had fallen. The two men were perturbed all through dinner. Katie gathered up bits and snatches. The recurring villain was an entity with the unlikely name of Parlor B.

"What on earth is Parlor B, Father?" she asked once. He told her curtly that it was a lunch club, and she took it that she wasn't to interrupt again.

Somebody called McQueen claimed it was in his power to throw the election the wrong way. Father questioned the assumption. "If he walks out on us, he's in the wilderness. We don't have to make any deal with McQueen."

"Parlor B don't care whether it's Democrats or Republicans they deal with, just so they get their pickings."

"Are you going to make McQueen a proposition or aren't you?" Mr. Parmiter demanded time after time. Father backed away from a direct answer. "It makes me puke," he said inelegantly. "When we're on the very verge of springing a trap on Parlor B."

Mr. Parmiter thought little of Father's trap. "I'd like somebody to show me," he caviled, "where those Lily-Whites of yours control thirty votes."

"They've made a good start. I haven't had time to work with them."

"They specialize in running off at the mouth. They swore themselves to secrecy, and signed it with their blood. Well, only today McQueen was twitting me about my big brave Civic Reform League. I told him it was no baby of mine."

"Has there been a leak?" Father asked sharply. "I particularly warned them——"

"All right, that's for later. What am I going to say to McQueen tomorrow morning? Election is just ten days off. Will you gamble on winning without the Twelfth Ward?"

Father drummed on the table. "Sell as dear as you can," he said finally. "Offer them the Water Board—that'll give them a good laugh. Step it up to Parks. They'll come back with a counterproposition."

"Father," Katie interrupted desperately, "how can you give anybody the waterworks?"

Horace answered her with controlled exasperation. "After the election, the mayor appoints commissioners to run the various city departments. . . . If you have to, Dan, settle for Public Works. There should be enough pickings in that to keep them quiet for a while. Whatever you do, don't let Parlor B get its hands on the Police Department, or we'll never succeed in cleaning up the town."

Mr. Parmiter grew quite chirpy now that the compromise was arrived at; he took a second drink, in defiance of doctors' orders. But poor Father was chagrined to the soul.

Katie obviously could not be of any help to her father in politics. She ought to be some comfort to him in Rampole Place. He had created the street for her benefit. So she tried to keep some stir of social life about the house. Her difficulty was that the Gang had disintegrated.

The big boys, the leaders, had graduated from the Cambridge School when Victor did, and all of them except Victor had gone away to college. Two of the big girls had turned overnight into young ladies, preoccupied with their coming-out parties; others had been taken to Europe.

The next younger subgroup still lived at home. But Delia Dysart had paired off with the youngest Breen boy, and the youngest Dysart boy had taken up with Dolly Sutton from Adams Avenue. The four of them were a closed square, hostile to outsiders.

There remained herself, Victor and Lissa. But that triumvirate had fallen apart. Katie was alarmed about Victor. Augustus made use of a frightening phrase: he said Victor was headed for hell in a hack.

As for Lissa, Katie made allowances for her standoffishness. If Katie had been Lissa, if her mother had decamped to New York, Katie would have done as Lissa was doing: she would have closed the shutters and denied herself to spectators.

The Grovers had a complication that Katie understood only vaguely: they were short of money. They kept no regular maid now—nothing but old Ella two days a week. Mr. Grover did the outside chores, and Lissa did the cooking.

Katie was too naïve to turn up her nose at poverty. What she did mind was Lissa's dropping out of the senior class at Miss Peebles' and transfering to an unknown institution called Northern High School. She left Katie riding alone to school in the family limousine.

Money was not the reason Lissa gave for this shift. She wanted to teach English; she had enough credits to graduate at midyear from Northern High, so that she could enter Meridian University for the second semester and get her degree in three years.

But Rampole Place saw through her subterfuges. Everyone knew that Philip Grover was strapped for money. Queenie was bleeding him white.

By fits and starts Lissa still seemed fond of Katie. But she was queer, her friendliness choked off unexpectedly. And she wouldn't so much as talk about Victor.

Katie was sore and unhappy about her brother, and she admitted he was misbehaving. But she did think Lissa, of all people, might have stood by. The friendship with Lissa was more and more of an uphill job.

Victor's delinquencies broke over Katie in successive phases, each a prelude to the next.

She knew, in the fall, that he and Jodie had broken up. He entered Meridian University, as befitted a Rampole. But if Victor's friends were typical, Katie never wanted to go to college.

He brought some shoals of them in his car. They abused their privileges systematically. They drank the liquor cupboard dry, and fell loutishly asleep on sofas. They stuck to Victor like burs, and they openly flouted Katie, who did not interest them. They made it a point of pride never to open a textbook.

Augustus, in his dry way, enlightened Katie. She mustn't judge the university by them, he said; every place had its rag, tag and bobtail. They hooked onto Vic because he had a car and a big house and money in his pocket. By June most of them would be back where they belonged, behind a soda counter. All Katie had to do was wait.

Katie waited. After election Father would have time to exert his Olympian power and straighten Victor out.

Victor brought coeds to the house. Katie put up with them, until the evening she blundered into the sitting room in the dark.

She flipped the light switch. She had thought the house was empty.

A voice said, "Oh, for God's sake!" The light had revealed a nasty clutter of couples in equivocal attitudes. They were tangled like a litter of newborn kittens; but unfortunately they were not newborn kittens. The whole house was befouled for Katie. She had the sitting-room piano moved upstairs to the playroom so that she should never need to expose herself to such another shock.

Victor was remorseful. He stopped bringing girls to the house. Instead, he stayed out late at night.

One night she was wakened by clumpings on the back stairs. A stumble, a recovery; a high silly giggle; Augustus coaxing somebody around corners; somebody being sick in the bathroom; somebody being maneuvered into Victor's room.

She put on her bathrobe and went out into the corridor. "Have we got burglars, Gus?" she demanded, hoping it was merely burglars.

"Go on back to bed. It's nobody but Vic."

"But he's sick, Gus. I'm going to call the doctor."

"He's drunk, that's all that's wrong with him. I've got him to bed."

"How loathsome!"

"Boys are entitled to sow their wild oats."

Katie went back to bed and spent the rest of the night in a shaking fit. When Victor did come to life she could hardly bear to look at him.

In the Adams-Avenue code, a gentleman knew how to carry his liquor. Even Horace, among the politicians, was deceptively abstemious, and he despised drunkards even while he played on their weakness.

The storm of election mounted, broke, and receded. The Republican ticket squeaked through in Meridian. Mayor Wellworth proceeded to the appointment of his commissioners, amid a scattered raising of editorial eyebrows. Horace washed his hands of the whole mess, and set his face toward Washington.

But at least he must take time to straighten Victor out before he left.

Late one night the gravel spattered in the driveway, and a car pulled up at the side steps under her window. Katie put her head out.

It was a policeman who had brought Victor home. Victor's car was wrapped around a lamppost, the policeman said. Victor had put his head through the windshield, and he was going to need a doctor. The policeman had wanted to take him to a hospital, but the boy had wanted to keep the accident off the police blotter. The policeman hoped, on an interrogatory note, that he had done right and that the Senator would be satisfied.

Augustus reassured him by an exchange of currency.

By this time Katie was downstairs. Gus let her call the doctor while he mopped away the blood that was seeping out under Victor's bandage. "I'll wake Father up," she said.

"No rush about that. The kid didn't hurt anybody but himself. His car is busted, and that will keep him out of mischief for a while. He'll learn his lesson quicker if you don't bring his dad down on him."

"If Victor kills himself some day, Father won't thank you for covering up for him."

"It won't come to that," Augustus said in a relaxed way.

This was a new idea—that it was her duty *not* to speak to her father. It left her with no recourse at all.

Next afternoon, the Wednesday before Thanksgiving, there were new developments. Father came home from the office as black as thunder, and summoned Victor into the smoking room. Katie huddled in the sitting room, listening to the rumble of male voices. "Oh, God," she kept repeating, "Oh, God!" Katie had no settled views on God, but this was a prayer from the heart.

They didn't come to dinner; they sent for sandwiches and coffee in the smoking room. Augustus served Katie all by herself.

"Is Father forbidding Vic to drive a car, do you think, Gus?"

"This ain't about the accident."

"What's he done now?"

Augustus stood at ease, chop platter in hand. "It's something happened the first of the week. The dean of the university was down to see your pa at the office this afternoon. Seems Vic was caught circulating a pocket flask in the back row of a classroom."

"Is he fired?"

"You don't fire the son of the president of the board of trustees. You—er—" here Augustus began impersonating his conception of a college dean—"you regret that his boyish spirits have got out of bounds, but you acknowledge that there's a great deal of good in the lad, and you confine yourself to—er—a sharp reprimand. . . . Your pa is handing the reprimand along."

"That's the worst of living like——" Katie had no words for the Rampole situation.

"It's the worst of being the biggest frog in the puddle."

"He never gets hauled over the coals properly. He always wriggles out of his scrapes."

"Plenty of people would like to be in his shoes. Don't take it so hard, Katie. Nobody can straighten Vic out except himself."

"If he doesn't destroy himself first!"

Augustus said, "I never heard tell of a Rampole destroying himself."

For years Katie had loathed the Thanksgiving Day gorge at Chestnut Point, which was a fossil relic of earlier hospitality. Jennie always turned out an exact duplicate of Grandmother Joe's menu—two turkeys and a ham, a vat of scalloped oysters, boiled onions and mashed turnips, pumpkin pie, and a glut of pioneer condiments.

The guest list had been frozen years ago, when Chloe died. On this holiday the Rampoles recognized their hereditary tie with the Cummagers and with a whole phalanx of obsolete cousins.

This year Katie actively dreaded it. Neither her father nor her brother made an appearance during the morning, and she had to go into the great conglomerate party without knowing what crisis might have developed under her own roof. For some time she was left to deal single-handedly with the elderly guests who congregated in the front parlor. Where was Father? Where was Victor?

Cousin Geneva told her she looked peaked. Cousin Corinne skittishly demanded to be brought up to date on Katie's parties and Katie's beaux. Granny Cummager, who had never forgiven Mrs. Bellamy for taking the dressing of Katie out of her hands, poked at the waist band of her frock and said it had no more hang to it than a meal sack.

Absently fending off these impertinences, Katie listened. Perhaps Victor wasn't in the house at all. Perhaps he had swarmed out his bedroom window and set off to seek his fortune. Perhaps—— Father appeared in the archway, in cutaway and white carnation, easy in his apologies, quite the statesman. Only Katie read the heavy, darkling look behind his urbanity.

Just as dinner was announced Victor came bucketing down the stairs, tying his tie. "Sorry, everybody," he said breezily, and was at once forgiven.

His bandage started a great cackle in the henroost. He wouldn't make a story of it—he said he banged his head through a window. The old ladies were putty in his hands. Wounded, gallant, with his rakehell handsomeness, he stirred the embers of their femininity to a glow. Cousin Corinne cried archly, "I'll warrant you make the girls' hearts go pitapat, you rascal you!"

Katie picked up her soupspoon with an exhalation of thankfulness. At least Father and Victor hadn't come to a break.

In fact, they seemed to have established a truce. They staged a political discussion for the benefit of their guests, who were able to go away saying, "I had it from Cousin Horace's own lips on Thanksgiving Day . . ."

At seven o'clock Augustus reminded the Senator that the car was waiting to take him to the train. He said a hasty good-by all round. Nothing had been settled. At the most it was a respite.

Victor had welcomed his father's summons to the smoking room. For weeks he had been daring the lightning to strike him down. Since Jodie left home, his misery had been so excruciating that tearing himself to pieces had been his only relief. When he rammed his car into the light pole he had been asking for trouble.

He needed a knock-down-and-drag-out fight with someone whom he could then blame for his wretchedness. The patriarchal structure being what it was, his father was his natural adversary.

The fight was a disappointment. He went into the smoking room, his eyes smoldering beneath his bloody bandage.

Horace Rampole did not bellow at him. He opened with a lot of stipulations that cut the ground from under Victor's feet. He well understood, he said carefully, that Victor had quarreled with Jodie Epps and that such an experience was shattering to a young man. He ran through the catalogue of Victor's misdoings, ending with his own interview with the dean of the university. "You can see," he said, "in my position, I'd rather ask for leniency for any boy in Meridian than for my own son."

Victor understood this Rampole hesitancy in claiming a Rampole advantage. It was too easy a way out of a scrape. He tried to bluster. "That's all very well, Father," he said, sitting slumped in his chair and shielding his eyes from the lamplight that sent shafts of pain through his eyeballs. "But I didn't ask to be born a Rampole. I have my own life to live."

"Well, precisely. What are you doing with your life?"

Victor was at a disadvantage. Other boys had gone as far as he had toward self-destruction, but his trouble was that he knew better. He had too much horse sense for his own comfort. He grew morose instead of combative, and the big fight on which he had counted began slipping away from him.

They talked a long time, first over highballs, then over sandwiches and coffee. They were not getting anywhere, but it was as if they were groping toward each other, missing contact but still needing each other.

Horace strayed into the future, sketching out a career for Victor. Naturally he would go into politics—politics was the real lifework for a man. . . .

Victor listened with half an ear. He found himself framing the unaskable, unforgivable question that lay beneath all the horse sense they were talking: Father, was my mother that man's mistress?

He had managed to bury the question from his own consciousness, till Jodie dredged it up into the open. He could never have any peace till that question was answered.

But he couldn't ask his father. The question would bring down the whole porticoed structure that was Horace Rampole and leave him in rubble. It would be the ultimate in filial impiety.

While Horace droned on about politics, Victor counted off the possibilities on his fingers. Either Jodie's story was a lie, a *Sun-Record* lie; or Augustus and Aunt Louisa had kept it from his father because they believed it was true; or his father had built up scar tissue between himself and the intolerable knowledge; or he had accepted it without taking it too much to heart. The last case would be the worst of all.

I'd rather not ask him. None of those answers would do me any good except the first one—and that's too good to hope for. So long as I don't ask, I have a one-in-four chance of believing in my mother, and I'm not bankrupt.

But meanwhile his father was building card castles. "Father," Victor said finally, "don't build your hopes on me. I'm a no-good. Politics doesn't interest me."

"Doesn't interest you!" Horace repeated blankly.

"I can't see myself making a lifework of trudging down the road behind William Howard Taft."

"He's a better President than you give him credit for," Horace said half automatically. He himself was getting tired of standing up for Taft. Pity was not the emotion a leader should evoke. "But in politics, things change faster than you'd think possible. That's the sport of it—engineering the changes."

"You'll have to excuse me."

Horace made one of the major concessions of his life. "Naturally I wouldn't force you into politics, son. It's going to be a full-time job handling the family trust funds after I'm gone."

Victor rejected the suggestion with a sidelong twitch of the head. "One squirrel cage is as good as another. I'll pick a cage when my time comes. But in the meanwhile, Father, I'll admit I've been playing the giddy fool. I'll promise you this much—and you can count on it. While you're out of town I won't give the family a black eye. I've tried going to the devil, and I've about run through the fun of it."

"That's something," his father said, "but it's not much—not for a boy in your shoes. I'm not a churchgoing man, but I—er—I often think of the parable of the talents. I was one of the ten-talent men, and I feel I have an accounting to make. You're another of them."

Victor gave his father a smile that was almost affectionate, but mocking. To whom did the old rhinoceros expect to render that accounting, and what would he claim credit for? For winning elections? For steering bills through committee? For platitudinous orations and shady back-room compromises? For the stadium at Meridian University? For the eight houses in Rampole Place?

It wouldn't be fair to take his father's lollipop away from him. Victor stood up. "If you don't mind," he said, "my head hurts, and I'm going to bed. Don't worry about me, Father. But on the other hand, don't build any hopes on me."

After the Senator left town, the house settled into its winter death-in-life. Katie didn't have night terrors about Victor any more. He came home earlier, and he came home sober. He drew away from his train of sycophants. From time to time he studied a little. He exerted himself fitfully to give small pleasures to Katie.

But it was impossible for her to be happy about Victor, and impossible to help him. He had a favorite chair in the sitting room, and there he sat in hourlong dolorous musings, his legs dangling over the arm, while she read his face furtively. Dark passions traversed it—cynicism, hatred and self-hatred. Twinges of torture. Sometimes he bit off an ejaculation of disgust. Sometimes he groaned without knowing it. Sometimes he slammed out of the house and scorched down the driveway in his patched-up car.

She would have shed her blood to help him. But he kept her at arm's length. He must walk his own path through hell.

Katie saw no particularly good reason why she should ever have been born. During the winter twilights in the funereal house she dallied with thoughts of suicide. There was no real agony in her that would have sustained her through slashing her veins or swallowing poison, but she would have been thankful to wake up some morning and find herself dead. She surveyed her wan corpse and found a certain pathos in it. She selected the flowers for her coffin.

Not white roses; white roses would be so inappropriate that they would make people snicker in spite of themselves.

Tiger lilies. Long-legged, rank-growing tiger lilies for an Indian. Wooden tiger lilies, she amended girmly: wooden tiger lilies for a wooden Indian.

Chapter 32

DURING the winter months of 1910 Philip Grover and Lissa sealed themselves away from their neighbors. Both of them were bleeding internally from the wound to love, and the wound to self-love.

The adjustments to a separation have a niggling nastiness about them. In Philip's case the niggling had to be about money. He hadn't been able to support one establishment; how was he to support two?

Queenie had established herself in an apartment hotel with dining-room service. It was a minimum apartment, she wrote—but naturally it had to be in a good neighborhood, or what was the use of living in New York at all? And she had had to buy a few little furnishings to make it homelike, for which she was sending the bills to Philip.

He soon realized the unwisdom of sending her half of his income as it came in. It arrived in large clots and small driblets—legal fees, property rentals which were often consumed by taxes and repairs. Sometimes he was put to it to meet his office pay roll. He knew Queenie would spend the full income of the fat months, and then face the lean months with wide-eyed bafflement. A monthly stipend was her best hope of solvency.

Lissa threw herself into household economies. It was she who proposed transferring to Northern High School for her senior year. She hunted out Ella Hedges, for two days a week of washing and cleaning. Lissa undertook to cook breakfasts and dinners, and she carried her lunch to school in a packet.

Philip was chagrined by these expedients. On Adams Avenue no householder except old Mr. Cummager had ever sunk so low as to let his womenfolk do the cooking; and Mr. Cummager was a symbol of total failure. The arrangement was unfair to Lissa, with her heavy load of schoolwork. Furthermore, Philip had been pampered all his life, and he did not particularly enjoy Lissa's cooking.

But he gritted his teeth and matched Lissa's sacrifices. He raked the leaves himself. When winter came on he shoveled snow, stoked the furnace and carried out the ashes. This public parade of economy ate into his Adams-Avenue pride. Queenie's departure was a verdict on his inadequacies, and carrying his own ash cans to the curb was a confirmation of the verdict. He and Lissa saved something like twenty or thirty dollars a week—a mere drop in the bucket of his obligations.

A theoretical remedy would have been to go out after more business at the office. But clients who had not turned to Philip Grover in his palmy days were slow to seek him out in his eclipse. So he let one of his clerks go and took back some of the leg work he had done as a young man.

Nevertheless, hope was alive under the surface of his mind. Already, Queenie's artless letters gave away her disillusionment with New York. She played up her occasional gaieties, but she demanded pity for the number of evenings she sat alone, playing solitaire, in her horrid tucked-up little sitting room. Sooner or later she would be back—chastened, ripened. He could afford to wait her out.

The one acitivity to which he really gave himself was his Civic Reform committee. This was work that needed doing, work he understood, work that would result in bringing Anson Epps down to dust.

That committee of his was hard to hold in leash. They wanted to come out shooting. The mayor's new appointments outraged them; Wurtenbacher, who had taken over the Department of Public Works, gave off a stench of graft as rank as creosote.

Philip patiently pointed out that their timing had been set by Senator Rampole. He would talk to the Senator—he would make an appointment with him the next time he was in town.

Horace was at home for Thanksgiving, but he couldn't be reached. Philip was obliged to forgive him. The Senator had private anxieties, which were no affair of Philip's committee.

Ella Hedges knew all there was to know, and more, about young Victor.

Victor was drinking like a fish, and Augustus Henning sat up every night to put him to bed. Victor had smashed his car to smithereens. Ella had it pretty straight that there was a girl involved and that the Senator was paying her hospital bills to keep the story hushed up. Victor was expelled from the university—or maybe it was only suspended; but at any rate he was in hot water up to his neck. Ella said it was a mercy Lissa had cut loose from Victor when she did.

But meanwhile Philip's committee was losing momentum. The members began telephoning excuses for cutting the meetings—we're only marking time anyway, they said.

Philip's heart was sore and remorseful for his Lissa. He knew she was carrying some sort of burden on her conscience; she had persuaded herself that the breakup of the family was her fault. But when he tried to force an entrance into her confidence her pupils dilated as if she were looking into the face of Medusa with the snaky locks. In pity, he let her alone. But he read her: she hated Anson Epps, she hated Victor Rampole and she hated herself. She was poisoning herself with the bread of hatred.

Lissa was paying penance, and she embraced the penance. The housework was a part of it: the crowded classrooms and shrieking corridors of the strange school, the noontime packet of sandwiches, the grueling streetcar rides. In some obscure way Victor's descent into hell was part of her penance—a pain she had had laid upon her.

Meanwhile, with unrecorded steps, her new life was restoring her. No one at the Northern High School threw her catastrophe in her teeth. She lost herself among strangers—and emerged as a prodigy of talent.

Her English teacher gave the class an assignment in writing verse. Back came thirty-nine abortions and one accomplished sonnet. She ran the sonnet in the December issue of the school literary monthly; and the new Lissa was born.

It was not a revealing sonnet. It was called "Endicott Beach" and it was about the beauties of nature. The Adams-Avenue in Lissa forever cut her off from the catharsis of parading her heart in public. But as sonnets went in 1910, it was a feather in the cap of the English Department. It was correctly constructed and delicately turned.

By the unpredictable mercy of God, that sonnet fetched Lissa up out of her morass. It was an arrow aimed at the future instead of the past. She sat late in her virginal bedroom, with the magazine open in the lamplight, reading herself in print. Every time she reread her sonnet she was more struck by its felicities. For the first time in months she went to sleep happy.

And when she woke next morning her overload of guilt had slipped from her shoulders. Of course, she was still sorry about Daddy and Queenie; she was sorry Victor Rampole was going to hell; she was sorry she had betrayed Queenie's half-formulated plans to Victor, and through Victor to Jodie, and through Jodie to the abominable Mr. Epps; but what was done was done.

"Daddy," she said as she carried Philip's coffee to the breakfast table, "do you know what I'd like?"

The lilt of her voice brought his eyes up from his paper. She was blithe as a bird; she had her girlhood back. He could not have refused her anything.

"I'd like you and me to go down to New York to spend Christmas with Queenie."

His first impulse was to raise objections—budgetary and emotional.

Then he berated himself for a curmudgeon. He had not made much of a success of his waiting policy. Perhaps Lissa's instinct was valid— perhaps this was the time for reconciliation.

There was, of course, his committee. He had hoped to pin Senator Rampole down during the Christmas recess. But after all, he had a vice-chairman, who would be all the better for a whiff of responsibility.

"I think I can arrange to get off," he said.

Daily he reframed what he would say to Queenie. He must hit the right note—not too cocky and not too abject; not, please God, truculent or recriminatory. He must be genuine, he must be spontaneous. He must let her know that without her he was nothing but the hollow shell of a man.

He and Lissa got off the train in the early morning and went up to the apartment in a cab. Queenie met them at the door in a ravishing dressing gown, and abounded in embraces.

"You see how tucked-up it is," she apologized. "Darling Lissa will have to sleep on the davenport, but I've got her this pretty screen to dress behind. I'm having breakfast sent up—that's one of the nicest features of living this way. Now, tell me simply everything." She leaned forward with her hands clasped, the picture of eagerness.

Philip looked for signs of her disillusionment. It was a little hard to admit to missing her when she showed no evidence of missing him. She was a hostess, quite at her ease.

Midway of breakfast, she took a telephone call. "No," she said. "No. Not this evening, and not tomorrow evening. Not till after New Year's. My adorable family is visiting me, and I'm saving every minute for them. . . . Oh, I almost forgot to thank you for your beautiful poinsettias. . . . Merry Chirstmas to *you*, Bert. If you see Jack, tell him I said hello."

Philip and Lissa sat arrested, their eyes on their plates. Queenie left the telephone without embarrassment, and poured out hot coffee. "Poor dear Bert!" she said. "He's a little bit ordinary, and I've had to put him in his place once or twice, but he's fun."

Lissa left the table for a tour of the apartment. She discovered a gas ring on the bathroom shelf, with a coffeepot. Queenie said she made coffee when she couldn't sleep.

"If you had a frying pan," Lissa said, "I could get our breakfasts. It would be cheaper."

"Darling! You didn't come to New York to *cook*."

"I make very good breakfasts—don't I, Daddy?"

"Is Ella getting slack?" Queenie asked sharply. "She must be taking advantage of you."

"Why, we wrote you that Ella comes only two days a week now."

"But certainly somebody must get your breakfasts!"

Philip tried to keep his hackles from rising; but he couldn't resist saying, "Lissa gets the meals, and I do the furnace."

"So you wrote." Queenie's fingers were playing a tune on her pink-satin knee. "I never took you seriously. 'They're being melodramatic,' I said to myself. 'It won't last three days.' Why, the house must be a pigsty."

Philip said tartly, "No house that Lissa kept would ever be a pigsty."

"But why, Philip, why? Lissa is my daughter too, and I simply will not permit you to sacrifice her to your fetish of economy."

Philip closed his mouth like a trap.

"But it's so sordid, Philip, so out of proportion. I don't suppose you save ten dollars a week by getting rid of Ella and old Watson. You know, darling, there's something I must say to you whether you like it or not. You remember your mother and her white kid gloves?"

Philip silently dared her to drag his mother into the discussion. She went on. "I was devoted to Mother Grover, but some of her little ways did amuse me. She did—she actually did—clean her own gloves in a pan of gasoline, to save cleaners' bills. They came out all crackly and they smelled so!—and I always thought it showed a lack of perspective."

"My mother——" he began hotly.

"What I'm trying to make you see, darling, is that you've inherited that penurious streak. Time after time you've made us all miserable to save ten dollars. Now you're letting Lissa squander her youth over a dishpan."

"Queenie, my expenses are larger than my income. I'm very grateful to Lissa for lightening the load."

Queenie suddenly tossed the intolerable subject over her shoulder with her hands. "Well, let's not spoil our holidays arguing about money. I've certainly economized till it hurt, and things will work out. What shall we do this morning?"

The days spun by, starred with matinees and little dinners. After their first spat, Philip leaned over backward not to be penurious; and Queenie pointedly selected inexpensive little restaurants. So they arrived at New Year's Eve, when of course they had to drink champagne and blow horns, and so to New Year's Day. Philip and Lissa were to take a train in the evening.

The moment of reconciliation had never come. They had been sweet to one another, but their sweetness had been forced and wary. Philip knew he ought to take the initiative, but how could he make overtures to a wife who made no concessions? Queenie had kept her irresponsibility intact.

Lissa was packing her suitcase, and Queenie was folding frocks. "Philip," she said, turning toward him with a dress across her extended hands. She had the large beauty of a Grecian marble. "You—you haven't asked me to come home with you."

She was giving him an opening. But he was shackled by qualifications, forebodings, unresolved grievances. He said in his pedestrian way, "You know we want you. We can't very well urge you. We haven't much to offer."

He exasperated her, as he had exasperated her for years. But at that moment he couldn't do any better.

He knew that when it was too late the warmth, the longing would flood back into his arid channels. He would lie awake in his bed, consumed with the desire for her presence. He would hear the silver tinkle of a voice where no voice was. But he had a hardwood honor of his own, which forbade him to simulate a nonexistent warmth.

"You don't really miss me," she said under her breath.

"We miss you every minute of every day. But how could we make you happy at home? Nothing would have changed since you made up your mind you'd be happier in New York."

A hardening had come over her—and no wonder. He had not made

228

much of a plea. "I am happier here," she said. "Naturally I miss you and Lissa. But at home—" she hunted for a phrase—"at home I can't be myself without getting people down on me. Here, there's more choice."

Philip's eye traveled to the poinsettia on the window sill. It seemed to him an inadequate compensation for home, security and love; but it had its value for Queenie.

He said into the silence, "I have no right to beg you to come home on our account. When you're ready, all you have to do is let us know, and we'll meet the train."

She gave him a sapless, conventional smile. No self-respecting woman could come home on an invitation like that. Love would have been more selfish in its demands.

Lissa said very little on the train that evening. She lay awake hour after hour in her berth.

She did not precisely judge her father—she understood too instinctively his refusal to set a trap with sugared bait.

Instead, she went off into a daydream of what a man should be. He must be all man; he must beat his woman and break her headstrong will; he must enforce his love upon her and exact her worship. It was an enthralling fantasy; it sent tingles through her.

It was folklore; it was fairy tales; it was *The Taming of the Shrew*. It didn't correspond with reality at any point. Fancy Daddy playing the cave man! She laughed a little, and nestled down into her pillow. He was sweet and he was inadequate; and she would make him as happy as she could. But from that evening she dismissed her own sense of guilt for wrecking her family. She was perhaps maimed, but she was almost frighteningly free.

Philip framed no excuses for himself. He accepted the fact that he had been permanently lessened by his visit to Queenie. Love had been the spring that moved him, and love had failed him. He went prepared for lesser failures, and failure came to meet him.

In the first place, with his committee. Professor Jenkins, his vice-chairman, reported sourly on the conference with Senator Rampole. "The man is stalling—we all sensed it. He won't give the word to pitch into Wutenbacher. He suggests that we start again from scratch on a new investigation."

"He probably has his reasons. Wheels within wheels, you know."

"Too many wheels, in our opinion. We suspect Rampole has made a deal with Wurtenbacher."

"That I can't believe."

"Well, we're being penalized. The new tax bills are out, and our assessments have been raised beyond all reason. I'm told the Board of Review can be made to see reason—handsome consultant's fee to an appraiser named Hannigan, and down comes your valuation. Well, we refuse to bribe our way out of trouble. But we're none of us rich men, Philip, and unless we're going to achieve results, we're not enlisting as martyrs."

The long and short of it was that the committee disbanded.

The disbanding of the committee was not enough to save Philip's hide; he was marked for vengeance. He was served with papers in three damage suits in one week. One of his tenants had had a mattress chewed up by rats; two others had been flooded out when a drain backed up. The *Sun-Record* had it: PROMINENT SCION SUED.

Philip managed to sell one of the old rattletrap buildings, and put the proceeds back into repairing the others. But in February he had to sell some of his rare books to piece out Queenie's allowance.

Once Lissa began attending the university, it became logical to move her nearer to her education. Fortunately the Suttons were willing to rent Philip's house—or rather, Queenie's house. He had put the title in her name so that if he went under financially, the rental of it would provide for her.

The move eased his sense of pressure. His friend Professor Jenkins sponsored him for an associate membership in the Faculty Club, and this group accepted the fact that he and his wife were separated. He stopped dragging a chain of errors behind him. He concentrated on his law practice, and even picked up some new business.

Lissa was happy at University Heights. She had a success not only among her father's friends but among the young instructors. She was disturbingly pretty and tantalizingly unkissable. Her father hoped that in moving away from Rampole Place she had forgotten Victor Rampole. He saw her, when her time came, marrying some promising young professor.

Above all, with his reduced scale of living, Philip was making ends meet and sending Queenie her check without a monthly cataclysm.

He was dead in a sense, drought-stricken, blasted at the heart. But he was as comfortable as a dead man could be, and still capable of the deceptive pantomime of life.

Chapter 33

In March Rampole Place took a shattering shock when the Grovers moved to University Heights. It was known, vaguely, that they had spent Christmas with Queenie in New York, and people had supposed they were patching up their differences.

This move, without so much as a by-your-leave, was an affront to the solidarity of the street. Philip had closed a door in his neighbor's faces. They let him go his way.

Curiously the move gave Lissa back to Katie. As soon as Lissa was settled she called Katie up and asked her to Saturday lunch in her new environment, which was out of the old shadow of Queenie, of Victor and of Anson Epps.

Something new was coming into Lissa. Now that she was in college she began to acquire beaux, dates and a social life. She went to faculty parties with her father. She wrote for the college magazine. She joined a poetry circle.

After Katie found her way to the apartment she went there often, with a sense of adventure. It was the ground floor of an old wooden house that needed paint. It was spacious, shabby, comfortable, full of brown-framed photographs of classical antiquities.

Mr. Grover and Lissa took some of their dinners at the Faculty Club. In a way he seemed to belong there. Certainly Lissa did.

The professors and their wives made a pet of Lissa. She was so lovely, they said, so much what a young girl ought to be but seldom was. They found something piquant in her attachment to Katie Rampole—the vestal and the dark barbarian princess, arm in arm. They were always conscious of the fact that Katie was the daughter of the president of the board of trustees.

Katie did not contribute much to the faculty parties, but she frequented them in Lissa's wake, and they gave her something new to think about. She began to consider going to the university herself next winter. There was very little else in sight for her.

After Katie graduated from Miss Peebles' she faced a summer of blankness at home. Concurrently with Jodie Epps's return from her finishing school in New York, Victor joined a foursome of boys who were setting off for a summer in Europe, and left Chestnut Point half dead behind him.

In July, however, Congress adjourned; Father came home and the smoking room came back to life. And Aunt Louisa invited herself for a visit. No action of Aunt Louisa's was unmotivated, and Katie suspected that she herself was the focus of Aunt Louisa's attention this summer.

Whatever Aunt Louisa had in mind Katie expected to dislike; but she was sure to be overruled. Aunt Louisa was renowned in Meridian for getting her own way. When she founded an orphanage she made it a going concern. When she gave a fancy-dress ball her guests climbed into periwigs and ruffles. It was family legend that she had outfaced Big Joe himself in the matter of her marriage. And not even Horace Rampole had been able to prevent her moving to California.

It was not long before Katie found out what was afoot. She was sorting sheet music in the front parlor while her father and her aunt took a final cup of coffee at the breakfast table. Katie might as well have been sitting at the table with them.

"She has no life of her own, Horace. She's like a spook in a graveyard."

You mind your own business, Aunt Louisa.

"I can't seem to lick it," Horace admitted. "The Gang has broken up."

"A childhood group always breaks up."

"Well, what comes next?"

Aunt Louisa said competently, "Katie must do exactly what I did at the same age. She must come out in society like a normal girl."

"At seventeen? Why, Louisa, she's nothing but a baby. She isn't hatched yet."

"She's through school."

"She's talking about taking a couple of years at the university."

"Horace Rampole, how outrageous! Poor Katie has enough handicaps as it is without your turning her into a bluestocking. Do you want to kill her chances of marriage?"

Horace was properly abashed. He asked uneasily, "Well, how do we go about getting up a debut?"

"There is no sacrifice I won't make for my own flesh and blood," Louisa said superbly. "I have always held myself ready to step back into the picture. I shall reopen the Adams Avenue house and present Katie with all the honors. And I shan't close it again till I have her suitably married off."

"Now, Louisa! I will not have my daughter shipped to market like a head of beef."

"Was I shipped to market like a head of beef when Mamma brought me out in the conventional way? I danced all winter, and by spring I was engaged to my beloved Ollie. It's a natural process for a young girl."

"I won't have Katie railroaded——"

"Dear Horace!" Katie heard Aunt Louisa's chair pushed back. "Do trust me. You may be quite sure I have my niece's happiness at heart."

If Victor had been at home, Katie would have called on him to be her champion. In his absence all she could do was compromise. She proposed to come out in a limited way—taking courses at the new Music Department of the university by day and putting in a brief appearance at parties in the evening.

"My dear child, that's unthinkable. You'll be dancing till three in the mornings. And we'll need ten days in New York to order your frocks and your cotillion favors. Then there will be luncheons given for you, and you can't be ungracious about accepting them. You'll be asked to assist at receptions. You'll have to rehearse for the tableaux at the Charity Ball. . . ."

"I will not make a public spectacle of myself, even for charity."

"No one is asking you to. The tableaux will be classical subjects, in the best of taste. My child, you don't seem to realize the sacrifices I am making for your benefit. This debut is no personal pleasure to me, I assure you."

. . . It wasn't, wasn't it? No more pleasure than a gorge of raw meat to a hungry lion.

Aunt Louisa gave herself to the redecorating of Chestnut Point for Katie's reception. Horace took shelter among the upstate politicians while she ripped out cornices and installed crystal chandeliers. She made a clean sweep of the old parlors. When she got through with them, old Mrs. Joseph would not have known them; they were completely up to date.

What worried Katie most was her music. She had already had to cancel three piano lessons. At any moment Miss Archibald might lose patience and dismiss her as a pupil.

She tried to placate Miss Archibald by describing the ramifications of the coming-out. "I have no control over it," she concluded bitterly. "I can't escape from it. I shall simply die."

Miss Archibald viewed her predicament with cheerful detachment. "There are worse deaths," she said, "than being smothered in creamed chicken and mushrooms. Think of it this way." She swung around to the keyboard and indicated a musical grand entrance. "You're in a circus tent. Here come the elephants—that's the dowagers, with your Aunt Louisa leading the line. Here comes a bevy of dancing girls—that's the debutantes." She tinkled in the treble very inventively. "Now they're making a deep curtsy to the dowagers."

Katie began to laugh helplessly. A spark of irony sent off sizzles inside her mind. "Here," she contributed, "is Miss Kate Rampole making her curtsy." She parodied the debutante theme with a discord and a flat-handed bump on the keys.

Miss Archibald chuckled. "That's my girl. That's the way to take it. We'll drop your lessons while the elephants go by."

Miss Archibald had given Katie the clue to the dolorous maze. As Aunt Louisa grand-marshaled the big parade, Katie satirized it at the piano. She made up a theme for the caterers' men and the carriage callers, and a fugue of gush which she called "Girls in the Dressing Room."

For Katie's ball Aunt Louisa had enlisted the talents of one Butworth Green, who had dedicated his life to leading cotillions. He came repeatedly to tea with Aunt Louisa, carrying charts he had worked out. "This one is tricky, Mrs. Lassigne," he would say, knitting his colorless eyebrows, "but I think you can count on me to bring it off. Say you trust me!"

Katie sat observant, taking notes on the leaping intervals of Butworth Green's voice. Later she played him on the piano, and laughed a good deal at her own wit.

Nothing went wrong with Aunt Louisa's big parade. Katie marched through it, insulated by the new irony Miss Archibald had planted in her.

The dances were the most trying features, because she knew she looked like a great gawk in a ball gown; and she knew the young men who favored her in the cotillions must be fortune hunters.

Mrs. Lassigne was not satisfied. She saw her sacrificial efforts wasted. Katie was determined to be unpopular; she kept her nose in the air, and bit off all overtures to conversation. She slung her beautiful clothes on her back anyhow, and scraped her hair into a great unfashionable bun at the back of her neck. She made no new friends, male or female.

Mrs. Lassigne said bitterly to one of her cronies, "This is the last time I put myself out for Katie Rampole. I wash my hands of her. I always said she was a throwback."

On the fifteen of January she had the wooden shutters screwed back into place on the Adams Avenue house, and shook the dust of Meridian from her feet. Katie's debut would go down in the annals as a triumph, but Aunt Louisa chalked it up as a final defeat.

Chapter 34

KATIE gloried in the resulting solitude. She got back to her piano lessons and consulted Miss Archibald as to what music courses she should enroll for at the university in February.

"Why," she said, looking up from the catalogue, "isn't this your nephew who's teaching some of the courses? Roy Godkin? I thought he played in an orchestra somewhere."

An odd conflict recorded itself on Miss Archibald's rugged features—a conflict of family pride and professional outrage. "He's just been appointed, but unless he mends his ways he'll be back playing in an orchestra. He's gone completely dissonant. He says—" she spoke with portentous irony—"he's *outgrown* Brahms and Beethoven. I don't want you to study with Roy Godkin. He'd be the ruination of you."

"I couldn't study with him if I wanted to. He doesn't teach any of the elementary courses." But Katie made a private note that she must hear some of Roy Godkin's music.

One day, just before the term opened, Lissa telephoned her. The Burches were giving a musical evening, and Mrs. Burch had suggested that the Grovers might like to bring Katie Rampole. "Do come, Katie, if you're not fed up with parties," Lissa said. "Some of the faculty from the Music Department are going to play, and Daddy and I will be out of our depth. We need you."

Katie needed no urging. This was the first invitation of the winter that had interested her.

She knew about the Burches. Professor Burch had married a rich widow who was very musical. Mrs. Burch had a music room with two pianos.

For once Katie gave consideration to what she had better wear. None of her ball gowns—and yet she wanted to look as well as she could.

The tableaux at the Charity Ball had required Katie to wear a garment which Aunt Louisa referred to as "that old green thing." Since she was tall and not very pretty, the director had used her for a strong note of color in the background. The costume hung straight, classic and unfashionable, held in by a jewel-crusted girdle.

Aunt Louisa had adopted in her youth the dogma that green made a dark complexion look sallow. After the tableaux the costume had been relegated to the attic. But at least it was severely plain, and Katie had taken a liking to the strong, bronzy peacock color. She decided to wear the old green thing. The small act of independence exhilarated her, and she expected to enjoy Mrs. Burch's party.

She called for Mr. Grover and Lissa in the limousine and took them on to the Burches'. It soon appeared that Mrs. Burch was not giving a conventional musicale. The guests sat on divans and ottomans around the big, bare, distinguished room. Out in the corridor a buffet was set up with glasses and bottles. Mrs. Burch towed Katie around the room, introducing her. "I particularly want Dr. Schweiz to meet you," she said, "since you're going to be one of his pupils."

Dr. Schweiz was the head of the Music Department, and a very great man indeed, as he was the first to admit. His hair was leonine, his voice had a waspish authority. He held up the musical proceedings for a long-winded anecdote, purportedly humorous, which turned on the fact that Felix Weingartner had a habit of seeking his advice. The anecdote was received with placatory departmental laughter.

Pretty soon Mrs. Burch and another woman fell to playing something for two pianos. Then the music got sidetracked in favor of an acrid general denunciation of the horn section in the local symphony orchestra.

"You'll give us something, Dr. Schweiz?" Mrs. Burch asked, to get her party back on the rails.

"Later, later," he said languidly, implying that the small fry should be given their scamper first.

All this while two young men had been glaring and thumping their fists at each other in a corner. Both of them wore their hair short and tried to look like young businessmen with no nonsense about them; but their passion betrayed them. The taller one Katie recognized instantly as Mr. Godkin—his steel-rimmed glasses, his quadrilateral face.

"Roy," Mrs. Burch suggested, "it's your turn."

Mr. Godkin assented carelessly, and rose.

"Nothing *too* queer, Roy."

"Nothing of my own, you mean. Is Debussy too queer for you?" he said as he made his way toward the piano. "How about the *Images?*" and in a minute he was playing.

Miss Archibald harped on touch, on tone, on dynamics. Mr. Godkin was not trying for any of these. His playing was almost arid. And yet it set Katie's imagination to work.

I know, she discovered suddenly. *It's like Miss Peebles reading Shakespeare aloud to the school. She doesn't compete with Sothern and Mar-*

lowe—she leaves the interpretation to us. Mr. Godkin is reading Debussy aloud to us. It's a composer's playing.

The Debussy was approved. "Are you strong enough for some Schönberg?" he asked half defiantly. And his hands began tearing at the strangest chords Katie had ever heard—chords that sounded like misprints. They racked Katie's ears—she would have to hear them again and again before she could judge them. But they stimulated her furiously. Her eyes fastened themselves hypnotically on the pianist.

So did all the other eyes. Dr. Schweiz dramatized his displeasure in a way that was meant to make his subordinate cringe. Mrs. Burch held her hands playfully over her ears. When he finished she cried—with his best interests at heart—"Now give us the antidote. Give us some Chopin, Roy—or are you above playing Chopin?"

"I'm not a Chopin player," he demurred. "Anyway, I've had my turn. Somebody else play."

Nobody volunteered.

"Miss Dineen?"

A thin, elderly lady, much beaded, with eyeglasses chained to her face, shook her head.

"Come on," Mr. Godkin said. "Honestly, I didn't mean to minimize Chopin. It's simply that I can't do right by him."

"Who can?" said Miss Dineen worshipfully.

"We have a Chopin player in the house," he said. And with a tiny smile he rockabyed the opening phrase of the Ballade and turned his head to look straight at Katie.

A voltage went through Katie that all but knocked her off her seat. He had given no indication that he remembered her. Her whole life was destroyed and remade in an instant. "I couldn't possibly," she stammered.

"I've heard you play it very well."

"I've hardly touched the piano for three months," she protested. But she was urged from all sides, and propelled to the piano.

"I haven't played the Ballade in years," she said. "I'll have to play something else."

Everyone urged the daughter of the president of the board of trustees to play something else, then. She could see them getting ready to applaud whatever she played. Let her play as badly as she liked, they would dutifully clap their hands.

She sat with her hands gripping the piano bench, her forehead lowered in thought, reviewing her repertoire. None of it was in shape. Certainly not the Beethoven. Not the Grieg.

All right, she thought, I'll give them just what they're looking for. A naughtiness mounted in her.

"The reason I'm out of practice," she said to her audience, "is that I've been through an absorbing experience." A power was coming into her—a Rampole platform manner. "I have been presented in society this winter. I will give you my impressions of coming out in society."

While they swallowed down their blankness she struck a few chords. "First," she said, speaking over her own playing, "we have the assembly of the dowagers." And she went into Miss Archibald's elephant march. Nobody knew quite how to take it.

"And now here come the debutantes." *Tinkle-tinkle-tinkle.* The audience began to laugh.

"This," she said, "is a cotillion leader planning his campaign." And she gave them Mr. Butworth Green and his charming anxieties. In musical terms this was the best part of her Début Suite. Mr. Godkin had his elbows on the tail of the piano. He gave an outright guffaw, and it echoed round the room.

"Now," Katie said impressively, "we arrive at the climax of the season, the debutante ball." She wove the dowagers, the debutantes, Mr. Butworth Green and the dance orchestra together higgledy-piggledy.

"You may like to meet the debutante in person," she said. She parodied the reigning waltz of the season, ending with a flat collision and a few descending titters from the debutantes. Miss Dineen took off her glasses and wiped the tears of laughter from her eyes.

"The season is over," Katie said sepulchrally. She played a few bars of Chopin's Raindrop Prelude, transposed into a minor, dying away like the drip from a rusted gutter.

The moment Katie stopped playing, her exhilaration flagged. What had possessed her to make a fool of herself in a gathering of really musical people? It hadn't been even funny—they had laughed for prudential reasons. Oh, that the floor would open up and let her through! She fled from the people who were crowding up to her, and took refuge in a corner with Mr. Grover and Lissa.

"I want to talk to you," Roy Godkin said. He forced himself into her triangular retreat, and took her firmly by the elbow.

She let him lead her to the execution block. "It was dreadfully cheap, I know. I can't imagine what got into me."

"It was dreadfully cheap," he corroborated her. "Here, come out in the hall and get a drink."

Katie was too stricken to protest that she didn't drink. She let him put a glass of red wine into her hand.

"What tantalizes me," he went on, "is that if you can do that—and it

238

was clever as hell—you can do something a lot better than that. You have a command of the keyboard. What's rarer, you have a certain amount of musical inventiveness. Your field is composition or nothing."

"I am taking Elementary Harmony this next term," she said, anxious for his approval.

"Harmony 101," he said in a slow and awful voice. "Oh, God, O Montreal. Harmony 101, my poor child, is a fate far worse than death. Harmony 101 is what is wrong with this mummified Music Department."

"It's a prerequisite for practically all the other courses."

"Certainly. It's the embalming department, so the corpses of the victims won't stink. First inversions, second inversions, progressions—I can teach you all that in three days. You know it already."

"But I shan't be studying with you."

"I shall have to take you on."

Katie saw what Miss Archibald had meant when she said that before long he would be back playing in an orchestra. Dr. Schweiz was not the man to put up with this sort of thing. She said hesitantly, "Miss Archibald helped me to pick out my courses."

He said, "My aunt taught me the first forty per cent of what I know about music, but she is not God the Father Almighty."

Katie couldn't help laughing.

"Well," he demanded, "are you going to travel with the sheep or the goats? I warn you, if you skip Harmony 101, they won't give you a degree."

"Degree!" said Katie blankly. "Why, of course I'll study with you if you'll have me." She was astonished that he should have any doubt about that.

"You are taking Harmony 105," he informed her, "a course that has been set up as of right this minute. Don't forget, now, when you register—Harmony 105."

The Senator, on his flying trips home, took heart. He had written off Katie's debut as a total loss. Now, weeks later, dividends were beginning to come in. She was as far as ever from rose-leaf cheeks and dimples; but there was something about her eyes that stopped one's breathing for a second. She reminded Horace of some of the foreign-diplomatic wives in Washington.

Katie was not conscious of having changed. It was the world that had changed, by setting open its gates and inviting her into its gardens. She had been passive throughout the ordeal of childhood, and now she accepted the rapture of youth.

She was not in love. All that had happened was that she had been accepted for Mr. Godkin's special course. Their relationship was strictly academic: "Good morning, Mr. Godkin, I hope I'm not late." . . . "Well, Miss Rampole, how's it going?"

There was heresy and rebellion in Harmony 105. If Miss Rampole had been anyone except the daughter of the president of the board of trustees, Dr. Schweiz would have made short work of Mr. Godkin's un-authorized course. As it was, he refused Mr. Godkin a proper classroom; so Harmony 105 met on two kitchen chairs in one of the basement prac-tice rooms. There was a piano, and Mr. Godkin salvaged a shaky old table from the boiler room. There was hardly space to turn around in. But there was room enough for a hop, skip and jump through the rudi-ments of Harmony 101, before proceeding to better things.

One morning, when Mr. Godkin was illustrating an advanced experi-ment in dissonance at the keyboard, Katie had the effrontery to say, "Miss Archibald says you will be the ruination of me."

She expected a hot-tempered rebuttal. Instead, Mr. Godkin held down a silent chord with his big hands. "She's quite a Cassandra," he said. "Only last night she was telling me *you* would be the ruination of *me*."

"Me!" Katie gasped.

"Forget I said that," he told her impatiently. "My aunt has a lot of romantic bees in her bonnet. She—" his voice had the driest possible tone—"she sees me falling in love with you. Which would be equivalent to selling my soul to the devil, don't you see, because you are a rich society girl and not serious about music?" His fingers made a mocking quirk on the keys. Without thinking, Katie inverted his quirk in the treble, to assure him she shared his mockery. They both grinned, and got back to work.

All the same, that bee from Miss Archibald's bonnet was an awkward insect to have on the premises. It produced a constraint between teacher and pupil. Mr. Godkin didn't seem to have his mind entirely on his teaching.

At the next break he said casually, "Where did you ever learn to talk on the piano? Nobody else plays at your house, do they?"

"I learned it years ago, at your house."

"You never were at my house," he said, staring. "I never set eyes on you till the day you couldn't remember the Ballade."

"Miss Archibald had a bunch of us girls at your house, rehearsing for a recital. She called you to supper on the piano, and you answered from upstairs on the flute." She whistled the notes for "Down-in-a-minute."

"For God's sake!"

"We were practicing a Tchaikovsky serenade that Miss Archibald had arranged for four hands. You were upstairs, and you played an obbligato on the flute. Don't you remember?"

Mr. Godkin didn't remember a thing about it. He appeared stricken with wonder, beyond what the small incident warranted.

"I'm going to take a chance on you," Mr Godkin said, when the term was a few weeks along. "I'm going to tow you out in deep water and dump you. For next week, instead of writing out exercises, I want you to write three variations on this theme by Mozart." He began writing the theme in her assignment book, in his rapid, idiosyncratic musical notation. "We'll see what happens. But don't you tell Dr. Schweiz— he'd snatch me bald-headed. This is third-year stuff, according to him."

Katie looked over his shoulder, and then went to the piano. "I do that for the Gang at the house. I did it with 'Yankee Doodle,' and I did it with 'Old Folks at Home.'" She began trifling with the Mozart theme.

Mr. Godkin gave out a sound of inarticulate fury. "You do that just once more," he snarled, "and I'll send you right back into Harmony 101. That's not music, it's a parlor trick—like threading a needle, with a glass of water balanced on your forehead. You function with your muscles, Miss Rampole, the way a caterpillar humps himself along a branch. If you're going to be a musician, you'll have to use the inside of your head. You are to compose these variations *at a desk,* in a room where there is *no piano.*"

"How would I know how it sounded?" she asked ingenuously.

This time she had gone too far. He got up and stamped about the tiny cell, and even went down the hall to the water cooler before he got himself in hand.

When he came back into the room she was genuinely frightened by the scorn in his eyes. He put his hands in his pockets and spoke with careful self-control.

"I'm being unjust to you," he said. "I'm demanding something you haven't got. I've been wearing myself to the bone—" which was a wild exaggeration—"and imperiling my position in the department, trying to blow the spark of music to life in you. You're not fundamentally musical. You have a nasty little knack of pretending to be musical at parties. Obviously it gives satisfaction to you and your—*Gang.*" He was venomous as a spider. "Go on back to your gang. Be the infant phenomenon at little parties. It's a good act—you can milk it for the next forty years."

She said absolutely nothing. Her eyes fastened themselves on his, enormous, as if she were facing a firing squad. This was death. This was annihilation. Mr. Godkin had found out that she was not musical.

He took an exasperated stride across the room, and then whirled to look down at her. She was facing him from the end of the piano bench. She had not moved at all. She had shriveled together.

"Well, say something, for God's sake!" he challenged her. "Fight back. Don't play on my sympathy. Don't just sit there as if I'd shot you through the heart."

She gave a numb little smile. She stretched out her left hand and played the saddest possible descending cadence, ending in mid-air. It was her farewell to music. Her hand had said, "But what have you left me to fight with?"

She had broken his anger. "All right," he said. "I take it back. You are somewhat musical. But seriously, Miss Rampole, I see that I'm exploiting you. I've wanted to use you as a demonstration of my teaching methods. You're basically musical—but you have too much besides music in your life, and music is going to reject you. To you, music is one more sport. You have too much."

"What have I, except music?" she asked bleakly.

That brought back his anger. "You have bread and coal and shoes for the asking. And the raiment of the Queen of Sheba. Everywhere you turn, you have flattery. You've had this whole town turning cart wheels all winter for your highness' entertainment. Don't think I haven't read the papers. You've been the next biggest thing to the presidential candidates. You have——"

Her left hand struck out harshly at the keys, obliterating all these glories.

"All right, then," he accepted her comment. "Say you have guts enough to cut loose from all that. What you can't cut loose from is being so damned beautiful. You're saddled with that."

She made a little sound that was not quite a groan. "Don't," she said almost too low to be heard.

"Anybody would think I was roasting you over a slow fire. Don't what?"

"Don't be sarcastic. Don't make fun of things I can't help. You can scold me about music as much as you like. That's what I come to you for. But——" She gripped her hands together. Her eyes began dodging past him, looking for an escape route.

He went over to the table and began ranging the scattered notebooks and music paper. "Let's be clear about this," he said. "Has anybody been teasing you about not being beautiful?"

"I'm an eyesore. It isn't as if I made any claims to being beautiful. I didn't ask to have a coming-out party."

"That's a point we can't argue very profitably," he said without turning around. "You're entitled to your own opinion. In fairness to myself, though——" His composure broke, and he began talking fast and hotly. "Do you know what you reminded me of when you sat down at the Burches' piano, with your long straight arms hanging down against your long peacock-colored dress, and your head tipped forward? The young Medea. The young barbarian princess who was a sorceress. Fascinating, frightening. That's why you gave me such a jolt when you began tweedling on the piano like any high-school cutup. I said to myself—well, never mind what I said to myself, Miss Rampole. We've had enough heroics for one day. Let's get back to work."

"Lissa, what can he possibly have meant? Is he blind? Has he got a warped taste in—in beauty? Miss Archibald thinks he has a warped taste in music."

Lissa answered whimsically, "I can't think of anything except that he must consider you *are* beautiful. All that matters is that he shouldn't suspect you of thinking you're too beautiful to work at your music, and you've cleared him up on that."

Two weeks later Katie brought her "Variations on a Theme by Mozart" to Mr. Godkin. She had worked at them morning, noon and night, but she had disobeyed Mr. Godkin in regard to working away from the piano.

By the time she had put eight bars on paper, she had to go to the piano to hear how it sounded. There the music flowed out under her fingers—it developed faster than she could write it down. She turned it under her hands, reshaping her rhythms and her phrases. She tried conscientiously to put in some dissonance on Mr. Godkin's account, but dissonance was harder to handle than harmony was. Before long her Variations were getting so beautiful that she gave them their head. She went to sleep at night hearing them, and rushed to the playroom piano before breakfast.

She made a fair copy the night before she handed it in. When she laid it before Mr. Godkin she was half quaking, half tingling. She had invented an imaginary scene in which he laid down the manuscript and said reverently, "Why, Miss Rampole, I was prepared for talent, but talent is hardly a big enough word to apply to this. . . ."

He ran his eye along the neat staffs. He turned the page, skimming with his eye.

"Well, you certainly got a long way from Mozart," he said, laying it down. "You seem to have arrived at about the year 1892. It reads the way my mother's quince preserves taste."

He knocked her breath out as if he had been a mule who kicked her with his hoof. She turned a scorching scarlet and reached out for the despised sheets of music.

He held them down with the flat of his hand. "Not so fast," he said. "There were some pretty good men writing music in 1892, notably—" he snapped the manuscript with his fingernail—"Peter Ilitch Tchaikovsky. They tell me," he went on speculatively, "that the human embryo recapitulates the biological history of the race. That's Sunday-supplement biology—take it or leave it. But it stands to reason that if you're going to arrive at the year 1912, you've got to pass the year 1892 at some point. Here, play it." He slung the music at her.

Katie had her dander up by this time—for a curious reason. In all the seventeen years of her life no one had had the vulgarity to mention a human embryo in her presence. She acquitted Mr. Godkin of intending to be coarse; but he was an uncouth young man. Hence—the reasoning struck her as unanswerable—he was not a final arbiter on her Variations.

She set the music defiantly on the rack, and her right hand announced the Mozart theme. Then she began to play her first variation; and whatever Mr. Godkin thought, she found it bewitching.

The second variation was movingly sad—*tristoso*. Her playing drenched it with honey. By the time she had got into the third variation she had forgotten Mr. Godkin. She whipped up a rising gale of arpeggios to the big proud chords of the finale.

Then she sat and waited, without turning around.

He cleared his throat. "Well, the one thing I didn't allow for," he said after a silence, "was that you might be genuinely in love. I can't cope with this sort of thing."

"I am *not* in love!" she snapped.

"Then, alternatively," Mr. Godkin said, "I must concede that you are musical, or at least imaginative. . . . Come, let's take this apart and see what we can do to fix it up. You've used some progressions that would set a giraffe's teeth on edge. You've doubled your thirds all through here—that's what makes it taste of quince preserves."

He went through her fair copy, scratching out whole passages and scrawling, "*Rewrite.*"

"It's flabby, this *tristoso*, it's insipid," he said. "It's a young girl's dream of a broken heart, with marshmallow. Suppose we try it like this." He went to the piano.

She slipped to the piano bench beside him, and her fingers argued with his in the upper octaves. She meant to show him (a) that he was not God the Father Almighty, (b) that she was musical, even if he located her in the year 1892, and (c) that she was not in love. She could be every bit as pedantic as he was.

244

He was making great improvements in her Variations. He had command of a fresh idiom. Little queernesses fell from his fingers that sent shivers through her. But she would not give him the satisfaction of telling him so. Her hands on the keyboard continued to argue with his.

Unexpectedly his playing broke up in laughter. She looked at him sidewise as if he had gone mad. "You know," he said, still chuckling, "this is more fun than I've had in a dog's age. It's all very well for you to say you're not a witch—you have the devil in your fingers. They make damned good jokes."

"Oh," she said coldly. "I understood I wasn't musical."

"Got your back up, have you? Here, take the thing home and rewrite it to suit yourself."

Katie sat down at the playroom piano and opened her Variations, all slashed and scrabbled as they were. She meant to work at her revisions; what she actually did was play the work through for the hundred and fiftieth time. It might not be technically correct, but just as it stood it shone like the arch of a rainbow. You can't bend a rainbow. All you can do is glory in it. The Variations had come from somewhere very deep in Katie.

He thought I was in love, she said to herself while she was playing. My music said to him that I was in love. How queer!

She finished the finale and saw that her hands were shaking. How ridiculous of Mr. Godkin to leap to the conclusion that she was in love!

A great swell from the depths was lifting her. Her head was whirling, her body was sinking. Pure sweetness engulfed her.

She rested her hands on the music rack and bowed her forehead on them.

The prospect of the next lesson was a torture with delicious overtones. She must keep a guard even on her fingers for fear they might betray that she was in love with Mr. Godkin. He knew already that she was in love; but if God was good, she could keep her last secret sacred— that she was in love with him.

She came along the echoing basement corridor with her notebooks. A few feet from the door she stopped short, her books clutched to her laboring breast.

Mr. Godkin was playing while he waited for her. He was working on her *tristoso*—or was it her *tristoso*? He had done something to it; he was improvising on it. The Mozart theme was transmuted now into some ancient mode; it strode along strange, beautiful and lonely, with odd off-harmonies.

She had never known he could play like that. It was lovely enough to melt the bones in your body. He played it with one finger, and stopped halfway.

While Katie stood listening in the brick-walled corridor, something big took possession of her. Something selfless and self-completing.

She could not be deceived about that playing. It told her he was unhappy and tormented. Just as her playing had told Mr. Godkin that she was in love, his playing told her that he was in love. She did not quibble over the unlikelihood of his falling in love with a girl as impossible as herself.

She knew just what she had to do. The necessary power flooded into her.

She opened the door. He was sitting slumped at the piano. He looked up, as self-conscious as if she had caught him going through her purse.

"That sounded heavenly," she said.

"I wish I could think what to do with it next," he said, looking straight into her eyes.

"I'll turn it over to you. You can handle it. You've—you've transformed it. It belongs to you." The *tristoso* lent itself to their meaning like an algebraic symbol they had in common. They were not misunderstanding each other.

"I have no right to it," he said, looking away from her.

"It's of no value to anybody but you."

"Don't talk like that," he exclaimed roughly. He swung back to the keyboard and knocked out a raucous variant of the Mozart theme, hitting the notes as if he hated them. "That's my material," he said. But he was begging her to contradict him.

"You're afraid of sweetness."

"Yes. Who wouldn't be?"

He fingered out a long suspension in D-flat, and left it dangling just short of the resolution.

She crossed over to the piano and struck the tonic chord that brought peace back into the room. "There it is," she said. "Is that what you wanted?"

"It's all I want. But it isn't fair."

"Why don't you let me be the judge of that, Roy?"

He gathered her outspread fingers into a cluster inside his hand. "I suppose I may call you Katie," he said with an impertinent grin.

Chapter 35

VICTOR was doing better, Katie was doing better. It was a mercy that Horace Rampole had these private alleviations, because the Republican party was down with a deadly illness.

The experts were in hot disagreement. Must Taft be nominated a second time? And if he were given the nomination, could he win? It was a matter of life and death for the party workers.

Horace, in Washington, felt that Dan Parmiter was blinding himself to the emergency. Dan was the state committeeman; and although he was slipping in Meridian, he was still a big figure upstate. Dan took the revolt against Taft as the perennial pre-election howdy-do. After election the Republicans could sweep up the clutter and resume the reins of government. He limited his job to delivering the state of Algonquin in November. Horace saw the problem in its national aspect.

Horace had been loyal to the administration, within limits, but he was sick and tired of defending it on both liberal and conservative fronts. Defending Roosevelt had been child's play: the conservatives might not like him, but they couldn't lick him. He could always pull a fresh triumph out of his hat to becloud his errors.

Much could be said, and honestly said, in defense of Taft. To the Progressives one could point out that he had busted more trusts than Teddy the Trust Buster. His court appointments had been good. He had extended the civil service.

One could tell the Regulars that he had left the new tariff much like the old one. He had supported Uncle Joe Cannon, the lifelong czar of the House—though his support had not saved Joe Cannon's bacon. He had stood punctiliously behind his Secretary of the Interior in the Ballinger fracas.

The unfortunate man was a misfit in the executive chair. He was temperamentally a judge, with an admirable faculty for seeing both sides of a question. But he was a man who could be nudged, hoodwinked and misled, because of his faith in other men's honesty. And he had no gift for the high art of ballyhoo, instinctive in a born politician. For instance, he had worked hard for the Canadian Reciprocity Treaty, and all he had accomplished was to stir up bad blood on both sides of the border.

There were two constitutional amendments that pinched Horace personally. One was the authorization for a federal income tax. It didn't look well for a man as rich as Horace to oppose it—but what led straighter to the extinction of the wealth that had raised the whole economy on its upthrusting shoulders?

The proposed amendment for the direct election of senators came even closer home. If it passed, Horace would have to get out and hustle for his own re-election in 1914. He could win, unquestionably; but he had been seated twice, with proper dignity, by vote of the state legislature. He dreaded the dust, sweat and demagoguery of a campaign.

Horace had taken the stand that what couldn't be cured must be endured. To replace Taft by another candidate would dishonor the party. Roosevelt had taken himself out of the country, on purpose to give his successor a free field. He had refused to intervene in the Ballinger-Pinchot row.

But now Roosevelt was back on his native soil, and the country was homesick for him. It was tired and bored by Taft. It missed the clangor of war among the archangels.

Even if Roosevelt had not lifted a finger, the yearning would still have arisen. Roosevelt being the man he was, it was inevitable that he should lift his finger. Passivity was not among his gifts.

The great ex-President accepted an editorship on a periodical called the *Outlook*. From this rostrum he began writing a sharp commentary on public affairs. This opened the floodgates. If Roosevelt himself was critical of Taft, surely the Insurgents had leave to look elsewhere for a candidate. And where should they look, except to Oyster Bay? One by one they took staff and scrip, and made pilgrimage to the shrine.

Danny said, "Don't let me catch you kissing Roosevelt's toe, Horry."

So that was it! Dan had lost control of his party machine and let the rascals into Meridian—a situation for which Horace was being blamed. But he was still playing cock of the walk and ordering Horace around.

"Dan, can't you put aside your bias and look to the good of the party? This is a ground swell. The voters want Roosevelt."

"So does Roosevelt want Roosevelt. But he's had his two terms. He's disqualified."

"He's not manipulating this boom. The people are in love with him."

"Yah! Can't you leave the bleeding heart and the crown of thorns to the Democrats? You kind of embarrass me."

"The third-term precedent doesn't govern. There's been an interregnum."

"Interregnum—exactly! Princess Alice and all the little princelings. I hope you get a fat job as Groom of the Chambers. You'd look nice in knee pants."

"I say the country is drafting him."

"The men that write the checks aren't drafting him. He's getting wilder every day."

The time for argument was running out. Seven Republican governors petitioned Roosevelt to run. The pilgrimage to Oyster Bay was turning into a stampede. If Horace decided to go, he had better go soon, or he would be trampled in the crowd.

State legislatures were rushing through the authorization for direct primaries, to by-pass the party regulars. And when the primaries were held, in state after state the delegates were instructed for Roosevelt.

The Insurgents brought in such a bill to the Algonquin legislature, but it died in committee. While Dan Parmiter drew breath and dispensed the party funds, he was going to hold the reins. "You'd rather lose the election than win it with Roosevelt," Horace said bitterly.

"The country has a normal Republican majority," Dan said placidly. "The party can survive a split."

Horace himslf began to have qualms. Roosevelt was certainly bidding high and recklessly.

In February he threw his hat into the ring. His platform gave Horace pause. He advocated not only the initiative, referendum and recall, but the recall of judicial decisions—which was as good as tossing justice to the frenzy of the mob. Property, he proclaimed, should be the servant and not the master of the commonwealth. High-sounding words, dangerous words.

"Had enough?" Dan taunted Horace. "I thought so. He pretty near took you into camp. But he's a mad dog on the loose."

Taft fought back with obvious compunction. He and Roosevelt had been the closest of personal friends. But Roosevelt had roared out accusations a man of honor had to refute. He had accused Taft of selling out to the Interests. "Megalomaniac," Taft said, like a gentlemanly little boy trying to use bad language. "Neurotic political emotionalist," he said. "Caesar, Napoleon," he said. He was doing his best. . . .

The Algonquin delegates—including Horace Rampole—were appointed and instructed for Taft.

The choice was out of Horace's hands. He had put on all the pressure he could, both in Meridian and in Washington. He was a good soldier, and he would obey orders.

The campus seethed with politics of a half-baked sort. All Victor's contemporaries had been under the spell of the Great Roughrider since their earliest childhood.

Victor set up to be knowing and cynical, though his grip was weakening. Roosevelt had pledged himself not to run again. The sound and fury was routine. In the end the insiders would grease the rails for the organization candidate—that was how politics worked.

But when Roosevelt tossed his hat into the ring Victor's old hero worship came back upon him. He hoped he could influence his father, and to this end he cultivated his father's company.

One May afternoon he happened into the pantry for a glass of milk. He found Augustus getting out the big candelabra. "Company tonight?" he asked.

"Old Parmiter. I'm giving him the works. I like to remind him who he is." And Augustus opened the jar of silver polish.

"Got any dope?"

"I thought you were above politics," Gus said wickedly.

"This is a crisis. I want to know where Father stands."

"Ask him, don't ask me."

"I know where Parmiter stands—he's an old fossil. How about you, Gus?"

Augustus circled away with his cloth. "If Teddy don't get the nomination, I'm going to vote Democratic—and you can quote me to your pa."

"You're not the only one. The state is for Roosevelt."

"Tell that to Parmiter."

"Parmiter! Could Parmiter have built the Panama Canal? Could Parmiter have settled the Russo-Japanese War?"

"Quite the young orator, ain't you?"

"I am going to smoke Parmiter out," Victor said direfully.

When Dan came into the smoking room Victor was lounging in one of the big charis, and he did not intend to budge. He gave Dan the greeting their old acquaintance called for, and kept on looking at the evening paper.

He knew Dan had the reverence for himself and Katie that Britons had for the blood royal. Big Joe's portrait overtopped the scene, and Dan made something approaching a genuflection before it. He eased himself into a chair and sat rubbing his kneecaps. "Ah, the shindies I've seen in here," he said with gusto.

Here it came—a yarn so old that it had recaptured its innocence. ". . . And Lem Hankins says he'll be damned if he'll perjure himself for a measly hundred bucks. So Big Joe takes another greenback out of his tin box and slaps it down on the desk. . . ."

He made Horace uneasy. "You made up that story, lock, stock and barrel. You've been putting a high shine on it for years. Before you know it, you'll reel it off to some reporter and he'll run it in the paper."

"It's true as gospel. I sat in this room and heard it with my own ears. I was a young shaver then, learning my trade," Dan protested perversely. "But you don't need to give me lessons, Horace Rampole, in what to put in the papers."

The story did not shock Victor nor even surprise him. It bore out his opinion of the bad old days and of Danny's bad old character.

They went in to dinner. Victor made his own opening.

"Mr. Parmiter," he asked clearly, "Algonquin is going to switch to Roosevelt, isn't it?"

Dan was not to be caught napping by a question. "Think we ought to?" he asked quizzically.

"I'm asking you what you think."

"Well now," said Danny, thus squarely confronted. "I'd like to hear what your dad thinks. He's been swinging like a rooster on a weather vane."

"It's a teaser," Horace said. "It's dynamite."

"There's always dynamite before election," Dan said composedly, "and it never blows up. Once Taft is nominated, we'll start hating the Democrats."

"But this is the only time you've fought Roosevelt," Victor proclaimed with fanatic fervor.

"The party is bigger than even Teddy Roosevelt."

"Then you're for Taft, right to the bitter end. And the bosses are bigger than the people. And party regularity is more important than a good President."

"Mind your manners, son," Horace intervened.

"Oh, leave him talk," Danny said with infuriating tolerance. "He's been reading the *Sun-Record,* that's all that's wrong with him. Talking is healthy."

For the rest of dinner Victor subsided into smoldering silence. He was through with Dan Parmiter and through with his father.

Sharp at ten o'clock, pursuant to doctors' orders, Dan drove off in his rattletrap car. Horace took his troubled cigar out into the mild May evening and promenaded the lawn.

He had read the condemnation in Victor's eyes. He had an unfulfilled longing to stand well with his son. He wanted one thing in the world: he wanted to come out for Roosevelt.

But he had not arrived at his present height by following the urgings of sentiment. He tried to be realistic.

It isn't, he reasoned, as if we had a choice of qualified candidates. We have Roosevelt—Taft—and some nameless scoundrelly Democrat as yet unnominated. Taft can't win, so we narrow down to Roosevelt or the Democrat. It's all very well for Dan to talk about waiting four years to get back in—our time is running out, his and mine.

Dan says Roosevelt is a wild man these days. But when he was President his bark was worse than his bite. He belongs in the White House; he's dangerous only when he's out of it.

An undertow was carrying Horace out to sea; there was no fighting it. Victor was the prototype of the ardent young, the custodians of the future, who had no use for a mossback party. New blood, he said to himself, puffing his cigar to a glow. His decision was made.

Now his mind functioned furiously. By the time he went up to Victor's room his plan was in shape.

He rapped, and heard a permissive grunt from inside.

Victor was sitting sidewise over the arm of the chair. His textbooks were spread open on the table, but he had not been working. He was brooding and bone-angry. He was a lost boy in search of a leader.

"Vic," Horace said, "I'm going to swing the state delegation to Roosevelt."

Victor looked at him unbelievingly. "You've missed the boat," he said. "You missed the last boat when you let old Parmiter block that primary bill. The delegation is signed, sealed and delivered to Taft." But the glint came into his eye; he wanted to be persuaded he was wrong. He pulled himself straight in his chair.

Horace said, "In '64, when I was younger than you are, my father took me to the convention that nominated Lincoln for his second term. Would you like to go to Chicago with me, Vic?"

Victor's face blazed up, then froze. "Not to see Taft nominated," he said.

"To see Roosevelt nominated. Now, Vic, you're old enough to keep your mouth shut—?"

Victor pledged his silence with a nod. Horace sat down on the foot of the bed. "Algonquin is pledged to Taft," he said, "but the delegates' hearts are not in their instructions. Half a dozen of them have come to me with their anxieties. They know the state isn't back of them."

"Why didn't you say some of this to Dan Permiter?"

"And put Dan on warning? Now listen to me. As you're aware, nearly two hundred seats at the convention are contested. The state organizations have accredited one set of delegates and the primaries have accredited another. Before the convention can act, the Credentials Committee will have to rule on seating the delegates. It will be a matter of several days. On averages, they're bound to seat a certain number of Roosevelt men.

"Now, I estimate that the first and second ballots will be deadlocked, and that will release the delegations from their pledges. Meantime the Roosevelt forces will be working like beavers—and I'll be working. The stage will be set for a spectacular break out of line."

Victor was leaning forward with his hands clasped, devouring his father's face with his eyes.

"Algonquin comes second on the roll call, directly after Alabama. By the third ballot, I figure I can engineer a stampede. If I can't carry the whole Algonquin delegation with me, at the very least I can split it. We'll poll the delegates, and the bulk of us will switch to TR. If Dan balks at announcing the switch, I'll stand up and shout, 'Mr. Chairman, Algonquin casts three votes for Taft and fourteen for—Theodore Roosevelt!' And when I say stampede, son, I mean stampede. Hell will break loose. Every delegation on the floor will go into a huddle. Parades will start surging through the aisles. The band will strike up. The galleries will go crazy. We'll nominate Roosevelt by acclamation!"

Victor was on his feet by this time. He saw himself leading the stampede from the gallery. "When do we start?" he cried.

Chapter 36

THE Rampoles were driving over to Chicago in the big touring car, with William in livery at the wheel. Horace had reserved a suite at the Congress Hotel, down the hall from the state headquarters where Danny presided. He had calculated very nicely the amount of hospitality he could dispense to the state delegates without rousing Dan's suspicions.

Victor was charged like a seltzer bottle; one touch on the lever, and he spurted effervescence. But he tried to look deceptively cool, because he was a co-conspirator.

The day before he left Meridian he had an odd encounter.

He had gone down to the Swimming Rocks for a preseason plunge. He was baking himself on the rocks, with his arm across his eyes, watching himself head the stampede for Roosevelt.

He heard voices coming along the trail—one a young man's, distinctively Eastern, the other a girl's. The girl was Jodie Epps.

Something turned over inside him, but it wasn't his heart—it was his pride. Time and politics had overlaid his passion for Jodie.

Let her come—let her cut him dead; he was impermeable. He had higher things to think about.

They were so near at hand now, he could hear what they were saying. Jodie was putting up a front for her Eastern visitor. "You've probably read about the Senator in the papers. Well, this was all his land originally.". . . Just as if she were a bosom friend of the family!

Victor kept his arm over his eyes. He heard her check herself. She had come into the clearing, she had seen him. He would be dead asleep. . . .

"Why," she said, "there's Victor Rampole now."

. . . So he was visible this year! He wasn't a worm in the path. Snubbing her would give their bygone feud too much importance.

He uncovered his eyes and rolled over on his elbow. "Well, Jodie," he said, "when did you get back?"

What he saw in Jodie's face was appeal. Her face was saying, Back me up, Victor, just this once. I have an out-of-town guest. Don't let him see that I'm not on speaking terms with the Rampoles.

"Victor," she said prettily, "I don't believe you know Jamie Nellison. He's just graduated from Harvard, and he's going into the State Department."

A Harvard graduate, was that it, and going into the State Department? That was a double handicap for a Meridian University sophomore in a wet bathing suit. Victor rose above his disadvantage. He got to his feet and shook hands with Jamie Nellison—Jamie Nellison, for God's sake! He exchanged banalities. He extended courtesies. "How long are you going to be here? . . . Your first trip west? . . . I hope you'll use our tennis court. I wish I were going to be around, but my father's taking me over to the convention in Chicago." Mr. Jamie Nellison might be going into the State Department, but he wasn't going to the Republican convention.

Mr. Nellison had had Jodie to Harvard Class Day. His attitude toward Victor was beautifully kind, as from a regnant suitor to one of the early rejects. I'd like to know, Victor thought, what kind of cock-and-bull story she's told him about me.

I wonder, he thought further, what Mr. Jamie Nellison is going to make of Onie Epps. Mr. Nellison is not common clay. He has pedigree written all over him.

Mr. Nellison was repulsively well turned out. He had a small gold emblem on his watch chain. His manner was that of the well-bred tourist entering graciously into native life. To an Algonquin ear his accent was farcically choice.

If this was Jodie's idea of a catch, she was welcome to him. "I've got to go back to the house," Victor said. "Nice to have seen you, Jodie."

Somehow she was clinging to his hand, as a bird grips its perch. "Have—have things been fun around here lately, Vic?" That pretty, pretty mouth of hers was trembling—not enough for Jamie Nellison to notice. But Victor knew Jodie's mouth pretty well.

"So-so. The Gang isn't what it used to be. People are pairing off."

He shouldn't have said that. It stirred up the recollection of his pairing off with Jodie and of his crashing break with her.

"What's Katie doing with herself?" Jodie persisted, dragging out the conversation.

"Oh, Katie—she's well up above the clouds these days! Katie's a composer, no less. She's studying at the university."

"She still sees Lissa Grover, though?"

Jodie had a nerve, bringing up Lissa's name!

She was trying to provoke a scene, that's what Jodie was up to. Nothing would infuriate her more than to have him keep his head.

"I believe she does," he said. "You know the Grovers have moved away from Rampole Place."

"I know. But you must run into Lissa on the campus—? Perhaps you drive her back and forth?"

He said negligently, "I haven't set eyes on Lissa in months. She has dates with the faculty."

"Mrs. Grover is distressed about Lissa. She says she's going to be an English teacher," Jodie said with innocent relish. "It seems too bad, doesn't it?—because she used to be so fond of you."

Drat the girl! Her tremors had been put on for effect. She was alive with malice and flirtatiousness. "Jamie," she said, catching Nellison's wrist in her other claw, "you mustn't mind my reminiscing with Victor. He was my first beau. Isn't he the handsomest thing you ever saw? . . . Well, enjoy yourself in Chicago, Vic. Come along, Jamie."

She retreated with flying banners. She had put Victor through his tricks like a trained seal, for the benefit of Mr. Jamie Nellison. The whole performance had been as cheeky as the devil.

It cleared the air wonderfully. Jodie Epps aroused no emotion in him except exasperation.

When the Rampoles rolled up to the Congress Hotel in Chicago they found the city insane with excitement. A shirt-sleeved populace milled in Michigan Avenue—hoisting placards, tailing after bands, buying newspaper extras, gaping and cheering from the curb, clotting beneath the hotel balcony where at any moment Roosevelt might appear.

For Roosevelt had arrived in the city that morning. He had set himself to await the call of his country at Sagamore Hill; then, characteristically, he had charged into the thick of the fight. When Victor heard that Roosevelt was on hand he felt that the battle was as good as won.

"Could you introduce me to him, Father?" he asked.

"Not yet, Vic. Plenty of time later." And of course Father was right. He couldn't show his colors yet.

Victor was proud to be his father's son. The Senator navigated the hotel lobbies as purposefully as a tug in a crowded harbor. He made his way from group to group, fraternizing at the cigar counter, dropping an adroit word at a restaurant table. Even in an upbound elevator he was working. He bought meals, he gave lifts in his lordly car, he handed out cigars and held a mtach to them, he kept his rooms stocked with liquor, coffee and sandwiches. He was giving a characterization of a ripe old sportsman, an amateur politician—harmless, likable, freehanded.

He was punctilious about frequenting the state headquarters where Danny held court. Danny didn't extend himself as the Senator did; he acted—poor old dupe—as if the Taft nomination were safely in the bag. He toddled about the hotel, paying his respects to the Old Guard; and he went early to bed.

Dan had no way of knowing that when the delegates left his levee they dropped in for a last drink in Senator Rampole's rooms. The air was blue with their smoke; Victor consecrated himself to keeping their glasses filled.

Victor's flood tide of politics broke for one moment over a sunken rock.

While he was passing sandwiches he heard his father's voice boom out: "Well, Arne, you old so-and-so! Where have you been keeping yourself? Arne, this is my boy Victor. Victor, this is Congressman Olsen, from the Nineteenth District, up around Doonville. Bourbon and branch water, I suppose, Arne?"

"So this is young Victor Rampole," the congressman said in a slow, upcountry voice. Victor felt his hand taken, and retained, in a big-muscled grip. He wanted furiously to snatch his hand away. He was seeing a borrowed stovepipe hat on a large square flaxen head. Six years ago—an eternity ago.

But Olsen held fast to his hand, and he had to flash one upward look.

"Takes after his mama, don't he?" Arne Olsen said with what seemed

256

to be delight. "Particularly about the eyes. Mighty pretty young thing she was."

Then a hitch came into his manner, as if he had remembered what a touchy subject Mrs. Rampole's death was. He relinquished Victor's hand and moved toward another group.

. . . Where did you meet my mother, Mr. Arne Olsen? Was it at a meeting at your house, with a young Mr. Ritter? Were they innocent? Or did you tell a lie to prevent a scandal, as Jodie Epps says you did? You can give me back my mother by convincing me she went to that meeting—but you'll drive me back into hating my father, because he didn't protect her. It's Father I have to live with, and he and I are just getting solid ground under our feet. . . .

The question couldn't be asked, it mustn't be answered. Let Chloe Rampole rest where she lay, poor lovely extinguished thing.

Victor went back to his hospitalities and his excitements.

Half a dozen of the delegation had an understanding by this time, and they were sounding out the others. No question about it—when Horace gave the word a good two thirds of the delegation would swing to Roosevelt.

"Enjoying yourself, son?" Horace asked when they were alone.

"It's all over but the shouting," Victor said, glowing.

"Don't kid yourself. I'm not at all pleased with what I hear out of the Credentials Committee."

"What could go wrong now?"

"Everything depends on who's elected Permanent Chairman."

"All the chairman does is count the votes—and we certainly have the votes."

Horace gave an ironic laugh. "I hope you're right. Look, Vic. Roosevelt is to speak at the Auditorium tonight. I can't show my face there, but you worm your way in and then report back to me."

No assignment could have pleased Victor more. He put all his muscle into his shoulders and elbows and got himself inside the hall just as Roosevelt came to the front of the platform.

The whole house rose and roared like one monster organism. Victor was a part of it—a part of America—cheering, crying, singing. Roosevelt stood waiting for the ovation to die down. A sympathy that could not be called by any lesser name than love passed between him and his audience.

He was not a cartoon of eyeglasses and teeth; he was a hero mainfest. Blunt head strongly set, bull-terrier build, boxer's thrust of body—and beyond that, a natural authority, a ruler's bearing.

His voice had no beauty. Its very intensity thinned it, and it broke into a falsetto range. But it was the vehicle of his purpose. He was not fighting for the Presidency, he said. Win or lose, he was fighting for certain principles of government. "We stand at Armageddon," he cried, "and we battle for the Lord."

It was a religious experience. The shouting swelled into an enormous singing: "Onward, Christian Soldiers!" . . . "Glory, Glory, Hallelujah!" . . . from five thousand throats, five thousand surging hearts. Such a leader could not lose—not with America at his back.

Next morning Victor set off for the coliseum with his gallery ticket. He was there as soon as the doors opened.

As a spectacle it didn't represent the majesty of the nation. The building was constructed like a train shed, with iron girders and bunting. The floor was set out with armies of kitchen chairs, aligned under the standards of the state delegations. Underlings were conferring on the rostrum. Reporters were joking in the press box. Early-bird delegates, dressed for comfort and not for style, were hobnobbing in the gangways and fanning themselves with their straw hats.

After Victor had died a hundred deaths of impatience, the floor and galleries did finally fill. He saw his father take his place. Pretty soon now Father would be making headlines. Danny came in with a seat cushion under his arm, as chipper as if he were not marked for defeat.

A temporary chairman called the session to order. The first significant business was the nomination of a Permanent Chairman. The Taft forces, the Roosevelt forces, the La Follette forces, each put a name in nomination. The Taft nominee was Elihu Root, Roosevelt's former Secretary of State—a renegade from Armageddon.

Partisan spirit broke out in hoots and catcalls. The voting was interminable, raucous, disorderly. When the votes were tallied, Root was inducted as chairman.

Senator Rampole looked black; Dan Parmiter looked smug. Root's voting strength roughly foretold Taft's.

Victor went out into Wabash Avenue for a side-arm lunch. When the two hundred contested delegates were accredited the picture would change. As between the claims of the party hacks and of the delegates elected at direct primaries, there could be no doubt which represented their constituents.

Victor was back in his seat when Root called for the report of the Credentials Committee.

The Credentials Committee had dealt with the contests by seating a whole roster of delegates accredited to Taft and a few accredited to Roosevelt. Wherever there was the slightest technical loophole, the committee had ruled in favor of the organization. It was barefaced robbery.

Pandemonium broke loose, parliamentary and extraparliamentary. From all over the floor the point was raised that the contested delegates should not be allowed to vote on the acceptance of the committee's report, which constituted their own validation. Voices bawled, "Mr. Chairman! Mr. Chairman——" and arms were brandished toward the oblivious rostrum.

The stentorian Rampole voice could have cut through the bedlam of noise. But Horace chewed his dead cigar, pulled at his nose and judged that the time was not ripe. His delegation comprised a solid core of five or six men secretly vowed to Roosevelt, about the same number of hard-shelled politicos who would stand against Roosevelt to the end, and a middle group who wanted to be on the winning side. This group would not jump aboard the glory train till it began to roll; and it wasn't rolling yet.

Elihu Root ruled that each contested delegate was debarred from voting on his own case, but qualified to vote on the seating of all the others.

A booing roar of anger rose from floor and galleries, continuous as the thunder of a cataract. The gray, long-beaked head of the chairman dominated the uproar. State by state he called for the vote.

State by state the contests were resolved in favor of Taft, amid cries of "Thief! Liar! Crook! Steam roller! *Toot-toot*—steam roller!"

The Roosevelt supporters huddled in frustrated furious groups. They had been outflanked before the battle so much as opened. A rumor swept the galleries that Roosevelt would force an entrance to the floor of the convention. No, that was rumor; but extra police had been called out in anticipation of riot. . . . Meanwhile the steam roller pursued its course.

Victor sat watching the murder of his hopes and praying for a Rampole miracle. But between sessions his father dodged him. He could not face the appeal in Victor's eyes. Give him time, for God's sake! The right moment for action might still come; and the Senator was too old a bird to go off half-cocked.

When Roosevelt was put in nomination Victor recovered his optimism. The surge of the demonstration was bound to sweep the waverers into line. Spontaneous parades broke out behind state standards, snaking through the screaming knotted crowd. The band struck up "Onward, Christian Soldiers." The woman next to Victor in the gallery screamed like a factory whistle for five minutes straight. Root banged with his gavel for three quarters of an hour before he got the demonstration under control.

What was Father waiting for? If that wasn't a stampede, what was? But the Senator was not marching, he was sitting.

At the end of an eternity the nominations were all in, and it was time for the voting. Victor had a tally card ready. He forbade himself to hope on the first ballot. On the third, Father would manifest himself and cast a block of Algonquin votes for Theodore Roosevelt.

The tally was running heavily in favor of Taft—and no wonder. But what was happening on the floor? Huddles, buzzing desperate groups hardening into a decision. Delegations from the Progressive states, when called on for their votes, withheld them in formal protest against the operation of the steam roller. Clusters of men marched off the floor of the convention, carrying their frustration, their anger and their enthusiasm outside the cursed building.

In the Algonquin section there was no bustle, no withdrawal. Algonquin stood pat, while the Roosevelt forces—the core of the Senator's stampede—walked out of the convention.

Victor forced his way to the front of the gallery and leaned over, screaming and waving. "Father, get going! In a minute it will be too late. Father, Father!"

He might as well have screamed into the face of Niagara. His voice, his violence left no trace on the universal roar. Roosevelt was betrayed; America was the captive of the Machine; and the Senator had not once taken the cigar out of his mouth.

Shaken to the depths of the heart, Victor blundered his way out into Wabash Avenue. Let them wind up their foul proceedings, let them nominate what Vice-President they liked. He tore up the rest of his bunch of gallery tickets and dropped them down a sewer.

He would have caught the first train out of town except that he heard one more rumor in the roaring streets. More than a rumor—a headline in a paper. He snatched a copy. The Bull Moosers were swarming like hornets. That evening Roosevelt was to address a Progressive rally at Orchestra Hall.

Victor rushed back to the hotel suite. He would give his father one more chance. The voice of the country would not be gagged forever; the Progressives would run Roosevelt on a ticket of their own.

The Senator came in late, fagged and shaken. "Don't wait to eat, Father!" Victor urged him. "You ought to see the jam in Michigan Avenue."

"You go if you like, son," Horace said. "I can't countenance a split in the party. Taft is our candidate."

He saw the scorn, the rejection, in his son's eyes. But his choice had been forged through half a century of party loyalty.

"I'd rather have had Roosevelt," he said. "But in a three-way split, nobody will win except the Democrats. Taft can't do the injury to the country that a Democrat can."

"I am going to the rally," Victor said, and set off for Orchestra Hall.

To cap a catastrophic day, he couldn't even get inside the hall. He had as much gristle as any boy, but thousands of his fellow countrymen were as determined as he was. At the birth of the Progressive party, Victor was wedged among the gapers on the sidewalk.

He plunged off westward into the city. He crossed cheap, garishly lighted streets and wandered into a region of warehouses as blind as mausoleums. He stood on the Madison Street bridge and looked with loathing at the greasy little river.

He had reached the end of his subservience to the family. The very name of Rampole was tainted with treachery. With fine-sounding pretensions and with deep unscrupulousness.

He would never go back to Chestnut Point, nor to Meridian University. He would strike off across country, as old Huck Rampole had done in the beginning. He would work out his destiny with his own two hands.

But first he would go back to Meridian and browbeat old O'Donnell into turning his money over to him.

Chapter 37

AT FOUR O'CLOCK the next afternoon Victor stood on the sidewalk outside the Cinnamon Block in downtown Meridian. He had just come down from Mr. O'Donnell's office in the building. He turned the small coins over in his pocket with fingers that had a tendency to tremble, and rejected the inclination to stop in somewhere for a drink.

One would have said that the heir to the Rampole fortune would be able to put his hand on ready cash. One would have been mistaken. All his life Victor had drawn money from Augustus as he needed it. Twice a year he received a hundred and fifty dollars; but the next payment fell in September, and this was June.

Mr. O'Donnell had been implacable about turning over his inheritance to him. Until Victor came of age only his father, who was his guardian, could release it. And Victor would not ask his father.

He still had an unbroken ten-dollar bill and a one-dollar bill in his wallet. He would have had more if he had not come chasing back to Meridian on a fool's errand. He had chosen to believe he could bluster his money out of Mr. O'Donnell's hands. After he broke his last ten-dollar bill he would be standing up in his shoes and very little else.

Well—he gave a laugh that had gravel in it—Huck Rampole stood up in his mocassins and walked west into the wilderness, and he did all right.

He had never meant to stay in Meridian. He had meant to try his luck in some city where he could break free from the Rampole web. Now he had spent his train fare; so he was tethered. He should never have left Chicago.

All right, he had left Chicago; in Meridian he would have to lose his Rampole identity. He would have to be Victor Roper, or Victor Rogers. He would have to get a room and a job on the wrong side of the river.

A job now: what kind of a job? He found himself turning into the drugstore for a cup of coffee. Over his coffee he would come to a decision about a job. . . .

He brought himself sternly back to the sidewalk and stood there with his feet foursquare and his forehead lowered. He might need that nickel. He could think just as well standing up. In one hour Victor had taken a whole course in the insecurities of the poor.

He knew boys who were working their way through the university; they got jobs through the dean's office. A fine figure Victor Rampole would cut walking into the dean's office and asking for student assistance.

He knew young fellows who went to work after they graduated—in their father's businesses, in the offices of their father's friends. Always by favor. Poor men got jobs through the Parmiter machine—favor again. The Rampole web.

A streetcar lumbered past him, loaded with straphangers; the working day was over. Those men in overalls, those white-collar underlings— they didn't rise by favor; they were too unimportant to be worth buying up.

They didn't rise at all; they passed their lives hanging from streetcar straps. But they brought themselves to market and made an honest bargain—pay check in exchange for a job. They kept their self-respect.

All well and good. They walked into an employment office and said they were answering the ad for a bookkeeper.

Victor laughed outright at this point. "Yes, Mr.—Roper, you say? Fill out this blank. You type, I presume. . . . No? Then you understand bookkeeping? You've worked in a shipping room? . . . Well, Mr. Roper,

I hardly think we have anything for you today. Thanks for stopping in."

After twenty years Victor had no skills to bring to market. No head, nothing but muscles. He could swing a pick, he could push a wheelbarrow. Huck Rampole had faced the wilderness with a better equipment; he had learned to shift for himself.

It would be easy to get his hands on a little more money before he took his plunge into the wilderness. He could get into his own room at Chestnut Point and out again with salable articles which were his: suits, tennis rackets, the big silver frame he had bought for Jodie's picture. Or he could get money out of Katie. . . .

The price was too high, in terms of integrity. He would rather head into the wilderness with his eleven dollars and develop his animal cunning as he went along. He would apply for a job as a common laborer.

Victor went into the lobby of the Cinnamon Block to buy a paper at the newsstand.

The headlines blared up at him: BULL MOOSERS ORGANIZE. His heart was sore for his lost archangel. But Theodore Roosevelt was finished: Horace Rampole and the standpatters had betrayed him. Victor discarded the front section of the paper and folded it open at Help Wanted—Male.

"*Sun-Record*," a man said behind his shoulder, tossing down two coppers. The familiar voice caught Victor off guard, and he looked around.

"Well, Victor!" Anson Epps said, as fatherly as you please. "I thought you were over in Chicago, settling the affairs of the nation."

This was fantastic. This was like a morality play, with Vice coming on stage in horns and a tail. It took Victor a minute to deflate his own sense of the sinister. There was no black magic in running into a Meridian businessman in the Cinnamon Block. The building was not a lamasery dedicated to private contemplation. Mr. Epps might just as easily have been Mr. Dysart or Mr. Coleman.

Victor nodded and turned away, hoping Mr. Epps had not read his misgivings in his face.

Mr. Epps had read something. "Still gun-shy of me, I see," he bantered. "Come out of it, Vic. Jodie tells me you and she are back on speaking terms. She's got another fellow now. Isn't it time to shake hands all round?"

What a mischief-maker the man was! What a rattler of old skeletons for the sheer pleasure of watching them dance!

Victor had to say something. He said, "I ran into the two of them down at the pool the other day." And he edged toward the street entrance.

Mr. Epps was leafing through the *Sun-Record* with a proprietary eye. "How did that young cooky pusher strike you?" he asked carelessly.

Victor said evasively, "I only talked to him for a minute."

"Look here," Mr. Epps said suddenly in a different tone, as if he had made up his mind about something. He folded his paper and thrust it into his side pocket. "Don't run out on me. I need some advice, and you're the man to give it to me. Come over to the Hofbrau and have a quick one." And he took Victor's arm.

While Victor was still resisting the too-friendly pressure, it broke over him that while he might not like Mr. Epps, he was the least dangerous man he could have run into in the Cinnamon lobby. He was excluded from the Rampole web; hence he had no power over Victor. As Jodie's father, he had once had power, but Jodie's dominance was broken.

At one time Victor had been his father's partisan against Epps and Eppsism. How Father had befooled him with his knightly battle against the hosts of evil! Father's conspiracy to deliver Meridian from the boodlers had gone the way of his conspiracy to nominate Theodore Roosevelt.

Beneath these high reasonings lurked two unacknowledged cravings: a craving for the free lunch on the Hofbrau bar, and an inquisitiveness about Jodie's new romance.

He let himself be shepherded down the street to the Hofbrau. Mr. Epps took the corner table and gave the waiter an order. Victor reached out and acquired a stuffed egg and a dill pickle on the way to the table.

"Now then, Vic——"

"Mr. Epps, you mustn't talk to me about Jodie. She'd be furious."

"I wasn't planning to tell her," Mr. Epps said dryly. "Now, Victor, don't shy off. I'm determined to ask you one question." He spun a salted cracker like a coin. After a moment he raised his eyes. "Jodie means more to me than anybody in this world except her mother. . . . Now, now! Don't waste your breath telling me you two have fallen out of love with each other—that's the very reason I want to talk to you. You know her romantic streak, and—well, let's call it her bitchiness. I'm as fond as hell of that kid, and I hate to see her make a mess of her life. She's got some of her mother in her, and her mother is pure gold. She's got some of me—and that's a black load for any girl to carry."

This was as near sincerity as Mr. Epps would ever come. All the same Victor said firmly, "Excuse me, sir. I'm the last person Jodie would want you to talk like this to."

"All right—answer me one question and I'll let you off the hook. Is

Jodie a girl who will be satisfied by a marriage of ambition? It's in the works. I can tip the scales either way."

"Marriage of ambition!" Victor stammered.

"Exactly. Your family isn't one-two-three with the Nellisons, Victor. He'll end up an ambassador."

"The chances are she's in love with him."

"Listen—I saw her when she was in love with you. He's as fair and square as a bar of Ivory Soap, and just about as fascinating. And the in-laws—they're grandees, that's what they are. They could make Jodie's life a hell if they had a mind to. And Jodie—damn it, she'd fight back! What would you say were the odds on a happy life for Jodie?"

"Mr. Epps, if you don't see the—the indecency of my discussing this with you, I can't explain it." And Victor pushed his glass away from him, preparing to make his escape.

Epps spun his salted cracker off the table. "Maybe I ask too many questions," he said. "It's always seemed to me the easiest way of finding out what you wanted to know." Then, sending the discussion after the salted cracker, he added, "Can I give you a ride out home?"

"No, thanks" would have been answer enough. But Victor had been strung tighter and tighter as this conference pursued its unseemly way, and his tongue spoke ahead of his wits. "I'm not going home," his tongue said, with horrifying expressiveness.

"So?" Epps said smoothly. He had not missed Victor's intonation. He fished in his pocket for silver to pay his bill, and darted looks at Victor from under his canted eyebrows. "Fed up, eh? I don't blame you."

"I didn't say a word about being fed up!"

"You didn't need to," Epps said, laying down two quarters, and a dime for the waiter. "I've been watching you for years, Vic. I knew the day would come when you'd walk out on the Rampole flummery."

"I did not say——"

"I don't ask you to say. Your father and I have had our knives into each other for years, and I don't doubt you've been filled up with fairy tales about my evil behavior. But at least I can say for myself—" his nostrils took on a brimstone pride—"that I'm not a sanctimonious hypocrite like the Rampoles. I admit that I work exclusively for the interests of Anson Epps, and to that extent I'm a better man than your father is." And into the silence that followed his words, he let drop the words, "I could put you to work, Victor."

Victor gagged on the acrid half-truth Epps had enunciated. He was in no mood to defend his clan, but neither would he deny his own blood. And as for working for Epps, he had not scrambled out of the Rampole frying pan to land in the fire of Eppsism.

"I'm not looking for a job," he lied desperately. "I have a job."

"My mistake. I noticed you reading the want ads."

"I'll have to be going now. Thanks for the drink."

"Need any money?" Epps inquired in the friendliest way.

"I have all the money I need, thank you." Victor started walking toward the swing door.

Epps fell into step beside him. "Well, you're lucky. When I was a young fellow with my way to make, I borrowed right and left. I paid it all back."

They had reached the sidewalk now. Epps would be turning left, so Victor turned right.

After they had separated he swung back. He could not retrace the flying leaps by which Epps had forced himself into his confidence—it was black art; but since he had learned so much, Victor must say something more.

"There's just one thing, sir. I'd be glad if the word didn't get back to my family that you've seen me. They're bound to find out about one business call I made this afternoon, but it would be simpler if my trail vanished at that point. I have some things to figure out, and I don't want to be bothered."

Epps gave one last grin. "You were never safer in your life, boy. I'm the last man Horace Rampole will come to for information about you." And he was gone, with an affable wave of the hand.

Victor set off on foot for the station. He must reclaim his bag from the checkroom and find lodging for the night. In the morning he would buy a pair of overalls and go out hunting a job.

Chapter 38

NORMALLY, Senator Rampole would have given Dan Parmiter a ride back to Meridian in his car. He made the trip alone.

Dan had too much the look of licking his whiskers. He didn't let out a single peep about the little stampede that never came off, but gratification stood out all over him. Invalided, was he? Superannuated? In the trial of strength he had shown himself the man of iron, and Horace was the man of straw.

Horace needed time to come to terms with his fiasco. He had plenty of time, because the car had three blowouts, and the trip took two full days.

He knew what came next: Dan would discipline him. Dan would rub his nose in the tedious chores of campaigning—money raising, speaking assignments in remote county seats.

The effort would be poured out on sand, irrecoverable. Dan might conceivably carry the state for Taft, but not the nation—not this year. He might as well be in his hammock drinking beer. And yet the politicians' code demanded that he keep up his tub thumping till Election Day.

Horace had no stomach for Taft, but he had lost faith in Roosevelt. Before the nomination every candidate was entitled to scramble for the nomination. But a candidate who would bolt the ticket and split the party was a willful miscreant.

Horace could not shake off the look of betrayal he had brought into Victor's eyes. Somehow he must reinstate himself. "I came up with the party, and I'll go down with the party." To Horace the words were hallowed with an old solemnity, like marriage vows. But would they be valid to Victor?

Not tonight, Horace decided, as the hours of the trip lengthened out. I'm too tired. I'll tackle him after I've had a night's sleep in my own bed. . . .

Late the second evening the car limped into the driveway of Chestnut Point. The distributor had gone wrong and the engine was hiccupping, but it had brought him home.

A disreputable roadster was standing in front of the portico. The Senator told William to drop him at the side door. "I can't face a howling gang of kids tonight," he said. "I'll have Gus bring me something to eat in the smoking room."

Augustus emerged from the pantry to welcome him. One of Augustus' perquisites was the privilege of skimming the cream off the Senator's news. And the convention was epochal news.

Horace was too tired for gossip. "Vic home?" was the first thing he asked.

"Vic! Didn't you bring him back with you?"

Horace said evasively, "I expected he'd be home ahead of me. Don't sit up for him—he has his key. Bring me some ham sandwiches and a pot of coffee, will you, Gus?" He dropped into a big chair without taking off his duster.

What melodramatic stunt had the boy pulled? Well, he would run out of money before long. He'd come home chastened.

"Who's in the front of the house?" Horace asked while Augustus was setting out the midnight snack.

"Just Katie and that everlasting beau of hers," Augustus told him, elaborately casual. But his eyes ferreted for the Senator's reaction.

Horace kept his face impassive. It ill became a Rampole to express surprise that the family debutante should have caught herself a fellow. He had been preoccupied before the convention; he hadn't kept a check on Katie's movements. "You go on to bed, Gus," he said. "I'll lock up."

Ordinarily he had great recuperative capacity. Tonight he smelled earthquake weather—nothing was stable.

He sat over his third cup of coffee, nagging at the problem Victor presented to him. The kid must have run off and joined the Bull Moosers, he decided. Victor had been roped in—that's what had happened.

He felt better, and drained his cup. All he wanted now was to get to bed.

There remained the tactical problem of getting Katie's caller out of the house, so that Horace could lock up. It was an ungodly hour—nearly one in the morning.

His fatigue was like an active sore, demanding treatment. He would make short work of that caller. In fact, the more he thought about the caller the more he suspected his motives. There was something fishy about any man who kept Katie up till one in the morning. Katie had no fund of small talk. The man must have designs on her.

He might of course be one of the neighborhood youths, smitten with love. Greater miracles had happened. Horace hesitated to scare him off by playing the heavy father. He must reconnoiter.

He began by stamping histrionically to the side door, slamming it, locking it and bolting it. All this by way of giving fair warning.

No results—no stir of departure from the front parlor, no car driving away.

Possibly the caller might have left already, while Horace was eating and musing. Possibly Katie might be snug in bed.

He reopened the side door and took a prowl around the four sides of the house. The car was still there. The only light in the front of the house came from the entrance hall. The basement windows were dark, so the young people were not raiding Jennie's icebox. From the back lawn he discovered a vague glow filtering through the sitting-room curtains. If Katie was entertaining her caller in the sitting room, she must have advanced him to domestic intimacy. The whole situation was troubling.

Be he who he might, it was time the young man went home. Horace re-entered the house, marched to the sitting-room door and opened it. The room was empty, although the lamp was on.

Nasty surmises forced themselves into his mind. He couldn't suspect Katie of impropriety, but he could easily imagine her, inexperienced as she was, in the clutches of some scoundrel.

Now if it were Vic, with one of those trashy coeds of his, he would be down at the Swimming Rocks, and no great harm done. But Katie—his unarmed, undefended Katie—she couldn't take care of herself.

Impetuously Horace set out to rescue Katie. He jerked open the big front door . . .

And stood arrested, his firmament tumbling about his ears.

The two figures in the vestibule were welded into an embrace that took no account of interruption.

After one thunderstruck second Horace demanded in a voice of doom, "Just what is going on here?"

The two figures broke apart, as innocent as Eden. Even at that shattering moment Horace's eye registered Katie's extraordinary beauty—a beauty independent of feature, a beauty that transfused her being.

"But we're going to get married, Father," she said, as if that fact should clear up all his outrage.

"Come inside," Horace said. He preceded the pair into the parlor and switched on the crystal chandeliers.

The young man richly deserved to be kicked down the front steps. But such rough justice might do measureless injury to Katie. This was her first lover. Horace must protect her pride.

They approached him hand in hand, both of them still moon-struck from their embrace. Horace looked the young man up and down, and his stomach actively revolted at the thought of such a fellow making free with Katie's person.

The fellow's hair was understandably tousled. He blinked through his spectacles at the prismatic light. His suit, his shirt, his tie, his socks and shoes were such as Horace bought ready-made for upstate campaigning. His chunky face had no handsomeness to it at all, and it did not look like Adams Avenue.

"Who is this man you've brought into the house?"

"Why, Father, you must know him. He came to my recital. He's Miss Archibald's nephew."

"I'm Roy Godkin, sir. I'm an instructor in the Music Department at the university."

This was what came of letting young women go to college.

The problem was not to be dealt with by kicking Mr. Godkin down

269

the steps. A teacher had a specious claim to social standing. Katie's in-fatuation must be handled like a case in court—with full preparation, taking of testimony, presentation of the points at issue.

While Horace hesitated, Godkin took the lead. "I'd meant to talk to you before now, sir. We expected you earlier in the evening."

"But while waiting," Horace said grimly, "you rather jumped the gun. I want it clearly understood that there is to be no engagement unless I'm satisfied with you."

"Father, it won't take Roy a minute to tell you about himself. It isn't as if he were a stranger."

"Not tonight, Katie. You've sprung this on me pretty suddenly, on top of a grueling ten days in Chicago. You'll have to give me time."

If Katie had not been under a bad magic, he would not have needed to make this appeal. Normally she took delight in anticipating his wishes. Now she transferred her allegiance to this adventurer by say-ing, "My engagement is just as important to me as politics is to you."

"Nothing is more important to me than your engagement. You can't ask me to O.K. it like an office memorandum. That's why I won't be rushed."

"Katie—" Godkin took charge of the scene—"Senator Rampole is right. I can't expect him to hand you over like a parcel. We have all our lives. We can afford to wait."

"But Father says we can't even be engaged."

"That's a matter of definition," the fellow said cheerfully. "He says we aren't, we say we are."

"I am engaged to you."

"I am engaged to you," he echoed her. "That being the case, suppose we give your father a chance to turn around. When you're ready to talk to me, sir, you can locate me through the university switchboard." He lifted Katie's face with his hand—it was nearly on a level with his—and planted a grave, decorous kiss on her mouth. Then he swung out of the room. His motor spun, engaged, roared, faded away.

Katie went over to her father. The emotion wavered across her face like the play of northern lights.

He enveloped her in the crook of his shoulder and took her free hand in his own. "Katie, Katie," he mourned. "I didn't expect this to hap-pen quite so soon—quite so upsettingly. You will have to let yourself be guided by my judgment. You know I want you to be happy."

"Father, it's not a tragedy."

"Let's not go into it tonight, Katie. I have anxieties I couldn't talk about in front of a stranger. You haven't heard from Vic, have you? He hasn't got in touch with you?"

"Victor?" With an effort she brought herself back into the everyday world. "Why, he's been over in Chicago with you. Has he—has he done anything dreadful? Has he been in another accident?"

"He walked out of the convention almost a week ago. I assumed he'd come home."

He had no grounds now for complaining of her lack of sympathy. "Didn't he tell you where he was going?"

"He didn't wait to speak to me. He was in quite a state of mind."

"Oh, he's so extreme about everything! You don't—you don't think anything can have happened to him?"

"It's not likely, but of course I'd like to be sure."

"Is there anybody you could ask?"

"I hate to put bloodhounds on his trail."

"But, Father, if he'd been in a car accident——" The old family catastrophe brushed them both with its baleful wing.

"I can't do anything before morning. He may come walking in by that time, or he may send us word. Let's go to bed. Good night."

"Good night, Father."

Horace stretched himself in his big bed. He seldom pitied himself, but this summer the cards were certainly running against him—and in a game where he couldn't settle his losses and drop out. His public life, his son, his daughter—trick after trick was falling to his opponents.

His lifelong irony came to his rescue. He was making the complaints that weak men make for their failures . . . old Cummager. . . . He might be licked in the end, but he would play his hand out.

Politics he put out of consideration; those tricks had been turned and quitted. More men than he had misplayed their hands in Chicago. Horace had acted by what light he had.

His children, though—he had done what a widower could to mother them. Chloe should have lived. . . .

He had never been able to get through to Victor. Try as he might, he ran against spiked armor. Not that the boy was coldhearted—he was a whirlwind of passions, enthusiasms and loyalties. Victor had some grudge against him that never came out into the open.

But Katie, the cherished, the best beloved, the undefended! Katie kidnaped by an outsider. Katie unrecognizable, Katie a changeling.

This fellow—this musician—he couldn't be sincerely in love with Katie. Katie had nothing to attract a stranger's love.

This stranger, of necessity, was courting her to get his hands on her money. He would break her undefended heart at his leisure. Everything in Horace Rampole shouted No! to the profanation.

271

Archibald . . . Godkin . . .

Archibald . . . Threads of association began to form.

Schontz Street. Miss Archibald's checks went to Schontz Street.

Nothing wrong with Schontz Street. A churchgoing, tax-paying neighborhood, meekly enduring the chuckholes in its pavement and the miasma from the soap factory. Schontz Street voted Republican, by and large, which was to its credit. But it was a street of little people. Children of God, no doubt, and freeborn American citizens, but little people. Adams Avenue did not intermarry with Schontz Street.

Archibald, now . . . Why, of course. When Horace was a boy he had driven down with Augustus to the old Archibald stonecutting yard. After fifty years and more he recalled the proprietor coming up covered with stone dust, his mallet in his hand. An upstanding young Scot, competent at his trade. He had cut the stone for the portico when Chestnut Point was a-building. Horace recalled the artillery roll of his tongue, the cock of his black burnished eyebrows. Of course! Miss Archibald had those eyebrows, and so did young Godkin.

Godkin . . . The most damaging thing about that name was that it was not rooted in Meridian. Hadn't he heard something about Miss Archibald's living with a widowed sister and supporting her? One of the Archibald daughters must have married a fly-by-night from out of town. Never trust a stranger. . . .

For Miss Archibald herself Horace had a real respect. A fine woman, in her proper place. . . .

Godkin . . . Some teasing little clue, just out of reach. . . . "Star-Spangled Banner" . . . banquet . . . hotel lobby . . . big display board . . . Dinner Music by Godkin's Quintette . . . Hotel Belvedere . . .

Instructor at the university, indeed! Was that the caliber of instructor the university was hiring with Horace's money?

At last the Senator turned over and went to sleep. Like so much else in Meridian, Mr. Godkin was within his overlordship.

Early in the morning he got Dr. Schweiz on the telephone. The great man was testy on being awakened—he kept musicians' hours. His tone changed miraculously when he heard who was calling. "Ah, Senator! . . . Yes, Senator. How kind of you! You have undoubtedly read my departmental report for the year."

Horace wished he had looked into the report which was lying on his desk. "Fine report!" he said heartily. "My congratulations, Doctor. But I'm calling to check on one of your young instructors, Mr.—let's see— Mr. Godkin. Roy Godkin."

Horace interpreted the silence that greeted this inquiry. Dr. Schweiz was wondering which way to jump. Did his august patron want praise or criticism of Mr. Godkin?

"I was wondering," he said, "whether this could be the chap who used to play in the orchestra in the Belvedere dining room? And that raises the question whether he's qualified to teach in your department."

He had unwittingly trod on Dr. Schweiz's toes. A musician took what work he could get; and he himself had played in a theater orchestra in his day.

He answered suavely, "I assure you, Senator, that I should not have engaged him unless he were fully qualified. He holds several degrees from excellent conservatories. Your daughter is one of his pupils. She can tell you whether his instruction is satisfactory."

It was Horace's turn for silent reflection. He didn't want to tip his hand—he didn't want to give Katie away.

Dr. Schweiz, still poised for a dash in either direction, continued. "I should value your advice on whether to reappoint Mr. Godkin next year. His contract is on my desk at the moment."

Horace's throat spoke for him, by giving out an involuntary but revealing noise: "Er-r-rumph!" Something on that order. It was all Dr. Schweiz needed.

He unleashed the wasp vibrations of his rich voice. "I myself have grave doubts of Mr. Godkin, apart from his academic qualifications. I am trying to build a team, Senator, and Mr. Godkin does not bear the yoke with patience."

No encouragement from the Senator—but no discouragement either. The Senator was waiting.

"I knew, naturally, when I engaged him, that Mr. Godkin was an adherent of the new cacophony. I am not narrow-minded. I don't want our school to stand with the reaction—and there is a vogue for dissonance." . . . Where does he dig up those words? thought the Senator, floundering behind him. . . . "But I made it clear that our department stood for a thorough grounding in the fundamentals. Only in their third year should students be exposed to the new idiom. Mr. Godkin has been recalcitrant in the matter of teaching elementary harmony. He undercuts me at every opportunity."

Another silence. But Dr. Schweiz's grievance was strong upon him, and he continued. "I regret exceedingly that Miss Rampole is not getting the basic instruction she is entitled to. She is cutting herself off from the possibility of a degree."

"How do you mean—cutting herself off?"

Dr. Schweiz knew now where he stood. The Senator's daughter had bamboozled him—Harmony 105 was not under protection. "Well," he said, "Mr. Godkin kidnaped Miss Rampole into an unauthorized course which has no existence in the curriculum. Harmony 105, he has the effrontery to call it. Harmony 105 consists, in plain terms, of Mr. Godkin meeting Miss Rampole for three hours a week in one of the basement practice rooms."

"How did this come about? It sounds like pretty slack administration in your department."

"I will describe to you exactly how it came about, and you will tell me, Senator, what I should have done differently. You must be aware that your son and your daughter occupy a privileged position at the university. The faculty assumes that their wishes represent your wishes, and we are under great obligations to you.

"I happen to have been present when Mr. Godkin cooked up his little scheme. I had intended, of course, to take charge of Miss Rampole's courses myself. It was at one of Mrs. Burch's musical evenings, shortly before the second semester opened. Mr. Godkin had been barely introduced to Miss Rampole, but he made what you Americans call a dead set at her. He invited her to improvise—and most charmingly she improvised, incidentally. For the rest of the evening he monopolized her— no one else could get a word in. He took her out in the hallway, and she did not reappear for half an hour. The next thing I knew, she had registered for this nonexistent Harmony 105, which Mr. Godkin had evolved out of his own consciousness."

Horace saw it all—the Pied Piper, whistling his Katie into servitude. He made an alarming noise in his throat, like that of a lion tearing at a carcass.

"On the whole," said Dr. Schweiz somewhat hastily, "I incline to get rid of Mr. Godkin. I will give him a warm recommendation to some other faculty. But he will never fit in with us." He waited for approval.

Horace was too sharp for him. "That's for you to decide, Dr. Schweiz. I make a point of never interfering with academic affairs." He felt certain that the name of Godkin would disappear from the next year's catalogue.

Chapter 39

VIC ROPER—until recently Victor Rampole—found his days long and his evenings longer. He had played a lot of tennis and swung an ax on timber, but never for ten hours at a stretch. Now a foreman saw to it that he earned his two dollars a day by shoveling mortar into a barrow, wheeling it up an inclined plank, dumping it into a trough and going back for more. At noon he sat in the shade of a wall and ate out of a tin lunch pail. He was so taciturn with the other workmen that they avoided him. He was certainly no laboring man—he must be an actor out of a job.

He worked, ate and slept on the disinherited east side of the river. He would not let himself cross the Cinnamon Bridge, for fear he should be recognized; he looked too much like his father's campaign posters.

He was a little hurt that there had been nothing about his disappearance in the papers. It looked as if his father were letting him stew in his own juice. When his bones ached, a fierce resentment kept him plodding behind his barrow.

After supper he sat on the front steps of his rooming house until the mosquitoes and the landlady drove him inside. Mrs. Schneider found him an irresistible enigma. His clothes and his suitcase marked him as a real gentleman. She theorized that he had run away from home because he was crossed in love. Any day she expected a pumpkin chariot to call for him.

To escape her probing he would go up to his stifling back bedroom and lie on the bed, reading the help-wanted ads and wondering how to qualify for a better job. He could just barely live on his pay; he was not accumulating anything toward a fresh start in life.

He held himself awake by way of shortening the black period of drift before he fell asleep, when his imagination ran wild. He didn't give a whoop whom Jodie married. Mr. Epps had been trying to get him back on the hook. Ten to one, Nellison had never proposed to Jodie at all. He did not look the type that went mad with careless love.

(Turn over. Thump pillow, beating down the lumps. Throw off sheet.)

If Jodie was fool enough to marry Nellison, she would be condemning herself to slow hell. And that, in a way, was too bad. Jodie was a venomous little flirt, but she had sweetness, she had fire. The right man could bring her out.

Not Victor—God forbid. (Turn over. Suffocating to death. Take off pajamas and sling them across the room, where they catch on the gas bracket.) Drafting of specifications for hypothetical man who could handle Jodie and bring out her womanly pliancy.

(Down the hall for a glass of water. This must stop. Think about something constructive. Say the multiplication table; say the Kings of

England. "William the Norman and William his son, Henry, Stephen and Henry, Richard and John . . .")

Jodie, I ask you to think twice before you marry that man. He takes you to Harvard Class Day, but that's not all there is to marriage—not by a long shot. . . .

(Damn everything! Room cooling off. Body naked. Pajamas out of reach. Pull up sheet—pull up sleazy old blanket . . .)

Well, that was better. Oblivion let down its velvet dews. Peace, till the alarm clock went off.

He came home after a blasting hot day behind his wheelbarrow. He had been lightheaded all afternoon. He had had trouble keeping the front wheel on the plank—and he would have begged off, except that the gang had its snickers ready for the expected collapse of the dude, the pretty-boy, the actor out of work.

His landlady met him, all smirks, with a scrawled telephone number. "This lady wants to get hold of you right away."

"Why, nobody knows I'm here," he blurted out without thinking.

"One person does. She asked for Victor Roper. Go on now, call her up. Don't be stiff-necked. She's ready to kiss and make up."

"You've got it all wrong." But Victor took the slip. His eyes wouldn't focus—the figures changed places—but he saw the Doochee exchange plainly.

It couldn't be Katie calling, or Jennie, or Lissa Grover, who had moved away. He knew well enough who it was. Somehow Epps, the old devil, had put the young devil on his track. Mr. Epps was in cahoots with all the contractors in town.

He sat on the edge of his bed, considering. He reviewed Jodie's wrongheadedness, her malice and jealousy and spite, her vulgarity, her cruelty. Her own father had called her a bitch. You couldn't trust Jodie.

Meanwhile he had been tossing a coin and catching it. He laughed when he saw what it was; it was the nickel with which he meant to call Jodie. All right, nickel, he said. But he would be terse and businesslike with her.

"Victor!" her voice came through at the first ring. She had been lying in wait for his call. She spoke guardedly.

"Roper speaking," he said, as if he were returning a business call.

"Victor—if even Delia Dysart asked a personal favor of you, you'd do it, wouldn't you? If her life depended on it?"

"What does Delia Dysart want me to do for her?" he asked dryly.

"I can't speak very freely."

"Your fiancé might overhear, is that it?"

"Yes. Just exactly that." She gave the news time to sink in. "But I've got to see you. Just once. It's the last favor I'll ever ask of you."

"My congratulations. Only—I can't come out there."

"Why not, Vic? I can't come to you."

"Because," he said conclusively.

"You don't want your family to find you. I understand all that—Daddy told me. I'm not asking you to come to the house. Listen carefully, Vic."

"Yes?"

"We're having a little celebration here tonight. I'll get everybody to playing that game where they turn the lights off and hunt for people. That will give me a chance to get away for a while without being missed."

"Away from Jamie?"

"I know you think I'm awful, Vic, but you won't when I explain."

"Where shall I meet you? Down at the Rocks?"

"That's too far, Vic. I couldn't get back in time."

"Where, then?"

"You know the beginning of the trail, back of our house? You know the first handrail, by the little bluff? Wait for me there."

"When?"

"Could you be there at nine o'clock? You may have to wait—it depends on how soon I can get away."

"I'll wait till nine-thirty," he said. "Anything else?"

"No. Good-by, Vic. Thanks for calling."

"My, my, don't we look nifty!" the landlady said when he came downstairs. "Somebody's going out sparking."

"You little know how wrong you are, Mrs. Schneider," he said, brushing past her.

He meant to eat something, then walk across the Cinnamon Bridge. He would take the eight-o'clock interurban and arrive at his rendezvous with ten minutes to spare.

He was still qualmish from his long day in the sun. The workingmen's restaurant had nothing to offer except fried fish and stewed squash, so he made out on iced tea and a bun.

To keep from being recognized during his trolley ride he stood on the front platform with his back to the other passengers. It was nearly dark, the afterglow was fading. At least, this small adventure was an improvement on his own hall bedroom. Life began to rise in him.

The big trolley lumbered out Madison Avenue, parallel to Adams. He felt like a revenant. He caught a glimpse of Bierbach's Dancing Academy. He passed the rear of his Aunt Louisa's extensive lawns. He saw the Cambridge School and Miss Peebles' School, and Toomey's Drugstore on the next corner. Sweet, guileless places, repositories of his youth.

At the end of another half hour—"Next stop, Doochee Bridge."

He swung off the car platform and skulked across the bridge, above the stagnant flats and the clear-running river, to the entrance gates of Rampole Place. His own house was a dark colossal silhouette at the end, with a glimmering of pillars. Almost no lights were on. He wondered how Katie was making out. He wondered how soon his father would send out an alarm for him—calloused old brute!

There were four cars in front of the Epps house. Shadows skimmed past the drawn curtains. Victor had plenty of time—Jodie hadn't started her hide-and-seek yet.

A crowd of young people streamed out of the Dysart house under the crackling street lights, toward the Breen house. Ping-pong, no doubt. Victor had better get away down the trail before he was caught. He dodged across the fringe of the Eppses' lawn.

He had to fight the nostalgic influence of the trail: it was as rank and sweet in his nostrils as the scent of heliotrope. He had laid out this trail. He and Jodie had kissed and quarreled here a hundred times.

He leaned his elbows on the handrail and listened to the river at the foot of the bluff. Voice of running water, going back as far in Victor as he could remember. Voice of great trees astir, sweet sleepy notes of nesting birds.

It was a long time before Jodie joined him; it was a quarter to ten. She could not have blamed him for leaving. But he liked these woods, he liked this river running through the dark. They had been his.

"Oh, Victor!" she startled him in the end. She was breathing fast, after her run from the house. "I was afraid you'd have gone by now."

"All right," he said. "We're both here. What's on your mind?" If she thought he was going to fall all over her, she would find out how mistaken she was.

She fastened both of her hands around his wrist. She was still short of breath. "Victor, you think I want you to make love to me. I wish you'd believe that I don't want to marry you. I'd be afraid to marry you. I want to ask you this: Ought I to marry Jamie? How much has a man a right to expect of his wife?"

"Everything. The whole works. Why did you get engaged to him if you're not in love with him?"

"Let's sit down," she suggested. Supple as always, she folded herself cross-legged at the foot of a great beech, without loosening her clasp of his wrist, so that he found himself drawn down beside her. He managed inoffensively to break her grip, because it made him feel foolish.

"Don't fly off the handle till I've finished," she said. "In a certain sense a girl can make herself be in love with any man who gives her a good time. All girls do it. If I'd met Jamie before I met you—if he'd made his kind of love to me—I'd have grown in the direction of being Mrs. Jamie. Well, Victor—you got me first."

"Where is this getting us? You aren't the only girl who hasn't married her first sweetheart."

"I've told myself that. When I said I'd marry Jamie, I did it in good faith. I like everything about him, and I thought his love-making would grow on me. Well, I keep waiting for the big lift that never comes. He kisses me—and I have to draw on what I remember about your kissing me. You didn't leave me the same that you found me. There's hell-fire in you, Vic, and there's hell-fire in me, and there's no hell-fire in Jamie Nellison."

A great hurrah resounded through Victor's depths. He ignored it as well as he could. "What's your alternative?" he asked. "What will you do with yourself if you break your engagement?"

"Sit and wait," she said, with a quirk of self-mockery.

"Sit and wait for another Jamie Nellison?"

She gave a tiny shrug.

"Don't think I'm going to tell you to break your engagement. You'll have plenty of consolations in the way of lands and gold and lordly gear. You can 'make yourself be in love with him'—the same way you made yourself be in love with me." He gave these words a nasty intonation.

"Victor Rampole!"

"I'm quoting your exact words."

"You're twisting them on purpose. You know I loved you. That's the whole trouble."

There was a poignancy in her voice that unmanned him. Jodie had not left him the same that she found him, either. His hands went out to her. He would kiss her once—he would kiss her good-by. . . .

What reversed his movement of reconciliation was more than he could say. His intention turned a total flip, like a fish fighting the hook. Mixed with the taste of honey was the aftertaste of gall. In bitter truth, he knew this girl too well. He knew her wiles and her falsities. He had heard her accuse his mother of having a lover.

Out of some cavern of mistrust came his accusation: "Your father put you up to this."

He heard her furious intake of breath.

279

"You've engaged yourself to another man," he went on relentlessly. "But you're not sure you can hold him. You're afraid he'll see through you the way I did. You're making one last try for good old Victor, just to be on the safe side."

How she found her aim he didn't know. But the blow landed—a full, stinging slap across the face.

He snatched at her. No girl was going to slap him twice. He pinioned her arms. She was, as slippery as a snake—they were wrestling, rough-and-tumble on the forest floor. She was fighting her way out of his grasp, a grasp as cruel as a lover's. Every inch of her was braced against him.

"Had enough?" he asked through his teeth. "Say you're sorry and I'll let you go."

Her answer stupefied him. It was a tiny, clarion laugh—the horns of elfland faintly blowing. "Sorry? Victor, you silly! You've never stopped loving me."

"You little bitch!" he said, and began kissing her.

Her head weaved, avoiding the insistence of his mouth. He would teach her to lure him out into the woods and then slap his face! He kissed her violently, brutally, as if he were punishing her.

The hell-fire was mounting in him and calling to the hell-fire in her. She was weakening. She enjoyed being bullied. She couldn't hold out against him. Now she was kissing him with complete abandon—wild, inordinate kisses after long thirst.

He felt the danger. The fire was coming too close. He asked her harshly, "Isn't it time you went back to the house—before it's too late?"

"Not while you're here," she murmured, almost too low for him to hear her. She drew him closer.

Well, she had asked for it.

The darkness was thick about them. God knew what time it was. Victor sat up cross-legged beside Jodie. She was lying as straight as a corpse, except for the long tremors that ran through her. She groped for his hand. "Victor, what are we going to do?"

There was no laughing this off. Both of them knew they had committed a dreadful sin. Victor had deflowered a virgin—a decent girl, a girl everybody knew. He had ruined her.

He had possessed her half in lust and rancor, half in a bewilderment of love. No point now in trying to untangle his motives; he had ruined her.

She had consented to her ruin with unvirginal warmth, but that was no excuse. Even if Mr. Epps had set the trap in which the two of them were caught, that was no excuse. Victor had smelled the trap and walked into it.

Victor did not want to marry Jodie. Now that he had taken her, his high-colored imaginings stood corrected by experience. The ecstasy was there; but after the ecstasy came the reaction, the shame, the something still indefinably missing. Jodie was still Jodie, with all her wrongheadedness, her malice, her deviousness. . . .

But he had ruined her. That was the ultimate fact.

"Don't worry," he said, almost kindly. "I'll make an honest woman of you."

"Victor——"

"Do we have to hash this over?"

"Yes, we do. The first thing I want to say is, I'm glad it happened. It was worth whatever it costs."

A bitter rejoinder came to his lips. Naturally she was glad it happened. She had outplayed him. She had hooked him.

But he bit back his recriminations. If he and Jodie were going to have to spend their lives in double harness, there was no merit in bandying hard words.

"The next thing is, I didn't bring you here for this. You must believe me, Victor."

Perhaps she did not see into herself any better than Victor saw into himself. He would give her the benefit of the doubt; but he had no heart for a bedtime chat.

"Jo-o-die!" a bellow rang through the woods. "All sorts in free. Jodie!"

"Good gracious, that's Daddy on the rampage."

"What's our story? Can we keep this to ourselves till you've given Nellison his walking papers?"

"Victor, how can I? I must have been out here an hour."

"You surely aren't planning to exhibit me in front of the guests who are celebrating your engagement to Nellison? Really, Jodie, there are limits——"

"However I break the news to Jamie, he'll hate me—and however I do it, he won't die of a broken heart. He's just busting with self-control, Jamie is."

"You're a tough little operator."

"This is an emergency—you don't seem to realize." She got to her feet and began tugging at him.

"I realize I have a slight emergency of my own. I'm not even supposed to be in Meridian."

"Victor, you're afraid of your father. Which means more to you—your father, or me?"

"He has a right to be told before the *Sun-Record* spreads the glad tidings." The shoe was on the other foot now, morally speaking. Victor had condemned his father and left him. His marriage to Jodie would be a compound betrayal of all his father held in reverence.

"Victor, are you going to sit there till somebody routs us out with a flashlight? Wouldn't you rather walk out across the lawn with me and let me tell them we're engaged?"

Her vivacity was coming back. Her ruined condition appeared to weigh but lightly upon her. She was readying herself for a grand entrance.

This was what Victor's break for freedom had come to. "Oh, God!" he said. "Let's go."

Chapter 40

ROY GODKIN telephoned Katie every morning at ten minutes past ten. The college term had closed, and he was unsnarling the departmental red tape at his desk.

Katie waited for his call in the sitting room with the door closed. She was working cross-stitched initials on guest towels, to make herself feel like an engaged girl. She did this needlework only when she was alone, because it would have been a dead giveaway if anyone caught her at it, and she meant to play fair with her father. Roy's call was the moment of the day that she lived for.

Roy, being a man, was not to be satisfied with telephone calls. "How much longer is he going to keep us in limbo? I thought in terms of a couple of days. He's had a week now."

"Roy, darling, we must be patient. It's because he's so fond of me and feels so responsible for me. You have no idea what a wonderful father he's been since my mother died."

"Hasn't he talked to you at all? Hasn't he asked you any questions?"

"Not yet, Roy. But he's studying me under his eyebrows."

"I'm not familiar with the kind of father that holds the keys of heaven and hell. If he forbade you to marry me, would you take it lying down?"

"Roy, you are the only meaning there is to my life."

"Then what are we waiting for? Haven't you got a Lord Chamberlain, for God's sake? Isn't there any way of presenting your humble petition to the throne? If I'm the only meaning in your life, let's see you get into action. I'm damned if I'll squat with the rest of the beggars in the courtyard. You are a major part of the meaning of my life, but you're not the whole of it. I can live without you if I have to."

"I'd like to see you try," she mocked him. His laugh came through to her, acknowledging her power over him. Katie had never had power over anyone before. The feel of it was delicious—it was love's miracle.

"Roy, I promise to speak seriously to Father when he comes home this evening. If he puts us off again, I'll let you come out here anyway."

"The devil you will! I won't set foot in his house till he invites me in."

"Do you have to be so cantankerous?"

"I'm starving to see you—but I have my pride. Isn't there anywhere else we could meet? The campus teashop?"

"William would have to drive me out there, and it would be all up and down Rampole Place that I was having a clandestine meeting with you."

Roy emitted several sulphurous words. "I'm not sure I like being engaged to the Princess Royal."

"I could meet you at Lissa Grover's apartment. William often drives me over there."

"Well, why didn't you say so sooner? I'll see you there at three tomorrow."

"Unless Father calls you first."

"In any case," he said firmly.

She went back to her stitchery and her daydreams. She felt like a young apple tree in bud. Nothing could prevent her unfolding now—nothing.

Augustus put his head in at the sitting-room door, and she whipped her sewing under the chair cushion. His face was a-pucker with anxiety. "Through with your phoning? Maybe you ought to go in to your pa. He's going to take this engagement pretty hard."

For one heartbeat Katie thought he meant her engagement. He did not. The Rampole Place grapevine was jigging: Victor was back in town. He had been living in a rooming house across the river and sneaking up to meet Jodie in the woods at night. Jodie had pulled the wool over everyone's eyes. Her own folks were announcing her engagement to that chappie from the East when—lo and behold, Victor cut him out! There had been big doings down at Number Two last night.

Katie got to her feet, white and quivering. At any time the story would have shaken her. Today it was almost too much to face. She was like some child who had just learned to put three building blocks together in the form of a house, when her big brother took the blocks for a tower of his own. Her father would have no patience for her now. Victor came first, by right of primogeniture, by right of sex, by right of headstrongness.

She knew Victor's engagement would be a mortal blow to her father, but she didn't know why. The feud with the Eppses was part of business, part of politics, part of the masculine world. She merely knew that Mr. Epps was a symbol of enmity.

All the same, she had promised Roy to speak to her father, and that was a promise she must not break.

"Hasn't Father gone to the office? Where is he? What can I do for him?"

"He's shut up in the smoking room. Can't bear to show his face, most likely, and watch people grin out the side of their mouths. This has hit him right in the middle."

"How did he hear it? Did Victor come home last night?"

"Victor knew better than to come home last night. I told the old boy myself, at breakfast. I figured it would come better from me than from a stranger. He's a proud man, your pa is."

"Are you sure it's true?"

"The *Sun-Record* has an extra out. I sent William down for it."

"I'd better see it."

Augustus fetched the paper from the pantry. The front page was taken up by a banner headline and three overlapping photographs—the happy couple and the jilted swain. Clandestine courtship . . . hated Eastern rival . . . the paper had gone to press with the announcement of the engagement of Miss Josephine Epps, only daughter of the publisher of the *Sun-Record,* to Mr. James Nellison III, of New York City and Pride's Crossing, Mass., when the great news broke. Additional pictures on back page.

"This is particularly disgusting," Katie said when she had plodded through the paper. "Has Father seen it?"

"No, he hasn't. But he'll have to, sooner or later."

"I'll take it in to him."

Quaking, she opened the smoking-room door. Long, long ago, on the mythical day when her mother was killed, she had tried to comfort her father and he had blasted her with an oath.

But he hadn't meant to hurt her. Afterward he had come upstairs and kissed her good night in the kindest way. However he blasted her this morning, she would understand.

He was not dangerous. He sat facing the fireplace, with Big Joe and Abraham Lincoln glooming down at him. His hands hung slack outside the arms of the chair. His face, usually so rugged, looked eroded by aeons of pain.

Katie sat down on the floor beside his chair and took one of his hands, without breaking silence. His fingers climbed over hers to stroke the back of her hand.

If she were ever to keep her promise of speaking to him about Roy, she must bring him up out of his lethargy. But that was a long way ahead.

Slow tears were coursing unregarded down the folds of his face. After a while he spoke, as if he were talking in his sleep. "Sly. Spiteful. Typical. Epps wouldn't have wanted it to happen in any straightforward way."

"Father! Don't take it to heart so. It's just Vic and Jodie, and he's always been in love with her. It would have been kinder if he'd told you first, but it wouldn't have made any difference."

"Maybe so," Horace said, looking at her for the first time. "Got to keep our chins up, anyhow. Perhaps you'd better go round and leave some calling cards—teach 'em manners." His mouth widened in a terrible effort at irony. He was coming back into the waking world.

"That's the spirit," Katie said, as her mother used to say when Katie fell down and hurt herself. "Do you know what I'm going to do? I'm going to send for some coffee. And while we drink it we're going to say all the nasty things about the Eppses that we can't say to anybody else."

He gave her hand a little humorous shake, silently thanking her. Augustus brought in a coffee tray, with hot muffins and strawberry jam. "You didn't eat a mite of breakfast, Horry," he said, reaching back fifty years for the old nickname.

While Horace drank his coffee, Katie buttered bits of muffin and laid them handy by. To her delight he unconsciously ate what she buttered. The copper-red was coming back into his face, the caverns were filling out. She intercepted one of his ordinary everyday looks—a scrutiny from under his eyebrows.

"Well now," he startled her by saying, "about this young man of yours."

"Father, we don't have to discuss him today. Roy and I can wait."

"What better time? This business of Victor's points my moral for me. I couldn't have spoken before this—you'd have said I was prejudiced."

"Spoken, Father?" She had a premonition of dreadfulness.

"I've tried to protect you children. In Vic's case I've been outsmarted. I'm going to make sure nobody collects your pelt."

Katie's lifelong bent was to submit to her father's views. Her voice shook, but she said resolutely, "Don't lump Roy Godkin with the Eppses.

You don't know a thing about him. You haven't taken the trouble to find out."

"I have found out enough about him."

"From—?" She read his face, and then said, "From his enemies."

"From his superiors. Let me tell you what I got from Dr. Emmanuel Schweiz." He took her heavy-handedly through his version of Mrs. Burch's musical party. Katie sat clutching the edge of the coffee table, her eyes fastened incredulously on her father's face. Once or twice she interrupted. "Oh, that wasn't the way of it!"

"Did he or did he not single you out and invite you to play?"

"Certainly. But——"

"Did he or did he not take you out of the room for half an hour?"

"We were talking about music."

"Did he enroll you in a special, unauthorized private course consisting of yourself and himself?"

"He disapproves of the first-year harmony class."

"Did he exert himself to rescue any other students except yourself from this deadening routine?"

"Father, this story of Dr. Schweiz's is like some horrible chemical that turns blue into pink. What happened was that we fell in love. Think of it that way, and all the facts fall into place. Dr. Schweiz is a jealous pompous old fuddy-duddy, and he hates Roy."

"And you're an utterly inexperienced young girl who doesn't know a fortune hunter when she sees one."

"You're determined to be unfair."

"Let me ask you a hypothetical question, as the lawyers say. Disregard love, for the moment. Take a penniless young musician—"

"Yes," Katie said proudly.

"—who has never known where his next meal was coming from. Supported through his childhood by a hard-working old-maid aunt. Putting himself through school by playing in honky-tonks."

"Would you have admired him more if he'd asked for charity?"

"He's ambitious. He has his way to make. He captures a plum—he gets a university appointment. By the greatest good luck he meets the daughter of the president of the board of trustees of his college. Let him get on the right side of that girl, and he's fixed for life."

She stirred, resisting the trend of his question.

"Assuming—assuming, as we agreed to do, that he is *not* in love—assuming that he is a young man with his eye on the main chance—how differently will he behave from the way Mr. Godkin behaved at Mrs. Burch's party?"

Her color came gloriously back. Her eyes glowed. Her voice pealed.

"Assuming," she came back at her father, "that he is a young man of the fiercest, touchiest pride, assuming that he has earned his appointment by years of training, assuming—and Dr. Schweiz neglected to tell you this—that he has enough creative talent to make a great name for himself, what, except love, would induce him to clutter up his professional future with a rich society girl like me?" It was an oratorical effort in the true Rampole tradition.

Unfortunately her father was self-immunized against Rampole oratory. She saw him weighing what he was about to say, and speaking with reluctance. "Katie, this is my last question: Has any other young man—any young man who had nothing to gain by making love to you—has any such man ever loved you at first sight?"

He might as well have knifed her. She fought back a descending blackness to say, "Roy is my equal. He's my superior. Your question doesn't apply."

"I've thought a great deal about your marriage, Katie. You have it in you to be a happy wife. A wonderful wife. Is it too much to ask you to wait until you've learned a little more about your world?"

"I know you want me to be happy. You built Rampole Place for my benefit. Yes, you did, Aunt Louisa said so. I worshiped you for doing that. For your sake I've tried to be the kind of daughter you were entitled to. I went through all this coming-out folderol, didn't I? And nothing happened. It couldn't—I wasn't alive. Then Roy Godkin and I looked at each other across a piano, and all at once I was born. I'm a human being, I'm a girl. Roy brought me to life, Father, and he has a claim on me."

She had exhausted her father's patience. His knuckles showed white from his grip on the arms of his chair. "You won't see reason," he said, "so I've got to be arbitrary. I don't want to hear of your seeing this Godkin again. Is that clear?"

"Yes, Father."

On any other day she would have defied him openly. If he had phrased his edict in any other words, she would have been forced to defy him.

But this was the day when Victor had broken Horace Rampole's heart. She could take advantage of the ambiguity of the edict. She would see Roy Godkin when she liked, and she would arrange that her father shouldn't hear about their meetings.

Chapter 41

WILLIAM drove the touring car up to the Grovers' door. "Don't wait," Katie told him. "I'm staying to supper. I'll telephone the house when I want to be picked up."

She climbed the shaky, hospitable wooden steps and crossed the porch. Lissa had pinned a notice above the bell: *Walk in, Katie.*

She had so much to tell Roy that she did not even try to prepare herself. She and Roy must not be as cruel to her Father as Victor and Jodie had been. Apart from that, she was Roy Godkin's to dispose of.

She was early. She had the apartment to herself, with its big battered chairs and window seats, its broad hearth, its framed photographs of the Erechtheum and of Trajan's Column. She walked into Lissa's room and took stock of herself in the mirror.

I'm beautiful, she said to herself, glorying in the incredible. My eyes are superb—Roy says so. He likes the color of my dress. I am going to marry Roy Godkin. Mrs. Roy Godkin . . .

She heard his footstep on the porch and ran out to welcome him. Even while she was in his arms she was beginning, "I have so much to tell you!"

He was not in a mood for love-making. He released her after one perfunctory kiss, and slung his hat across the big room. "I have plenty to tell you. Your father has had me fired."

She had never seen him look as he did. His eyes had the unbelieving stare of a man who had been robbed of his life's treasure. He had never looked so young.

"Roy, he couldn't have! He never intervenes——"

"He intervened this time, all right." Roy flung himself down into a wicker chair. "Come here!" he ordered her brusquely. She swarmed into his arms. "Old Schweiz refused to renew my contract," he said. "I've a good mind to sue the university. I had a verbal understanding with him in April, at a time when I could have got another job."

"Darling, Schweiz has always hated you. Father can't have had anything to do with firing you. He hasn't had time."

Roy mimicked viciously, " 'I have taken this step, Mr. Godkin, only after conference with our benefactor, Senator Rampole.' With the dirtiest possible look, to make sure I got the implications."

"Father can't have done it!"

"Are you telling me he's consented to our engagement?"

"Yesterday was a terrible day at our house. Perhaps you saw in the papers about my brother Victor?"

"Well, I saw that he was engaged to an uncommonly pretty girl. Drove his rival from the scene, and all that. Is that your idea of a terrible day?"

"But Father and Mr. Epps are the worst kind of enemies. The paper didn't put that in. This isn't just a boy-and-girl romance, it's a catastrophe. It's a victory for the wrong side. Father is shattered."

"Great God above! What a jolly life you Rampoles lead, up there at the palace!"

If Katie had not been in love with Roy Godkin she would have taken umbrage at his mockery.

"I did have a long talk with Father about us," she said. "It wasn't the time I'd have chosen, but he opened the subject himself."

"Can you give me the gist of it?"

"The gist of it is simple enough—he doesn't want to hear of my seeing you any more."

"And you took that lying down?"

"I'm here, aren't I?"

"Does he know you're here?"

"No."

Roy uncrossed his legs so violently that he nearly threw her off his lap. She landed standing up, distinctly ruffled.

"Sorry if I hurt you," he said in a cursory way. "But I don't like this, Katie. I said I wouldn't go to your house till I was invited. Instead of standing up to him, you sneak out to meet me behind your father's back."

"You should have heard me standing up for you. I did twice as good a job as you could have done for yourself."

"Let's hear about it."

"I'd rather not tell you. It was nasty. Father was still staggering from seeing Victor carried off by a designing girl——"

"And he saw you threatened by a designing young man?"

"Well, darling, Dr. Schweiz had given a sinister twist to the story of the evening at Mrs. Burch's. He had Father convinced that you were——"

"A fortune hunter. Well, naturally. Good thing for you that Dr. Schweiz saw through me so fast. Tell me every word your father said."

"I can't, it was too degrading. Let's talk about what to do next."

He smiled at her, not happily. "Come and sit down again. I'll be more careful."

She wanted to, very much; but she was not used to being bounced off men's laps. She said with proper dignity, "I'd rather sit over here."

He said, "Well, your father has us pretty well boxed in. He's fixed it so we can't get married."

"Why can't we?" she cried out.

"Because I can't support you. I have no job. Hence, no money. Ever hear of money, Highness?"

"That's ridiculous. If you wanted to marry me, you wouldn't let money stop you."

"You think I don't want to marry you!" he said, wondering at her.

"Well, you just said——"

"Being a fortune hunter," he said nastily, "naturally I hesitate to marry you against your father's wishes. It's your money I'm after, my girl."

"Roy, don't say things like that, even to be funny!" She shuddered, and put her hands over her face. She could feel her large nose thrusting out between her palms. It was the first time in weeks that she had thought about her nose. For a few seconds she was not beautiful, she was not loved—she was the old, impossible Katie Rampole.

He was up on his feet. "For God's sake! Katie, are you taking me seriously? Is there no limit to your stupidity? Can you possibly think that I don't love you?" He pulled her hands down from her face, and his eyes probed into hers. "Haven't you any touchstone? Can't you detect the real thing when it comes your way?" He took a turn across the room. "I suppose I ought to make allowances. I suppose a girl like you attracts a lot of the wrong sort of attention."

"Roy, nobody pays me any attentions, except you. Nobody thinks I'm beautiful, except you. You're just deluded about me, and I live in dread of the day when you'll lose interest in me. Why should anybody want to marry me?"

"Who's done this to you?" he shouted. "Who's persuaded you that you're not worth loving on your own account? Katie . . ."

"Yes, Roy?"

"Katie, will you marry me tomorrow? On nothing, mind you. No job, no savings. I can sell my violin—that will keep us till I land a job in the fall."

"You don't want me to, Roy."

"Naturally I don't want you to. I've never had to ask a woman to make one can of beans do for two days. You are a very ignorant girl,

Katie Rampole. All the same, if nothing but marrying you will convince you that you're worth loving, I love you enough to marry you."

Katie sat nonplussed, twisting her fingers. In all her daydreams, no Prince Charming had ever offered matrimony on these terms. At Chestnut Point an undue concern for money was thought to be sordid and ignoble.

Roy resumed his persuasions. "Your brother has guts enough to take a chance. I see by the papers that he's getting married on two dollars a day. The papers find that immensely romantic."

"Oh, but that's different," she said artlessly. "Father will come round—or else Mr. Epps will." She stopped, appalled by what she was implying.

He read her face like clear print. "That's right," he said sardonically. "You're on the right track. Think it through. The designing Mr. Godkin realizes that Father will come around. It's a good gamble for Mr. Godkin. He'll take the girl on the chance of getting the money."

She got unsteadily to her feet. "Roy, must we go on hurting each other like this?"

"Yes," he said, and took her into his arms again. "You're hurting me like hell, and I'm scratching and biting. But I love you, and I suspect you love me. Marry me, Katie. Tomorrow. Before you get undermined again."

"Not tomorrow, Roy. On account of Father. I will marry you, truly I will—but not tomorrow."

"And not ever? I begin to see why your brother had to present his father with a *fait accompli*. You'll have to make a stand against your father's influence, Katie. He's an old tartar."

She threw his quip back at him. "You are a very ignorant man, Roy Godkin. No one has been so kind to me as Father has. I cannot, I simply cannot marry you two days after Victor has got engaged to Jodie Epps." She strained away from his beloved embrace. She felt almost literally torn in two.

"Katie, do you know what the word 'allegiance' means?"

"Of course."

"Where does your allegiance lie?"

He was making her look at him. She tried to hold her eyes steady in his, with all her heart in them; but he stared her down. Her glance slid sidewise. "You're so drastic," she said. "There's a right way and a wrong way of changing allegiance."

"Marriage is a case of all or nothing at all, in my book."

"Yes, Roy, but . . ."

"But what? Go on."

"But . . ."

He was out of temper now. He sang out, "Last chance at this desirable new-model fortune hunter. What am I offered? Going . . . What, no bids? Going . . . Come, ladies and gentlemen, this opportunity may not occur again. What am I offered? . . . Withdrawn from auction. Bids insufficient. . . . Go on home to your father."

He snatched up his hat and stormed out of the house.

She wanted to run after him. An old habit stopped her. If she ran after him she would make herself ridiculous. Katie Rampole had never had any power of attraction. Her only recourse had been a rigid avoidance of anything that would make her look ridiculous.

Chapter 42

PHILIP GROVER and Lissa were an anomaly at University Heights; they had entry to the faculty circle, without membership. The faculty wives enjoyed dissecting them, in a well-disposed way.

Three or four of these ladies were taking coffee in the lounge of the Faculty Club, while Philip and Lissa ate their dinner within eyeshot. Most of the outbound diners stopped at the Grovers' table to exchange a word or two. A nice-looking young instructor engaged Lissa in a five-minute conversation. She was charming to him, she was responsive; but it was plain that the initiative was all his, and at the end of the little colloquy he straggled forlornly away, dismissed. Lissa turned back to her father and picked up their conversation where the young man had interrupted it.

"They're not like father and daughter. They've closed the gap in their ages."

"They're more like husband and wife."

"Agnes! You mustn't go around saying things like that. You could be dreadfully misunderstood."

"I don't mean anything unprintable. I mean they're so Darby-and-Joan."

"I say Lissa's more like a mother with a handicapped son. Lissa protects him, she draws him out in company—haven't you noticed? She's sorry for him."

"Well, his wife left him, you know."

"I'm not surprised. He's the kind of man a woman could hardly resist leaving. He has no gimp."

"I think you're horrid. I'm always glad when I sit next him at dinner. He's as kind as can be, and he has quite an intelligent mind."

"All I'm afraid of is that he'll drain the life out of Lissa. How can she marry, with him on her hands?"

"Oh, Lissa's a thousand miles from getting married."

"And yet she's very attractive to men. I can't quite explain her attraction, but you have to admit she's got it."

"Anybody as pretty as Lissa can afford to be aloof."

"Pretty! She's a sweet thing, but how can you call her pretty? She isn't flesh and blood, she's a wreath of morning cloud."

"Agnes darling, you were raised on the Gibson Girl tradition. Ask the young fellows whether they think she's pretty. You know Edmund is the advisor for the Poetry Circle, and he comes home laughing over a gorgeous young bandit from the football squad who is trying to write free verse, simply because that lets him sit in the same room with Lissa Grover once a week."

The conversation swung in the direction of free verse. In the year of grace 1912 rhyme and rhythm had flown out the window; Browning and Meredith were suddenly old-hat, and one owed it to oneself to subscribe to little magazines bound in Manila paper.

Lissa was no Gibson Girl, but she was the precursor of an incoming style of beauty: she foreshadowed Irene Castle. She was stripling-built, light as thistledown, simple and exquisite in movement. Her step had a lilt to it, her head rode like a flower.

She had no coquetries. She unabashedly put on glasses in the library. But nothing deterred the young men from lallygagging after her. If she wouldn't go to football games, they trailed her to concerts and art exhibitions, and worked on the literary magazine for her sweet sake. She liked them all very much, and discussed the new aesthetic movements with enthusiasm. Now and then she hurt an admirer's feelings by absently calling him Bill when his name was Harry; and occasionally she had a little trouble in persuading a young man that she had no intention of kissing him.

She didn't expect to marry. Centuries ago she had loved a boy named Victor Rampole too much, and learned her lesson. Her life was full enough without marriage. After she took her Master's she would go into the English Department; and she had her father to look after.

She loved Daddy, and her heart ached for him. With just a little help from her, Philip Grover would pass for a man like any other.

It was true that she chattered with him as a wife chatters with a husband. He needed to be tied in to the pattern of human predicament.

She made an agreement with herself that telling him other people's secrets was no violation of trust.

The two of them had followed Katie Rampole's romance from the evening of Mrs. Burch's party. What Lissa knew about Harmony 105 Philip learned at dinner.

When Victor Rampole's sensational engagement broke into the news she knew her father would be concerned on her account. The two of them maintained their reticences; they seldom discussed Queenie, and they never discussed Victor. But she saw his hovering eye at the breakfast table.

She tried to assure him, in pantomime, that her interest in Victor was a matter of prehistory. She passed the *Sun-Record* across to him, with its interlaced photographs and Cupid's darts, and propped a textbook open against the coffeepot on her own side of the table. When she finally spoke it was about the theme she was writing.

"Oh," she remembered as he was leaving for the office. "Katie has borrowed our living room for a session with Roy Godkin this afternoon. I'll be over at the library. Make plenty of noise before you come into the room."

"I suppose this Victor business will add to Katie's difficulties," he said. "Horace Rampole will be like an enraged tiger, and he's bound to take it out on Katie."

"It couldn't have happened at a worse time. Katie had worked up just barely self-confidence enough to marry Roy, with all the omens favorable. I really dread what this may do to her."

"Poor old Rampole! To lose his son to the Eppses, and then to have his daughter carried off by a band leader."

"Daddy, Roy is a university instructor."

"In Adams-Avenue terms, my dear, he's a band leader. My guess is that Rampole has thrown Godkin out of the house, or they wouldn't be meeting over here. It's rather an unpleasant responsibility for us to take."

Lissa's chin lifted a little. She would not conform to her father's hesitancies beyond a certain point. "Nothing we do is going to make or break Katie's marriage. If they didn't meet here, they'd meet on a park bench."

That afternoon Philip remembered to whistle penetratingly as he came up the front walk. Lissa came out on the porch to meet him. "Katie's lying down on my bed," she whispered. "Come out to the arbor, where we can talk."

"Godkin gone?" Philip asked as they skirted the house.

"Very much gone, I'm afraid. Katie's lying there like one of those fossil remains in the museum, with her eyes fastened on the ceiling. She frightens me."

"Do you think her father forced her to break her engagement?"

Lissa said gravely, "I'm afraid she isn't the one that broke the engagement. When I came in and found her this way I said I was going to telephone Roy. And she positively cringed, as if—as if he were her enemy."

Sitting together in the ramshackle arbor they spun out their inferences: thus, thus and thus events must have moved among the Rampoles. They knew the Rampole pride and the Godkin pride, they knew Katie's disbelief in herself. They arrived at something pretty near the truth.

"Well, it's a pity, but probably it was inevitable. This was a pretty implausible marriage for Katie Rampole, you must admit."

"It isn't as if Katie were ever going to make a likely marriage. They were fathoms deep in love. You know, Daddy, Katie has been transformed since the moment she met him. It was as if Roy evoked her, living and breathing and loving, out of a chrysalis."

"Well, my dear, it's too bad, but it's out of our hands."

"It's that lack of faith in herself that's at the root of it all," she went on, as if her father had not spoken. "If Senator Rampole told Katie that Roy was after her money—and I don't exactly blame him, because I'm sure he spoke in tenderest love—she has nothing in her that would make her say, 'Roy loves me for what I am, and I'm worth loving.' She's never liked herself till this winter."

"Well, Horace has never liked her. He's loved her, but she's never come up to his specifications for a Rampole daughter. That's why he's put so much effort into remodeling her. She must have sensed that."

"Daddy, do *you* think Roy would make Katie a good husband?"

"That's neither here nor there, Meliss."

"I wish you'd answer me honestly."

"Well, he's not my dish of tea. I wouldn't want you to marry him. He's gauche, he's quarrelsome, he's profane. He's not Adams-Avenue, if that's what you're getting at."

Lissa said impatiently, "What good is Adams Avenue to Katie Rampole? How about his character? Is he honest? Is he loyal? Is he——"

"Oh, as to that—I don't doubt he's a heart of oak."

"That's all I wanted to be sure of." And a resilience came into Lissa that alarmed her father. "I'm going to patch things up."

"Now, Melissa, don't meddle."

Lissa's fine-cut mouth, so like her father's, set in an expression of resolve most unlike his. "There are times when I feel called on to meddle. This was no calf love, Daddy, it was predestined. It was the point where her music and her self-confidence came together and made a girl out of her. If she loses this chance, she'll be like a flower you try to tie back on its stalk after it's been cut."

"You're taking too much on yourself."

Year after year Lissa had spared her father's feelings. Now her eyes looked into his for one instant and told him that he had always taken too little on himself, and that that was why he was empty now. He looked away before she did, and withdrew his opposition. "All right," he said abruptly. "So you're going to patch it up. What's your first step?"

"One step," she said, and her smile was touched with naughtiness, "would be for you to go and reason with Senator Rampole."

"Me! I could no more go and tell Horace Rampole to let his daughter marry a band leader than I could dance on the points of my toes."

"You've never tried either," she said, contemplating him. "You might turn out unexpectedly good at both."

"We'll rule that out, if you don't mind."

"All right then, my next suggestion is that you should talk to—to Victor Rampole. I have no use for Victor, but I will say he's always been a good brother to Katie. And he has the most surprising flashes of . . ."

"Flashes of what?"

She had a momentary difficulty in bringing out, "Flashes of intuition. Flashes of perceptiveness."

"Let him exercise them, then. He's her brother. He must know what's in the wind. He must know the trouble his engagement has brought down on her."

"How can he possibly know? Haven't you read the papers? He hasn't been at home. He hasn't communicated with his family. He's been living in a rooming house and chasing Jodie Epps through the woods and groves. Probably he's never heard the name of Roy Godkin."

"Nevertheless I am not going to speak to him."

She looked at him for several seconds, to make sure he was in earnest. "All right," she said, "I'll speak to him myself. Will you oblige me so far as to ask him to meet me at your office? I should like to advance under at least a small parental umbrella."

"Lissa, are you sure you want to talk to him? Do you want to dig up that corpse?"

"I can't imagine what you're talking about," she said coldly.

Her father shrugged, and conceded her her privacy. He agreed to try to arrange the appointment.

Chapter 43

ONE consequence of Victor's engagement was that he retired from his wheelbarrowing and went to work for his prospective father-in-law.

He could have refused. Taking this job made nonsense of his recent high-flown break for freedom, and it was a public infamy to his own father.

But when Victor said he'd rather not be beholden to anybody for a job, Mr. Epps was taken aback and deeply wounded: if you couldn't count on your own son-in-law, who could you count on?

In the spirit of solving a brain teaser: How Old Is Ann?—Victor dallied with the riddle of whether Anson Epps had made use of Jodie that night when the engagement was announced, or whether Jodie had made use of him. Had the man gambled with his daughter's virtue to further his own ambitions? How deep could infamy extend?

Neither Jodie nor her father would ever tell him. They both appeared thoroughly pleased with the situation; and if Anson had any suspicions of what had gone on in the woods that night, he covered them. Who cared how old Ann was? . . . Victor fidgeted with the riddle, and tossed it aside.

A black vulture of cynicism had set its claws in Victor. This was where his posturing about integrity had landed him—exactly where he belonged, down among the damned. He had the Rampole blight in his marrow; he was all promise and no performance. He had danced to Anson Epps's piping all the way, and he had passed the point of decision.

Whatever integrity he had carried away with him from Chicago was tarnished by the spectacle of his engagement. He had been a godsend to the yellow press. The papers had interviewed his landlady Mrs. Schneider; they had run photographs of his hall bedroom and his wheelbarrow. Lochinvar in Overalls—that was the caption for Victor Rampole through time and eternity.

Chestnut Point looked much more like a paradise now that he had locked himself out of it. But at least he would not move in with the Eppses, as Onie kindly urged him to do. He moved, instead, to a white-collar rooming house on Adams Avenue. He would take his medicine; he would gag down the congratulations that the friends of the Eppses pressed upon him. But he had to get off by himself for some part of the twenty-four hours.

He did his best to go through his paces prettily when Jodie brought him into the show ring. He supposed she was entitled to gush and twitter and go into raptures for the benefit of her mother's friends; she was an engaged girl.

He could have been more patient with Jodie if she had shown any private evidences of bad conscience. But her sense of guilt had evaporated the moment he undertook to make an honest woman of her. She was all gurgles. She and her mother began to talk trousseau. She pressed for the earliest possible wedding date. Well, she'd better!

For the benefit of spectators, she developed a trick of dropping a kiss on his nose as she flitted past him. When he recoiled she would cry, "Oh, you old bear, you!"

On the third evening of their engagement they were sitting in the sun parlor, isolated by universal tact. "Victor . . ." she said.

"What, Jodie?"

"How long shall we give your father to come around and see us?"

He gave her an openmouthed stare. Didn't she take in any of the realities of the case?

"Well, you know, the man's family is supposed to come to call on the girl's family. It's a little awkward until they do. I hardly know what line to take with our friends up and down Rampole Place."

"Jodie, have you forgotten that even before we got engaged, I wasn't on speaking terms with my father? May I remind you that I'd run away from home?"

"But you can't keep that up forever. Everything's different now. You've stopped pushing your wheelbarrow."

"If you're waiting for my father to kill the fatted calf, you're in for a long wait."

"But, Vic darling, oughtn't we to patch things up somehow? And I don't like to sound mercenary—but one way or another I shall simply have to get hold of an engagement ring, even if it's only a garnet. I can't face people."

"Have you laid out a course of action?" he inquired blackly.

"Well, I thought we could drop around at your house, and sort of ask the Senator's forgiveness. At the very least we could have a nice visit with Katie. I want to be on good terms with your family, Vic."

Victor got to his feet. "You should have looked a little farther ahead before you let me make love to you. If you did it to get on terms with the Rampole family, you misplayed your hand."

She was on her feet too. It was like one of their old quarrels—for a moment they were fully alive and white-hot with hatred. Her hand rose a few inches from her side, quivering with the urge to hit him across the face.

She brought it down with a tremendous effort at self-control. "You can't mean the things you say. What gets into you, Victor?"

"Something that ought to have got into you by this time. You're no good, and I'm no good. We've got ourselves into a mess, and we're doing the only thing we can do to avoid a scandal. But we have no claim to special consideration from anybody, including my family. It sets my teeth on edge to hear you chirruping over a dirty situation."

All the color drained out of her face, till even her lips were gray. It was some time before she was able to say, "If we hadn't loved each other, that would have made it dirty. But we did love each other, and the other night on the trail we still loved each other. So what we did was nothing worse than a—a sort of a preview."

He pitied her so much that the anger went out of him. Perhaps Jodie was cleaner than he because she had not sold her birthright. He answered her gently. "Perhaps the difference is that we used to be matrimonial volunteers, and now we're conscripts. Keep your chin up—this is the bad stretch. We're going to be happier than you think."

He kissed her. For a moment she fitted into his arms, into his heart.

But she was not happy—and small wonder. Before long she said she had a headache coming on, and if Victor didn't mind, she would go up to bed.

It was the next morning that Philip Grover called Victor at the office.

Victor's work was pure farce comedy. He wouldn't have blamed the rest of the staff for submitting their resignations in a body, on having such a greenhorn interpolated into the office. But apparently the staff accepted nepotism as one of the inevitables of life. They patiently showed him where the postage stamps were kept and where the water cooler was. When Mr. Epps sent him to the files he had to ask not only where the files were but how a filing system worked.

Victor suspected that Anson Epps's office was the field headquarters of iniquity. What wouldn't the Civic Reform League have given for one look into those files? Beyond a doubt they contained evidence on judges corrupted, witnesses suborned and disorderly houses protected. But he had to admit that the files he had handled so far related to builders' supplies.

He was well aware that his only value to Mr. Epps was as a trophy—a tarpon stuffed, varnished and mounted on a board, a big catch. That was why he was summoned so often to the inner office. . . . "You've met

Vic Rampole, Alfred? He's going to marry my girl, you know, and he's learning the ropes." . . . Victor ground his teeth and shook hands with Alfred. Once damned, totally damned.

At ten o'clock in the morning his desk telephone rang. "Mr. Rampole? Mr. Grover is calling—one moment, please."

While he was waiting for the connection, Victor made a dozen lightning guesses as to Mr. Grover's business with him. Could his father be getting at him roundabout? And if so, what attitude was Victor to take?

"I want it understood, Victor, that I'm a mouthpiece and nothing more. The—er—well, the long and short of it is, Lissa thinks you're the person to talk to Katie. She's completely prostrated, and Lissa is worried about her."

"Katie? You can't mean over my engagement."

"No, no—over the breaking of her own engagement. Your timing worked out unfortunately for Katie."

It was a good thing Mr. Grover could not see Victor through the telephone. Victor had stopped listening. Katie engaged? Incredible! Katie's engagement broken?

This was what came of selling one's birthright. Victor had reserved the right to make ducks and drakes of his own life, but he had intended never to let Katie down. . . . Katie engaged? To whom, for God's sake? Victor had plumbed the various levels of guilt, but now he had hit bottom.

". . . so don't ask me what she expects you to do," Mr. Grover was still blathering along. "But she won't be satisfied till she talks to you."

"You mean Katie?"

"No, I mean Lissa. So I undertook to ask you if you could come around to my office some time today for a conference with her."

Mr. Grover's hesitance made it clear that he thought the request an impertinence and that Victor was free to refuse.

It wasn't an impertinence, but it was a dilemma. It was like an old dream inside a new dream. Victor sat turning a paper clip over in his fingers. Jodie would be jealous and angry, as she had been when Victor went into conference with Lissa before.

There was, however, one advantage in being a conscript fiancé: Jodie might be as angry as she liked, but she depended on him to make an honest woman of her. And she had been plaguing him to patch things up with Katie. . . .

Katie was in trouble—that was the conclusive point.

"I could get over during my lunch hour," he said. "Say about twelve-fifteen, if that's all right with Lissa."

"I'm sure it will be," Mr. Grover said. "She's kept the whole day open. I'll let her know."

Chapter 44

THE Pendleton Building had been one of the sights of Meridian when Philip Grover's grandfather built it, because it had five stories and the first elevator in town. The elevator now had an antiquarian interest, since it was operated by a rope. It would have been a pity to replace it, even if Philip had had the money. The two top floors had stood vacant for years, and the stairs were adequate for any business the building was likely to attract.

Victor went into Mr. Grover's outer office, and Mr. Grover came out to meet him with his hat in his hand. "I'm going over to lunch at the club," he said. "You and Lissa can make yourselves at home in my office."

Lissa was standing in profile against the sunlight of the office window, nerving herself to face Victor. He knew her well enough to be sure she felt very forward in having sent for him; her dress, her bearing begged him to believe that she was acting only in Katie's behalf. From his griddle in hell he indulged himself in an inward laugh that had a good deal of affection in it. She little knew how deep the gulf was that kept them from endangering each other; it was the gulf between the upper and the nether worlds. He could look at her with as much detachment as if she were a photograph printed in a magazine.

A surprisingly pretty photograph, incidentally. He had been unconsciously expecting to meet a sixteen-year-old in a white tennis dress. She still had the same nose and ears and eyelids, but they had come into a new relation. Call it beauty.

Not flamboyant beauty. Lissa would have had poor success as a carnival queen on a float. Her beauty was like a melody so ethereal that you couldn't hear it above the sound of your own breathing—a beauty that perhaps the damned could best appreciate, from across a gulf. Not great beauty, but flawless of its kind. Honey and alabaster.

"I'm awfully glad you sent for me, Lissa," he said to her. She came around to face him. "Will you start at the beginning and tell me what this is all about? I'm ashamed to say I don't even know who Katie was engaged to."

Her self-consciousness left her. She sat down in her father's chair; and without the aureole of sunlight behind her, she was nothing more than a girl in a neat gray dress and a neat gray hat. "Nobody knew," she told him. "Daddy and I happened to, because we were with her the night it began."

Victor took the visitor's chair and interrogated her until he had the story clear. By hindsight he remembered how much happier Katie had looked this spring, and how many hours she had put in at the playroom piano, doing her assignments for Harmony 105.

"What kind of a guy is Godkin?" he demanded. "He sounds pretty brash, and yet you like him."

"He has power—original power. He's like a tide coming in. He's strong enough to lift Katie out of herself, and that's what she's always needed."

"Can you see any way of bringing them back together?"

Lissa worried at the clasp of her handbag before she raised her eyes. "Somebody will have to work on Katie—that's why I thought of you. She doesn't believe in herself. To love anybody else, you've got to love yourself a little first."

Victor didn't know where Lissa—so reserved, so withdrawn from the tempest of the heart—had come upon this wisdom. But it sank down into him, glinting as it sank, till it vanished like a gold key at the bottom of a well. Some day he must go down after it. In the meantime, it effected a little silence between them.

She brought her eyes up to his again. "Daddy said something enlightening. He said Senator Rampole loved her without liking her—certainly without admiring her. Perhaps that was true of you, too. You and your father were kind about carrying Katie on your backs, but you never encouraged her to walk on her own kind of legs. It was old Miss Archibald who taught Katie to walk."

Victor did not contradict her. She went on again—with a pinkness coming into her face, because she was about to say something sentimental, "Then Roy Godkin held out his arms, and Katie walked straight into them, as proud as Punch because she'd made it across the floor by herself."

"That was very kind of Godkin, but does it quite warrant his marrying Katie? Oughtn't she to walk around a little first?"

"But she's stopped walking entirely. She got the breath knocked out of her after her first try. If you haven't seen Katie, Victor, you can't appreciate what this has done to her."

"And your theory is that Godkin broke the engagement because he thought Katie ought to be able to see he was no fortune hunter?"

302

"It's pure theory, Victor, but it's the only theory that fits. Roy doesn't know he's dealing with a toddling child. He thinks of Katie as a sophisticated society girl. So he gets hurt feelings and roars at her."

"And you're sure he *isn't* a fortune hunter."

"That's one thing he's not. He's bumptiously self-respecting."

"They'd better wait," Victor said decidedly. "Thay may be made for each other, but they're not ripe for each other."

"But what good will waiting do Katie unless she gets a new lease on life? She'll drop farther and farther behind the procession. She'll huddle closer and closer to her father, for fear of getting another knock."

"I never knew you were such a romantic, Lissa. You won't be satisfied till Godkin carries her off on a white charger."

"It would have been a very good idea," Lissa said, pink but stubborn. "In fact, Victor, I think that's just what would have happened, the day she met him at our apartment, if the story of your engagement hadn't broken that same morning."

"Lissa, the world is a much nastier place than you think it is, and the answers aren't as pat as you think they are. I can't take the responsibility of advising Katie to run off with an orchestra leader. Who am I to advise anybody?"

"Who better? You've learned to walk alone. You've struck out for yourself. You've chosen a wife, certainly against your father's wishes. You must know how it's done."

Her ingenuousness grated on him. It would have given him perverse satisfaction to throw the facts straight in her teeth, so that she would stop admiring him: he was being forced into a shotgun wedding; he had sold himself to the devil.

But a condemned spirit has no right to yell obscenities across the gulf. Lissa's eyes, artlessly glowing, were fastened on his, waiting for him to undertake a miracle. A pressure was closing down on him.

"You've sprung this on me all at once," he said. "I can't talk to Katie at the drop of the hat—I might do her a lifetime of harm. I'll—I'll have to whip my ideas into shape."

"If you can't help her, nobody can," Lissa said. "And don't wait too long—Katie might do something desperate."

Chapter 45

THE Pit and the Pendulum, Victor said to himself. The walls closing in, and the big blade swinging closer. You gather strength for what's coming, and then things tighten up another notch.

When he left the Pendleton Building he had already overstayed his noon hour. But he could not possibly go back to being a stuffed tarpon in Anson Epps's office just yet. He drifted toward the esplanade on the river front and settled down on a bench with the rest of the derelicts.

It was melodramatic to tell himself that he was between pit and pendulum. He had had a row with his father; he had engaged himself to the only girl he had ever wanted to marry; his sister had fallen in love with her music teacher. These three items did not add up to tragedy.

The three items were symptoms of a hidden malignancy. It was time he took a straight look at them.

He gazed across the river. He knew where the streetcar ran that crossed the Cinnamon Bridge. He knew where to get a dinner of fried fish and stewed squash for a quarter. He didn't know much about love.

What was it Lissa had said—how did it go? To love anybody else, you have to love yourself a little first. Queer for Lissa to say anything as penetrating as that.

The aphorism had no application to Victor, in any case. Before he could begin loving himself, he would have to obliterate his entire record—the record that had condemned him to hell. You can't un-rot a carcass, he told himself.

A pressure was mounting inside his head. Not intermittent—relentless and inescapable like the swing of the pendulum. Nothing could arrest it.

He fought against an irrelevant memory of the moment, in his father's suite in Chicago, when his eye had refused to focus on Arne Olsen's large, Norse, well-intentioned face. Wasn't there something else he could think about besides Arne Olsen?

Victor knew how the walnut feels under the nutcracker, just before its shell goes to fragments. When your head feels like that, you don't pick and choose your topic. There was a question he could have asked of Arne Olsen, any time this last thousand years, and Arne could have answered it.

He still resisted the idea of Arne Olsen, a clodhopper, a stranger. There must be someone else he could ask, someone more civilized.

Not his father. Aside from all other objections, Victor doubted that his father had a firm answer, any more than he did.

Dan Parmiter knew. But Dan Parmiter was an old reptile.

If it were only myself, I could endure what I'm going through, and I have it coming to me. But it's a whole stage army—it's Father, and then Jodie, and then Katie; and then Father, and then Jodie, and then Katie. . . .

Even if I went up to Doonville to talk to him, he wouldn't be there—he'd be off campaigning for Roosevelt.

But Victor knew politics too well to put himself off with that excuse. Congressman Olsen would be going great guns among the Bull Moosers. The way to reach him was through the new Progressive Headquarters on Bridge Street, near the railroad station.

Even before Victor had made the decision, his legs were carrying him across the plaza. His feet struck the pavement in a quickening cadence; he was all but running.

It was impossible to miss the Progressive Party Headquarters. It was wearing spectacles—the eyeballs being mammoth posters of Roosevelt and Hiram Johnson, and the rims being bunting looped by some inexpert hand. It had been set up in a vacant store.

The noise inside was deafening. There was a knot of evangelizers around every table, and a messiah screaming into every telephone. There were wall maps, there were file boxes, there were bales of posters barricading the windows.

Victor approached a young woman who was trying to address envelopes. From the motions of her lips, he judged that she was asking him whether he wanted to sign up.

Victor brayed above the clamor, "I'm trying to locate—*Congressman— Olsen.*"

The girl pointed her penholder toward a glass partition at the rear of the room.

Victor looked through the partition. A committee was sitting around a long table covered with papers. Olsen had pushed his chair back; he had his thumbs hooked into his suspenders; his chin was down, and his eyes were attentive. He was a behemoth of a creature, but there was ripeness in him, and the others deferred to him.

"Oh, my goodness!" the girl said. She cast a glance at the clock on the wall and began signaling Arne Olsen. None of the Progressive volunteers walked when they could run, or spoke when they could scream; they were caught in a cosmic high wind.

The congressman nodded composedly at her through the glass. "He has to catch the three-twelve train," she said. "He'll never make it. You'd think he had all day."

Olsen climbed into his coat and picked up some papers, talking all the while. He reached down for his suitcase in the corner and came into the outer office.

It was four minutes past three. The best Victor could do would be to make an appointment, and he would make the appointment if he had to dogtrot at Olsen's heels all the way to the station. "Mr. Olsen!" he said. "When can I talk to you?"

"Well, Victor Rampole!"

"Congressman! You'll miss your train!" the girl intervened nervously.

Olsen said to Victor, "Walk along to the station with me," and shouldered his way toward the door. Victor followed him into the street. "Can't hear yourself think in there," he said composedly. "It's all healthy, but I'm a three-miler and I don't run myself to death at the start."

"I don't want to keep you," Victor said, talking fast. "I just wanted to make an appointment with you about a personal matter."

"Now, now—there's no rush. They don't know it, back in there, but I'm taking the four-seventeen. I haven't had a square meal in three days, and I'm headed for the station restaurant. I'm going to relax, and get the yammer out of my head."

"Well, I won't bother you, Congressman. If you'll just give me an appointment . . ."

"No time like the present. Come along, you can talk while I eat." Victor took the congressman's suitcase and fell into step beside him.

"Volunteering for the campaign, I suppose," Olsen said, with that slow, friendly shrewdness of his. "I heard you bolted the convention."

"Mr. Olsen, you said you knew my mother?"

"Why, yes." Olsen was returning his receiving apparatus; it took him a perceptible time. "Why, yes, I knew your mother."

Now that Victor was face to face with his question, he found it unsurmountable, like the straight face of a cliff. He made a detour. "You must have known Harold Ritter."

"Harold Ritter! Why, he and I swam in the same swimming hole, before he went off to college. Smartest boy ever graduated from Doonville High—everybody looked for him to make his way right to the top. Sounds funny, but I wouldn't have any trouble imagining Harold Ritter President of the United States, if things had come out different."

This was not in the least what Victor had expected to hear. He felt as if he had opened what he took to be a closet door in a strange house, and found it leading outdoors. He had to enlarge his terms.

"What was it you wanted to know?" Olsen prompted him gravely.

Victor took a drowning breath and said, "I wanted to know whether you actually held a meeting at your house the night Mother was killed. People say there wasn't any meeting."

"You sure you want to dig that up, Victor? It was a tangled sort of a business, and a tragic business."

"I ask you before God to answer me honestly. Things are in a mess, and I have to straighten them out."

Olsen walked several steps without looking at Victor. They were almost at the entrance to the station. "There was no meeting. It seemed best to say there was, on account of your father. Maybe we were wrong."

There it was. Victor stopped dead, fighting down the brackish taste that came into his mouth. His mother had made herself common. His mother was defiled.

Olsen gave him an anxious look. "If you didn't want to know, you shouldn't have asked," he said.

"I had to know."

"I felt pretty bad about Harold. Particularly because I had to tell so many lies. It seemed to me Harold deserved better than to be hushed up and whispered about. . . . And so he did!" Olsen said with a burst of intensity. "Look here, Victor! If you've got to know any of it, I'd rather you knew all of it. It was pretty sad, and I've never known just what to think."

"Take your bag, sir?" a redcap said.

"No, thanks. We're going into the lunchroom. . . . Come on, son. What you need is a cup of coffee." He convoyed Victor into the restaurant and gave the waitress an order.

"There wasn't any meeting," he said, "but I saw them that night."

Victor made a motion to escape. He didn't want that night to be any more vivid to him than it was. Then he sat down again.

"Harold stopped in at the house and asked for the key to my rowboat. I kept one padlocked down by the bridge in those days. They wanted to go on the river, because it was such a fine starry night—poor young things. They were all of a dazzle. Maybe I shouldn't have let them take the boat. But they were kind of heartbreaking, and I had a feeling it was out of my hands."

"Did—did—" Victor cleared his troublesome throat. He had to go on listening. In some way the full story mitigated what he had heard already. At least it had been stars and clean-running water, instead of a shoddy hotel room and a leering clerk. "Did they come often?"

"Often? It was the first time they'd been out together. Harold bought that classy new car on purpose to take her out. He wasn't much of a hand at driving." His dinner came, and he pitched into it. After a little while he said, "You know, when Harold first fell in love with Chloe I took a grudge against her. She's a fashionable woman, I said to myself, she's had experience, she has no right to make a fool of that boy. . . . But after I got one look at her, I knew she had no more experience than a baby."

"She hadn't. She'd lived all her life inside a sort of play yard, with only the nicest playmates. She had no dealings with Father's politicians. I've never even understood how she came to meet Harold Ritter."

"He ran into her on her own side steps, when she was coming in from the garden with a basket of flowers. He held the door open for her—and he came downtown lunatic with love. He'd never seen anything like her, of course. There weren't many like her. We kidded him about his crush, the way you'd kid a boy for having a crush on Julia Marlowe. What floored me was that she would go out alone with him. I guess they couldn't fight it."

"I used to blame my father for not looking after her better. That was when I thought he sent her off to a meeting. I was wrong about the meeting."

"No. It's hard to say what your father did wrong. He couldn't make himself any younger than he was."

Olsen went back to his pot roast and mashed potatoes. Victor nursed his cup of coffee between his hands.

"Recollect what our Lord said?" Olsen demanded suddenly. "'He that is without sin among you, let him cast the first stone.' That's what I hung onto while I was telling all those lies. I know they did wrong, and I'm sorry I lent them my boat, and it's a pity everybody doesn't live by the book of rules. But one thing I will say to my dying day: what they did may have been wrong, but it wasn't dirty. They were true lovers, and love is a pretty rare commodity."

If Arne Olsen had been a man of finer grain, Victor might have broached to him the idea that was running through his own mind—that quite possibly Chloe and Harold Ritter had had no guilty intimacy at all—nothing guiltier than a kiss. Victor remembered his mother's Victorian fastidiousness; he remembered the ballads she sang after dinner— tears and years, heart and part, forsake me never, farewell forever. Perhaps they had drifted down the river under the high-hung stars, and kissed, and gone back to their duty and their death.

Arne had come to terms with their adultery and forgiven it. He had made a legend out of it.

No one would ever know. No one need care. The story had turned

to favor and to prettiness. It was like an old valentine in a trunk. Victor
wished he had talked to Arne Olsen years ago.

Chapter 46

"WELL, Mr. Olsen," Victor said, getting up from the table,
"I won't take any more of your time. Thanks for the coffee."

He owed Mr. Olsen thanks for much more than that. His thanks
were too complicated to express.

The idea of going back to the office never crossed his mind. A man
was entitled to be alone with himself on the day he came to himself. He
stood a while in the train shed, his eyes following the recurrent cycles
of arrival and departure. He felt lightheaded and yet curiously real.
That feeling must come from the sudden cessation of pain.

His new insights were like a spring run of fish crowding an estuary:
he could dip in at random and pick up a shining netful. He had too
much treasure.

"What they did may have been wrong, but it wasn't dirty"—that was
what Arne Olsen had given him. "They were true lovers." If Victor
could have arrived at that simple point the day Chloe was killed, how
much ravage he would have saved! But he couldn't reach that point
till he had gone down to hell and back—till he had dishonored a girl he
should have loved.

He had held it against Jodie that she didn't feel dishonored. . . .

This was the pause, the long rest in the music—the conductor holding
the orchestra frozen until he brought his baton down. The expectation
mounting, the breath arrested until the moment of release.

Here came the down beat: Jodie was not dishonored, because she
had loved him truly.

That, and nothing but that, was the consistent key to Jodie. She had
loved him since the first evening at dancing school. Her father had
manipulated her love, perhaps, but he had not invented it. He had not
connived against her virtue—she had expended it without counting the
cost. Her provocations, her cruel coquetries, had been defenses against
his own arbitrary outbursts. When she summoned him to meet her in
the woods she had made a last effort of love.

It was half past three. He was to dine with the Eppses. The intervening time was his own, and he needed every minute of it for sorting his catch of revelations.

It occurred to him to walk all the way out from downtown—eight miles, two hours. That would bring him to Chestnut Point by five-thirty and give him a chance to clear up Katie's affairs, so that he could have the rest of his evening, the rest of his life, for Jodie.

He swung off northward, out Adams Avenue. His legs worked like pistons. He breathed deep and free—freer than he had breathed in years. He was off to set the bad world right.

He made a re-evaluation with every house he passed. Aunt Louisa's. Aunt Louisa hadn't done so badly, the night Mother was killed. She had scented scandal, and nipped the scandal back. Victor remembered how he had lit into the censorious ladies in the back parlor. He must dismiss his grudge against those ladies.

Granny Cummager's house. He knew his mother's wedding photograph would be sitting on the piano between the pierced-china nutbowl and the stereoscope. Chloe was the bright lost angel of that house, the lodestar and the recompense. Let Granny worship at that shrine. Mother's sweetness had been authentic. Even her fall from brightness had been a feather's harmless drift through space.

"The Grovers' old house, three stories and a cupola in dark-green clapboard. He was sorry about the Grovers. They had been through a lot of trouble. The trouble had shriveled Mr. Grover. At one time Victor had thought of him as an oracle. No one would go to him now for a divine word.

At times Victor had avoided Lissa because she brought him bad luck. He had found her devotion a little boring. What a girl she had grown into! Her action today had not been easy; it had been wise, generous and brave.

Above all, the Eppses' old house. The front-parlor window had a doctor's sign in it now. Victor stood holding the spikes of the iron fence in his two fists, reliving the evenings when he had escorted Jodie up those precipitous steps, wondering whether he dared to kiss her. Jodie's young mercurial moods, her melting moments, the come-and-go of living scarlet in her cheeks. . . "Jumping jiminy!" he said aloud.

He had broken with her when she said his mother had had a lover.

Well, his mother had had a lover. She had sinned, in thought and in act. Her early death left her preserved under a glass bell, a figurine in tinted wax. Life would have destroyed her gracefulness.

Jodie had borne with him long and generously. Beginning today, he could love her with his whole heart, because his heart had been made whole and apt for love.

He must straighten out his workaday relations. He could not go on letting his father and Mr. Epps contest the ownership of him—the position was too humiliating. He would have to leave Meridian. Jodie would go with him.

He walked slowly now, head bent, hands in pockets—the image of the Senator in cogitation. That five-thousand-dollar inheritance—no one could keep it out of his hands next March, when he came of age. He would put it into some small trading enterprise, in the Huck Rampole tradition, and run it into a fortune. Slim pickings at the start, of course—but Jodie had said she would love him if he were a poor boy selling newspapers.

His father. He pitied his father now. Horace Rampole was no lover for a young wife. A bargain had been implicit in his marriage—Rampole position for Cummager beauty—a middle-aged affection on both sides. The only miscalculation had been that Chloe was not middle-aged. Father was no paladin, but he was no scoundrel either. He did his best.

Tramping now along the drab reaches of upper Adams Avenue, Victor began scheduling those interviews which were to enlighten so many. Would Father be at home and free? If he went first to the Eppses', could he talk alone to Jodie? There was no ideal sequence. He would have to take his interviews as they came.

He reached the Doochee Bridge in a glow of perspiration, cleansed of all impurity.

He turned into the Epps entrance, and asked for Jodie. Mrs. Epps came out of the sun parlor in a fluster. Her fat pretty face was turgid. "What have you been doing to Jodie?" she demanded. "She's locked herself into her room, and I hear the most extraordinary thumping sounds. I do wish you two could be nicer to each other."

"I've treated her abominably, but that's over now. Let me run upstairs, Mrs. Epps, and speak to her through the door."

"Certainly not. I've given you young people entirely too much freedom. A girl has her reputation to consider. All this nasty publicity——"

"After all, Mrs. Epps, I'm engaged to her."

"I'm not so sure you are."

"Mrs. Epps, I'm going upstairs."

"That you are not." And Mrs. Epps barricaded the stairway with her splendid bulk. "You can just wait till Ance gets home, and abide by what he says."

It was infuriating; but after all, a half hour didn't matter. "Then I'll run up to the house," he said, "and come back later."

"To the house! Since when have you made peace with your family?"

"I'm going to make peace by dinnertime."

"Jodie might as well be engaged to a Mexican jumping bean," Mrs. Epps complained. "I don't think you're going to be a very dependable husband for my little girl, Victor."

"I'm a reformed character, Mrs. Epps. I'm going to surprise you."

"Jodie's pretty good at surprising people, too," Jodie's mother said bodingly.

Victor couldn't take Onie Epps's warnings seriously. He knew what she didn't—that as a conscript Jodie had limits to her freedom of action. She would have to give him a chance to put things right; she couldn't help herself.

He walked through to the pantry at Chestnut Point. The familiar scents came to him across an abyss of time.

"Well, Gus . . ."

"Well, Vic . . ." Augustus was laying out the silver for dinner. His casual stance proclaimed that he was not slaying any fatted calf for Victor.

"Father home?"

"He's upstate, speechifying."

"Oh," said Victor, forestalled. "Katie in the house?"

"Now don't you go upsetting Katie. I'm having a hard enough time with her without you sticking your nose in. I've had the doctor twice, and he's prescribed her a tonic. She won't even take it."

"I'll doctor her," Victor undertook, and bounded up the stairs.

He knew where to look for Katie. When she had the megrims she stayed by herself in the old playroom.

And there she was, sure enough. Her black head was visible over the back of an armchair that was turned to the bay window, looking out toward the sunset behind the western forest. She was not doing anything at all.

"Katie . . ."

She sprang up to face him, her hands clamped together against her ribs. She looked—the horrid comparison forced itself upon the mind— she looked like a sick horse in the corner of a stone wall. "Did Father say you could come back?" she asked him stupidly.

"I'll talk to him later. I'm here to talk about you. I'm going to fix you up."

"You don't even know what's wrong with me."

"Yes, I do. Lissa Grover told me."

"Lissa doesn't know. Nobody knows."

"You'd be surprised how much Lissa knows."

"Nobody can fix me up."

"That's what I thought about myself—and how wrong I was!"

"You! You're all right." Her bitterness spilled out of her. "You ride roughshod over everything that gets in your way. You're headed somewhere. Let me alone." Her hands knotted themselves tighter against her rib cage. Her teeth began to chatter.

Victor crossed the room in long strides. He put his arm around her shoulders and took both those agonized hands in one of his. "Steady!" He gave her the word of command. "I'm going to make Father see reason about you and Roy Godkin."

Never, not even after her mother was killed, had she failed to answer his command. But she was different—something had broken her. She began to cry terribly. Only his arms around her kept her knees from buckling.

He somehow worked her and himself down into the big chair and let her cry against his shoulder. She was in worse shape than he'd had any idea of. He had brought this trouble down on Katie. He must lift it.

Augustus came anxiously into the room with a tumbler. "Here, give her this. Sometimes it straightens her out. It's spirits of ammonia. I wish your pa was home. Something has got to be done about that girl and done quick. She sounds like a timber wolf in a crate."

Katie drank off the draught. She put her hands over her face for a moment, and then straightened herself. "I'll be all right now, Gus," she said.

When her breathing was steady again Victor said, "Katie, I've been through hell, and I've dragged everybody down behind me. Now I'm out, and I'm going to get the rest of you out."

Yes, she was listening.

"It goes back to when Mother was killed," he said. "Ever since then, we've tried for the wrong things. I cared too much about Mother, and you cared too much about Father, and Father cared about you and me to the point where he warped us out of shape. It was the best we could do—but it's time to do better."

She was listening intently now. He took a short cut to his conclusion. "When it comes to growing up and getting married, the time for caring as much as that is past. We've got to face forward instead of backward. I've done rotten things to Jodie, because without knowing it I was facing backward. You and Roy Godkin fall in love—and then you let Father face you around backward again."

"Father has nothing to do with this, Vic. When I face forward I have nowhere to go. It's just that I'm not a girl anybody would want to marry."

"You didn't use to be, but this spring you were. If you let yourself face backward now, you're a goner."

"I knew you didn't understand," she said. "Roy doesn't want to marry me. He's found me out. He's through with me. And probably it's just as well—I could never have been sure how much of his love was love and how much was self-interest. I couldn't have lived through that, Victor."

Victor knotted his black brows and stared out into the westward trees. What he had to say was so clear to him, and so incommunicable! "I can't speak for Godkin—and I don't have to. You're the only person who can size him up, and you'll never size him up correctly till you come to believe in yourself."

" 'Believe in yourself!' That's easy for you to say, Vic. You have something to believe in. What have I got?"

"You hardly know yourself. You were just coming alive this year. Lissa said you were like a kid learning to walk. You're not ready to get married—you must wait till you can walk better. But you mustn't cut yourself off from Godkin, because he's the man that started you walking."

"He won't even be in Meridian. Father has had him fired from the univeristy, and he's looking for another job."

"Oh, if that's all! Leave that to me. Once Father gets me off his mind he'll take the pressure off you and Roy Godkin. I'm entirely different, Katie. It takes too long to explain, but you'll have to believe me. I'll see that Father gets Godkin's job back for him, and I'll see that he lets you go on studying with him. By the end of another year, you and Godkin will have had a chance to make up your minds about each other. I'll make Father see that Godkin is—well, like that Pygmalion fellow. He created you, and he has a right to you."

He was not prepared for his effect on Katie. She didn't so much rise out of his arms as ascend. Gravity had loosed its hold on her. Half an hour earlier she had reminded Victor of a sick horse. Now she was the young Artemis bending her bow.

"Victor!" she cried. "How right you are—how right! I'm not going to follow a word of your advice, but I thank you a hundred thousand times."

"Hold on, now," he cried sharply. What had come over the girl? "Don't go off half-cocked. Wait till I've talked to Father. You can't— you wouldn't——"

"I can and I would," she caroled. "You said just one true word—you said Roy created me. I'm going to gamble everything I've got on Roy Godkin. I'm going to him this minute."

He held her by the elbows and tried to force her to look at him. Her eyes were almost incandescent, and they did not see him at all. Victor had a sense of profanation in laying a hand on her; this was not his sister Katie.

He put all his old authority into his voice. "I said to—go—slow! I said to get acquainted with yourself. I said you might find——"

"And I say I'll put my creation back in Roy's hands. If he can't make a good job of me, nobody can. We may not know each other, but we love each other." And she broke out of Victor's hold.

"Where are you going, for heaven's sake?"

"I'm going straight down to his house. . . . Lend me some money, Victor. I'm taking the interurban."

This anticlimax was what convinced Victor he had launched a hurricane. The roofs were flying over the treetops, if Katie was taking the interurban.

"I haven't any money. You'll have to get it from Gus, and I hope to God he doesn't give you any."

"He will," said Katie. Victor heard her going down the stairs in long, light-footed leaps.

Chapter 47

Short of pursuing Katie across country and wrestling with her, Victor had no way of halting her nuptial flight. He wished his father were at home. He wished he had gone at Katie in some slower way. What he had overlooked was that a person—a girl—was not an inert vessel into which one could spoon a measured dosage of enlightenment. A girl was combustible. When he came to talk to Jodie be must bear that fact in mind.

It was long after six o'clock—he must go straight to Jodie. He had been ruthless with her yesterday evening. This evening he must be wise, he must open his whole being to her. He must convince her that he was worth loving.

So musing, he made his way down Rampole Place and rang the doorbell of Number Two.

It was not Withers who opened the door, it was Anson Epps himself— a rattlesnake coiled for the strike. "Yes?" he asked nastily, as if Victor had been a peddler.

"May I talk to Jodie, Mr. Epps? She's expecting me."

"You may not. Incidentally, you're fired—in case that means anything in your life."

"I'm sorry I didn't get back to the office this afternoon, Mr. Epps. But it was the best day's work I ever did for Jodie."

"Jodie is not interested. Go on back to Chestnut Point and lap your cream out of your saucer. You'll hear from me later, and so will your father."

"Mr. Epps, Jodie will never forgive you if you come between us now. I never knew how much I loved her until today."

"You needn't blat your love from the front doorstep. Come inside. There are a couple of things I'd like to make clear to you myself." And he kicked the door full open.

As he followed him to the study at the back of the house, Victor tried to guess the grounds for Anson Epps's indignation. Mr. Epps had plenty of grounds: he might be resenting Victor's call at Philip Grover's office; he might be resenting his overtures to the Rampole family; he might well be resenting Victor's seduction of his daughter. Which of Victor's defections had Mr. Epps uncovered? He must let Mr. Epps do the talking.

While Mr. Epps was closing the study door, Victor took his stand in front of the fireplace. He felt a little as if he were being shut into the cage with a tiger, but he was full of obstinate courage.

"I've had just about enough of you, Victor," Mr. Epps said. "There isn't room enough in this town for the Rampoles and the Eppses—and you needn't think I'm going to bow myself out of the picture."

"This isn't Epps-versus-Rampole, sir, it's between Jodie and me."

"That's what you say. But let's take a look at the facts. You broke with your father. I fell for your little game—I hired you. What happens next? You go into conference with Philip Grover—a two-for-a-nickel reformer who has made me his particular target. If you think, Victor Rampole, that you can make an appointment with Philip Grover through my own switchboard without my hearing about it, you're a simpleton. The very same day, you go sidling home to Papa—all is forgiven. Next thing is, you come around bleating about how you never loved Jodie as you do today. While I have breath in my body, you're not going to use my daughter as a cat's-paw. . . . And she's seen through you—she's finished with you."

This Machiavellian reading of his actions was so plausible that Victor laughed out. The laugh threw Epps off his stride for a moment.

"Mr. Epps, you're completely off. My father doesn't even know I've been back to the house. I went to straighten Katie out about some of her personal affairs. So far as I know, Mr. Grover hasn't spoken a word to Father in six months. I'm not going back into my father's camp, if that's what's worrying you. I'm going to set up for myself in some town where there are no Rampoles and no Eppses, and I'm going to ask Jodie to go with me."

"Taking your wheelbarrow along? So that's your big offer to Jodie! You broke up her marriage to a man who could have given her everything a girl wants. Now you're giving her the privilege of packing a workman's lunch for you every morning. You're a spoiled, self-centered brat, and you shall not make her that offer."

Victor held himself steady. "Jodie doesn't care for power and glory the way you do, Mr. Epps. I won't leave this house unless Jodie tells me to go."

Anson Epps stood working at the corner of a rug with the toe of his shoe. It curled up, and he trod it flat; it curled up again. All at once he laughed. "You'll never stay turned down till Jodie turns you down," he conceded. "Come on upstairs. I don't think you can twist her around your finger, but if you do, I'll take a hand at the rebuttal."

Victor followed Mr. Epps upstairs. Jodie had been hurt and angry the night before. This was possibly the last chance he would have for presenting his case to her. He knew the fury of her impatience. Would she give him time to convince her that he was a man newborn?

Mr. Epps rapped, and spoke softly through Jodie's door: "Let Daddy in chickie?"

For one moment Victor liked Anson Epps. He might be a scaly customer, but he loved his daughter as fiercely as Senator Rampole loved Katie. And Victor had done him a great wrong.

They heard a scurrying inside the room, and mysterious bumping sounds. Then the click of a key. Mr. Epps went in, and left Victor standing in the corridor.

In a minute he came out, and the green glint of triumphant malice in his eye permitted Victor to stop liking him. "She says to send you in," he said—claiming game, set and match before the play was finished. We'll see about that! Victor told himself.

Victor stood abashed on the threshold. He had gone to the limit of physical intimacy with Jodie, but he had never been inside her room. He had dreamed about it, but it outdid his dreams. He had not known a room could be so satiny, so exquisite. It smelled of the perfume he breathed when he kissed her.

But where was Jodie? He closed the door and looked for her.

"I'm in here," she called from the bathroom. "I'm in a terrible hurry.

If you want to talk to me, you'll have to talk while I'm washing my hair."

He could hardly believe that even Anson Epps would have admitted him to Jodie's bedroom while Jodie was in her chemise and petticoat, but such was the case. He was embarrassed to his Adams-Avenue marrow. Was Mr. Epps counting on the seduction of Jodie's personal charms? And to what end?

The charms were in evidence. When she bent over the washbasin he had a liberal view of her young bosom. It wasn't like Jodie to exploit herself in this fashion.

He had to admit, wryly, that she was well protected. Her hair was falling forward over her entire face, and lying in dark ropes in the basin. She turned her face sidewise to look at him, and wiped some lather from her forehead with her upper arm. Not even Romeo could have embraced Juliet while she was covered with suds.

Victor leaned against the doorjamb and began speaking his piece. "Jodie, I was inexcusable to you last night, but it's never going to happen again. Today I went right down to the bottom of myself and found out what had kept me from loving you."

Midway of his speech, she groped for the rubber spray and showered hot water over her skull, which was small and sleek like a wet cat's. She had not heard him very well. "It certainly is never going to happen again," she said grimly, and began scouring away at her scalp with her finger tips.

It had been unpleasant enough to suspect Jodie of trying to seduce him. It was more unpleasant to conclude that she was not responding to him in any way at all. She was letting him see her half naked because he was negligible—like a servant who brought in wood for the fire while she was dressing, like a dog that had strayed into the room.

"Jodie!" He laid his hand on her sleek wet shoulder—a mermaid's shoulder. "Are you sore because Lissa Grover talked to me about Katie? You wanted me to get back on terms with Katie, and she's in quite a pickle."

She stopped scrubbing long enough to take that in. She said, "This is the first I've heard about your talking to Lissa. No, I'm not sore. I've graduated from all that." Her fingers went back to their circling movement above her ears. It was like trying to talk to someone on the far side of a window.

"I went today and talked to a man who knew how my mother was killed. That's what's been between us, Jodie, every time we quarreled. I didn't trust you because, down underneath, I didn't trust my mother. She had to be perfect, do you see? But I couldn't be sure, and I wouldn't ask for fear of finding out. I was going to keep her propped up on a pedestal if it killed me.

"Well, Jodie, nobody will ever know whether she had a lover or not, in the *Sun-Record* sense, but it doesn't matter. She and Harold Ritter loved each other. She gave off sweetness the way a flower does. Nobody looked to her for strength. She never outgrew her childhood. She died the way she lived here with us—gay and tender and loving. And if she'd lived, she'd have been broken like a flower. I can love her for just what she was, and I'm not going to spend any more time shoring up that pedestal. So now, Jodie, you and I can be happier than you have any idea of."

Was Jodie listening to him at all? She doused her head with shampoo lotion, sozzled it with the spray, and scrubbed up new seas of lather.

He resisted an impulse to take her slim, wet neck in his hands and shake some sense into her head. He pushed ahead. "I walked all the way out from town this afternoon—going over every minute we ever spent together, every fight we ever fought, and seeing that you were right every time. I used to think I loved you, but I had a—a divided heart. You just give me a chance, and I'll show you what love is!"

She turned on the spray again, moving it methodically about her head. The lather dropped in loose flakes into the basin.

"Good God, Jodie, haven't you heard a word I said? Aren't you even listening?" He gave her arm a shake.

She finally turned off the spray. "I'm sure it was very interesting," she said, wringing the rope of hair between her hands. "But you aren't the only person who gets great new light on things. Must you really go on orating to me, Victor? It isn't doing any good, you know."

"I am going to say it all over again, and you are going to listen."

"Well, have it your own way. Reach me that bath towel."

She wound the towel into a turban and tucked in the ends. She put on a quilted satin bathrobe and belted it around her with a cord. She led the way into the bedroom and perched herself on the chaise longue beside the fireplace. He followed her, and took the far end of the chaise longue.

"How much *did* you hear?" he demanded. "I don't want to bore you, but this is a very important conversation."

"Talking was your idea, not mine. Daddy said he couldn't get rid of you, so I said to send you up. Can you take a hint, or shall I spell it out for you? I am through with you." She picked up a long, flexible nail file and began shaping her nails, raising her eyelashes only long enough to punctuate what she had to say.

He reached out and took the file away from her. "You are engaged to me," he reminded her. "I am making allowances for your being angry at me, but I demand that you give me a chance to explain."

She reclaimed the vicious little blade. "It's just as well you came over," she said, sawing away. "You'll have to know sooner or later. I'm not engaged to you any more, Victor. I'm—— Now, if you won't pass this along to Daddy, I'll tell you something. . . . I can't have him getting out an extra."

"What is it I'm not to pass on—that you washed your head and manicured your nails?" A black doom was closing in on him, but he fought it back.

"You solemnly promise not to tell? You won't let anybody get it out of you?"

"Sure, I promise. Whatever it is, you'll take it back before I'm through with you. You're engaged to me."

"I've packed all my suitcases. When Daddy knocked on the door I had to hide them in the closet. Tomorrow I'm going to marry Jamie Nellison." She underlined the atrocious statement by a direct look across the nail file.

"No."

"I telephoned him this morning. I'm to meet his train early tomorrow morning, and we're to drive around till we find a justice of the peace in a town where there isn't any newspaper. His family is going to be in fits about this."

Victor said in horror, "You have no right to marry Nellison. You have no right to marry anybody but me."

"No?" she asked, meeting his eyes defiantly.

The small word gave Victor his orders and his *congé*. It denied that he had any rights over her. It was as final as a bullet through the head.

"Jodie," he pleaded in desperation, "you think it's me you're punishing, but it's yourself. Aside from the fact that it's a dirty deal for Nellison and a dirty deal for me, it will be the destruction of you."

"It's a fine time of day for you to begin worrying about my destruction. You've done everything you could to destroy me. You have my permission to relax."

"But—" he cried. "But——" She was like a child, dancing willfully on the verge of a precipice, stopping her ears with her fingers against the agonized entreaties of love. He had no recourse except brutality for snatching her back from the abyss. He would hurt her, and he would be glad to hurt her. He said between his teeth, "All right, you're asking for it. How will Jamie Nellison like it when he finds he has a piece of damaged goods on his hands?"

Her face flamed under its turban; he thought she was going to fly at him with her nails. Then the color drained out of her, as it had done the night before. She might have been modeled in clay, even her berry lips. She set down the nail file, because her hands were shaking. She clasped them together in her lap.

"I can handle Jamie," she said with that colorless mouth.

"You don't love him. You love me."

"I used to love you. Loving you was pure torture. Love is nothing to base a marriage on—it puts a girl at a man's mercy."

"But I never really loved you until today. For your own sake, Jodie, give me another try."

"Why should I trust myself to you?" she asked him. Tears took their course across her lower lashes. He had never seen her so beautiful—with the beauty of chiseled bone, with the beauty of death. "People don't change overnight. You despised me, that night in the woods. I closed my eyes to it, but last night I had to face it. You were beastly last night. Perhaps you couldn't help it, but you've put me through too much. I'm free of you at last, and that's what you've got to accept."

"This revenge of yours is going to cost you too much. You'll live the life of a French doll with a smile painted on—and that's not you, Jodie. You'll break under it. Wire Nellison. Tell him——"

Damn the girl! Just when he had her down, her brows took on their saucy quirk. She was a hummingbird, impossible to catch in any net. "I can't really run out on Jamie—not twice in a row," she said, dimpling. "I crossed my Rubicon when I telephoned him. It was a very unmaidenly thing to do, and it sent him into a delirium of joy."

"You're throwing away your happiness and mine."

"I doubt that," she said coolly. "I'll have Jamie, and you—you'll always have your Lissa Grover. Stop worrying, Victor. I'll tell you something interesting." To emphasize her self-command, she took up the file again and set to work. Her eyelashes shot one dart at him.

"I'm beginning to believe that something did change in you today. I don't recognize you. You won't quarrel. You're benign and grandfatherly, you have only my best interests at heart. But where does that leave you and me? The hell-fire has gone out of you—and I'm afraid that was what I was in love with. Except for that, only a fool would take you when she could get Jamie Nellison."

She blew at her finger tip and launched a tiny cloud of filings. "This is going to work out splendidly," she said, moving to the next finger. "When you get another great enlightenment about your mother you can go and talk it over with Lissa Grover. That's just the sort of warmed-up gravy she likes."

Chapter 48

VICTOR made his way past Anson Epps, who was standing sentinel in the corridor. Let Mr. Epps lick his chops while he could. It was no part of Victor's duty to warn him that his daughter was on the verge of eloping with Jamie Nellison.

Victor could not face his own house yet. He might still have time to snatch Katie back from her rashness. But even if he caught up with Katie, he had no views to enforce on her. He had never been so entirely wrong as on this day when he set out to put the world in order.

He took refuge in the deep forest behind his own house, but he could not escape the nightmare of Jodie's marriage. It was like watching while she was swept over the brink of a cataract. It was like being gagged and tied to a tree, and watching her while she was raped before his eyes.

The torture of it was that Jodie was not married yet. There was still time to save her, but he was bound and gagged. He would not be allowed inside her room again. If he confronted her, she would not listen to what he had to say. Even if he chloroformed her and abducted her physically, he couldn't compel her to trust him.

He came into a little clearing where the men had been cutting timber into lengths with a power saw, ready to split for firewood. Some of the great cylindrical chunks had fallen across the lane the truck would have to use when it drove in.

There was no logic to what Victor did—he was under torture. He went to work with maniac obstinacy to make an orderly stack out of those logs.

It was an impossible job for one man—that was why it suited him. The massive hardwood drums weighed hundreds of pounds apiece. It became important that Victor should range them in a pyramid—four at the base, then three, then two, then one to top off. He would demonstrate that he could bring order into one corner of the refractory universe.

The lowest tier gave him no great trouble—he tugged and kicked the logs into line with savage exultation.

The second tier took more ingenuity and more muscle. It was backbreaking labor. The lower tier spread under the impact and let one of the upper logs through to the ground level. I'll teach you where you belong, Victor growled through his teeth. He realigned the base and compelled the rebellious log to take the position he had planned for it.

By this time he was so exhausted that it was a pain to draw air into his lungs. Except for his obstinacy he could have dropped to the ground and fallen dead asleep. But he was getting somewhere, and he tackled the third tier.

No amount of management was going to get that third tier into place—the pile was waist-high. It was a matter of brute man power—Victor Rampole versus the force of gravity.

He took a grip, bent his back, and heaved as Atlas must have heaved to get the world aboard his shoulders. He managed to hoist one end across the edge of the stack; and with that advantage he began forcing the log into place.

This is crazy, he said. Every muscle in his body was quivering involuntarily. The crazier the better.

He forced the log into position inch by inch. All at once the pile disintegrated. Victor jumped back with what agility he had left, but the log in his hands came down and bashed his foot cruelly. After one rumbling minute, all he had to show for his labors was a row of logs lying on the ground looking up at him. They said to him, quietly but unmistakably, Exactly what was it you were going to show us, Mr. Victor Rampole?

He had spent himself. On account of his foot he couldn't even make it back to the house. He let himself drop in the center of the wagon track and fought to bring his trembling muscles under control. His breathing sounded like crying. He couldn't be crying—he had winded himself in an attempt to build a log pile.

The sunset was deepening; the wandering airs stood still. The birds were putting themselves to sleep with a few last absent-minded warblings. A twig snapped, in unhurried progress toward dissolution.

Victor lay on his back and looked through the branches into a pool of upper sky. He glimpsed a star, lost it, and glimpsed it again. It was like a silver minnow flashing under water.

The forest told him that he would never get Jodie back. She had set her face toward her own destruction. That was what the log pile had proved—that there were forces too big for you to fight. For a while they might seem to be on your side, but all that meant was that you were temporarily on their side. They had no obligation to serve your purposes. Jodie was destroyed.

Night took possession of the rolling world. Victor dropped off to sleep for a little while.

323

The chill of the dew wakened him. That, and the throbbing of his smashed foot. He kicked off his shoe, but the foot had a pulse of pain in it.

He spent some time in tracing destiny back to its sources—destiny that had slipped one cog in synchronization. He and Jodie had meshed together, and then the great mechanism had wrenched them apart at the moment when they should have locked finally. It was a waste, it was a waste—of force and fire and love.

It was easy enough to make excuses. Victor rejected all excuses. He heaped the blame on himself. He had treated Jodie abominably, long before he technically ruined her.

And yet he had not drawn up the schedule for his own enlightenment. It was like the local train that arrives at the junction five minutes after the express has gone through. Love had left by the earlier train.

He got to his feet somehow, flinching at the pain. He found himself a lopped branch for a crutch. He made his way out of the forest.

He hobbled into the house and found Augustus sitting disconsolate on the pantry stool, looking well over a hundred years old. "Well, good grief!" said Augustus. "This puts the clincher on things. Who's been massacring you?"

"I smashed my foot up in the woods. A log fell on it."

Augustus got Victor as far as the smoking-room sofa, and called the doctor. Then he went off for his old panacea, a pot of coffee. "Get this down if you can, Vic," he said. "You and I have got to talk about Katie. Where did she go kiting off to? It's after two in the morning, and she ain't home yet."

"Hand me the telephone, will you?"

Miss Archibald answered the first ring, and she began speaking her mind before Victor had his question fairly out of his mouth. "Pure selfishness!" she growled. "Juggling with his professional future as if it were a ping-pong ball!"

"But where is she, Miss Archibald?"

"How should I know? They didn't do me the honor to confide in me. She went storming up the stairs to his room—which was not a very ladylike thing to do. Five minutes later the two of them pelted downstairs and set off in Roy's car."

"It's time they were back."

"I quite agree with you. I'm dead against Roy's marrying Katie, but when they do come back they'd better have a marriage certificate with them, that's all I have to say. The *Archibalds* have never made a field day for the *Sun-Record*. We have always been able to hold our heads up among our neighbors."

"Did they look as if they were running off to get married?"

"They looked completely mad, if that answers your question."

"Well, thank you. If you hear anything, would you mind letting us know? We're disturbed about Katie."

"We're just as disturbed about Roy He's had brutal injustice from your father already." And Miss Archibald hung up.

"We ought to telephone Father," Victor told Augustus.

"Horace has had enough wallops lately. Either they're married by now or they ain't "

"But Katie's not fit to get married—she's an infant in arms."

"So how you going to stop her? Do you want to chain her up and leave her howling like a wolf? Look here, Vic—how many perfect marriages can you count on your fingers?"

After cogitation Victor said, "You and Jen come as near it as anybody I can think of."

Augustus made a noise that was half snort and half sneer. "All right, I'll tell you about that perfect marriage. I'm not very proud of this story. When Jen first married me she tried to stop my drinking. She was a blue-ribbon teetotaler, Jen was. So I come home drunk one night, and she begun reading the riot act to me, and I saw red, and I knocked her straight across the room into a stand of fire irons. She was laid up for weeks. I've always thought maybe that was why we never had any kids."

"Gus!"

"We don't talk about it. Only reason I bring it up now is to ease your mind. By that I mean a marriage don't have to be perfect to be pretty damn good. If Katie marries that young knucklehead of hers, she'll make out as well as most folks do."

"It will just about finish Father."

"Coming from you, that sounds good," Augustus said at his driest. At this point the doctor came in and began splinting Victor's foot.

Victor lived through the day when Jodie was to marry Jamie Nellison with his foot bandaged and propped on a stool. He could hardly keep from telephoning the Epps house and asking for Jodie. There was still a chance that the hummingbird might have streaked off at a tangent.

By four o'clock the suspense of hope was over. Augustus came into the smoking room with a pink newspaper in his hand and a mighty queer look in his eye. "I reckon you know about this," he said delicately.

JODIE WEDS JAMIE

It jumped at Victor halfway across the room. "I expected it," he said.

Augustus fiddled about the room with his eye cocked. "I see now why you come home," he hazarded. His inquisitiveness was nearly killing him. "This will kind of clear away the wreckage between you and your pa."

Well, so it would. Much of the tension between Victor and his father would never need to be resolved in words. He wasn't working for Epps any longer, he wasn't marrying Jodie. Chloe Rampole's death was a matter for each of them to deal with as he chose.

They still had plenty to negotiate. Their political cleavage—but that was stale news. Victor's new start in a new city—there was no rush about that. While he was obsessed by his own guilt and by the loss of Jodie, he couldn't think ahead.

As for Katie's disappearance, his guilt lay lightly on him. He had done nothing more than spark an explosion that had been in the making for months. The explosion was at least an alternative to melancholia. Victor was sorry for his father and he hoped he could make peace between him and Katie, but he did not blame himself too much.

For another day it was an open question whether Katie was married at all. Then a sharp-eyed reporter in an Ohio county town spotted the marriage license, interviewed the crossroads pastor who had performed the ceremony and gave the news to a waiting world:

KATIE WEDS BANDSMAN

The press was able to report that Roy Godkin had taken his bride to Cleveland and signed up with a dance orchestra for the summer. The two Rampole Place elopements were a godsend to the entire country, eclipsing even the presidential campaign. The nation rolled young love over its palate.

His father reached home that evening and shut himself into the smoking room.

Chapter 49

HORACE RAMPOLE was very nearly a broken man. The whole grandiose project of building Rampole Place had miscarried. Katie had declassed herself; she had married a nobody, a confidence man, a low-grade Lothario, a fortune hunter. At least the fortune hunter should never lay hands on a penny of the Rampole money.

And yet—Horace couldn't have Katie going barefoot through the streets of Cleveland. In the very act of drafting an ironclad new will he broke off to write her a grudging note, in which he hoped never to see her face again, and enclosed a check for a thousand dollars.

In the course of four days this check was returned, with a polite note thanking Father, but saying Katie didn't need any money.

Horace might have been permanently broken. He was letting his campaigning slide; he stayed closeted in his own smoking room. It was Anson Epps who stung him back to life.

Horace had not asked how it came about that Jodie gave Victor the go-by and married Mr. James Nellison III. The answer seemed self-evident—a simple jilting in favor of a better catch. Victor looked as glum as an owl, bearing out this theory. It did not occur to Horace that Anson Epps might be carrying a grudge against the Rampoles.

Then one afternoon he sat long over the *Sun-Record,* realizing that he had miscalculated. This was spite work of the subtlest kind.

PARK BELT PUSHED

It was being pushed in a knowing, a disarming way. Young Councilman Flint had taken up the plan that the *Sun-Record* had advocated for so long, and sponsored it before the City Council. It was a plan so well drawn up that if Horace had been a councilman, he would have had trouble in finding grounds for voting against it. There was a map on the back page, overprinted with green ink. Horace himself, with all his knowledge of the city, could not have improved it except in one particular.

The plan threw a great green arc along the western boundary of the city, taking advantage of groves, glades and running brooks.

Only—the Senator would have brought the arc back to the highway south of the Doochee Ford, leaving Chestnut Point unviolated.

There was a ring of green ink around the Doochee Ford—the historic, the scenic, the almost mythical Doochee Ford, now in private hands. Not a peep, so far, about an access through the obsolete right of way.

Horace was not deceived. He understood the timing of a newspaper campaign. The more dramatic aspects were being held back. The trap was set for the gentry of Rampole Place. The paper probably had photostats locked in its vaults, of plats altered forty years ago to the public disadvantage. Maybe even an affidavit from some cranky old county employee. Win or lose a lawsuit, the Rampole name would be dragged through the mud; and the Epps machine would win at the polls in November.

And Rampole Place would rend the Senator limb from limb. With every right—he had betrayed it to the mob.

I am not licked yet, Horace pronounced to the empty smoking room; but his voice rang hollow. Big Joe's eye looked puffed and cynical. Big Joe was saying, plainly and unpalatably, Have you forgotten all I ever taught you, Horry? When you can't lick 'em, join 'em. It's time for a horse trade.

The Senator's pride, half noble and half ignoble, revolted from horse trading with Epps, but his realism drove him toward a trade. He would have to talk to Dan Parmiter.

He rang Dan's house three times before he got an answer. This was unheard of; Mrs. Magruder rarely left the premises.

"Mrs. Magruder, could you ask Dan to drop around some time to-day?" Dan must have seen the headline; he'd understand.

"Mercy on us, Senator, hadn't ye heard?" Her voice was all but strangled with grief. "I've been down to St. Joseph's with him all day. I just come home to pick up me night clothes."

"Why didn't you get word to me?" Horace asked her sharply. He was more moved than he would have thought possible. He and Dan had had their feuds, but Dan was his bench mark. The word cancer hung in the air between him and Mrs. Magruder, but he withheld it.

"They hauled him off to the hospital at the crack of dawn. He'd been in a groaning anguish all night. They've been X-raying him, and I've been holding his poor hand. Tomorrow morning they're to open him up." She let off a keening wail. "If they'd but give him back to me, he could die cozy in his own good bed. The doctors are onto him like flies on a beef bone. All they do is stick him with great needles, and he lies there and pats my hand."

In twenty minutes Horace was charging through the muted corridors of St. Joseph's. The black-robed sisters dodged out of his path. He walked through the "No Visitors" sign and into Danny's room.

A screen stood against the light. He distinguished a high white bed, and under the sheet a shrunken contour that must be Danny—he was a tiny man. His head lay on the pillow, parched and nubbled like a gourd, with the eyes closed. The needle had done its work of mercy—the anguish, at least, was not on him.

After a few seconds the old eyelids lifted, and a sky-blue spark came into the eyes. He stretched out his hand a few inches, and Horace took it. "Glad to see you, lad. They finally caught up with me."

"Don't try to talk. I'll just sit here."

"I need to talk to you." Dan's voice was like a faint telephone connection, but his grip held firm. "Talking won't help nor hinder what ails me. I'm plugged full of dope, and you'll bear with me if I'm dim in the wits, but I have things to say."

"They can wait," Horace said, sitting beside the bed.

"They don't mean to let me out of here alive. So listen to me, Horry. I've left you some money."

"I don't need your money, Dan."

"Nor you won't get it," Dan retorted impishly. "Now listen close. My money came out of Meridian, and the most of it is going back to Meridian. For a park, or a library, or whatever. But you'll get the handling of around a hundred thousand dollars—and that's for Kathleen, and you're to slip it to her on the q.t. I don't want to spoil her good name, that she's been so careful of, by leaving her a pot of money in my will. She's as decent a woman as ever lived, and she has many years of life in her yet."

"I'll see that she gets it, Dan. How much will you leave?"

The imp smile flicked across Dan's face. "Wait and find out. I've saved while you spent, Horry. I'll leave damned near as much as you will."

"Good enough," Horace said heartily. All the same he was shocked. It did not become a penniless man to save as much in one lifetime as the Rampoles had done in four. Dan must have unobtrusively bled the city for half a century. No matter—he was giving it back.

"You'll get Taft elected, Horry? This Wilson fellow ought to be a pushover—old jawbones in nose glasses!"

"Come, you'll be getting out the vote yourself."

Dan moved his head negatively on the pillow. "I've let this go too long, Horry. I was scared of the knife. . . . Horry! would you call me a hypocrite if I was to let 'em baptize me before I go? It'd mean a lot to Kathleen, because then I could keep a date with her in Paradise."

"She's deserved that much," Horace said.

It was no time for talking about park belts and rights of way. These stood diminished in the face of eternity.

"It's a long road we've walked together," the faint voice meandered on. "Last night when I couldn't sleep I caught a taste of those griddle-cakes Big Joe bought me in the depot."

Both of them knew the old story; they could traverse it together. That had been the turning point of young Dan Parmiter's life.

Big Joe was on his way to the convention of 1864, where Lincoln was renominated. The Civil War had not yet been won. There was disaffection in the North—draft riots, peace-at-any-price.

Horace had been a young shaver stepping down the train shed with his father's carpetbag, in short breeches, round jacket and Windsor tie. Dan was a fresh-faced country jake with a cockscomb curl, too young to vote but old enough to land a poke on the nose of the Copperheads. He had drawn his savings out of the bank and come to watch the convention.

Young Dan, bewildered in the roaring city, pulled off his hat and politely asked the way to the convention hall. Big Joe sounded his foghorn laugh and took the likable youngster in tow. "You can run errands for me between the hotels," he said. "I'll give you a dollar a day and your keep."

How the old time came back—the heady feel of youth in the veins! Even Big Joe had been young in those days, and relatively innocent. He had done well in the matter of army contracts, but he had believed in the War of Emancipation. He had no apologies to make, then or later, for the party record. The Republicans were the new men in those days, the patriots; it was they who saved the Union. His party and his country were synonymous.

"We elected Old Abe," Danny said. "Recollect the big torchlight parade down Bridge Street? By jinks, we don't have fun like that these days."

"What I'll never forget is Lincoln's funeral train. I stood in the rain along the tracks and cried like a motherless child."

"It was your dad brought the train through Meridian. We were a one-horse town then, we were off the main line. Even Joe couldn't get the train to stop, but he did get it routed through Meridian. Joe was a great one for getting his own way."

"Gus and I stood on ladders and hung festoons of crape all over the City Hall."

"And the rain fell, and the bells tolled in the steeples for his passing. We were a part of greatness that day, lad." Tears, an old man's tears, made their quiet way down Dan's cheeks. He cried out poignantly, "What the devil has happened to us since then, Horace? Time was, in this town, when the lowest a man could sink was into the Democratic party."

His hand clutched at Horace's as a spasm struck him. "Damn them gripes, they're coming back on me."

"I'll ring the bell. You ought to have another shot."

The sister came in with a flannel stir of drapery. Horace waited till the hypodermic laid hold of the pain, and then went out into the gaslit evening streets.

A curtain was coming down on a great pageant. For better or for worse, now, Horace was alone in Meridian.

Chapter 50

DAN PARMITER's funeral took up the energies of the city for several days. Not since Big Joe died had there been such an assembling of politicians in silk hats. The Epps faction outdid itself in ribboned floral pieces. The rites took place in the Roman Catholic cathedral, to the great gratification of Mrs. Magruder and to the disgust of right-thinking Protestants. Dan Parmiter had not been a devout or even a moral man, but at least he had not turned Catholic till he was kidnaped on his deathbed.

Victor was sorry for his father. Horace not only buried Dan with all the honors, he truly mourned him. The funeral was the end of a powerful old dynasty, and Victor himself had precipitated its fall. If he had not been the prize at stake, Anson Epps might not have challenged the Rampole dominion. Victor's enlightenments had come so late that they served only to illuminate the wreckage.

The Epps war engine was rolling against Rampole Place, and the civilian population was in revolt against Horace Rampole.

They didn't know yet about the right of way, but the desecration of the Doochee Ford violated all their sensibilities. They would lose the Swimming Rocks; it would be impossible to keep trespassers off the trails. They would never have built in Rampole Place if they had known how it was to be cheapened. They suspected that once Meridian got its public park, it would demand an access from Adams Avenue. The Senator had let his neighbors down.

For some days, while his neighbors vilified him hysterically, Horace kept up a front of confidence. He administered the old reliable opiate—leave everything to him. But no one trusted his omnipotence any more.

The *Sun-Record* stepped up the tempo of its campaign. The City Council set a date for a public hearing on Councilman Flint's proposal. Horace could predict the exact date on which the paper would break the damning story of the old right of way: it would be the day before the hearing. That left him six days for countermeasures—and he had no plan.

Late one night he went rambling out across his property. He paced the oval, where the new houses nestled on their lawns like so many portly sleeping fowls. He followed his own driveway back, and took the Indian trail as far as the Doochee Ford, where he stood smoking beside the summerhouse, scanning the scroll of memory and time.

First he remembered his two small children, hip-deep in the current of the ford, tugging stones into place for a dam. Victor giving orders to Katie. Chloe overseeing them from the summerhouse, where she sat with her needlework. The reflected sunlight struck laughter from her brook-water eyes. "Little skeezixes!" she said. "Horace, they think they're going to dam the Doochee."

Behind that, the picnic of a graduating class from the old high school. Horace—Horace in his early forties—doing the honors as his father's deputy. Young Chloe coming forward in her summer muslin with the huge puffed sleeves, to render formal thanks on behalf of the class: "Mr. Rampole, we all want to thank you for letting us have our picnic in this beautiful place—" and the blinding moment of decision when Horace knew this was the girl he had to marry. Poor little Chloe!

Behind that, the hilarious whooping of young boys diving naked into the pool. Young Horace Rampole, young Augustus Henning and a raft of boys from the farmsteads roundabout. Behind them, the yells of drunken Indians and the crack of rifleshots. Behind them, Huck Rampole's long silent stride on the fallen leaves.

Behind all that, the river cresting over the rocks and dropping into the quiet pool, as it had done before the Indians came. The river had engraved fifty thousand years of records on its rocks. The Rampoles were one bubble on the river's breast.

Something went off inside Horace like a charge of dynamite. His plan came to him full-born. It was a Rampole hunch—he couldn't be deceived.

This hunch was so farfetched that by lifelong habit he proposed to check it with Danny—and then realized he couldn't.

You can bury a man, but the death doesn't come home to you till you turn to him and he isn't there.

Once when Horace was a boy he had his leg in a cast for six weeks. He remembered the day the cast came off, he remembered stepping down on the leg without any assurance that it would bear his weight. The old panic recurred.

Well, he'd walked, hadn't he? The leg had carried him for another fifty years. He could manage without Danny, and move the freer. For the first time he was not accountable to any organization. He must make his own decisions and foot his own losses. He was his own man. Horace Rampole, old and discredited, was going to give people the surprise of their lives.

His fighting heart rose up in him. Strategy unfolded faster than he could follow his own processes. Epps thought he had him licked, did he?

He needed some days for laying his mines. He had until next Tuesday.

Unless he moved secretly, he would have fewer days than that. If one hint leaked out, the *Sun-Record* might spring its right-of-way story ahead of schedule. Horace must play for time—he must appear to be a beaten man, ready to trade.

This was an assignment suited to Horace's gifts. He had practiced pulling the wool over people's eyes while Anson Epps was in short breeches. He walked up and down, giving a short, jarring laugh now and then at Epps's expense. Let's see now—he must talk to O'Donnell; he must call a meeting of the Rampole Place Improvement Association. And in the meantime he must make himself teasingly accessible in the Belvedere Grill. He must appear willing to surrender the Parmiter machine in exchange for a revision of the park-belt plan that would protect Chestnut Point. He must earn time by giving a convincing performance as a politician in a blue funk.

The right way, the Rampole way, of calling the meeting would have been to drop in on his neighbors, one after another, and ask them up to his house on Tuesday evening. But if he put his nose inside a house, he would be harangued and blackguarded for half an hour before he could get away. And he couldn't reassure his neighbors without giving away his strategy.

If he had Miss Wupper call them, or Augustus, they would think he was ducking them again.

"Victor," he said next morning, "could you help me out? I'm calling a meeting here about Rampole Place. Could you do the telephoning for me? Ask everybody in the street—husbands, wives, any of the children that are old enough to take an interest. Eight o'clock Tuesday evening, and refreshments to follow."

Victor was almost concerned for his father's sanity. The old boy looked cocky—he must have taken flight from reality. Didn't he realize that the neighbors were ready to tar and feather him? "I wouldn't do that, Father," he said. "It's going to take more than a champagne supper to bring them back into line."

"They're entitled to speak their minds. All I'm asking you is whether you'll do the telephoning."

"Well, all right, it's your funeral. Yes, I'll do the telephoning. Shall I call the Suttons?"

"No. Queenie Grover holds title to Number Four. You'd better call Philip Grover—he handles her affairs."

"I'd better accidentally overlook calling Anson Epps, hadn't I?"

"Not in the least. He's entitled to be present."

"I don't get it." Victor didn't in the least want to call the Epps house. "Aren't you holding the meeting to get the better of him?"

"I forgot—I shouldn't have asked you to call Epps. Miss Wupper can give him a ring. He wouldn't miss this meeting for worlds—and I wouldn't miss having him here."

Even in his pit of gloom Victor couldn't help wondering what his father was cooking up now. He knew the signs—something big was on the fire. It would upset before it cooked, like so many of the Senator's grandiose conspiracies; but Victor wasn't going to line up against him this time. Father needed somebody on his side.

Victor's message set off detonations the length of the street. His ignorance was his shield. "No, I don't know what Father has in mind, Mrs. Breen, but it's something about protecting everybody's interests."

"He'd better have something in mind. He's let us down inexcusably. We'd never have considered building here . . ." But Mrs. Breen did agree to give the Senator one more chance; she and Cap would come to the meeting.

Yes, everybody was going. But if Horace Rampole let them down this time, they would dump their houses on the market and bring suit against him for selling to them under false pretenses.

They must stand up to the Senator. They mustn't let him talk them around. This was a question of their homes. Men postponed business trips to be on hand for the meeting. Women breathed resolution into their husbands. And they all furbished up their best clothes, because they knew they were going to be subjected to the best, or presidential, treatment at Chestnut Point.

Victor had checked off all the names on his list except Grover. He called Philip's office and learned that Mr. Grover was out of town for three days—he was arguing before the Supreme Court of Algonquin. Was there any message?

Victor beat a tattoo with his pencil and wondered what message to leave. Queenie Grover, the legal owner of Number Four, was in New York. The notice was a matter of form—her husband would represent her; but Victor didn't like to send her a message through her husband's office girl. He said thanks, there was no message. He would call Lissa at the apartment and leave it to her to notify one parent or both as she saw fit.

While he was looking up the telephone number, he gave a harsh little laugh. The time was behind him when he could get into trouble with Jodie by talking to Lissa Grover. He could talk to Lissa twice a day if he chose. And Lissa was nothing to him but a check mark on a long list. It was all a part of the grand maladjustment of the universe.

"Lissa?"

"Why, Victor, how spooky! I've just this minute opened a letter from Katie. Have you heard from her?"

"I hardly expect to," he said dryly. "She flew directly in the teeth of my brotherly advice. How is she?"

"At least she's pleased so far," Lissa said, obviously skimming the letter while she talked. "I can't help being glad about Katie. I don't know how they'll make out, but at least they've started."

"I don't wonder you're pleased—she did just what you wanted her to."

"Are you angry at me, Victor?"

"Angry? No. So many things have come loose lately, I've given up being angry." He hadn't meant to say that, but it made no difference what he said.

"I suppose I shouldn't have abetted her about Roy. But most of the trouble I've seen has come from tiptoeing away from difficulties. I've reached the point where I'd rather see people make one good smashing mistake."

Victor laughed and said, "There speaks a Grover. I'm a Rampole, and we bull our way into trouble. Oh, that reminds me—" and he gave her his father's message about the meeting.

She received it in silence. "You father's out of town," he amplified, "and I didn't know whether your mother ought to be notified."

"I'm thinking," Lissa said. "I'm giving myself a dose of my own medicine. I'm thinking I'll send Queenie a telegram and say it's important for her to come home."

He hung up the receiver, chuckling a little. What a dynamo Lissa was turning out to be, under her deceiving mildness! In some devious way she had made Katie elope. Now she was fetching her mother back to Meridian.

I suppose, he reflected, she coasted downhill behind her father and mother till she couldn't stand it any longer, and then she planted her feet and stopped sliding.

This was the only encouraging evidence the universe had laid before him in some time. It had a normal feel to it—a feel of enterprise. He thought about Lissa Grover for several minutes. He remembered the wicked way she used to take points from him at tennis.

He even thought it was a pity he had ever met Jodie Epps at Little Bierbach's dancing class. Except for Jodie he might have fallen mildly in love with Lissa Grover—enough in love to marry her, without knowing his own full capacity for love and for despair. Jodie had not left him the same that she found him. She and he had come too near—too heartbreakingly near—to the full sweep of an uncommon passion.

He was down in his pit again, looking across the gulf at the low green landscape of Eden. The quintessence of damnation was to be able to see across that gulf.

Chestnut Point was being put in shape for the meeting, and even a condemned soul like Victor could lend a hand at polishing floors and moving furniture. Like everyone else in the house, he was eaten up with curiosity as to what Horace Ramploe could be up to.

Augustus went unhappily about his work. He was afraid of the temper of Rampole Place. He had too long a loyalty to the Rampoles to enjoy watching while the big ship went down.

On Tuesday evening Mr. O'Donnell came out to dine with the Rampoles. He was splendid in white tie and tails, but he was obviously uneasy. He made a chance to say to Victor, "I'd like you to know, Victor, that I'm co-operating under protest. It's dead against my judgment."

"It's all Greek to me, Mr. O'Donnell," Victor said cheerfully. "But if it suits Father, it suits me."

Shortly before eight o'clock the neighbors began converging. The evening dresses, bare shoulders and white shirt fronts moved upon Chestnut Point in an irregular phalanx through the summer dusk. Horace came out to the portico to play host; and if he was conscious of the forced civility of the greetings, he gave no sign of sensitiveness.

Victor was sensitive. This was the first time he had been on general view. He read his neighbors' minds: Now we mustn't say a word about elopements; we can't talk about the Presidential campaign; God keep us from mentioning wheelbarrows. . . .

He carried his chin high, and went through his Rampole hospitalities. He wished this evening were well over.

Suddenly every group in the portico turned, like actors on a stage, to look at the foot of the steps.

An extremely old roadster had driven up, and Philip Grover was helping Queenie to alight. He and she and Lissa climbed the broad steps under a drumfire of eyes. The neighbors had to take time from their grievances to look at Queenie Grover.

If—as was generally assumed—Queenie had trod the primrose path in New York, it had left no mark on her. She was wearing one of her flowered billowing dresses, showing a great deal of shoulder, and a tulle scarf over her hair. She looked precisely as she used to.

Eyes met, and broke away. What was the status of the old boycott? No one could say that Philip was unchanged. He had aged, and drawn in upon himself. But he looked touchingly happy—as if he had his fingers crossed, as if he were afraid of waking up.

And Lissa—it wasn't her dress, though the dress was obviously something her mother had brought her from New York, ivory organdy, with a peach-bloom sash and slippers. It was her beauty that stopped everyone in his tracks. Since she closed the door of Rampole Place behind her, she had come into her looks. She walked like a flower on the move. She came up the steps as if she were afloat on a wind of happiness.

Rampole Place had no heart for mowing down that flower. The grounds for the boycott grew blurred. . . . Hadn't that horrid Anson Epps been at the bottom of the trouble?

"Why, Queenie Grover!" Horace exclaimed, as courtly as you please. And in his keyed-up condition he bent to print a kiss on Queenie's velvet cheek.

Following his lead, people came forward to give Queenie a wayfarer's welcome. Queenie had been tense, but in a moment she was all becks and dimples. "It's heavenly to be back," she tinkled. "How big and beautiful and quiet everything is here!"

Horace looked at his watch. "We can't wait much longer," he said. "Will you all come into the parlor?"

But he delayed in opening the meeting until Anson Epps slipped into a chair beside the door. Epps's eyes flickered in all directions. When he saw Queenie Grover he bowed sardonically. He settled into his chair as if the curtain were about to go up on a play of which he expected a good deal.

"We all know," Horace began urbanely, "that the park-belt proposal, otherwise so sound, threatens our privacy. Many of you have called on me to protect your interests, and I recognize my obligation. I sold you the land."

He was a natural spellbinder. He played them—watching their faces, gauging their hostility, making them wait. He indulged himself in a little oratory about the beauties of the Doochee Ford.

"Since the ford is on my land, the injury is primarily to me. But we are all involved. Mr. O'Donnell assures me that our titles are good, and defensible in court. Of course, they are subject to condemnation proceedings, like any property—and if the city starts condemning property, there's no guarantee that they will stop with my land. They'll want an access to the new park.

"Now, we could fight the condemnation through the courts. We couldn't win, but we could make such a nuisance of ourselves and cost the city so much time and money that they might decide to terminate the park belt south of the Doochee River. This course would be both expensive and offensive, and it would keep us on the anxious seat for years. Those of us who wanted to sell would have poor prospects of finding a buyer."

If this was his proposition, the householders rejected it in advance. They did not want a long, expensive and offensive lawsuit with a doubtful outcome.

"I have asked myself," Horace went on, "if there wasn't some alternative course, fairer and pleasanter to all concerned. I have such a course to lay before you."

Anson Epps's eyes flicked uneasily—Horace was watching his face. Horace put his hands in his pockets for a discursion.

"I may look at this matter differently from some of you," he went on, "more sentimentally, if you choose to call it so. Long before my father built out here, I used to ride my pony out from the city. In those days the country boys had the run of the ford. They'd come barefoot up the lane with their fishing poles. I swam naked with them in the pool, as boys do.

"There was a right of way across the land in those days." He shot a glance at Anson Epps, whose thunder he was stealing. "It was an old Indian trail to my great-grandfather's trading post. And I've never shaken off the feeling that the public has a right of access to the Doochee Ford."

It was going to take more than urbanity to get Horace over this hurdle. Knife points of anger glinted all around the room.

Horace was sublimely cool. The face he was watching was Anson Epps's. That face had chalked on it, Go on—I'm listening, old cock. You're not getting anywhere. . . . But his bravado had a tension to it.

"There is no perfect solution to the conflict between public interests and private interests. The land is mine. The final decision will have to be mine. It's quite proper that the major concessions should come from me.

"As you know, I hold title to the central esplanade of Rampole Place. I have had Mr. O'Donnell draw up—" here he took a legal document from the table in front of him—"a deed of gift to the city of Meridian covering the fifty acres where Rampole Creek meets the Doochee River, and a hundred-foot access from the front gates, across my lawn and through the forest to the park proper."

A flash fire of outrage swept the room. The men were on their feet, their arms thrashing, their faces suffused with rage. Women's voices shrilled the men into battle. Things were going well—unbelievably well—for Anson Epps.

With a tremendous thrust of personal authority the Senator subdued the clamor. "I recognize that this gift works injury to all of you—it destroys your privacy. As your neighbor, I want to give you what satisfaction I can.

"I have therefore—" he took up some papers clipped together—"I am therefore submitting an offer with no strings attached. I ask you to consider it in good faith. I offer to buy back from each and every one of you your holdings in Rampole Place, at a price twenty per cent higher than its total cost to you. Victor, will you hand these papers around?"

"Mr. Epps?" Victor said politely on his circuit of the room. Epps took the paper and scrutinized it sourly.

Victor felt the thwarted exasperation in the room. The Senator's offer had a specious princeliness—it was both too much and too little. It frustrated their open fury, but it did not give them back their homes. They had gone to the trouble of building houses exactly as they wanted them, with woods, water and privacy. They clamored for the floor.

"Take all the time you want," Horace said. "Make up your minds at your own convenience. My offer is good for three years."

Epps got to his feet. "Mr. Chairman," he said. The room froze.

He swept the circle with his brilliant eyes. "Possibly I am speaking for many of us. It strikes me, Senator, that you are being generous at your neighbors' expense. On the face of it you're making a handsome offer. But you know, as you have never allowed your neighbors to know, that the old right of way was never properly vacated by your father. You are making a merit of proclaiming it, because you knew you were about to be exposed. You are throwing away a trick to get the lead back. You are buying political popularity at your neighbors' expense. You are, in effect, bamboozling the rest of us out of our homes."

Victor, leaning against the doorpost, was shaken. Anson Epps was a master in his own field.

Then Victor felt a change moving across the room, as a breeze cuts into the sultry heat of summer. There was one field Epps had not mastered: the field of old Adams Avenue. The same views, presented by Cap Breen or Stewart Whitty, could have precipitated a spiritual lynching party. But Adams Avenue did not thank Anson Epps for being its

339

spokesman. Epps had fouled Rampole Place from the day he moved into it. He stood for notoriety, chicanery and loose living. It was unthinkable that Rampole Place should take up arms against the Rampoles under the banner of Anson Epps.

He stood waiting confidently for support from the floor. The herd was milling, but it wouldn't stampede. It needed another voice.

The voice, when it came, was the very last they had expected to hear. "Senator," said Queenie Grover, rising with charming hesitation.

"Queenie," Horace recognized her, amid a silence of total amazement.

"I don't know much about business," Queenie chirped. "All I want to say is that I've been living in New York City. Well, in New York, people think they're lucky if they live on a park—they even pay more rent to live there. They like it. They walk their dogs and their babies there. I wouldn't have the slightest objection to living on a nice parkway. Parkway or no parkway, Rampole Place is the nicest location in the whole city. You try living in an apartment and you'll know what I mean. The rest of you can do as you like, but as soon as the Suttons' lease runs out, I'm going to move my family back into our own house. I think it's perfectly beautiful out here." And she sat down, flustered and billowing.

Who would have thought it of Queenie? She was so right—she sounded the note of loyalty. She was moving back. The breeze of approval stirred the room.

Cap Breen was on his feet now. "May I make a suggestion? It will come out of the Senator's pocket, but it won't cost so much as buying us all out. If he will put up a good-looking stone fence along our front boundary lines, and a similar fence between us and the new park, I for one will consider myself sufficiently protected. Queenie's right—there isn't any better place to live."

"An excellent suggestion, Cap," Horace said. "I'd be getting off easy. . . . Well, perhaps there's no need for formal action. If any of you want to sell out after the fence is built, you have my signed offer in your hands. With your concurrence, I'll give this story to the *Morning Telegram,* because it will be big news for Meridian. Shall we continue our discussion in the dining room?"

The refreshments developed into a love feast, with toasts, champagne and an upsurge of public spirit. Everyone observed with pleasure that that horrid Anson Epps had gone home early.

Departures began to impend. People made a point of saying something pleasant to the Grovers. . . . "It will be such fun to have you back,

340

Queenie. Philip has been lost without you. Doesn't he look twenty years younger?"

Queenie was afloat like a cloud in a summer heaven. Her welcome reminded her of when she came to Meridian as a bride. A blessed amnesia was closing in around the difficult years; in another week the memory would be irrecoverable. "As soon as we get back into Number Four I'm going to give a party," she twittered. "I can't call it a house-warming, exactly, so I'll call it a housewarming-over." And in the benign atmosphere of the Senator's party this passed for wit.

"We ought to be going," Philip said, "if we don't want to be swept out. Where's Lissa got to? Victor, have you seen Lissa?"

Victor hadn't seen Lissa, but he undertook to find her.

She had been giving off an iridescence of joy all evening. Knowing her as intuitively as he did, he knew that she was so happy she needed to be alone. He would find her in one of the various hide-outs around the place. Outdoors.

The Swimming Rocks? The summerhouse above the ford? The little arbor that stood between lawn and forest at Number Four?

No, Lissa had been most herself around the tennis court. That was where he would look first.

It was a magnificent summer night, a picture-book night. The moon was riding the zenith, ringed about by diaphanous arabesques of cloud.

He found Lissa lying back in one of the spectators' chairs under the trees at the edge of the court. She had the moon-infiltrated quality that the clouds had; she had no weight nor earthliness.

She hadn't moved, but she had seen him. He went across the velvet grass. "Pretty pleased with yourself, aren't you?" he said to her.

Without preamble she said in an enchanted voice, "For once I did something, and it turned out right. I needn't have been frightened. The moment came."

He gave a kind of laugh, saturated with irony.

"Oh, Victor, I'm sorry," she cried with instant compunction. Her spirit stopped floating, and re-entered her human body. "I shouldn't be rhapsodizing like this, when everything has gone so wrong for you. You haven't had your moment yet. When it comes, you'll like it."

"Why, it's come!" he exclaimed, surprised that she should need to be told. His irony went out of him, and he added slowly and honestly, "And it was all right. It wasn't like your moment—it was packed with dynamite, but that's because I was packed with dynamite. It exploded because it had to. But it left the air a lot clearer."

She didn't say anything, she didn't press him. It was as if she partook of the essence of his moment without words. Her very silence teased him to pour himself out to her. He had the scroll of destiny in his hands, but he had not deciphered it yet. Lissa was not a participant in his destiny; she was a sensitized observer. She, if anyone, could help him with his interpretations. As long as he had known her, she had had the gift of charming his secrets out of him—and now he need not resent this witchery of hers.

But tonight was not the time; her family was waiting to take her home. "Your father's looking for you," he said. "I'm glad you're so happy."

He gave her a hand up out of the long chair, and they crossed the moon-drenched lawn together. Once they were inside the house, the neighborhood world engulfed them. This was Horace Rampole's great evening, and it would have been ungenerous to hold aloof from it.

The guests had gone; Ausustus was turning out lights in the front of the house. Victor followed his father into the smoking room and found him teetering gloriously on his toes and heels in front of Big Joe's portrait.

A tingle ran through Victor. He had been proud tonight of his Rampole blood. "I still don't see how you swung it," he said. "It was like when the magician saws the lady in two and then leads her up to the footlights in one piece."

"That was no sleight of hand," Horace said testily. "It was a bona-fide offer to buy my neighbors out, and it was at your expense and Katie's. I wouldn't have had much money to leave you—but both of you have made it pretty plain you have no use for my money. As for myself, I don't mind a public parkway across the lawn—it will bring out the votes."

"It's going to be a sensation. Meridian will run you for President of the United States."

"President? Not on your tintype. You know something, Vic? I'm not even going to run for re-election to the Senate in 1914. It's a mug's game now. And now that Dan's gone, somebody's got to look after Meridian."

"You'd go back into municipal politics?" Victor demanded.

"Meridian is in my bones," Horace said. "I've neglected it lately."

"I don't know what's got into you."

"I'll tell you what it is—Dan's gone. Funny thing—I was about ready to pay up my losses and pull out of the game, till Dan died. Then all at once I was on my own. No coaching from the side lines, bad or good. I'm going to have fun from now on. Sooner or later, Vic, the time comes when there's nowhere to go but forward."

Nowhere to go but forward! Victor's blood made a leap of response. Funny, that it should be his father who put that into words.

"You can't rush it," Horace went on, holding his cigar unlighted. "It came late for me. But when it comes, you recognize it. . . . Katie, now. I went all to pieces over this Katie business. A couple of days ago it came over me that Katie is a Rampole, and the Rampoles do best when they play their hunches. I'm not going to stand in her light the way my father and Dan Parmiter stood in mine. She has plenty of stuff in her, and she'll have to get it out in her own way. . . . So the long and short of it is," he concluded sheepishly, "I wired her to come home."

The last painful stringency went out of Victor. If that was the conclusion Father had come to about Katie, he and Victor would have no trouble in settling their account.

He found Horace eyeing him with the hesitance that had marked their relationship for years. "Do you—do you know yet where you're heading for, son?"

This was a question Victor would have liked to postpone for a few days longer. The elements of his answer had been emerging out of his subterranean turmoil ever since he talked to Arne Olsen, but he had not framed them handsomely. The conclusion to which he was being forced was an anticlimax to his spectacular break away from the Rampole pattern.

He took several turns across the smoking-room rug, with his head down and his hands in his pockets, while his father watched and kept silence.

This was his opening, if he chose to take it, for demanding his five thousand dollars and his independence. But Jodie had been right when she said the hell-fire had gone out of him. The grand gesture of rebellion had become fatuous. His Rampole heritage no longer strangled him; he had acquired the power of breathing free within its limitations. He could never be anything except a Rampole, but he had a choice of what sort of Rampole he was to be.

Everything that had been driving him out of Meridian had changed, from his father to Jodie, and himself most of all. His first twenty years had been a curtain raiser, a boy's tragedy of confusion. Before the curtain went up on his life, he needed time for training, time for healing, time for growing straight.

His answer spoke itself—not a heroic answer but an honest one. "I expect I'd better go back to college in the fall. I got a little ahead of myself."

"Good idea."

"You and I didn't see eye to eye about the convention, Father. I've got even worse news for you. I've been thinking a lot about the election. It looks to me as if Taft and Roosevelt had cut each other's throats and destroyed their value to the country. I like the looks of Woodrow Wilson very much. I reserve the right to go out and ring doorbells for the Democrats this fall—and if you want to throw me out of the house, you'll just have to throw me out."

This blasphemy came unpremeditated to Victor's lips. Its echoes rebounded from the bust of Abraham Lincoln in his toga, and sent a quiver through the portrait of Big Joe Rampole. Horace appeared to dilate under interior pressure, and his face congested with mulberry-purple color. For an appreciable moment it seemed likely that he would take up Victor's challenge by throwing him out.

He set his teeth for a moment, and closed his eyes. Then, as a man and a realist, he swallowed the dose. "Well, a young fellow has to sow his wild oats," he managed to say.

Lissa Grover went into her own bedroom. Through the wall she could hear her father and mother twittering like two birds settling down for the night.

Her heart was beating full and strong. She and Victor had said almost nothing to each other at the tennis court, but there was no wall between them now. She uncapped her fountain pen, opened her diary and wrote:

> *Love alters not with his brief hours and weeks,*
> *But bears it out even to the edge of doom.*

She sat dreaming over the timeless words. Doom was a long way ahead; she could afford to wait.

She even thought that the time might come when she could give destiny a little nudge.